THE DIRECTOR

DAVID IGNATIUS

THE DIRECTOR

A NOVEL

W. W. NORTON & COMPANY

NEW YORK   LONDON

For Lincoln Caplan and Jamie Gorelick

For information about permission to reproduce selections from this book,
write to Permissions, W. W. Norton & Company, Inc.,
500 Fifth Avenue, New York, NY 10110

For information about special discounts for bulk purchases, please contact
W. W. Norton Special Sales at specialsales@wwnorton.com or 800-233-4830

Manufacturing by Courier Westford
Production manager: Louise Parasmo

Library of Congress Cataloging-in-Publication Data

Ignatius, David, 1950–
The Director : a novel / David Ignatius. — First Edition.
pages cm
ISBN 978-0-393-07814-5 (hardcover)
1. United States. Central Intelligence Agency—Fiction.
2. Computer hackers—Fiction. 3. Computer crimes—Fiction.
4. Computer networks—Security measures—Fiction. I. Title.
PS3559.G54D57 2014
813'.54—dc23

2014005434

W. W. Norton & Company, Inc.
500 Fifth Avenue, New York, N.Y. 10110
www.wwnorton.com

W. W. Norton & Company Ltd.
Castle House, 75/76 Wells Street, London W1T 3QT

1 2 3 4 5 6 7 8 9 0

It takes something more than intelligence to act intelligently.

—FYODOR DOSTOYEVSKY, *CRIME AND PUNISHMENT*

THE DIRECTOR

Graham Weber first encountered James Morris at Caesar's Palace Hotel in Las Vegas. Weber was watching the controlled chaos of the Palace casino just beyond the lobby. This was the gambling proletariat: The heavy hitters were deeper in the hotel at the Forum casino or in private rooms. Weber studied the people at the tables with the curiosity of a successful businessman who didn't like to gamble except on a sure thing. A younger man approached Weber from behind, tapped him on the shoulder, showed him his government identification and offered to carry his bag.

Weber was just under six feet, wearing an azure-blue sports jacket over a pair of tan slacks. He had the blond hair, ruddy cheeks and good health of a man who in his youth might have been a high school football quarterback, or an assistant golf pro. His eyes were an aqua blue that seemed to sparkle from reflected light in the same way as water in the sunlight. Weber was in fact a businessman in the communications industry, closing in on his first $500 million, when he met Morris. He had come to town to give a speech on Internet privacy to a convention of computer hackers.

"I'd turn off your cell phones, sir," said Morris. "Take the batteries out, too, if you want to be safe." He had led Weber out of the crowded din of the casino, back toward the fountain by the reception desk, whose perpetual cascade covered their conversation.

Morris was tall and thin, with close-cut brown hair and a pair of glasses that floated on his long nose in a way that resembled the cartoon character Michael

Doonesbury. He was wearing a black T-shirt that read AREA 51 WAITING AREA, under a gray linen jacket. He worked for the Central Intelligence Agency, as director of its Information Operations Center. He had been assigned by his bosses to escort Weber, who served as a member of the President's Intelligence Advisory Board.

"Why turn off the phones?" asked Weber. "I need to communicate with my office while I'm here."

"Because they'll get pounded," said Morris. "This is a convention of hackers. These people come here to steal stuff. Take a look."

Morris gestured to the crowd swirling through the lobby, and it was true, they didn't look like the normal Vegas visitors. Many were wearing cargo shorts and T-shirts; some had Mohawk haircuts; others had gelled their hair to the stiffness of porcupine quills. They were cut and pierced and tattooed across every inch of flesh.

"I have a BlackBerry and an iPhone," Weber protested, "straight to AT&T and Verizon. The messages are encrypted. The phones are password-protected."

"They're wide open, Mr. Weber. People have set up bogus Wi-Fi and cellular access points all over Las Vegas this week. Your phone may think it's connecting with Verizon, but it could be a spoof. And on the passwords and encryption, I'm sorry, but forget it."

Weber looked at his earnest, bespectacled guide and nodded assent. He opened the back of his BlackBerry and withdrew the battery. He looked quizzically at the iPhone with its nonremovable power source. Morris reached into his pack and handed him a small black bag with a Velcro top.

"Put the iPhone in this," Morris said. "It's a signal-blocking pouch. It prevents your phone from talking to any friendly or unfriendly networks."

"Handy," said Weber appreciatively. He inserted his phone in the pouch.

"You want to know how vulnerable you are, Mr. Weber? I'll show you later at the Rio. What you see there will frighten you, I promise."

"That's why I came," said Weber.

An hour later, after Weber had unpacked his bag and made some business calls on the hotel phone back home to Seattle, the two men were in a taxi taking the short ride from Caesar's across I-15 to the Rio, which was hosting the main events of the convention. Morris led the way. He'd changed into a black hoodie. On the way in, he got nods from occasional passersby. Weber wondered whether these were other intelligence officers trolling for talent, or agents inside the hacker world, or perhaps just kindred spirits.

They stopped to register at a VIP booth just outside the main convention area. Weber felt uncomfortable, watching the Mohawks and bullet heads walk past. Their T-shirts advertised their passion for undoing the ordered world: HACKITO ERGO SUM, *read one.* HACK THE CLOUD, *boasted another.* CARNAL KNOWLEDGE OF DEATH, *warned a third.*

A convention organizer handed Weber his entry badge. It was an odd-shaped device, with plastic representations of Egyptian gods and mummies below an electronic pod with a circuit board packed with chips and transmitters. There was space for three AAA electric batteries on the back. Weber began to insert the batteries he had been given as part of his registration kit.

"Don't turn it on," said Morris. "It's a mini-computer that will connect to the mesh network. It can track wherever you go here. It may have a camera and microphone. Leave it off. You're a speaker. You don't need the badge turned on. I'll get you through if there's any hassle."

Weber put the odd-shaped device, unwired, around his neck and passed through the entry portal, to respectful nods from the gatekeepers toward his guide.

"I take it you've been here before," Weber said, joining the stream of the crowd entering the convention space.

"I've been coming to DEF CON for ten years," said Morris, leaning toward Weber and speaking quietly. "It's my favorite honeypot."

"You recruit here?" asked Weber.

"I've hired some of my best people off the floor." He pointed to an overweight, pimple-faced young man in baggy cargo shorts and sandals, and a Goth girl shrouded in black who was sucking on a lollypop. "These people may not look like much, but when they write code, it's poetry."

Weber nodded to Morris as if to say, I get it. This was why he had accepted the invitation to speak at the hacker convention. As a member of the Intelligence Advisory Board, he wanted to see the future of intelligence. He had asked the board's director if the intelligence community could suggest a smart young tech specialist who knew the scene. They had assigned him James Morris, who had already earned a reputation at the CIA's Information Operations Center for his technical prowess.

"Come on, sir, I want to show you something scary," said Morris, leading the older man down a long, black-walled corridor to a crowded area at the center of the convention space. They moved through a knot of people who had dressed as if for a Halloween party; eventually they came upon a jumbo screen framed by

cardboard cartoon cutouts of sheep standing in trench coats and sunglasses. On the screen was a scroll of names and numbers.

"What the hell is this?" asked Weber.

"It's called the Wall of Sheep." Morris pointed to the information scrolling above them in a continuous thread. "Those are the log-in names and passwords of people whose communications are being intercepted, right now, in real time."

Weber shook his head. His hand went to the cell phones in his pocket.

"It's that easy?" he asked.

"This is slow. You should see what I can do with my machines at the agency."

Morris guided Weber through some of the other exhibits. They wandered into an area called Lockpick Village, which was devoted to cracking physical locks on doors, windows, safes and anything else that could be "locked." They strolled past booths where vendors offered specialized computer gear, cheap circuit boards, T-shirts, beer. In another room, teams were arrayed at different tables playing a specialized version of Capture the Flag, in which they competed to break into each other's servers and protect their own from attack.

Morris handed Weber a program listing the lectures going on in various rooms. It was a school for mischief: Hacking Bluetooth connections on phones. Hacking RFID tags on cargo containers. Building your own drone. Controlling automobiles remotely through their electronic systems. Hacking routers. Installing backdoors in hardware and software. Breaking the "secure" architecture of cloud computing. Manipulating unrandom "random-number" generators and unreliable computer clocks. Breaking wireless encryption keys. The list of lecture sessions went on for pages.

"This is dangerous stuff," said Weber. "Can anyone attend this convention?"

"Look around. You'll see Chinese, Russians, Germans, Israelis. Basically, they let you in if you pay the cash registration fee. There's no point in trying to keep people out physically. They'd just get the information on the Net. This way, at least we know who's here."

"And they're all trying to get inside our pants?"

"Yes, sir. And vice versa, in theory."

Weber nodded. It was indeed the ultimate honey trap. "Is the agency keeping up with this?" he asked.

"Sort of," said Morris. "The agency moves like an elephant."

"What about Jankowski? He's the director. He should be all over this crowd."

Morris pulled Weber aside and spoke in his ear.

"Director Jankowski is just trying to keep his head above water. The FBI is looking at his bank accounts."

Weber pulled back in surprise. "How do you know about that?"

"I just know," said Morris. "People say Jankowski won't last."

It was true, what Morris had said. The Intelligence Advisory Board had been briefed on the preliminary investigation several weeks before. It was one of the most closely held secrets in the government, and here was Morris whispering it in his ear.

"The agency needs a new director, sir," Morris said quietly. "Everyone knows that."

Weber was silent for a moment. He felt like he was getting pitched, which made him uneasy, but he liked the younger man's intelligence and intensity.

"The CIA needs a lot more than a new boss," said Weber. "It needs to enter the twenty-first century. Listen to my speech this afternoon, if you want to know what I think."

Morris nodded. "I reserved a front-row seat."

They wandered for another half hour, looking at exhibits, and then it was time for Weber to go to the Green Room and get ready for his talk. Morris left him at the door and proposed that they meet up afterward and see more of DEF CON.

Weber delivered his speech in a theater that sat several hundred. It was packed with young people, row after row of black T-shirts and hoodies. He took off his Italian sports jacket before he began speaking and rolled up his shirtsleeves. His corporate communications staff had written a speech titled "Stakeholders in Internet Freedom," with an accompanying PowerPoint presentation, but Weber junked it. Instead, he gave what he liked to call his "American dream" speech about how security and liberty could coexist. He had delivered versions of it before, for different audiences, but never one quite like this.

The room quieted. Weber hadn't been sure what to expect. He had visions of a mosh pit at a Megadeth concert. But they were hushed and respectful.

Weber used his own company as a case study. When he began twenty-five years ago, he reminded the kids in the audience, the Internet browser didn't exist and most of what people describe as IT hadn't been invented yet. But it was obvious that people were going to communicate more, and that the government would make a mistake only if it tried to limit or control communications . . . or spy on what people were saying to each other. But thank goodness, the government had been smart back then. It had let technology morph and multiply in a million ways that nobody could have predicted. Weber had expanded his business by doing the obvious, no-brain thing, which was to build some of the pipe through which the communications would travel, whatever they might be—buy spectrum and bandwidth, and let other people decide how to fill it.

And then the government got stupid, after September 11, 2001, Weber said. Intelligence officials got nervous and decided that the open information space was dangerous and needed to be controlled. It wasn't the government's fault; the whole country was frightened. But in its ferocious self-protection, it had built a surveillance colossus that struggled just to keep track of the dangerous people. The surveillance was too big and bureaucratic. And it began to eat up the free space that the new technology had created.

The audience was listening, even the geekiest kids with the spikiest hair. Weber could tell because they had stopped looking at their devices and were watching him.

"I didn't like what was happening," Weber said. And then he told the story that most of them knew, which was the reason, really, why they had come to hear him—about how he had protested the government's surveillance orders, at first in secret, and then in litigation that made its way through the courts, and then by working with members of Congress and finally by refusing outright to comply with what his lawyers told him were illegal orders and daring the government to shut his company down, all while he was a member of the Intelligence Advisory Board. He said they could fire him from that position, too, in addition to closing his business, but he wouldn't quit voluntarily. In the end, they didn't do either.

Weber looked at James Morris as he began the last part of his speech, about intelligence. He saw that the young man was smiling and nodding. There was a sparkle in his eyes, and his mouth was open slightly. It was a look you sometimes see in a church when believers are moved, or at a concert when listeners get lost in the flow of the notes.

"I have tried to help my country in every lawful way I could," Weber said. "I have tried to help the CIA, NSA and FBI do their jobs. I have served on one of the most sensitive oversight boards in the government. I will keep those secrets, and I would say yes tomorrow if someone asked me to help with proper activities. But I will not do things that are unconstitutional. I can't run my business in a country that controls information. I'd rather shut it down. As you know if you've been

reading the news, we're winning that fight. And I think that now, maybe, people are realizing that security and liberty aren't at war with each other . . . because in America, you can't have one without the other."

The DEF CON audience loved the speech. People stood and clapped so loudly that it embarrassed Weber. When he was finished, a man in a suit came up to him from the wings and presented his card. He said he worked for Timothy O'Keefe, the national security adviser. He said Weber had given a great speech that put into words what the president believed. He asked if he could share a video of the speech with his colleagues at the White House, and Weber said of course, it was for anyone who wanted to listen. The man asked if perhaps Weber might be willing to join O'Keefe for lunch sometime soon to discuss how the administration might chart a new path in intelligence.

Weber was flattered. But he was a businessman, not a politician. He always worried when people were too friendly. That meant that they would come looking for something down the line.

Morris was waiting outside the Green Room. He stood unobtrusively apart from the crowd that had gathered to congratulate Weber, or give him business cards, or otherwise ingratiate themselves. It was only when Weber was finally alone that the younger man approached him.

"That was a hell of a speech," said Morris.

"People at your agency wouldn't like it. They'd feel threatened."

Morris smiled, an inward, almost coy look of someone who had a new secret.

"Too bad for them," he said. "Let me show you what the hackers are up to."

They walked the halls for several more hours, meeting people, drinking beer and talking about technology. As the evening progressed, they moved deeper into the convention space. Eventually they came to a large hall in the back, where they heard hundreds of people shouting, "Don't fuck it up!"

Weber was curious; he moved toward the hall and in through the door. A packed house of very drunk-looking people was screaming at contestants on stage, who were trying to answer geeky questions about computer hacking and technology. Some of the contestants had their shirts off, men and a few women, bare skin. Out in the audience, people were bouncing a huge rubber ball from aisle to aisle, shouting and chugging down more beer, while onstage a woman in a black bra and garter belt was vamping around the contestants.

"What's this all about?" asked Weber, wide-eyed as he watched the fracas.

"It's Hacker Jeopardy," explained Morris. "It features free beer and a woman named Miss Kitty with a big paddle. It's humiliate or be humiliated."

"That's the hacker ethos, I take it," said Weber. "Humiliate or be humiliated."

"Yes, sir." Morris nodded. "I won this game three years running. Now they won't let me play."

Another hour of wandering, and Weber had seen enough. He bought dinner for Morris and himself at Nobu, back at Caesar's Palace. The young man was talking faster now, pumped by all that he had seen, and Weber couldn't track everything he was saying.

"Do they let you do your thing at the agency?" Weber asked as he was paying the bill. He was relaxed after his speech, enjoying his day of slumming in the hacker world.

"Not really. They're scared of me. What I do is subversive, by definition. It doesn't have boundaries. It cuts across directorates. They don't like that."

"But that's what the CIA is for, right?" said Weber. "It's their job to be in the space that other people can't get to. If you can knock on the front door, then send the State Department."

"Yes, sir. But these people are scared of the future. They aren't sure how to live in an open world. For most of them, the clock is still stuck at 1989. For some of them, it's still 1945. Their big event every year is the OSS Dinner. I mean, that's sad. They act like it's still a social club."

Weber listened to what the young man said. It worried him. Despite his private battles with the government over the past few years, he wanted a strong intelligence agency.

"How does it get fixed?" he asked.

"Honestly? People could start by doing what you said today, trying to think about what a modern American intelligence agency would look like. Maybe you haven't noticed, but the CIA operates like a second-rate copy of MI6. We're un-American."

Weber looked at his watch. This last comment made him nervous. He had let Morris get tipsy, and now he was going too far.

"I should crash," he said. "I have an early flight back to Seattle tomorrow. This was an eye-opener. I'm grateful to whoever made the arrangements."

"Thank my deputy, Dr. Ariel Weiss. She's the person in my geek shop who gets things done."

"Well, tell Dr. Weiss that she's a superstar."

Morris nodded, but he wasn't quite ready to let Weber go.

"You know what?" he said, leaning toward Weber, his eyes swimming behind those thick glasses. *"I hate working for stupid people. It offends me. That's why we need a new director."*

Morris reached his hand into the pocket of his hoodie and then extended it and shook Weber's hand. In his palm was the medallion of the Information Operations Center, with the center's name along the lower circumference and "Central Intelligence Agency" around the top. On the face of the coin was a blue bald eagle atop a globe formed of zeroes and ones. Above the eagle's head were the words "Stealth," "Knowledge" and "Innovation," above them a large silver key.

Morris let the coin slip from his palm into Weber's as they shook hands.

Weber took the gift. He studied Morris, reticent and opaque as he withdrew his hand and retreated back behind his black-framed spectacles. Weber's eyes fell to the coin, gleaming gold, silver and blue, topped by that big, mysterious key. It was the first moment in which he thought seriously about the possibility of running the CIA, and the idea grew to become a passion in the months ahead—until one October morning, fifteen months later, it became a fact.

James Morris spent one more day in Las Vegas. He wanted to see an old friend from Stanford named Ramona Kyle. She was speaking at DEF CON, too, on civil liberties and the Internet. Morris sat in the audience for her talk. She spoke so fast, the other panelists had trouble keeping up with her. She was a wiry, intense woman, a passionate intelligence packed into a tiny frame. Her hair was tumbling red curls, like Orphan Annie.

When it came time for questions, several attendees with neat haircuts asked about investments. She was something of a cult figure in the venture capital world. She had joined a fund out of Stanford, and discovered start-ups in Budapest, Mumbai, São Paolo, Santiago—all the places, she liked to say, that produced chess champions and didn't have their own investment banks yet. Sometimes she created the companies on her own, bringing people together in a coffee shop in Rio or a bar in Dubai. Eventually she started her own venture fund, and the money flowed so fast she stopped counting it—and started thinking about more serious things.

Kyle had a knack for making money, and people wanted to know her secrets even at this hacker's conference. But she waved off business questions. They bored her. She wanted to talk about the surveillance state, the threat to liberties, the new information order of the world.

A questioner asked her if it was true what was rumored in the chat rooms, that she was the biggest secret funder of WikiLeaks.

"Are you a cop?" responded Kyle. "Next question."

When the panel was over, she handed out cards with the name of an organization she had recently founded, called Too Many Secrets. It took its name from the rearranged anagram of "Setec Astronomy," which was a puzzle at the denouement of the classic hacker movie Sneakers. The organization didn't have a phone number or email address, but if Kyle met someone interesting, she wrote down her contact information in a tiny, precise hand.

Ramona Kyle didn't go out of her way for most people, but Morris was an exception. For years after they graduated she had stayed in touch, mostly at meetings for high-tech eccentrics. She had messaged him a few weeks before the Las Vegas gathering, suggesting that they meet for drinks after her talk. She proposed a bar called Peppermill in the north strip of Las Vegas, a seedy cowboy-hooker part of town where nobody would recognize either of them.

The place was nearly empty. In the center of the bar was a fire pit surrounded by unoccupied pink couches. Kyle was sitting in a dark corner in the back drinking pomegranate juice, no ice. She looked like a homeless girl: tiny body, rag-doll clothes, red hair still wet from a shower after the speech.

Morris sat down next to her on the banquette. At Stanford, he had momentarily wanted to sleep with Ramona Kyle, back when she was anorexic and pure brain energy. Now that she was healthier, she wasn't quite as sexy. As he moved closer to her, she disappeared deeper into the shadows of the booth.

"Did you take precautions?" she asked.

"Of course. I took two cabs and a bus."

"They are out of control," she said. "You have to be careful."

"Stop worrying," said Morris. "I'm here."

1

WASHINGTON

Graham Weber's new colleagues thought that he was joking when he said at his first staff meeting that he wanted to remove the statue of William J. Donovan from the lobby. The old-timers, who weren't really that old but were cynical bastards nonetheless, assumed that he wouldn't actually do it. Donovan was the company founder, for heaven's sake. The statue of him, square-legged with one hand resting on his belt, handsome as a bronze god, ready to win World War II all by himself, had been in the lobby since Allen Dulles built the damn building. You couldn't just get rid of it.

But the new director was serious. He said the agency had to join the twenty-first century, and that change began with symbols. The senior staff who were assembled in the seventh-floor conference room rolled their eyes, but nobody said anything. They figured they would give the new man enough rope to hang himself. Somebody leaked the story to the *Washington Post* the next day, which seemed to amuse the director and also reinforced his judgment about how messed up the place was. To everyone's amazement, he went ahead and removed the iconic figure of "Wild Bill" from its place by the left front door. An announcement said the statue was being removed temporarily for cleaning, but the days passed, and the spot where the pedestal had stood remained a discolored piece of empty floor.

The Central Intelligence Agency behaves in some ways like a prep school. Senior staff members made up nicknames for Weber behind his back that first week, as if he were a new teacher, such as Webfoot, Web-head and, for good measure, Moneybags. Men and women joined in the hazing; it was an equal-opportunity workplace when it came to malcontents. The director didn't appear to care. His actual childhood nickname had been Rocky, but nobody had called him that in years. He thought about bringing it back. The more the old boys and girls tried to rough him up, the more confident he became about his mission to fix what he had called, at that first meeting with his staff, the most disoriented agency in the government. Nobody disagreed with that, by the way. How could they? It was true.

Weber was described in newspaper profiles as a "change agent," which was what thoughtful people (meaning a half dozen leading newspaper columnists) thought the agency needed. The CIA was battered and bruised. It needed new blood, and Weber seemed like a man who might be able to turn things around. He had made his name in business by buying a mediocre communications company and leveraging it to purchase broadband spectrum that nobody else wanted. He had gotten rich, like so many thousands of others, but what made him different was that he had stood up to the government when it mattered. People in the intelligence community had trusted him, so when he said no about surveillance policy, it changed people's minds.

He looked too healthy to be CIA director: He had that sandy blond hair, prominent chin and cheekbones and those ice-blue eyes. It was a boyish face, with strands of hair that flopped across the forehead, and cheeks that colored easily when he blushed or had too much to drink, but he didn't do either very often. You might have taken him for a Scandinavian, maybe a Swede, who grew up in North Dakota: He had that solid, contained look of the northern plains that doesn't give anything away. He was actually German-Irish, from the suburbs of Pittsburgh, originally. He had migrated from there into the borderless land of ambition and money and had lived mostly on airplanes. And now he worked in Langley, Virginia, though some of the corridor gossips predicted he wouldn't last very long.

———————

The president had announced that he was appointing Graham Weber because he wanted to rebuild the CIA. The previous director, Ted Jankowski, had been fired because of a scandal that appeared to involve kickbacks from agency contractors and foreign operations. People said "appeared to involve" because the Jankowski case was still before a grand jury then and nobody had been indicted yet. But even by CIA standards, it was a big mess. Congress was screaming for a new director who could root out the corruption, and they wanted an outsider. Over the past year, Weber had been making speeches about intelligence policy and showing up at the White House for briefings. When the president appointed a commission to study surveillance policy, Weber was on it. By the time Jankowski resigned, he had become the front-runner for the position.

The vetting process took a month of annoying forms and questions. Weber agreed to sell all his company stock; it looked like a market top to him, anyway, and he set up a "blind trust" for the proceeds, as dictated by the ethics police. It embarrassed him, to see how rich he was. The only thing that seemed to agitate the vetters was his divorce from his wife, nearly five years before. They wanted a guilty party, a "story" that would explain why a seemingly happy marriage to a beautiful woman had self-destructed. He referred the White House inquisitors to the court papers in Seattle, knowing that they didn't answer the question, and he left blank their written request for additional information. It wasn't their business, or anyone's, to know that his wife left him for another man, whether to pull Weber's attention away from devotion to his business or because of love, he never knew. The world had assumed that it was his fault; that was the only gift Weber could give his wife at the end of their shared failure, to take the blame. He had tried to date in the five years since, but his heart wasn't in it. "Isn't there anything more?" asked the personnel lawyer. He looked disappointed when Weber shook his head and said firmly: "No."

"That place is like a haunted house," the president told Weber in their last conversation before the appointment was announced. "Somebody needs to clean out the ghosts. Can you do that? Can you fix it?"

Weber was flushed by the challenge; it was provocation to a man like him to attempt the impossible. His children were grown and his house in Seattle was empty most of the time. He had time on his hands, and like many people who have succeeded in business, he wanted to be famous for something other than making money. So with the impulsive hunger and self-confidence of a businessman who had only known success, he agreed to take the job running what the president, in a final, sorrowful comment, described as the "ghost hotel."

The old-timers warned Weber that the agency truly was in bad shape. The foreign wars of the previous decade in Iraq and Afghanistan had gone badly, demoralizing even the nominally successful covert-action side of the agency. The CIA had been asked to do things that previous generations of officers had been accused of but had only imagined, like torturing people for information or conducting systematic assassination campaigns. It would have been bad enough if this Murder, Inc., era had been successful; but aside from getting Osama bin Laden, the main accomplishment had been to create hundreds of millions of new enemies for the United States. The world was newly angry at America, and also contemptuous of its power, which was a bad combination.

Now, in retreat, the CIA needed permission for everything. That was what surprised Graham Weber most in his first days. He was used to the executive authority that comes with running a big company, the license to take risks that is part of creative management. But he was now in a very different place. The modern CIA worked more for Congress than for the president. Out of curiosity, Weber asked at his first covert-action briefing whether the agency had penetrated the networks of anonymous leakers who were stealing warehouses full of America's most classified secrets and publishing them to the world. He was told no, it was too risky for the agency. If the CIA tried to penetrate WikiLeaks, that fact might . . . leak.

Defeated countries are sullen beasts, and America had suffered a kind of defeat. It was like after Vietnam—the country wanted to pull up the covers and watch television—but the CIA couldn't do that, or, at least, it wasn't supposed to. It had a network of officers around the world who were paid to steal secrets. Even the agency's young guns knew this was a time to play it safe, find a lily pad where they could watch and wait. And then along came Graham Weber.

2

WASHINGTON

It took Graham Weber most of the first week to get settled. He had to learn how to use the classified computer system, meet the staff, pay courtesy calls on members of Congress and generally ingratiate himself to a Washington that knew little about him. At the office that first week, Weber made a practice of not wearing a tie. That was how executives had dressed at his company and at most of the other successful communications and technology businesses he knew, but it shook up the CIA workforce, as Weber had intended. After a few days, other men started going tieless to ingratiate themselves to the boss. On Thursday Weber wore a tie, just to confuse them.

He bought an apartment at the Watergate because he liked the view of the Potomac. He hired an interior decorator, who gave it the lifeless perfection favored by the trade. It was much more space than he needed; he was divorced and didn't like to entertain. His two children stayed overnight after his swearing-in ceremony, and they told him he had a cool view, but they went back to school in New Hampshire the next day. The Office of Security insisted on renting an apartment down the hall, to install the director's secure communications and provide a place for his security detail to nap. What Weber liked best was the long balcony that wrapped the living and dining rooms and looked out over the river. But his security chief warned him against sitting there unless he had a guard with him, so he rarely used it. Late at night, he would put a chair by the window and watch the dark flow of the water.

On Friday of his first week, Weber wanted to see his new workplace in Langley at first light, before any of his minions and courtiers were assembled. He arrived at the office at five-thirty a.m. when it was dead empty, to see the sun rise over his new domain. The low-slung concrete of the Old Headquarters Building was a lowering gray in the predawn, a few lights visible on the bottom floors but the top of the building empty and waiting. What would Weber do, now that he was responsible for managing this lumpy pudding of secrecy and bureaucracy? He didn't know.

Weber was accompanied that morning by the security detail that was an inescapable feature of his new life. The head of the detail was a Filipino-American named Jack Fong, built like a human refrigerator, a lifer from the Office of Security. Fong escorted him that morning to the director's private elevator entrance in the garage. It was so quiet in the cab that Weber could hear the tick of his watch. He turned to Fong. Like everyone else in those first days, the security chief was solicitous.

"You want anything, sir?" Fong meant coffee, or pastries, or a bottle of water. But Weber, lost in a reverie, answered with what was really on his mind.

"Maybe I should just blow this place up. Turn it into a theme park and start somewhere else. What do you think of that, Chief?"

The security man, thick-necked and credulous, looked startled. Directors didn't make jokes. There was a bare shadow of a smile on Weber's face, but all the security man saw were the aqua-blue eyes.

"Theme park. Yes, sir. Definitely."

They rode the rest of the way in silence.

Weber sat down at the big desk on the seventh floor and gazed out the shatterproof windows across the treetops to the east, where the first volt of morning was a trace on the horizon. He switched off the lights. The walls were bare and newly painted, stripped of any mark of Jankowski, who had resigned two months before. Now it was his office. The first light flickered across the wall like the lantern beam of an intruder.

Weber studied the desk. It was a massive pediment of oak that might have been requisitioned from Wild Bill's law offices at Donovan, Leisure. There were a few stains on the top, where someone had placed mugs of hot coffee or tea. The side drawers were locked but the middle one was loose. With all the commotion of those first days, Weber hadn't thought to open it. He pulled out the wooden drawer, expecting to find it as empty as the rest of the office.

At the very back of the drawer he found a sealed envelope with his name on the front. He tore open the sealing flap and removed a crisp sheet of paper. It was freshly typed. He read the words carefully:

> *A nation can survive its fools, and even the ambitious. But it cannot survive treason from within. An enemy at the gates is less formidable, for he is known and carries his banner openly. But the traitor moves amongst those within the gate freely, his sly whispers rustling through all the alleys, heard in the very halls of government itself.*
> —*Marcus Tullius Cicero*

Weber turned over the page, feeling a momentary chill, as if a draft of cold wind had just blown through the room. What was he supposed to make of this Roman admonition—and, more to the point, who had surreptitiously placed it in his desk drawer for him to find in his first days at work?

The place was truly haunted, he thought to himself: so many ghosts; so many myths and legends riddling the walls. Not a theme park, but a horror show.

Weber read the message one more time and put it back in the desk. His first wisp of anxiety had given way to curiosity, suffused with anger. Was this a real warning or a general proverb about loyalty? Was Weber meant to be the traitor? Or was it was some sort of practical joke, played on every newly minted director to rattle his nerves?

Weber had thought a good deal about traitors already. He'd had multiple security briefings that first week. This was the post-Snowden era. Finding potential leakers was the first order of business. The workforce was suspect. The decade of war had produced a reaction—an invisible army of whistleblowers and self-appointed do-gooders. The result, as any newspaper reader could see, was that America's intelligence agencies could no longer keep secrets. Security briefers assured the new director it couldn't happen again; CIA employees were watched and assessed, under surveillance every time they logged onto a computer or made a phone call or ordered a pizza.

Weber asked if all this internal surveillance was legal, and he was told, of course it was; employees signed away any right to privacy when they joined the agency.

Weber mused about this "Wiki" enemy that fought with the zeroes and ones of computer code. They were (or could be) anywhere. The result inside government was a new Red Scare. Where people in the 1950s had whispered the name "Rosenberg," now it was "Snowden," or "Manning." Somehow the intelligence community would have to learn how to live with fewer secrets; that was the new way of the world. But Weber was careful about expressing such skeptical views to his staff. These people had been traumatized. Their world had been turned upside down.

Weber tried to get to work, but the words echoed in his mind: "The traitor moves amongst those within the gate freely, his sly whispers rustling through all the alleys . . . in the very halls of government itself." Somebody was messing with his head, trying to knock him off balance. It had to be that.

Graham Weber greeted the secretaries, Marie and Diana, when they arrived at 7:55. They looked mildly embarrassed that the boss was already at work. But they had been through multiple directors and they knew that nobody lasts forever in the big office on the seventh floor, no matter how early they get to work. The "girls," as they had been known until not very long ago, were part of the CIA's invisible army of support staff who typed the cables and hid the secrets and cleaned up after those more exalted on the organization chart.

Weber was in shirtsleeves, tieless, two buttons unstuck. He shook Marie's hand, and then Diana's, still feeling like a visitor a week in.

"Good morning, ladies," he said. "I let myself in."

"You can start whenever you like, Mr. Weber," said Marie, the older of the two, who was now working for her fifth director. "We come in at eight."

"Marie, a word," he said, motioning for the senior woman.

"Yes, Director."

Marie was a blonde in her late fifties, smart and tough enough to run the place herself, people imagined, except for the fact that she'd never gone beyond junior college. She was the CIA's version of a senior non-commissioned officer. She had long ago dumped her first husband, an alcoholic case officer, and had given up on finding a second one. Diana, a much younger African-American woman, retreated to her desk. She was married to a senior officer in Support; they were planning to retire in another year and come back as contractors with green badges.

"In my office," said Weber, nodding toward the big room.

Marie followed him in, switching on the fluorescent lights as she entered. He closed the door.

"I want to ask you something," he said. "Privately, please."

"Everything is private with me, Mr. Weber. I work for one director at a time."

"Who has access to my office? Besides you and Diana, I mean."

Marie thought a moment. He wouldn't be asking if there wasn't a problem.

"The Office of Security," she said. "They swept it last week, one last time, to make sure."

"And who conducted the sweep?"

She looked genuinely embarrassed not to know the answer.

"I'm not sure. We have to scoot when they make their rounds."

"And remind me, Marie, who does the Office of Security report to?"

She looked at him quizzically, as if it were a trick question.

"They report to you, of course, as of last Monday."

"Right. But before this week?"

"Well, technically, the top of the chain would have been the acting director, Mr. Pingray. But as I think you know, he recused himself on most management issues, owing to his close relationship to Mr. Jankowski. He's trying to do the right thing, Mr. Pingray."

"Got it. So who did the Office of Security really report to, then, before Monday morning, if not Mr. Pingray?"

Her mouth wrinkled at the edges while she thought about that one.

"I suppose they reported to the director of National Intelligence, Mr. Hoffman. He's your boss, on paper, so he must be everyone's, ultimately."

Weber thought a moment. Could he ask Cyril Hoffman, the man who was responsible for oversight of sixteen intelligence agencies, whether he had been sending secret messages? No, of course he couldn't. He thought of asking the bright young computer maven he had met a year before in Las Vegas, James Morris, but that wasn't appropriate.

"Thank you, Marie," he said.

She headed for the door and then stopped and turned back toward him.

"Mr. Director," she said. "I just want to say, we're all very glad that you're here. People want you to succeed. They think you can fix things."

Weber laughed, not happily.

"That's what the president said. He also told me this place was like a haunted house. Do you think that's true, Marie?"

She nodded, with what Weber thought was a look of institutional pride.

Weber went to the window and looked at the cars of the early arrivals beginning to fill the parking spaces in the agency's Candy Land collection of color-coded lots. It was interesting how many agency officers drove foreign cars. You wouldn't find that at an Air Force base, or a Navy yard. The CIA didn't know whether it wanted to be a blue state or a red state. That was part of its problem.

Weber returned to the desk, which was a toasty brown in the spreading light. How was he going to get this place working again, really? Atop his desk was a notepad crowned with the agency seal and its pugnacious eagle. He took out a pen and wrote down phrases that came to him, and then crumpled the sheet: A week at the CIA and he was thinking in Power-Point. He was about to throw the note in the burn bag when it occurred to him that someone might find it and read it, so he put in his pocket.

3

HAMBURG

Far from Washington, a young man skittered toward the U.S. Consulate in Hamburg like a shorebird blown by the North Sea wind. He was dressed in low-slung jeans and a zip-up gray hoodie, his hands thrust deep in his pockets. His eyes were dark-rimmed with fatigue, and he was shivering in the cold October breeze that raked the inland lake along the Alster-ufer. At the gate, the guard stopped the visitor, but he showed his Swiss passport and said he had an urgent appointment.

Inside the guardhouse, the Marine told the youth to lower his hood so that his face was visible. The top of his head was thin stubble, like a layer of soot. In his right ear were three metal studs. Tattooed on his neck were a dotted line and the Russian words, Вырезать здесь. His passport identified him as Rudolf Biel. The guard wanted to send him away, but the young man said slowly and emphatically that he needed to talk to the director of the Central Intelligence Agency.

"I have a message for Graham Weber, CIA director, no one else but him."

He was a mess. His eyes were bulging and red-veined. His pallid skin was dotted with acne scars, as if he had lived his entire life in a cave. He spoke English with a German accent. His passport said he was from Zurich.

"Do you have an appointment with Mr. Weber?" asked the Marine guard behind the glass. It was a dumb question, but the Marine was confused. He had never seen a walk-in, twenty-five years after the Cold War.

"I must see him, the new CIA director. Mr. Clean. He will want to talk to me, sir, believe me."

The Marine behind the glass shook his head. He thought for a moment and then handed the man a form with an email address and phone number and told him to make an appointment. But this only made the visitor more agitated and insistent.

"Listen to me: This is a big secret. Email is not safe. I want a face-to-face meeting only, with Mr. Weber." He pointed his finger as he spoke, to emphasize his point. "No Internet. No electronic message. Otherwise, I am finished." He said these last words in deadly earnest.

The Marine pointed to the Russian words tattooed on the man's neck. At least he could start with that.

"What does that mean, in English?"

"It says, 'Cut here.'" The Swiss youth gave a cockeyed grin and then glowered at the guard. "I mean it," he said. "I am a dead man if you don't let me in."

The guard stared at him a moment longer and then nodded. He told the man to wait outside while he called the regional security officer. He didn't want to be blamed for letting in the scruffy young man or keeping him out.

The Swiss boy stood shuffling outside, hands stuffed into the pockets of his sweatshirt. The visitor glanced every few seconds over his shoulder, down the Alsterufer toward the bridge on Kennedybrücke, a long block away. A passerby glanced at him and made a distasteful face when he saw the shaved head and scruffy clothes. This was Hamburg's fanciest neighborhood. What was this clod of dirt doing here?

The visitor stuck his hands deeper against the wind. The waters of the Alster were like corrugated tin. The sun had vanished behind thick clouds, shadowing the lakeside walk in the flat gray of late afternoon. To the south were the towers of old Hamburg, to the west the great docks and freight yards along the Elbe River, and, beyond that, the North Sea and escape.

The regional security officer arrived at the guardhouse, carrying the red binder with the code phrases. He looked at the young man's passport and summoned him back inside the security hut. He'd been working at the State Department for nearly thirty years, long enough to remember what a defector was.

"Mr. Weber doesn't work here," said the security officer. "He works in Washington. Why do you want to see him?"

"I have special information. It is too dangerous to tell anyone else. I know a very big secret." The Swiss boy stared the State Department functionary dead in the eyes. His hands were open before him, as if he were holding an invisible gift that he wanted to present.

The officer nodded. There was something about the young man's intensity that made him believable. He looked in his red folder and dialed the number of one of the nominal political officers, K. J. Sandoval.

"Mr. Bolt is here. He says he has a package for Mr. Green."

There was a long pause. The CIA officer inside had forgotten the walk-in procedures, too, and she needed to look at her own cheat sheet.

"Is this a joke?" she muttered into the phone while searching. "The Cold War is over."

"No, ma'am." His voice was clipped. "No joke."

"Okay. Sorry." A few more seconds passed, until she found her script. "Did Mr. Bolt say what was in the package?"

"Nope. Just says it's important."

There was another pause, as she looked in the list of code phrases for what she wanted to ask. It wasn't there.

"Is he a nut?"

The security officer studied the man standing on the other side of the glass barrier. He had unzipped his hoodie, revealing a dirty black T-shirt with the faded inscription DEF CON XX and a skull and cross-bones. On his wrist was a bracelet with metal studs. He was a normal adult's bad dream, yet his eyes—as fearful and strung out as they were—were alive with intelligence.

"It's hard to say what he is," answered the security officer. "He looks like a punk, basically. He's standing here. Check him out yourself on the closed circuit. It's your call. I can send him packing if you want."

She studied the grainy camera image. He looked like a loser, but she was a new base chief, and she'd never had a walk-in. And she was bored with the ever-repeating loop of the European economic crisis. It was the only topic on which anyone in Washington ever queried the consulate or Embassy Berlin these days. It would be a pleasure to think about something different.

"What the hell?" she said. "Bring him up. I'll be in Conference Room A."

4

HAMBURG

K. J. Sandoval was waiting behind a polished teak table when the walk-in arrived upstairs, gangly and frightened, escorted by the security officer. The "K" stood for "Kitten," her given name. The base chief was a handsome Latina woman in her late thirties, lips freshly glossed, appropriate black suit. She was nearly ten years into her career as a CIA officer, in that awkward period between just getting started and waiting it out until retirement. She knew how to be patient: She was the oldest daughter of a Mexican immigrant from Monterrey who had joined the Marine Corps and risen to gunnery sergeant, E-7, before retiring to Tucson. Her mother had been a waitress until she got her high school equivalency certificate; now she worked for an insurance company. Sandoval had made her way in the agency by hard work and a friendly smile but she was stuck.

Rudolf Biel was buried in the hood of his sweatshirt when he entered the room, but he lowered it when he saw Sandoval. He looked even less healthy close up than he had on camera. Under the fluorescent light of the conference room, his pale, blemished skin had the mottled look of an albino lizard.

"I'm Helen Sturdevant," she said, giving him a card with her alias name and a phone number and email. He rolled his eyes and made a slight jerk of his head, as if to say, *Right!* She motioned for him to sit down and took a chair opposite. She looked at his passport.

"You're from Zurich, right? What do you do there?"

"I am a hacker. Okay? *Hakzor.* Sometimes Zurich, sometimes Berlin, sometimes Saint Petersburg. If you knew, well, you would know."

"Do you want to talk German? *Ich spreche Deutsch.*"

"I like English. *Hakzor spreche English.*"

"What do you hack?"

"Everything. With banks, I am the best. I am Swiss, what else? I am expert in ACH hack. Automated Clearing House. You know what that is?"

"No. Explain."

"Too complicated. No time."

"I have plenty of time."

"No, you don't, lady. You have a problem, and no time."

She looked at the passport again, and then at his face. He was smart, whoever he was.

"You said you wanted to meet Mr. Weber, our new director."

He nodded. "Yes, only Graham Weber. He needs me. It is worse than he thinks at CIA. I can help."

Sandoval suppressed a smile. Who did this kid think he was, marching into the consulate and demanding to see the director? He looked to be stoned, from the redness of his eyes. Download him and get rid of him.

"What you ask is not possible. Mr. Weber is in Washington. I'm his personal representative here in Hamburg. You can give me your message, and then I'll tell Mr. Weber. How's that?"

He shook his head. Under the stubble of hair, you could see the bones of his skull. It wasn't just that he was unshaven; he was dirty. He pointed a long finger at Sandoval.

"Excuse me, miss, you don't have time to be wasting it. They are coming for you."

"Who is coming for us?"

"That's what I must tell Mr. Weber. How will you deliver my message? If it is in person, this is okay. Otherwise, no deal."

She studied him. He was cocky, for a beat-up kid in a smelly T-shirt, demanding to talk to a new CIA director who had been in the job less than a week. He must think he had something important; either that or he was tripping. She wanted to throw him out, but she had already messaged Headquarters about the meeting.

"What does it say on your T-shirt?" she said, playing for time while she thought about what to do.

"'DEF CON.' It's where hackers go to show off."

"Sorry, never heard of it. Where is it?"

"Las Vegas." He smiled. "One of my friends gave it to me."

Sandoval nodded, though what he said didn't make sense: Why would a hacker go to a convention in Las Vegas? She looked at her watch; it was still morning in Washington. She had never handled a walk-in before, but she knew she needed to establish some kind of control and figure out what intelligence, if any, this dirty weirdo possessed.

"Look, Mr. Biel, let's get serious, okay? Otherwise we'll never trust each other. So I'll explain it to you. First, I'll send Mr. Weber a message, maybe later if he's interested I'll talk to him by phone. And then, maybe, if he's really interested, we can both talk to him in person. But to get started, I have to know why you're here. What's this message that's so special that it has to be delivered to Mr. Weber? You tell me that, and then we'll see what we can do."

He put his stubbly head in his hands, scratching the tiny hairs as if he could help the brain inside to think. He looked up and leaned toward her, so the tattoo on his neck was in front of her face.

"You do not understand."

"No, I don't. That's why I want you to explain it to me."

"You see my tattoo?" He pulled back the sweatshirt so she could see the dotted lines on his neck. "It means, 'Cut here.' The people who wrote that on me, they will do it, yes, in a minute, and nobody will know. That's why I communicate in person. No email. No message. Direct."

She reached out and tried to take his hand. Empathy, rapport: That had worked with a young woman from the Iranian Embassy in Madrid. But this one was too skittish; he pulled his hand back.

"Why is it so dangerous, Mr. Biel? You have to help me out. Otherwise, I'm going to have to ask you to leave."

He closed his eyes. He thought a long moment. Fifteen seconds, maybe twenty, a time that feels like forever when you're waiting for an answer. Then he spoke, slowly, knowing the weight of his words.

"People are inside your system. Your messages can be read. They are not secret. That is what I need to tell Mr. Weber."

Kitten Sandoval sat back in her chair. Now he had her attention.

"What do you mean, they're not secret? I assure you, Mr. Biel, our communications are very secure. The most secure in the world."

Now there was a trace of a smile on his lips. He had power.

"That is what you think. But you are wrong. You have been hacked. Your messages can be read. People are coming at you. They are planning something. That is what I know, which I must tell to Mr. Weber."

"But why to him? He's only been on the job a few days."

"They are afraid of him. Weber is the clean one. Not scared of anybody. That is why they are rushing. That is why I had to come now."

"We have a secure website, Mr. Biel. You can send him a message that way."

"Poof! Not so secure. I looked at it. Secure Socket Layer. What a joke! For my friends, it is an open book."

"How do you know all this? You must tell me that, or I won't believe you."

He pointed a finger to his head, as if to the brain inside.

"Hey, are you stupid? I know it because I am a hacker man. I know the ones who have stolen the key. 'Swiss Maggot,' you know that name? That is me."

He wrote it down in Leet, the hacker-beloved mix of letters and symbols: *5W155 ma99O7.*

"Sorry, that's a new one for me."

"Okay, 'Friends of Cerberus,' you know who they are? You need to make this connection. I tell you. How about 'the Exchange'? Eh?"

"No. What are 'Friends of Cerberus'?" You've got me there. And I don't know any 'Exchange.' Help me out."

He threw up his hands and sat up tall in his chair, his spindly, half-shaved body like a giant bug. He glowered at her.

"You don't know anything. That's why I need to talk to Graham

Weber. He will understand why these people are, what is it you say? Your 'worst nightmare.'"

"I don't have nightmares, Mr. Biel. Now calm down and explain: Why are you coming to us now with this information about our communications? Do you want money?"

"No!" he scoffed. "I could make more than you as a simple carder stealing your Visa shit, believe me."

"Then what do you want?"

He gripped the table, as if holding on for life. "I want protection. I want to get out. I need to escape."

"Do you have anything you can show me? So that I will know that what you say is real?"

He closed his eyes for a moment, pallid lids folding onto the gray pouches below.

"Bona fides." He took a piece of paper out of his pocket. It was folded and creased, and discolored from the grime of his jeans. He handed it to her.

"What's this?" she asked.

"This is a list of your agency officers in Germany and Switzerland. You look at this, then tell me what you think."

She opened the piece of paper and scanned the list. Midway through the list she found her own name. Her face lost color. The carefully painted nails fluttered slightly at the edges of the paper. She put it down and looked him in the face.

"This is impossible," she said.

"No, it is real, Miss Sturdevant. You are inside us and we are inside you."

"Do you know how this is done? How this information was obtained?"

"Of course I do know. That is why I am here. It is because I know this secret that my life is in danger."

"Why is your life in danger, Mr. Biel?"

"They think I have gone soft on them. So they try to kill me, already, in Saint Petersburg a week ago. That is why I come to you. Otherwise, I am a dead man. Maybe now you see?"

"Yes, now I see."

"Okay, Miss Sturdevant. Even though I know you are really named Kitten Sandoval. What kind of a name is that? You sound like a stripper, but I know you work for CIA."

She asked if she could make a call to Headquarters, but he said no, he didn't trust any message, he needed an answer now. So she had to improvise. She said she would give him five thousand dollars immediately. She would contact Graham Weber's office directly after their meeting, speaking only to his confidential assistant, not sending any message that could be intercepted. She would request an immediate exfiltration for Rudolf Biel and secure transportation to Washington, where he could tell his story and be paid.

"How much?" he demanded. "I cannot hack 'black hat' after this, too dangerous, so I need 'white hat' money." He was bolder, now that he knew that his information had value.

"I can't make that decision. But we will pay you enough that you won't have to worry about money. You explain how our computer systems have been compromised, walk us through it and tell us about this attack that's coming, and we'll make you a consultant and you'll never have to work for anyone again."

"Okay, I stay here at American Consulate on Alsterufer until you get answer."

"I'm sorry, that's not possible. No visitor is allowed to remain overnight on the compound, ever. But we will put you in a safe house here in Hamburg, with food and beer and everything you need, and then when it's time, we'll come get you. How's that?"

He shook his head.

"You did not understand me. Your safe house is not safe. They can find them. I can't stay there."

"Are you kidding? How can they know the location of our safe houses? Even I don't know where all of them are. You'll be okay there. Trust me."

"GTFO."

"What does that mean?"

"Get the fuck out." He ran the words together in his German-accented English.

She was about to laugh despite herself, but the young man was already moving. He rose from the chair across from her and put his hand on his sunken chest, against the DEF CON logo.

"I will take care of myself. I come back in three days, on Monday morning, after the weekend. I will come at ten a.m. Tell your people to let me in right away, no waiting, no chances. If you are not ready to take me in then, forget it. I go away forever, and your systems can all be hacked and all your information out on the street, what do I care?"

"Can we give you a phone, so we can contact you?"

"No. I told you, they can read it. They can track the GPS. Safer to be a lone dog, with no electronic signals coming off me."

"I'd be happier if we were protecting you."

He laughed, in his fashion, a choked, mirthless little cough.

"Who do you kid, Miss Sandoval? You cannot protect yourself."

He wanted to leave right away. She offered to transport him anywhere he wanted to go in Hamburg, in a secure vehicle without diplomatic tags. She offered a bodyguard to accompany at a distance, or watchers to see if anyone was following him, but he refused all that. Finally, she said she would send him out of the consulate compound through a tunnel with a hidden exit.

This last proposal he accepted. He took the money from her, and signed a receipt, though he wrote with such a scrawl it was impossible to read. Sandoval asked for an Internet address, a phone number, anything, but he refused. She thought of putting a GPS tracker on him, but the trackers were locked up in the storeroom.

Accompanied now by several security men, they walked down several flights of stairs and into a passageway that led to a tunnel under the back of the consulate property.

As Biel's spindly body moved the last few yards up the tunnel incline toward the exit door, Sandoval had a tightness in her stomach. She wanted to call him back and tell him to stop, that it was too dangerous to leave, that she would find some way to let him stay at the consulate, regardless of what the rules said. But the lead security officer was already opening the door, and the Swiss had pulled up his hood to hide himself.

"Wait," she said. But the Swiss boy was up the ladder and through the hatch and out onto the Warburgstrasse, which ran behind the consulate. She waved goodbye to him, but he didn't look back.

5

FREDERICK, MARYLAND

Ramona Kyle didn't visit Washington very often. It made her feel ill, physically, to be there: cramps in her stomach and sometimes a migraine that didn't ease until she had left the city. Washington represented everything that she thought was wrong about where America had headed over the decades she had been alive. Each year, it became more remote and arrogant. Its rituals and institutions were for show. Members of Congress pretended to oversee the executive branch; the courts performed the rites of judicial review; presidents reported each January about how they had enlarged life, liberty and happiness. It was like a victory parade in a people's democratic republic. Any connection with reality was disappearing. The truth was that America was losing touch more every year with the values the founders had cherished.

The last time Kyle had come to Washington she had visited the Jefferson Memorial in the late afternoon and sat on its steps and wept. The tears had come again each time she looked up at the walls of the rotunda and saw the libertarian president's words chiseled in the stone. Finally one of the guards got nervous about the presence of this sobbing woman and asked her to leave.

Kyle needed to see people who worked in Washington, but she wasn't ready to infect herself with a visit to D.C. So she asked a few essential contacts to come to her, taking appropriate precautions. She set herself up in the town of Frederick, about an hour northwest of the capital. Her personal assistant found a boutique inn outside Frederick and made a reservation in her own name, to shield Kyle's privacy. It was a weekend hideaway where the bedrooms were named after fictional couples. Kyle chose the bedroom named for Nick and Nora Charles, not because she was expecting any romantic visitors—she didn't *do* that— but out of respect for the author, Dashiell Hammett, who had refused to testify against his Communist friends and colleagues during the McCarthy era.

Kyle met her visitors away from the hotel, in spots that ringed the town. Her first caller was the staff director of Too Many Secrets, though he didn't carry that title because the organization didn't officially have any staff, much less a director. What it had was money from Kyle's substantial personal fortune to give away to groups and people fighting for what Kyle, in her speeches and op-ed pieces, called "Open America."

She reviewed the anti-secrecy agenda with her Washington man in a pavilion decked with red, white and blue bunting in Shafer Park in Boonsboro. Next to the pavilion was a towering American flag, and beyond that a baseball diamond where kids were noisily playing ball. The diminutive woman sat under the shade of the gazebo and discussed with her lieutenant how to keep up the flow of funds for legal defenses of people who had been charged with leaking government information. She scanned the half dozen accounts she used to send money to people on the front lines against secrecy, "our heroes," she liked to say, though she was careful even with this closest assistant not to identify who they were.

The second caller was the legislative assistant of one of the senators who represented her home state of California and now served on the Senate Intelligence Committee. Ramona Kyle had been a generous contributor to his campaigns, and she asked for little in return, other than that her favorite senator monitor abuses by intelligence agencies. She never requested classified information, but she always seemed to know what was on the committee's agenda, which made it easier for her to press her points. The aide explained that the senator would soon be introducing a new bill to restrict funding for the National Security Agency. That pleased Kyle, even though she knew it was for show, and that the senator, like most influential members of Congress, only pretended to oppose what she regarded as illegal surveillance.

Late that afternoon, Ramona Kyle met her old Stanford classmate James Morris. She had messaged him through an email account they had shared since graduate school. She proposed that they rendezvous at the Antietam National Battlefield, a few miles south of where she was staying. It was an anonymous enough destination, the sort any tourist would visit. Morris drove his Prius up I-270 from his apartment in Dupont Circle, and Kyle took a taxi from her inn in Boonsboro.

They met on the walkway that skirted the battlefield monuments. Morris was wearing a cardigan sweater and jeans, and his favorite pair of hiking boots. His hair was blowing in the afternoon breeze, and he looked almost handsome. Kyle appeared half his size, cloaked in a bulky wool turtleneck that obscured the shape of her body. Her frizzy red hair was tied back in a ponytail, and she was wearing a cap with the words ASTON VILLA, which was the name of her favorite soccer team, a sport she followed passionately.

It was flat ground, fields and orchards framed by the Blue Ridge in the distance, a natural arena in which two armies might collide. The humble white brick church around which the battle had been fought stood just beyond them on a rise. Kyle was wearing dark glasses and scarcely looked up from the walkway.

They immediately fell into intense conversation, as if they were taking up the thread of a dialogue that had been momentarily interrupted. They walked close together, the spindly man occasionally bumping into the tiny woman, each of them stopping suddenly to make a particular point. Ramona Kyle famously had no friends at Stanford save one, James Morris, and she seemed to shed her shyness and disdain for people when he was present. She was the only child of a brilliant, reclusive composer, and she treated Morris much as if he were the brother she didn't have. Morris, who also lived in a world where he had few close friends or intellectual equals, reciprocated the intimacy. He called her "K" and she called him "Jimmy," names they used with no one else.

"How do you survive it?" Kyle said after they had been talking for a time about Morris's life in Washington. By "it" she meant all the aspects of government that she found repellent.

"I multitask," he answered. "The right hand doesn't talk to the left hand, but the juggler never drops the ball."

"You scare me," she said. "You're such a good . . . spy."

They walked on toward the obelisks and pillars that marked the battle that had been fought on this ground on September 17, 1862. Ramona had seemed oblivious of the surroundings, but now she spoke up.

"Do you know how many people died here, Jimmy? It was twenty-three thousand, counting both sides. That's the most people that were killed in one day in any battle, ever, anywhere."

She took his hand and pulled him to a stop.

"Close your eyes and you can see the bodies. They're heaped up, one on top of the other. They're pleading for water. They want someone to come and shoot them dead, it hurts so much. That's what war is. Don't forget that."

"I don't," said Morris.

Kyle still had her eyes closed, smelling death in her nostrils. She took off her dark glasses and looked him full in the face.

"Listen to me, Jimmy: It was five days after Antietam when Lincoln issued the first draft of the Emancipation Proclamation. Do you know why? I think it's because it had to *mean* something, all this suffering. There was no turning back. It's the same for you. You can't stop now."

"I know."

Her voice fell. She took his hand.

"Did you bring me anything?"

"Yes," he said. He took a thumb drive out of the pocket of his jeans and, in one invisible motion, put it in her open palm, which closed around it. She thrust the hand into her own pocket under the bulky sweater.

"There's someone I want you to meet," she said. "He can tell you the real story, the secret history."

"Of what, K?"

"Of the CIA. He's a historian. He used to work at the agency, retired now. He was a friend of my father's. It will rock you, what he says. His name is Arthur Peabody. I'll have someone send you his number."

"Not now," said Morris, shaking his head. "In a week or two. It's too busy now. I have a new boss. The place is vibrating."

"Is Weber for real?" asked Kyle. "If he's serious, they'll destroy him."

"I don't know," answered Morris. "I guess we'll find out."

They walked a little longer, but it was getting dark. She nudged him back toward the parking lot and told him to get home before it was too late. "You're a shit driver," she said. "They shouldn't let you have a car."

She stood on her tiptoes and gave him a kiss.

Kyle called the Boonsboro taxi to come pick her up. She ate dinner alone, as she did most meals. The only decent restaurant in town was a steak house. She was a vegetarian, but they let her make a meal of grilled mushrooms and steamed broccoli.

The next morning Kyle met a fourth visitor. This one was more careful about the rendezvous even than she was. He took a bus to Frederick, then a taxi to Boonsboro, then walked the three miles northeast to Greenbrier State Park, an isolated pocket of woods that was empty even on a good day. He was of medium height, solidly built, his features obscured by a cap and sunglasses. Someone who knew him would have noticed that his well-cut hair was concealed by a shaggy wig. He spoke to others only when he had to, in language-school English that was nearly flawless, so that you barely heard the foreign accent. He called himself "Roger," in this identity.

The man waited under a wooden shelter as the low October sun cast its beam on the water. The morning was still, almost windless. He didn't turn when the taxi crested the access road from Route 40 and turned into the parking lot to deposit a passenger. A woman emerged from the backseat and, as the car revved back toward the highway, she strolled toward the lake, taking the long way toward the pavilion to make sure the park was empty.

Kyle sat down on the park bench across from the visitor.

"We only have fifteen minutes," she said. She leaned toward him across the picnic table and spoke so quietly that even someone sitting at the next bench could not have heard what she said.

6

WASHINGTON

K. J. Sandoval's message arrived at Headquarters late Friday morning, Washington time. She sent it in her pseudonym, which wasn't Kitten or even Helen, but "Mildred G. Mansfield." It was transmitted on the "restricted handling" channel, personal for the director. In cablese, she described the Swiss walk-in (REF A) to the Hamburg consulate (LOC B); she summarized his claim that the agency's internal communications had been compromised, including true names of officers of an organization she referenced only by cryptonym.

She sent Rudolf Biel's true name and the location where he had appeared in separate cables for security. She described his warning that agency systems were insecure, and his supporting evidence in the list of officers' names in Germany and Switzerland. She noted his references to Friends of Cerberus and the Exchange, but left out his self-description as "Swiss Maggot." She asked that any traces on him be run off-line. She concluded by saying that he had refused to stay in an agency residence, believing that it was unsafe, and that he would return to the consulate on Monday morning.

The message was restrained and professional, but it rang alarm bells. It was routed to Graham Weber through the Europe Division, to which Sandoval reported, with a copy to the director's chief of staff, Sandra Bock. When the message landed on the seventh floor, Weber was at lunch on Capitol Hill visiting the chairman and ranking member of the House Intelligence Committee. The communications clerk made sure the chief of staff was notified that the director had an RH message in his queue.

Bock knew the information was urgent as soon as she read it. The worst calamity for an intelligence agency is a penetration agent or a code break, and this hinted at both. She cabled the base in Hamburg and told Sandoval to stay put, pending instructions. Bock was not an excitable person. She was a twenty-year CIA veteran who had risen in the organization through brute competence, starting as a Near East South Asia analyst, then moving to Science and Technology, then serving as station chief in Tunis and finally running the Support directorate. She was a sturdy woman, big all over and allergic to dieting. She dressed in black pants suits every day, as if she were wearing a uniform.

Bock considered alerting the director while he was at lunch. But she decided it would be unsettling for him and might only make the members of Congress ask questions. She checked to see if the head of the Office of Security was in the building, but he was traveling. As a backup, she checked the Information Operations Center, which was located in an office block a few miles away. The director, James Morris, was at lunch, so she left a message asking him to call as soon as he returned.

Finally, she called Weber's security detail and asked the chief to alert her when the boss was leaving the Capitol on his way back to Langley. She was waiting in his outer office when he returned.

Weber was removing the necktie he had worn for his luncheon at the Capitol when he walked in the door. His cheeks were red. At the congressmen's insistence, he'd had a glass of wine at lunch. He was hurrying. His face said, *Don't bother me.*

"What's up?" he asked Bock, barely looking at her. He wanted her answer to be nothing, so that he could get to work on the pile of paper in his in-box. Listening to the congressmen lecture him about how to run the agency had put him in a bad mood. But she was such a large presence he couldn't very well walk around her.

"I think you need to take a look at this, Mr. Director," she said. "It arrived while you were at lunch." She handed him the cable, clad in a red folder, and followed him into his interior office.

Weber sat down at his big desk and studied the cable and attachments. When he finished, he looked up at her, focusing those marble-blue eyes. He trusted Bock, a tough woman manager who didn't know how to cut corners. He was sensible enough, in his first week, to take her advice before issuing any orders.

"What the hell does this mean?" he asked.

He motioned for Bock to sit down, but she remained standing.

"We don't know. But we have to assume that it could be bad."

"I thought CIA communications were unbreakable. That's what people have been telling me all week."

"Nothing is unbreakable, sir. Our systems are supposed to be secure, unless someone is inside the gap."

CIA systems, in theory, were protected by what was known as an "air gap," which meant that they were entirely separate, electronically, from the Internet or any other nonsecure computing systems.

Weber thought a moment. There wasn't passion or anxiety on his face, just the cold calculation of options and possibilities.

"Could this be some kind of provocation from another service?" he asked.

"Maybe," answered Bock. "Most of our people are declared to the Germans and Swiss. Someone could get those officers' names through liaison. But I don't understand how this walk-in would have that information from any normal channel."

"Why did she let him leave the consulate?"

"She thought she had no choice."

"Mistake," said Weber. "There's always a choice."

The director thought some more. He put a finger to his lip and traced its outline while his chief of staff waited like a big black crow across from his desk.

"Who's the best person to manage this? You know the staff. I don't. Who's the right one? Start with the case officer. Who's she?"

"I pulled her file," said Bock. "Her name is K. J. Sandoval. The 'K' is for Kitten, and don't ask me because I don't know. She's a hard worker, good fitness reports, GS-13 but will probably never make supergrade. She has a few recruitments, but nothing spectacular. I'm told EUR gave her the base in Hamburg as a reward for not making trouble."

"She sounds like mediocrity, squared."

"I can't disagree with that, Director."

"Who else? The Clandestine Service is just sitting around waiting for me to make a mistake. Who's a superstar over there?"

"The NCS doesn't do superstars anymore. Operations officers decided that sticking their necks out was dangerous to their health. I'd suggest you ask Mr. Beasley, for starters."

"Black Jack Beasley is a card counter," said Weber. "That's what everyone says. He'll always stand on seventeen."

Earl Beasley was the first African-American to head the National Clandestine Service. His nickname "Black Jack" came not from his skin color, but because in his younger days he had hustled every casino from Las Vegas to Atlantic City. He was a math prodigy who had dropped out of Princeton to play cards. His secret advantage had been racism. People just couldn't imagine back then that a black man could actually keep track of all the numbers. Later, before joining the agency, Beasley had a brief but very lucrative stint as a trader for an investment bank. He was a risk-taker, which Weber liked, but he had become a creature of the CIA culture.

"Who else can we bring in? I want someone who's smart enough to see around corners. This walk-in is a serious hacker, from what Sandoval says in her cable. What about the young guy who runs Information Ops? I met him last year. He seemed smart as hell."

"James Morris," she said, taking a step toward his desk. "He's the director of the Information Operations Center. The book on him is that he's a computer genius. He used to be a mathematician, then some kind of hacker. He's spooky smart, that's what everyone says."

Weber's eyes narrowed. It was part of his character, as a smart man himself, to believe that other smart people could solve problems. He'd been known at his company for picking the brightest kids and giving them lots of responsibility. That was part of his management style, hiring the special while bypassing the ordinary.

"I liked this kid when I met him," said Weber. "He's hard to read, but he knows a lot. Get him over here."

"I called him while you were on the Hill. He was at lunch, but I left an urgent message."

"Find him. I want to talk with him as soon as I can this afternoon. I have to meet with employees at four. After that let's have a senior staff meeting at five with Beasley and the general counsel and the DDI and whoever else should be on the card, plus Morris. Does that make sense?"

"Yes, Mr. Director, I'll let you know when Morris is on his way." She spoke crisply, without a trace of emotion on her face. That was the problem with Bock. She was so immune to charm and manipulation that she didn't give any clues what she was thinking beneath the surface.

"And call the base chief in Hamburg. Tell her you've briefed me, and to sit tight while we figure out what to do."

Marie knocked on the director's door just after three and said that Mr. Morris had arrived. Weber had a sense of anticipation, the way he used to feel before launching a new business deal.

James Morris hadn't changed from what Weber remembered. He was tall and thin. The glasses were tinted now, and he was wearing a plain black T-shirt and a black linen jacket. He didn't look like anyone else that Weber had met in his first week at the CIA.

"What do you know?" asked Weber. It was his habitual, informal greeting. He took Morris's hand. "Good to see you again."

"You got the big office," said Morris, trying to reciprocate the informality. "Quieter than Caesar's Palace."

"Not anymore," said Weber.

Weber motioned for Morris to take a seat on the couch, while he settled into the big easy chair. Weber's office was still undecorated except for a large map of the world and a photograph of the president. What drew the eye was the outdoors, glimpsed through the glass windows. With the trees nearly stripped of their leaves in mid-October, it was a scene painted with a palette of reddish brown, rather than green.

"What have you been doing the past year?" said Weber.

"Working hard, trying some new things, but spinning my wheels a lot of the time. People have been, you know, distracted with the Jankowski thing."

"That's why I'm here," said Weber. "To push 'restart.' Tell me about yourself. The details you weren't supposed to tell me before."

Morris offered a shy half smile. He had a sparkle in his eye, a glitter. Weber had seen it before with very smart people. They were plugged into an energy that wasn't on the normal grid.

"I'm the agency computer guy. That's what you heard, I'm sure. And it's basically true. I was a math major at Stanford, then I spent a couple of years in China working for Microsoft, then went to Carnegie Mellon to do my doctorate in electrical engineering but instead got recruited by Clowns in Action."

"Clowns in Action?"

"Sorry, Mr. Director, inside joke. I apologize."

"Don't. I may use it myself. So keep going. What did you do when you got to the agency?"

"I did Operations. They wanted to send me to S and T, but I could have stayed at CMU if I'd wanted to be an engineer. It turned out that I was good at recruiting systems administrators. We spoke the same language. The Clandestine Service sent me to Paris and Hong Kong. Then they brought me home for a while, and then I worked at the White House on the national security staff for two years. Then they brought me back to run Information Operations. That's me."

"I already know you won Hacker Jeopardy three years in a row."

Morris smiled.

"I didn't tell you my screen name was 'Pownzor.' That's still my nickname at the Information Operations Center. The new kids think it's cool."

"What does it mean, 'Pownzor'?"

"It means, 'I own you.' On the Net, people say you 'pown' someone when you take down his system, and the guy who does it is the pownzor."

Weber was nodding, liking what he heard. Those cold blue eyes were appraising Morris.

"Impressive," said Weber. "And are you still a hacker?"

Morris smiled that wary, coy smile again. "What's the right answer?" he asked.

"There isn't one."

"Then, yes, of course I'm still a hacker. I work for the CIA, for god's sake. That's the biggest hack in the world, right? We own everyone."

"I lied," said Weber. "There was a right answer."

The young man smiled, just an instant. He was losing his shyness. He looked the director in the eye.

"You did something brave this week, Mr. Director."

"What's that? Showing up?"

"You removed the statue of 'Wild Bill' Donovan. He represents some serious agency juju, all the way back to our godparents in London. Some people aren't going to like that."

"Hell, that's just an old piece of sculpture. I'll put it back in a year or two. This place just needs some new faces, a little airing out."

"It's more than that. It's cutting the cord. It's a declaration of independence. It's—" The young man was going to go on, but he stopped suddenly, as if he were about to utter something dangerous, and closed his mouth.

The director got up and called to Marie for some coffee, and in an instant she carried in a tray of beverages, hot and cold, accompanied by cookies and finger sandwiches. Weber poured himself a cup of coffee. As he stirred the grains of sweetener into the black liquid, he made up his mind.

"So I have a problem," said the director. "And I've decided that it's about to become your problem."

Weber waited for Morris to say something, but he didn't, so the director continued. He handed Morris a copy of the cable that had been sent a few hours before from Germany.

"We had a walk-in at our base in Hamburg today. A young man asked to meet with me personally, but the base chief said that was impossible. He was a kid, a hacker from Zurich. He claimed to have urgent information."

"What did he want to tell you?" Morris leaned forward intently and adjusted his glasses.

"He said we had been hacked. Someone had gotten inside our systems. I don't know all the details yet, but he had a list of names of our officers in Switzerland and Germany that my chief of staff Sandra Bock says was legit."

Morris nodded. He didn't speak for a long moment, and then he turned to the director and said, "Of course."

"What does that mean?" asked Weber.

"Of course I'll help, if you want me to."

Weber sat back in his chair, off balance. He wasn't used to someone accepting an assignment he hadn't formally made yet. But he liked the young man's enthusiasm and spontaneity.

"Good. I want fresh eyes on this. I want you to be aggressive, but not stupid. This building would love to see me declare a three-alarm fire and lock all the doors and windows so that nothing will change, ever."

Morris blinked. He looked down at the cable, then back at the director. "Where is the walk-in now?" he asked.

"We don't know. He wouldn't go to one of our safe houses. He said we were penetrated and that we couldn't protect him."

"I'll try to find him, Mr. Director. Bring him out. It's dangerous for him to be alone."

"How are you going to locate someone who disappeared?"

"That's my job, to be inside these networks."

"I thought the hacker underground was off-limits. People have been telling me that all week."

Morris's voice fell to a lower register.

"We have some special operations. They're run outside the building so we don't have to clear them with intelligence committees. I have a few platforms and nonofficial cover slots. Ask Mr. Hoffman. He approved it."

Weber nodded. A week into the job, and the secrets were beginning to come out of hiding.

"Is this kosher? I want you to be aggressive, but legal. This place doesn't need more scandals."

"It's what it is, sir. Like most things around here. I just don't want you to get blindsided."

Weber took the cable in his hand and searched for the name of walk-in.

"Have you ever heard of this Swiss kid, Rudolf Biel?"

"No, sir. But I think I know the organization he's telling us about. They spin around a German hacker group. They have Russian connections, too. We've been pinging them for a while."

Weber drummed his fingers on the table. Morris took a set of jade worry beads from his pocket and then thought better of it and put them back in his pocket.

Weber broke the silence.

"Walk me through it: We need to get him out, but carefully, or his organization will know we're on to them."

"Correct, sir. They will take appropriate precautions."

"But we can't just throw him back. He's a dead man if we do that. So what do you recommend to the new director?"

Morris disappeared behind those glasses for a moment as he pondered the problem. Then he began talking quickly, in a light, staccato voice, almost a patter.

"So . . . maybe we arrange his exfiltration so it looks like he's dead. We prepare something: a car crash or a boat sinking or a drug overdose. We dummy up the paper for the Germans so they confirm he's dead, and meanwhile we get him out on the sly. Then we watch his friends to see if they swallow the lie."

"That works," said Weber. "I like you. You're ready to roll the dice. Let's get you some help."

Weber punched the intercom for Marie. "Get me Beasley," he said.

Morris shook his head and mouthed the word, *No.*

"Hold that," said Weber into the phone. He turned to Morris.

"Don't you need Beasley? He's the head of the Clandestine Service. How are you going to run your exfiltration without him?"

"This should be an IOC case. Beasley would do it old-style, break a lot of furniture."

"But he runs operations."

Morris answered with the assertive tone of a man who wanted to build a new franchise.

"We know the hacker underground, Mr. Director. We aren't afraid of it. Hell, sir, we are it. We have a new capability: I call it our 'special access unit.' We have some ex-military people who help us out. We can use them."

"Christ, how did you get all that? It's not on any budget I've seen."

"It was part of the same authority that gave us the IOC platforms overseas. Right before Director Jankowski left. It was a package. Everyone signed off on it."

"Except me."

The director leaned back and ran his fingers through his blond hair and then patted it in place. He wanted to trust the young computer wizard, but this was his first week on the job.

"I wish we had more time."

Morris's tone was calmer now, more reassuring.

"I can do it, Mr. Director. It's on me, if something goes wrong. My resignation will be on your desk."

Weber laughed at the false bravado.

"Oh, come on, Morris. Don't overdo it. I'll tell Sandra Bock to prepare the paperwork. Just don't screw it up."

Morris offered a thin smile. "Thanks, Mr. Director." He flipped a half salute. "How soon should I get started?"

"Fly to Germany tomorrow. Meet the base chief. Her name is Sandoval. Help her out."

Morris adjusted his glasses. The stubble on his face looked darker, as the afternoon light deepened.

"Who's running the case, me or her?"

"You are. Find him, if you can. And work up your plan for getting him out and debriefing him."

"And you're okay that Mr. Beasley will be unhappy with this. The Hamburg base chief reports to him."

"That's my problem. I'm the director. Be back here at five for a staff meeting. Beasley will be here, along with the other 'clowns.' I'll tell everyone this is the way I want to run it. You can explain your plan."

Morris looked at the director curiously. He was a controlled, restrained man, but there was a flicker in one eye, almost a tremor.

"This will rock the boat, Mr. Director. People won't be pleased."

"Good. I get paid to take risks. You're my first one at the agency. So like I said, don't screw up."

Morris smiled. The momentary tremor had vanished. He gave the director a thumbs-up, and then shook his hand.

"You need to own this, Pownzor," said the director. "I mean it."

Morris nodded gravely. Then the shy smile returned as he walked out the door.

7

WASHINGTON

Marie knocked on Graham Weber's door again a little before four and said they were ready for him downstairs in the bubble. He had scheduled the first of a series of "town hall meetings" with the CIA workforce. He'd held similar sessions for years at his company, open and relaxed, and it had always been part of his management style. The deputy director, Peter Pingray, had offered to introduce him onstage, as a way to help Weber get settled, but Weber had declined. Pingray was an emblem of a past that Weber wanted to eradicate. Sandra Bock, his chief of staff, escorted him to the private elevator and rode down with him to the terrace just to the left of the main lobby. As they descended, Weber thought about the confluence of events that day: the note in his drawer; the visitor in Hamburg. He had modeled what he wanted to do at the CIA, but he couldn't control what his economist friends liked to call the "exogenous" variables.

"What are you going to say?" asked Bock.

"Nothing they'll like very much," Weber answered with a wink. "But at least I'll scare them a little."

Weber heard a smattering of applause when he stepped into the lobby; it got louder at first, and then quieter, and then stopped altogether. People really didn't know what to expect. They were curious, nervous, pissed off, but mostly they wanted to get a glimpse of the man.

The new director walked across the marble floor, past where the Donovan statue used to be. The crowd parted to allow him to exit the front door. People were standing on the statue of Nathan Hale, just to the left outside, to get a better view. Weber continued past the statue to the door of the round-domed auditorium. He hadn't fully realized how needy the place was until he saw all those wary, expectant looks.

It was hot inside the bubble, with so many people. Weber was already tieless, but he took off his jacket when he got to the podium and laid it over a chair. He had the easy, boyish smile he adopted in public. A soft face had always been a useful mask for him.

Weber looked around the room. They were so young, the people in the audience. What was he going to tell them? Not the same old shibboleths about intelligence that they'd been hearing for decades. He wasn't one of the old boys; they weren't his lies to tell and he had no reason not to be honest.

Weber put up his hands for people to stop clapping, but they didn't, so he just started speaking. "Stop, please, and sit down, or I'll think you're all just trying to suck up and will lose respect for everyone in this room."

He meant it as a joke, sort of. It got people to take their seats. Nobody in the CIA wanted to look like an ass-kisser, though the place was as filled with them as any bureaucracy, maybe more so.

"I asked to meet with you at the end of my first week as director, before I forgot why I took the job. This is the real version of what I think, before it gets rubbed down. So take notes, if you like. Tell your retiree friends to call the *Washington Post*. And I know who you leakers are, by the way, especially you, Jim."

He pointed to Jim Duncan, the Africa Division chief in the Clandestine Service, who was a notorious gossip, according to his chief of staff, Bock. That drew laughter from people who knew Duncan, and even those who didn't, it was so unexpected to call him out that way. Agency employees were terrible gossips, especially when they didn't like a new director. They would eviscerate their bosses, leak by leak, and they had already started on Weber.

"Let me begin by stating frankly what everyone in this room knows. There is something seriously wrong at the CIA. Our former director is under criminal investigation. Many agency employees have testified before the grand jury. Even our lawyers are hiring lawyers. Morale is awful. I'm told that operations in some parts of the world have essentially stopped. The only thing that's keeping us alive, people tell me, is our Information Operations, but that's not much help to the rest of the building.

"And the president has asked me to fix it. I want to start by telling you what I told the president. I'm not sure I can."

There were a few groans in the audience. People looked puzzled. They were accustomed to upbeat rhetoric from new directors, wrapped with a lame joke or two, but not to getting hit with a two-by-four.

"You all know that I got the job by saying no to the intelligence community. That's a strange credential, I realize, and a lot of you probably are suspicious about it. But the president decided he liked what I said, and when I told him that I thought the CIA was stuck in the past, he liked that, too. So as uncomfortable as many of you may be with an outsider as director, I have to say: Get over it, please. I got the job, and I have orders from the president to make changes. If you think you can work with me, great. If not, there are a lot of wonderful places to work outside the CIA and you may want to look around."

That brought a general murmuring. These were government workers. The very idea they might lose their jobs was heresy. Weber raised his hand for silence.

"A lot of you will say it's not your fault. And yes, it's true that the agency gets mistreated in Washington. The only thing liberals and conservatives agree on these days is that they don't like the CIA. But that's part of the agency's job, isn't it, to take shots from politicians? If people just had nice things to say, they could say them to the State Department or the Pentagon. Am I right? I think so."

Where was he going with this? From the nervous silence, it was obvious that people didn't know.

"No, the CIA's problem isn't the undeserved blame. It's the deserved blame. From what I have seen and heard, too much of the work product is mediocre. Too little real intelligence work gets done, because people are so busy trying to protect the past and avoid getting hit by the congressional investigation. It's like working at a company that's losing money. It's no fun. Under previous management, it appears that people were so contemptuous of the organization they were actually ripping it off. That's how bad it's gotten. People have been looting their own workplace."

A few people began to applaud, not sure what else to do, and then they stopped. He waited and let the silence build until it was embarrassing and people were fidgeting in their seats, which was exactly what he wanted.

"The president told me that we have a morale problem, and that I should fix it. But with all due respect to anyone in the audience from the White House, that is inaccurate. The CIA has a performance problem. The bad morale is a symptom. The disease is something else. And from what people tell me, it has been going on for a long time.

"Now the question is, why does the CIA have a performance problem? Why is it that so many of the things the agency does turn out badly? Iraq, Afghanistan, Egypt, Syria. How can you do better for policy makers—but forget about them, for the moment—do better for yourselves?"

"Kill more bad guys," said a voice in the back.

"Oh, very good," answered Weber, without missing a beat. "Let's turn the agency into a force of paramilitary killers, full-time. Give up on spying and just shoot people, twenty-four/seven. Sorry, friends, but that's part of the problem. This is an intelligence agency, not Murder, Incorporated. We're supposed to gather the secret information that can protect the country; we're not operating a shooting gallery."

"What's your answer, Mr. Director?" asked Pingray in the front row. "How do you propose to get the agency back on track? That's what everyone would like to hear."

Pingray was a tidy man; short, bald, round-faced. He asked the question sincerely, with the voice of someone who knew how many obstacles Weber would encounter, even if the new director didn't. But Weber didn't really hear him. He jumped on the question.

"The answer is the same as in any failing organization. Find out what's wrong. Then promote the good people who can fix it and fire the bad ones who can't. What's the point of taking the job, otherwise? Not just me as director, but all of you: Why work for this unpopular, low-pay organization—except to do great work, and be respected for it?

"At the risk of sounding immodest, let me tell you all something: I know how to fix organizations that are broken. I've been doing it all my life. But it's like a twelve-step process. You have to want to get better. You have to admit to yourself that if you don't change, you're going to end up dead. For the CIA, the past is an addiction. You're going to have to quit.

"So that's the end of my little pep talk. But you'll be hearing more from me, I promise. And please, no applause or I'll know you didn't hear anything I just said. Now, any questions?"

The air had been sucked out of the room. Nobody spoke, or even moved for a moment.

"Nobody?" He looked around the auditorium. "When you kick an old dog, at least you get a few growls. Come on, people."

There were a few hands. Employees asked predictable questions about pay freezes and furloughs and benefits changes, all of which Weber said could be better answered by HR. Someone asked him his views on "targeted killing," which was a euphemism for drones. He said it was too early for him to know what he thought; ask in another month. One person praised him for speaking so frankly, to tepid applause. Nobody was ready to call him on the heart of what he'd said about performance, because most of them knew it was true. They were working for a failing enterprise; he said he was going to turn it around. They had to hope he pulled it off, even the ones who resented him.

As Weber made his way out of the bubble, there was stone-cold silence like the quiet after a funeral, and then a low hum when he was out the door and everyone was murmuring, asking whether he meant it, if this was for real, if the agency was actually going to have a director who would kick ass in a way that no current employee could remember.

Weber walked back across the marble floor of the lobby. The CIA had been built in the brutalist modern style of the 1960s that eschewed ornamentation. There were no murals or paintings; only the stars in the wall to mark the agency officers who had died on duty, and the empty space where the Donovan statue had stood.

As Weber walked past the security gate where employees badged in each morning, his eyes focused on a sign beside the guard desk. It listed all the incongruous things that were forbidden inside the build-ing: EXPLOSIVES AND INCENDIARY DEVICES, ANIMALS OTHER THAN GUIDE DOGS, SOLICITING AND DISTRIBUTING HANDBILLS, DISTUR-BANCES, GAMBLING. He'd seen this warning sign every day that week as he moved about the building. He turned to the bulky, assuring form of Bock, who was walking next to him.

"That sign is ridiculous," said Weber.

"Say what, sir?"

"'Gambling' and 'creating disturbances'? I thought that was what intelligence officers did for a living. And 'distributing handbills'? Is that really a problem here? When was the last time someone gave you a handbill, Sandra? It makes us look asinine, to have a moronic sign like that where visitors can see it."

"You're in a pissy mood, sir." It was the first time Bock had been even modestly disrespectful.

Weber laughed.

"Maybe, but I'm right about that sign. It's silly. Get rid of it."

And the sign was gone the next day.

8

WASHINGTON

The senior staff gathered in the conference room across from the director's office as five o'clock approached. People were trying not to talk about the director's speech, but the mood was stiff and awkward, and they swiveled in their chairs or poured themselves glasses of water. The room was antiseptic and impersonal as only a government meeting room can be: a big table with a glass top; overstuffed leather chairs; television monitors for the now-inevitable video-teleconferencing hookups. Weber was a few minutes late, and people were looking at their watches when Sandra Bock arrived and said the director wanted everyone to gather instead across the hall.

The director's office wasn't big enough for the group, really. People had to sit three on a sofa and perch on the arms of chairs. But Weber liked it better this way, crowded and informal. He pulled up one of the chairs next to his big oak desk and parked himself in the arc of the circle. He still looked too young for the job: lean, fit, still some of his West Coast tan and that blond-haired baby face, peculiar for a middle-aged man.

He panned the group: At the center was Beasley, the chief of the Clandestine Service, resplendent in one of his tailor-made English suits and a Turnbull & Asser shirt with blue stripes and a pure white collar that set off his handsome brown face. Beasley looked at the new director and shook his head.

"Hell of a speech in the bubble just now, Mr. Director. Pow! Knocked me out. It made me want to commit suicide, actually, but that's my problem, right?"

"Right," said Weber.

Next to Beasley was Ruth Savin, the general counsel. She was a handsome woman, with jet-black hair and dark Mediterranean features that made her stand out among the Mormons, Catholics and fading WASPs who still, somehow, seemed to think of the agency as their place. She had come to the agency ten years before after a stint as staff director of the Senate Intelligence Committee, and had shaped the legal framework of every piece of secret business since her arrival.

The heads of other directorates filled up the seats: Loomis Braden, the top analyst, who was deputy director for intelligence and known to all as "the DDI"; Marcia Klein, who ran Support; Tom Avery, who headed Science and Technology. These were the people who once upon a time would have been known as barons, but now were more like caretakers.

Standing just outside the inner circle was the tall, ascetic figure of James Morris, the head of Information Operations. His casual dress, T-shirt and linen jacket signaled that he was different in age, temperament and so many other qualities. He had one hand behind his back; hidden from view, he was turning a quarter over his fingers, the way a magician will sometimes do.

As Weber was about to start the meeting, the door opened and in walked a large man, dressed in a three-piece pin-striped suit with a gold watch chain across the vest. He was carrying in his hand a brown fedora, which he had worn outdoors. On his arm was an umbrella. He was round-faced, hair trimmed to a short buzz; he had a habit, even entering a room unannounced, of looking over the tops of his glasses, so that his eyebrows seemed perpetually raised in a quizzical look.

"Hello, Cyril," said Weber. "Glad you could make it."

"Howdy do," said Cyril Hoffman genially, with a flourish of his hat. People made way for him on the large sofa. Hoffman fluffed his ample coat jacket out behind him as he sat down, like a concert pianist in tails taking his seat at the piano.

At the last minute, Weber had decided to invite Hoffman, the director of National Intelligence. It was partly an instinct for self-protection that he wanted Hoffman with him inside the tent as he faced his first real problem. But he also respected Hoffman's judgment. The DNI had been around the intelligence community for his entire adult life. He was the closest thing the country had to a permanent undersecretary for intelligence. There were very few secrets that he didn't know, and few messes that he hadn't helped clean up.

Weber cleared his throat. He was nervous, for just an instant.

"We have a problem," he began "It just arrived today. Some of you have seen the cable traffic, but for those who haven't, let me explain what happened. Today in Hamburg, Germany, a young man walked into our consulate and asked to see me personally, the new director. He told the base chief that we have a security breach. He's a 'hacker,' or claims to be, so he didn't put it that way. He said we have been hacked. He said the names of our personnel have been compromised in Germany and Switzerland, and he had a list to prove it. He wouldn't stay in one of our safe houses, as the base chief proposed, because he said our information wasn't secure."

Weber looked to Bock, who was standing motionless like an iron pillar.

"Is that more or less it, for the basics, Sandra?"

"Yes, sir," she answered.

"After considering this matter, I have decided to send James Morris, the head of Information Operations, to Hamburg to assist the base chief in the debriefing and exfiltration."

Every eye in the room turned toward the casually dressed young man standing beyond the couches. He had drawn some resentment over the past several years from colleagues for pushing his authority. Now he was being given what amounted to a battlefield promotion by the new director.

"Big responsibility," said Weber. "Unconventional decision, I guess. But my instinct is that the person who deals with hacker penetration of the agency needs to be able to swim in that sea, and the person here who fits that description is James Morris. Earl Beasley has generously agreed to help Morris work out the details. Thanks for that, Earl."

"I just work here," said Beasley slowly. "I do what the boss says."

Beasley let the words hang in the air, an implied rebuke, and then softened. "It's not crazy. The IOC should be more involved in operations. We've been saying that for years. Well, shit, now we gonna do it."

Weber nodded his thanks. Beasley was a good politician, whatever else he might be. On the couch, Cyril Hoffman watched Beasley with what seemed a look of sly amusement. Evidently he doubted that the chief of the Clandestine Service had spoken in complete sincerity.

Weber turned to Morris.

"So, James, why don't you explain to the group what you plan to do."

"Nobody calls me James, Mr. Director. Everyone in my office calls me Pownzor. Even people on the seventh floor do, too."

"I'll stick with James," said Weber. "Explain the drill."

Morris adjusted his glasses and took a step toward the center of the circle. For an awkward man, a "nerd," in common parlance, he also had a presence and a sense of theater.

"So the good news about hackers is that they can be hacked. Based on what the walk-in told the base chief in Hamburg this morning, we have a pretty good idea of who he is and the circles he runs in. He's connected to a group of hackers with roots in Russia who started with credit-card scams a decade ago, stealing people's data and buying expensive stuff they could fence in a hurry. They graduated to much bigger frauds; they extort banks, gambling sites, anything that loses money fast if it goes off-line. But they're not just scammers anymore. It's a movement."

"Meaning what?" asked Beasley. He didn't believe in movements.

Morris's eyes were gleaming behind the frames of his glasses. This was the part he understood best.

"They are motivated. They hate authority. To be specific, they hate us, the CIA."

"Everybody hates the CIA," said Beasley. "What else is new?"

Morris continued with his narrative, ignoring Beasley and looking at Weber.

"I'm flying to Germany tomorrow. The director is lending me his plane. I'll be working with the base chief. The walk-in is supposed to be back at the consulate Monday morning, but we'll try to find him before then. Once we get him, we'll bring him out. I'd like to make his exfiltration look like he died: in a car accident, that's the easiest. We don't want these people to know that one of their kids has flipped and come over to us."

"You know what I think?" muttered Beasley, his voice dropping an octave to a menacing low bass. "I think we should fuck . . . them . . . up."

Beasley was a Princeton man, out of a prep school before that, but he knew how to sound street-tough.

Morris adjusted his glasses. He was at pains to correct Beasley.

"These hackers may look funny, with their tattoos and spike hair, but they are serious people. They have weapons. They fight back. That's why we need to download this man as quickly as we can. Then, well, then you can slit their throats if you like. But I suggest it would be wiser to get inside their computer networks."

People nodded. Nobody in the room had ever heard Morris talk about slitting throats, or imagined that he was a man who thought in those terms, but he was playing the role the director had given him.

"Why would hackers go after the CIA?" asked Ruth Savin. "Isn't that a reach?" The general counsel hadn't spoken until now. She was the watcher and note-taker at meetings like this, and she enjoyed asking uncomfortable questions.

Weber looked at Morris, who remained silent. He didn't respond to questions if he didn't have an answer.

"Are they working for another government?" pressed Savin.

Weber looked again to his Information Operations chief, but the tall young man was impassive.

"I don't think we know," said Weber. "That's why we've got to get this walk-in out of Germany and hear what he has to say."

"We need to be careful about how we try to penetrate these groups," said Savin. "Beasley has been ordered to stay away from WikiLeaks and their friends. There is a huge flap potential if anything surfaces."

"I'll be careful," said Morris. "But we need to develop sources."

Heads nodded in agreement, even Beasley's.

There was a rustling sound, as Cyril Hoffman moved about on the couch. Hoffman hadn't said a word until now. He had sat quietly on the couch with his hands clasped together, listening to the discussion.

He was a large man, and the folds of his voluminous jacket covered him like a cape.

"May I?" Hoffman asked, looking to Weber.

"Please. I want to know what you think about all this."

"I feel badly for you, Graham," Hoffman began. "What a welcoming present. I am reminded of the opening bars of Beethoven's Fifth Symphony: a crescendo right at the beginning, with the whole orchestra racing along behind. Yet all anyone remembers is those first few notes."

"I'm not much on classical music," said Weber.

"No one is perfect, Mr. Director. Now, you asked me what I think about this Hamburg business, so I'll tell you. To quote the indispensable Talleyrand, 'One can do everything with a bayonet except sit on it.'"

"What does that mean?"

"It means that you have to respond, but carefully. This is either a big problem that threatens the agency's communications, or a small problem created by a young man in Germany with fanciful ideas. But unfortunately, you don't know which yet. So you have to protect against the worst without damaging yourself in the process."

"Forgive the mundane. But what would Talleyrand say about operational security?"

"Treat this as a code break. Change encryption keys. Sweep the facilities in Germany and Switzerland. Do a damage assessment on the officers' names that have been revealed. Who have they recruited? What operations have been compromised? Beasley can do all that for you. Damage control is one of his specialties."

Hoffman looked at Beasley, with whom he had been doing business for nearly two decades. Beasley nodded.

"Okay," said Weber. "What else?"

"I am intrigued by your plan to give principal responsibility to our young colleague, Mr. Pownzor. That's unusual." Hoffman looked toward Morris indulgently.

"Meaning that you think it's a mistake?" asked the director.

"Not necessarily. It sends a message: You're the change agent! So here's a bit of change, right off the bat: entrusting a sensitive problem to a young man who has the 'right stuff.' It tells the workforce that you are the new man; you mean what you say. Bravo to that!"

Hoffman clapped his hands, barely audibly, pat-pat-pat.

"Thank you," said Weber, knowing that the director of intelligence had just given him the authority and opportunity to destroy himself.

Cyril Hoffman was an unlikely intelligence czar. He was an eccentric, theatrical personality—rumored to be gay, but such a Protean character that any such effort at categorization was misplaced. He was a student of Philip Glass operas and the history of Italian city-states; he was an amateur poet and cellist; he was a man of parts. This improbable figure had survived at the agency, and indeed had eventually been promoted to director of National Intelligence, because he understood the nature of power in a secret bureaucracy. Nearly everyone in the U.S. government owed him a favor. Abroad, he had his own back channels with the heads of a dozen foreign spy services. Above all, Hoffman understood that the eleventh commandment for spies was, in the words of Lord Palmerston: "Do not get caught."

Weber took up the rope of command that Hoffman had handed him. He asked Beasley to summarize the damage-control measures he would take in EUR Division, and he asked Morris to go over one more time what they knew about the walk-in and the milieu from which he had emerged.

"Any other items of business?" asked Weber when these recitations were finished. "It's my first Friday afternoon, so let's clear the decks."

"I have some operational approvals that need your sign-off," said Beasley. "The Special Activities Review Committee sent five tasking orders to the general counsel's office. Ruth has cleared them all. They're all Internet-related. We can do that now or save it for another time."

"Go ahead. Empty the in-box. What have you got?"

Beasley took five slim red folders from Savin and handed them to the director. The pure white cuff of his London shirt extended from his blue suit.

"As I said, it's five items. Two are about facilitating cover, two are about case officer movements, one is a general authority."

"Do they involve U.S. corporations?" asked Weber. He was used to being on the receiving end of operations like this.

"Yes, sir," said Beasley. "For the cover integration, we need to massage some social networking sites and search engines to backstop the legends. We're doing the work overseas, so it's under existing authorities and approvals."

Beasley was talking fast. Weber interrupted. This was his meeting, and he wanted to run it.

"Is that right?" Weber asked Savin. "Is this all legal?"

"Yes, sir. It accords with our existing identities-protection program, and with Executive Order 12333, as amended."

"Are the companies witting?"

"Not in every case," she answered.

"Which means what?"

"Which means that some of the general counsels' offices have personnel who have served in government and hold the necessary clearances and are familiar with our procedures."

"Do they tell their bosses?"

"Where appropriate. In many cases, the CEOs have been briefed extensively, and so they are witting, yes. I know you remember that from your former life."

"That's why it makes me nervous," said Weber. "So you talk to friendly CEOs, and in other cases, not so much."

"Yes, sir."

"But it's overseas, so it doesn't really matter, because under Title Fifty we can do whatever we want," said the director as if reading a legal primer.

"Pretty much," chimed in Beasley, a twinkle in his eye.

"Let's give this one a closer look," said Weber. "I'll sit down with Ruth and go over the rules."

People looked at each other. Directors didn't question operational approvals that had been okayed by the general counsel.

"Let's move on," said Weber. "What about the movements of case officers? What's that?"

"Two requests," said Beasley. "Change retinal-scan database in Dubai for a traveling officer who has already transited that point under a different identity, and alter a fingerprint database in Russia, same reason."

"What if we get busted?"

"We won't," said a voice from the back. It was Morris, who was still standing just back from the couch. "Our tradecraft is well developed.

Our alteration software erases its tracks as it changes the data. We are invisible, in and out."

Morris seemed to light up when he talked about technical issues. It was part of his uncanny, almost spooky self-confidence.

Weber held up the last red file marked Information Operations and Global Financial Market Integrity.

"This looks dubious," said the director. "What is it, Earl?"

"Ask Morris," said Beasley. "This one will go through his shop."

Morris looked at the floor awkwardly.

"To be clear: This was not my idea, but it will use IOC resources. Basically, it's a general authority for collection of economic intelligence via the Internet."

"Why are we doing that? I thought we left that sort of thing to the French and Chinese."

"The markets are . . . nervous," said Morris. "Everyone is looking over their shoulders. So . . . inevitably, people are hacking other people's databases and market platforms. They're installing beacons; getting ready to change zeroes and ones, if they ever need to."

"Why is that inevitable?"

Morris peered back at the director from behind those black glasses. He was trying to read his new boss.

"Because, Mr. Director, if people can play games with any system, they will. It's a sport for younger people. They like to attack systems just to show how stupid other people are. Director Jankowski thought we needed to be prepared."

"He's gone now," said Weber. "What about us? Are we altering other people's data? Are we penetrating their 'databases and market platforms'?"

Ruth Savin, the general counsel, answered before anyone else could speak.

"We do not collect intelligence on behalf of American companies," she said.

"Is that a formal prohibition?" asked Weber.

The room was silent. Most eyes turned to the senior official present, Cyril Hoffman.

"Is this the time for a full review?" sighed Hoffman. He was looking at his watch. "This is a story for another day, surely. Mr. Morris needs to get working so he can catch his plane tomorrow."

Savin took the cue from the DNI. She reached toward the director to take back the five red folders, but Weber held them close.

"I want to check the small print," said Weber.

"Of course, sir. We'll set up a time in the reading room."

"But suppose I want to read them now."

"The practice has always been to return operational files at the end of the meeting. These files are subject to the special controls for the Special Activities Review Committee. Would you like to change those procedures, Director?"

Weber looked at Hoffman, whose mouth was turned down at the corners in something approaching a scowl.

"Leave the procedures unchanged," said the director. "I'll schedule a time to come read."

"Thank you, sir," she said.

"And I'll want to read into the back files, too, to review information operations that were approved previously and are on the books."

Savin looked to Hoffman, who was stone-faced. Their silence peeved Weber.

"Hey, folks, let's be clear. I'm not going to stay in a job if I can't read the files. Not a chance. I'll call the president. He can find someone else."

Hoffman puckered his lips. He didn't like public displays, and he didn't like it when officials who had been in their jobs for one week threatened to quit. But little showed on that round, genial face.

"Of course that can be managed," he said calmly, measuring each word. "Ruth, make whatever arrangements are necessary to read the director in."

Hoffman gave a little bow toward Graham Weber. There was bland look on his face, a mask of cordiality.

"And again, welcome, Mr. Director," he said, extending his hand. "You have taken on a very big job. I don't want to see you fail."

It was an expression of confidence, if you parsed the words, but Weber sensed that he was perilously close to making an enemy. He clasped Hoffman's elbow as people were heading toward the door.

"Thank you," said Weber.

———————

"Perhaps I might stay for a few private words," said Hoffman as the last of the other visitors left the room. He walked to the door and closed it.

The two men took seats opposite each other. They formed a contrasting portrait: one man large and ceremonious, the other compact and informal. But it was also a juxtaposition of two generations and cultures: an older one rooted in a past that, whatever its recent difficulties, had the weight and momentum of history; the other proposing an uncertain future with both opportunities and dislocations.

Hoffman spoke first. He was more intimate in private, no longer playing a role.

"You really must be careful, you know," said Hoffman. "We all understand that the world has to change. I supported the president's decision to bring you in, because I know we need a fresh start. But if you pull too hard on the thread, you will soon find that you don't have any sweater left."

Weber nodded. He needed Hoffman's help but wasn't sure how to get it without compromising his own goals.

"I don't want to scare people, Cyril, especially not you. But if you don't frighten people a little in the beginning, they won't take you seriously. You have to send things back at first, and tell people they can do better. Otherwise you're stuck."

"Yes, yes." Hoffman smiled. "I know that's what they teach at the Harvard Business School. But this is different. You are now responsible for the security of your country. The world is a very dangerous place these days, and, thanks to our leaker friends, the NSA and CIA have lost their ability to monitor some of the truly menacing people. That's not government propaganda, it's a simple fact. The leakers have taken our most precious secrets and exposed them to the whole world. The programs that have been revealed cost many billions of dollars. People gave their lives to protect those secrets, and now they are being published in the newspapers willy-nilly."

"You probably blame me for opening the floodgate," said Weber. "Most of my new colleagues do. But you have to understand: I'm trying to make the country stronger, not weaker."

"Of course you are. And nobody blames you for anything. But you must consider what it would be like if the country were attacked again, and make sure that you would be comfortable with your actions. That's all."

Hoffman stood. He had given his speech, and it was time to go. But Weber had one more question.

"Am I doing the right thing sending Morris to Germany?" he asked.

"Probably. Morris is a useful young man. We gave him some special authority this past year, and he has been quite creative with it. But be careful with Morris. He is not of your generation, let alone mine. We may not entirely understand him."

Hoffman extended his hand once more. Weber clasped it.

"Thanks for helping," said Weber.

"I'm not helping! I am merely observing. If you ever truly need my help, it is certainly available. But that would be most unfortunate, because it would mean that you had failed."

Hoffman turned and let himself out the door. Weber returned to his desk. Night had fallen, in the time since he had begun his senior staff meeting. The parking lots were emptying out, and the lights were twinkling across the river from the civilian world that agency employees liked to describe collectively as "downtown."

In Hamburg, Sandoval waited at the consulate for an answer until it was nearly midnight in Germany and quitting time at Headquarters. She ate potato chips and drank diet sodas from the vending machine and tried to get ready to handle all the questions from the seventh floor about her first big case. In a nervous binge, she finished three packs of chips. At midnight when there was still no reply, she ordered a pizza from the local Joey's.

Sandoval received an answer from Washington just before two a.m. Saturday, Hamburg time. The message informed her that the case would be handled by James Morris, the head of the Information Operations Center, who would be arriving in Germany on Sunday morning.

"Those bastards," Sandoval muttered to herself when she read the message. Headquarters had decided the Latina girl couldn't handle it, so they were sending in an Anglo male branch chief. A decade's worth of CIA self-doubt suffused her: She was just window dressing for the promotion boards and diversity reviews, given assignments but not trusted.

Sandoval brooded for a few minutes, and then called the Ops Center on the secure phone and asked to be connected with James Morris in Information Operations. The line was dead for perhaps a minute, and then Morris came on the line, his voice flat.

"This is Morris," he said.

"You're taking my case away," said Sandoval coldly.

"No theatrics, please. This is business."

"Excuse me? I'm not being theatrical, I'm being angry. This is my walk-in and my case. Why am I being relieved?"

"Sorry about that. No offense meant. But this is an IOC case now, restricted handling. It involves some issues outside your lane."

"My message was for the director personally," she said icily. "How did it end up in your hands?"

"Because the director gave it to me."

"What if I protest? Complain to my division chief. This is obvious sexism. Girl gets case, boy takes over case. That's bullshit."

"Take it to whoever you want. You'll lose. I'm bringing him out of Germany in the director's G-5. That's orders. If it seems unfair, you can complain to the inspector general. Be my guest. I arrive Sunday morning. But please: I'm not your enemy."

9

HAMBURG

James Morris was a loner when it came to operations. Perhaps it was all those years as a young man closeted alone with a computer, spinning his threads of code out into the world. It was a solitary pursuit, and one that led a person to live inside himself. Morris managed the operational details using a tablet computer the techs had rigged for him that synched every sixty seconds with the agency's system. Because he was so fast with his fingers and could type almost as quickly as he could think, he was constantly sending out tasking orders, directives and updates to his staff at the IOC's headquarters. He kept his operational traffic overseas in separate compartments to which he had special access, so it was difficult for anyone else to keep up with him.

That was the secret of the power Morris had assembled in the Information Operations Center: He could do things that others simply couldn't match, or even imagine, and he had pushed operations into areas that previously had been empty space, using broad authorities that were in the shadowy space between the CIA and NSA.

When Morris left the director's office late that afternoon, he began assembling the team he would need in Hamburg. He didn't ask for help from Beasley or the EUR Division. The planning went late into Friday night and resumed early Saturday morning. It didn't occur to him to review his plans with Sandoval, the case officer in Hamburg who had met with Rudolf Biel when he walked in the door of the consulate. She worked for Beasley. She wasn't his problem.

Morris lived on Cap'n Crunch cereal when he was on the road. He ate it with milk, with water, plain, in preformed wafers like granola bars. Partly it was because he liked the taste, and partly it was in homage to the hacker cult of Cap'n Crunch; in the early days, hackers had used the free whistles inside each box, which sounded at a frequency of 2,600 herz, to spoof telephone switches and make free calls. He knocked back a box of the cereal while flying Saturday night on the director's G-5, washing it down with a cocktail of bourbon and diet ginger ale.

The escape plan Morris had devised was a conjuring trick. When the Swiss youth arrived at the consulate Monday morning, Morris and his techs would fit him with a disguise that changed his hair color and clothing—and then move him from the consulate to a holding area near the airport, north of the city, where the plane would be waiting. A paramilitary officer on loan to Morris, head shaved and dressed up in a disguise to resemble Biel, would rent a car using his name and driver's license. On the E22 motorway near the Dutch border, the car would have a fiery flameout that destroyed the vehicle and everything in it. Doctored bits of Biel's DNA would be left in the vehicle for the police to find: hair, fingernails, skin, just enough to allow identification.

James Morris showed up at the consulate in Hamburg Sunday, as promised. He was gaunt from too little sleep and he had an overcaffein-ated glint in his eye. To Sandoval, who was several years older, the won-der boy looked like someone who should be carrying a skateboard. He set up shop in her office, and installed two techs he had brought along from Langley in the communications room next door.

Morris disappeared in the late afternoon Sunday for a meeting out-side the consulate. He didn't inform anyone who he was seeing. But his little team from Langley guessed that he was trying to locate Biel using electronic magic that he couldn't share with others.

Sandoval protested her displacement to the consul general. He told her to take the empty office of the economic officer, who was home on leave. He'd gotten a call from Washington requesting full cooperation.

Sandoval assented, but demanded permission to be present with Morris when the walk-in returned on Monday. Otherwise, she said, she would file a grievance with the ambassador in Berlin and the CIA inspector general. The consul general assured her that nobody in the "country team" wanted that.

Morris was there waiting early Monday morning. He looked edgy from the moment he walked into the building. He studied the closed-circuit cameras that monitored the sidewalk along the Alsterufer; occasionally he peered out the window, as if he could summon Biel by staring long enough in the right place.

"I'm nervous," he muttered several times as the ten o'clock scheduled arrival time passed, audibly enough that Sandoval heard him in the communications room next door. "Why is he late?"

At eleven, Morris sent out a team of his people, cut to him from the Global Response Staff, to begin looking for Biel in the Rotherbaum neighborhood surrounding the consulate. By early afternoon, the dragnet was widened to the city as a whole.

Morris pulled Sandoval aside as his concern mounted.

"Do the Russians have a consulate here?" he asked.

"I don't think so," she said. "But the Russians are all over everywhere."

"I know," said Morris. He walked away shaking his head. Sandoval worried that she had done something new to offend him.

Weber checked in twice Monday on the secure line to ask whether the defector had arrived, and Morris assured the director each time that it was just a hitch, Biel would show up soon. He said he had his watchers monitoring digital and wireless signals from anyone associated with Biel's underground life.

Morris quizzed Sandoval, pressing for more details about Biel that might hint where he might be. He watched the video of her interview with the Swiss fugitive twice, start to finish, looking for clues. He removed the CD from the surveillance monitor when he was done and told Sandoval he was taking it back to Headquarters for analysis.

"Where is that little fucker?" said Morris loudly, his voice echoing down the hall, just before five when it was time for the consulate to close its gates. He asked the Marine guard to stay on duty for another hour.

When the consulate closed its doors at six, there was still no sign of him.

Morris received a call that night on a cell phone whose number he had given to only one person. The caller was a member of the operations group Morris called his "special access unit." The unit's expenses and personnel were not on the CIA budget. Its operations were coordinated by a special NSA base in Denver, which ran interagency signals intelligence at the request of the Office of the Director of National Intelligence.

The unit had access to signals that were not officially collected, such as those involving underground hacking groups. In the case of the young man from Switzerland, Rudolf Biel, the special unit had been receiving and analyzing his messages for more than a month, along with those of a few others in the circle of activists within which he moved. The chatter in the last few days had been about a new source for the network, someone recruited by an American civil liberties group, who had access to *everything.*

"We can't find him," said the caller. His voice was agitated.

"Where the hell is he?" demanded Morris. "He's going to get smoked."

"We don't know. We've pulsed everyone we can, but we're not getting anything back. They're all dead circuits."

"Keep trying," said Morris. "My ass is on the line."

"I'm hot. People are going to have my coordinates soon."

"Then don't call me again on this number. Don't call me on any number. Do what Denver tells you to do. Everyone gets one chance to screw up. You just used up yours. Don't do it again."

Morris and his security team brought in the Germans the next day, as discreetly as they could. He had Sandoval contact the local Landesamt für Verfassungsschutz, or State Office for the Protection of the Constitution, the unlikely name of the local version of the FBI. They were given a photograph of Biel and asked to check whether he had used any transport nodes out of the city—air, train, bus, motorway—they could monitor. Later in the day, the LfV distributed the photograph to the Hamburg police and the neighboring states of Schleswig-Holstein and Lower Saxony. But after twenty-four more hours of looking, none of these agencies had turned up any trace of young Herr Biel.

Morris was reluctant for many hours to admit to others that there was a problem, but he finally ordered a search—first the old city near the consulate, then Hamburg proper, then the suburbs—until finally, by late Tuesday, he had drawn in the German police in three states.

"You should eat something," Sandoval urged the hollow-eyed Information chief on Tuesday. He had gone through his store of Cap'n Crunch and was living on caffeine, in various forms, and granola bars. Sandoval had forgiven Morris by then for poaching on her case; she didn't want to have him collapse in her midst. She offered to cook him a proper meal at her apartment, a steak and baked potato, but he shook his head.

"I think he's gone," Morris told Weber on the secure phone Tuesday evening.

"What do you mean, 'gone'?" asked the director.

"I think he's dead. Someone got to him. They realized he had come in to us, so they took him out." Morris made the sound of a pistol shot on the phone. "It's my fault. I should have found him in time."

"I'm bringing in Beasley and the Clandestine Service," said Weber. "I should have done that from the beginning. This is crazy."

"No, Director, please," Morris implored. "Give me two more days to work this. Let me use the assets I have in place. If Beasley's people come in now they'll just make things worse, believe me. This is my mess. Let me clean it up."

Weber paused, trying to take in the intensity and insistence of the young man to whom he had given so much responsibility. He wanted to trust Morris, and in that way confirm that his own judgment had been right.

"Explain to me. How will Beasley make things worse?"

"We have contacts inside these groups. They could get compromised. We have ongoing technical operations. They could get blown. We have our own liaison relationships with foreign services. We need soft hands right now, Director."

"Soft hands? We aren't running a beauty salon. Beasley called me an hour ago. He told me that in this business, when they shove you, you shove back. That's the rule."

"Beasley isn't Superman, Mr. Director. We have operations working. People could get burned. And who knows? Biel may have been a plant, trying to draw us off base. The world is full of smart kids who hate the CIA. We don't know who's involved."

Morris's voice had a new tone of concern and intensity. Weber heard it, and wanted to understand.

"Okay. So, what if another service was involved?"

Morris went dead silent for a moment.

"What do you mean?" he asked evenly.

"What if another service wanted to protect someone they have inside the agency, a penetration that Biel was about to blow, and they took him out?"

"Worst case," said Morris quietly. "That's why I'm asking for a couple more days before you bring in the big dogs. Please trust me."

Weber sighed.

"Goddamn it. I'm out on a limb. Trust comes with an obligation. You know what that is?"

"You told me already: Don't screw up."

"Correct. Find him. And if it goes bad, it's on you."

"I know that. You have to understand, Mr. Director, these people operate under Rule Five of the Internet."

"That means absolutely nothing to me, sorry."

"Rule Five says that Anonymous never forgives. It means that hackers can be deadly."

"Look, Morris, I don't care about these screwballs except that we stop them from harming the agency. That's my only job now. I have just one question for you. Do you have what it takes to get this done?"

Morris's voice was firm and unambiguous.

"Yes, sir, absolutely."

Morris disappeared from the consulate Tuesday. He didn't say where he was, and Sandoval in Hamburg and the station chief in Berlin didn't ask. It was easy for Morris to travel light: He ran agents as if they were part of a virtual "second life." He had only a few officers, but they all had nonofficial cover, with commercial platforms that allowed them to move anywhere. Back home at the IOC, he had people tracking networks and monitoring beacons from machines around the world. He was listening for electronic chatter, and what the underground world was saying about Biel. The only traces he picked up were conspiracy talk about the CIA. Morris's conclusion was that nobody knew anything real about where Biel was or why he had disappeared.

Morris left the mundane management of the IOC to his deputy, Dr. Ariel Weiss. She was as geeky as he was, but less of a lone wolf. She acted as the HR buffer for him, soothing bruised egos, negotiating hiring, transfer and severance packages, and meeting with other U.S. and foreign government officials whom Morris found tedious. He liked to say that she was Sheryl Sandberg to his Mark Zuckerberg, but that flattered him and, if anything, undervalued her. Weiss was a superb operative in her own right. It was just that she didn't get much chance to demonstrate it, with her boss always disappearing into some cave or another.

By Thursday, Morris messaged Weber from somewhere—the operations center thought the message had originated in Berlin—that he had done everything he could and would be coming home soon. He thanked Weber for his trust, pushing that button one more time.

Biel's body washed ashore on Friday near where the Elbe meets the North Sea. He had been shot twice, once in the head and once in the chest.

The body was found near a nature preserve called Nordkehdingen. This was farmland, and the corpse might have stayed on the sand for a week, but it was seen by a fisherman who was bringing his boat back from the North Sea and happened to glimpse something on the bank of the big river. The nearest police station was a little outpost in Balje, a few kilometers away, but they sent in a second unit from the town of Cadenberge, and then a whole squad from Hamburg who turned the windswept little beach into a crime scene.

The body was so cold and battered from the sea that the German police said they couldn't be sure when Biel had died. It could have been the previous weekend, just after he'd visited the consulate, or later. The Germans traced the bullets to a gun that Interpol had registered as having been used by a Russian mobster based in Romania. That pulled all the chains: The German Federal Office for the Protection of the Constitution, known as the BfV, and its foreign intelligence counterpart, the unpronounceable *Bundesnachrichtendienst*, or BND, reported a few hours later that the man who owned the gun had worked with the Russian hacker underground, which communicated through a website called mazafaka.ru, whose anonymous leadership was known as "the Root." The group had morphed into other, nastier splinter groups.

Morris came along with Sandoval to the briefing with the BfV and the BND. It was held in a gleaming new building near the city center that housed the Hamburg State Office for the Protection of the Constitution. Morris sat stone-faced through the German account, occasionally asking Sandoval to translate a forensic term that wasn't familiar. He didn't ask questions or offer comments, and didn't betray any emotion whatsoever inside the government office.

It was only when they were outside that Sandoval saw that Morris's eyes were lit with a pale fire she had not seen before. He was shaking his head back and forth, as if he couldn't believe the chain of consequences that had formed in his mind. The worst thing in life is when someone is searching for the explanation of why something bad has happened, and they realize that for reasons they could not have imagined, *they* may be the cause. There was something of that stunned revelation in Morris's face.

Sandoval didn't talk to him about the case until they were back at the consulate in a SCIF, as the secret world described the omnipresent space known as a "secure compartmented information facility."

"Who got him?" asked Sandoval.

"The bad guys knew something," he answered slowly. "They smelled a rat. They took him out before we could rescue him."

"This is my fault," Sandoval muttered, half to herself. She had been brooding since Friday night about her decision not to override the rule about letting people stay overnight inside the compound. She had caught the CIA disease of being overly cautious.

"No," said Morris, shaking his head. "You're wrong. There was nothing you could have done."

"Was he right? Are they reading our traffic?" she asked.

"I can't talk about that," said Morris, still visibly shaken. "We'll follow up aggressively. That's all I can say."

When they got back to the consulate, Morris called Weber to give him a report. When Morris finished with the details, he paused, cleared his throat and then spoke dully as if reading from a script.

"I am offering you my resignation, as of today," said Morris.

Weber didn't answer, so Morris repeated himself.

"I broke your trust. I let you down. So I am offering to resign." He paused a moment, and then started again. "I am resigning . . . effective as soon as you name my successor."

Weber still didn't answer. He was pondering.

"I need to think about it," said Weber eventually. "I stuck my neck out for you."

"Yes, sir." Morris's voice was thin and brittle, like a bowstring that had been stretched too tight.

"We talked about how another service might be involved. What about the Russians?"

Morris didn't answer for a moment. The silence was oppressive.

"I don't know," said Morris. "I just . . . don't know."

"You sound exhausted. You need some rest. It's terrible to lose someone like this. Come home. We'll talk about it next week."

"Yes, sir."

"This case is just beginning. I need people who know what they're doing. Does that still include you?"

"Yes, sir, if you want me." Morris cleared his throat. "I'm just getting started."

"So am I," said the director. "Don't write the resignation letter. Let me think about it."

Morris left Hamburg immediately. The G-5 had already flown home without him, so he had to fly commercial. He tried to sleep on the plane, but his head was spinning.

When Morris arrived back in Washington, he took a taxi to the outskirts of his neighborhood. He went to a pay phone on Fourteenth Street and called the most private number he had for his closest friend in the world, Ramona Kyle. He didn't know where in the world she was, and he knew that it was risky to call, but he needed to talk.

She didn't answer, and he didn't leave a message. She called the pay phone a minute later from a second number. Morris answered on the first ring.

"Something bad happened," he said.

"I know."

"There's a leak inside the agency, to some very dangerous people. Am I the leak?"

"Don't ask me that."

"I need to know."

"No, you don't. Get off the phone. This is bigger than you. You can't stop now. Go see that man I told you about, Peabody, the historian. He knows things. Don't be frightened. This is what you've wanted. Don't stop, now that it's really happening. You can't turn back. You have to go forward."

"I need to see you."

"That's impossible. No more calls. I won't answer. Hang up the phone and go home now. You have a chance to make a difference in the world, forever. I believe in you."

The line went dead. Morris hung up the phone. Everything she had said was true. He had no choice. He thought of a fragment from a W. H. Auden poem that Ramona Kyle liked to read aloud to him when they hid in her dorm room at Stanford and pretended the world had disappeared. "Yesterday all the past . . ."

Morris walked away from the phone kiosk and wandered down P Street until he came to Dupont Circle. Two African-American men were playing speed chess at a stone table in the middle of the plaza, beside the fountain. They were astonishingly good, brilliant men, obviously, yet they were dressed in ragged clothes and appeared to be homeless. Something was wrong in the order of things. Morris watched them for a while, moving their pieces, bam-bam-bam, feeling a strengthening resolve, and then walked home to his apartment.

10

WASHINGTON

Graham Weber's chief of staff, Sandra Bock, lingered in his office after he'd heard the final dismal news from Germany. She knew that he was upset, but he wasn't a man who invited intimacy or sought consolation. She decided to offer him some unsolicited and anonymous advice. She left on his desk a copy of a book cable that had been sent to all stations and bases ten years before. It had been written by the operations chief in Baghdad for case officers who were deployed to combat zones. It was brief, and to the point:

> *Three Rules for When You Are Under Fire:*
> *1) Always have a plan for what to do if something bad happens.*
> *2) Always be the first to move; don't wait until the situation is clear,*
>   *because by then it may be too late.*
> *3) Keep moving until you find cover or you're out of the fire zone.*

Weber didn't say anything to Bock, but he must have known the message came from her because she promptly received a brief, hand-written note on a stiff crème-colored card with the director's initials that read, *Thank you. Graham.*

The director needed a walk to clear his head. Jack Fong, the bearish chief of his security detail, insisted on following behind. That seemed

silly to Weber, given that he would remain within the protected compound of agency Headquarters, but he was already getting worn down
by procedures. It was harder to fix the big problems, he had discovered,
when you were nettled with so many little ones.

Weber took a long circumnavigation of the building, turning left
out the front door and then left again in a wide arc that skirted the
Green lot, the Brown lot, the Purple lot, the Black lot, the Tan lot and the
Yellow lot. This color-coded, enforced cheerfulness was characteristic
of the agency's bureaucracy, in its attempt to pretend that this was just
like any other workplace. The agency's bureaucracy tried so hard to be
normal, which was the one goal it could not possibly achieve.

While his black SUV followed thirty yards behind, Weber hummed
a hymn he remembered from his days as an altar boy at St. Aloysius Par-
ish on Mount Troy Road in Pittsburgh. He was brooding all the while,
wondering whom to consult and what to say.

Weber wished he had a board of directors. He had been reporting to
boards for the whole of his business career. When something bad happened, or trouble seemed to be lurking around the next corner, he had
learned that it was wise to ask board members for counsel. That made it
harder for them to blame you later if things went wrong, and sometimes
you got some good advice. But Weber didn't have a board. He served at
the pleasure of the president, and the president wasn't seeing much of
anyone outside the White House these days. He was traveling and giving speeches, lost in the misty uplands of his second term. Weber wasn't
sure where else to turn.

When Weber got back to his office, he placed a call to Cyril Hoffman, the director of National Intelligence. Hoffman was technically
Weber's boss, but more than that, he was a seasoned bureaucrat who
had seen his share of catastrophes over the years. Weber asked if he
could stop by the DNI's office at Liberty Crossing, a few miles away. The
response was theatrical, as always; Hoffman invoked Jesus, Mary and
Joseph in one sentence, but he agreed to the visit.

The black Escalade was waiting in the basement garage next to the
director's elevator. Weber got in the backseat and closed his eyes while
Oscar, his driver, got the all-clear from the garage-door guard. The
big SUV rolled out of the concrete bunker toward Route 123, and then

motored the few miles west to the anodyne office complex that housed the DNI and his staff. This ODNI entourage had grown in the dark of secrecy like a vast field of mushrooms sprouting in a cave, and now numbered more than a thousand.

Weber's trip had been organized in such a hurry that nobody had precleared his arrival, so he went in the front door, through the metal detectors and past the chubby security guards, like any other visitor.

When Weber arrived upstairs at Hoffman's office, he could hear the low hum of what sounded like cello music. Entering the room, he realized that he was listening to one of the Bach cello suites. It was an incongruous match of sight and sound. The office was appointed in the government's preferred sunny, cheerless décor, with navy blue carpeting, polished cherrywood tables and maroon leather furniture that was so new and shiny it seemed closer to plastic than any natural substance.

Behind the desk at the far side of the room loomed the fastidious, ample form of Cyril Hoffman. He was dressed in a brown suit today, as ever the gold chain across his waist, its bright links marking his girth. He ambled slowly toward Weber, his feet splayed outward slightly in a way that made his whole body seem to list slightly, left and right, as he took each step. He extended his hand toward Weber.

Hoffman's secretary and chief of staff were hovering at the door.

"A well-timed visit," said Hoffman. "Everyone, leave now, please, chop-chop." He shooed away his two aides, who retreated backward as if leaving a royal personage. Hoffman winked at his visitor.

"The exercise of power is operatic, don't you think? There are so many supernumeraries and props. It's just so . . . overdone. Would you like an espresso? I make it myself. I have my own machine."

Hoffman pointed to a large appliance along the wall, the sort of espresso machine you might find in a café in Paris. It had large handles and spouts and stainless steel fixtures.

"The security people insisted on taking it apart before they let me bring it up to the office. They thought it might be dangerous. How could that be? You put in beans and water, and out comes coffee. Quite good coffee, too, I would say. Would you like a cup?"

"No, thanks," said Weber. "Maybe some water."

"Water, of course. Important to hydrate. Still or sparkling?" He spoke in a patter, as if he were talking to himself.

"Still," said Weber, taking a seat on one of the maroon leather couches.

"Yes, still, certainly. What was I thinking?"

Hoffman poured from a bottle of Italian mineral water; on the label were testimonials from various Roman medical specialists. He handed the glass to Weber with a proprietary nod of the head.

"So what brings you barreling over here, barely two weeks into the job, to see your Uncle Cyril? It can't be that you've encountered a problem. You are the future of intelligence. The president told me so himself, just a few days ago."

There was a note of sarcasm in Hoffman's voice. He was a generous man, but he liked dealing with people on his own terms, and Weber didn't owe him anything.

"I need advice," said Weber.

Hoffman leaned forward, so that his belly, neatly wrapped in the brown pin-striped vest, seemed to be resting on the edge of the coffee table.

"I am all ears," he said.

"Hamburg went south. You probably heard."

"Indeed. I'm sorry for that young Swiss fellow. Should have taken our advice and stayed in a safe house."

"I'm wondering whether to fire James Morris. He offered me his resignation today. I told him I wanted to check with a few people."

Hoffman struck his palm against his forehead.

"Good god, man. This isn't Japan. People don't have to fall on their swords when something goes wrong. It wasn't Morris's fault, was it?"

"Not really. As you said, the walk-in should have stayed where we could protect him. But it happened on Morris's watch. He's supposed to know these hacker groups, supposed to be inside them, he claims. So it's partly on him. I've been saying since I got here that the agency needs more accountability. Well, here's my chance to show it."

"A word to the wise—three words, actually: Don't do it."

"I thought you'd say that. But isn't that the problem with the government? Nobody ever gets fired when something goes wrong. The agency has no gag reflex. It will swallow anything. I want to change that."

"Starting with Morris?"

"Maybe."

Hoffman looked over the top of his glasses, eyebrows bristling.

"Don't do it," he repeated. "Young Mr. Morris may be an odd duck. But he is also well connected."

"How so?"

"The White House likes him. Timothy O'Keefe, the national security adviser, most especially. He thinks Morris is the new generation. He gives a great briefing, as you might expect. I'm told that when he holds forth in the Situation Room about cyber matters, you could hear a pin drop."

"Morris briefs the president?"

"Sometimes. He's quite the eager beaver: apple polisher, crowd-pleaser, all that."

"He seems shy."

"He's a mysterious chap, this Morris. A Protean character. They tell me he's a reader, and a brooder, always roaming in the archives looking for this and that. He has some peculiar notions. A tad conspiratorial, or so they say."

"So *who* says?"

"My spies. They're everywhere."

Hoffman chuckled at this notion that he maintained his own private network of information, though Weber was sure it was true.

"One more suggestion," continued Hoffman. "Go see O'Keefe before you do anything. Make sure he's on board. Morris has been running some sensitive operations. They're not all on Ruth Savin's official books. Ask Beasley about them. You will be, what should I say? Amused. He's quite a creative fellow, young Morris, no matter how many threads he occasionally drops."

Weber was pleased, inwardly, to hear this testimonial to Morris's ingenuity and political clout. It affirmed his initial instinct in giving him responsibility, even if things hadn't worked out as planned.

"I'll see O'Keefe," said Weber. "And I have one more request. What should I do to protect our communications systems from whatever is coming at us? I don't want to panic people at the agency, but we need an independent scrub. Since you oversee the NSA, I thought maybe they could help us."

"Do you want the correct answer or the real answer?"

"The real answer, obviously."

"The correct answer is yes, of course, we can call in the NSA and sweep up everything in sight. Panic the children and small animals. The real answer is no. Be careful. Do this discreetly until you know what it is."

Weber nodded. This was all new to him, but he understood immediately that Hoffman was right.

"How should I proceed?"

"Do what I advised last week. Sweep this and that. Concentrate on the known leaks from Germany and Switzerland. Don't sit on the bayonet. I will lend you a technical team from my staff, on condition that they report back to me, each step of the way, what they're finding. How does that sound?"

"It sounds like good advice, actually. I appreciate the help."

"Don't sound so surprised," said Hoffman merrily. "Want a last bit of counsel?"

"Of course. I need all I can get."

"The thing that you have to remember about this job is that you are not just a manager, but also a magician. And as any professional magician will tell you, every magic trick has three parts: what people see; what they remember; and what they tell others about what they saw. You want the audience to swear the body disappeared, or the rabbit jumped out of the hat. But they will say so only because, at the critical moment, you made them look somewhere else."

"I'll think about that, Cyril. I'll remember it, even better. But to me, you sound like a good manager."

"Ah, excellent," said Hoffman, smiling. "That means you did not see the trick."

Weber bade the DNI goodbye, grateful for his advice, but not at all sure whether he was dealing with an ally or an adversary. When Weber left the office, Hoffman turned up the cello music again.

11

WASHINGTON

Graham Weber had visited the White House over the years as a business leader. He had even been to a state dinner once for the president of China, when the entire house had been decorated in a phantasm of American hospitality, but he had never felt comfortable in the place. This time, he felt he had no choice. He was an employee. He had Marie call the office of Timothy O'Keefe to make an appointment as Cyril Hoffman had advised. The national security adviser suggested that he stop by the next afternoon, around six p.m., when the other business of the day was done. O'Keefe seemed to be expecting Weber's call, but that wasn't a surprise. Hoffman would have given him a preview.

O'Keefe was waiting in the national security adviser's office at the north end of the West Wing. The walls smelled of fresh paint, a creamy off-white; O'Keefe had the painters in every few months, just after the security team. He had the proper décor for a senior national security official: a chunk of the Berlin Wall; a page from Osama bin Laden's personal diary; a Frederic Remington sculpture of a cowboy atop a bucking horse; and finally, several nautical paintings of American warships under sail.

O'Keefe welcomed Weber, but just as they were about to sit down the phone rang. It was the president, and O'Keefe scurried off to the Oval Office while Weber waited in the narrow hall next to the stairs that led down to the Situation Room. The national security adviser returned perhaps three minutes later, looking flushed as he bustled back into his chamber. He was a fussy man, and he was obviously in a bad mood.

"What was that about?" asked Weber, taking a seat across from O'Keefe at a small wooden conference table.

"The markets," muttered O'Keefe, rolling his eyes. "The president keeps getting calls from overseas. He is . . . worried. There's a witching hour this week, all the central bank notes roll over; much whining from our British friends, as usual." He didn't elaborate, and Weber didn't ask.

O'Keefe was waiting impatiently for the visitor to state his business, so Weber plunged ahead.

"I'm sorry to bother you." Weber could see that his host was stressed.

"That's my job, to be bothered, so that the president isn't. What is it?"

"Cyril Hoffman told me to come see you. He probably explained what it's about. I have a young man working for me named James Morris. I gather he used to work at the White House, and that people here think highly of him. Hoffman said I shouldn't do anything without talking to you, so here I am."

O'Keefe looked away, toward the window and the front lawn of the White House. This was his palace and his prison. He turned back to Weber.

"Clever boy, Morris. He's a bit dark sometimes, moody. Handle with care."

"He just offered me his resignation. He made a mistake on a very important case. I'm wondering whether it's best for the agency if I let him go."

O'Keefe's face was like a white balloon, with a thin moustache above the lip that looked like it might have been drawn with a pencil. He took off his wire-rimmed glasses and wiped the lenses with the end of his tie while he pondered the move that would be most useful to him and the president. Weber was bringing him a problem that he didn't need, at the end of a busy day.

"Well, my friend, it didn't take you long to get in trouble, did it?" His voice sounded grouchy, like someone who hadn't had enough sleep.

"I'm sorry, Tim. I promised you a new beginning out there, but it's a moving target."

"And now you want my permission to fire someone important, two weeks into the job."

"I want to do the right thing. The agency feels like a company in Chapter Eleven. Someone has to say no."

"You prize your independence, from everything I hear. You don't take orders from anyone. That's your style, right?"

"I guess so," answered Weber. He was trying to remain genial.

"But the reality, my friend, is that you are *not* independent. You work for the president; which, as a practical matter, means that you work for me."

Weber raised his hand.

"Sorry, Tim, I didn't come here to pick a fight. I wanted your counsel. I know I work for the president. I follow his orders, so long as they're legal and proper. If I decide I can't follow an order, I quit and you find someone else. Simple."

"I must say, you have an annoying habit of threatening to resign, for someone who just got his job. Hoffman tells me you did it a week ago. Please don't do it again."

Weber held silent. This was not a playground argument. He was in the White House. He served at the president's pleasure. He waited for O'Keefe to continue.

"What you need to understand," said the national security adviser, "is that there is a political side to everything. If Morris resigned from the CIA, it would become public, inevitably. And then people would ask why he resigned. And then some people might realize that an agent he had traveled to meet had ended up *dead*, and the president hadn't done anything about it. And then all of this would be *my* problem."

"I wouldn't announce it," responded Weber. "I think Morris is under cover, so the newspapers couldn't report his name, legally. He runs the Information Operations Center, which is a part of the agency that we don't talk about. So maybe it would stay secret. But what difference does that make? If we need to replace him, we should do it."

O'Keefe raised a finger.

"Please! Of course it would become public. What century do you think this is? The Senate and House Intelligence Committees would hear about it before the day was out, and they'd call you and me both, asking why they weren't consulted. And then they'd want to know what Morris was doing in—where was he?"

O'Keefe was getting flushed again. He couldn't help himself.

"Hamburg," answered Weber.

"Yes, the committees would ask what he was doing in Hamburg. Who got killed there, and was he really trying to defect, for god's sake? And for that matter, what was Morris doing in general? What were these Information Operations of his that the White House had not thought necessary to disclose? Sorry, Senator, sorry, Congresswoman. I guess we should have briefed you about those, now that it's all blown up. Oops."

O'Keefe continued, wagging his finger now, trying to stay cool but not succeeding.

"And then there would be a staff investigation, and then a closed hearing, and then a newspaper leak, and then a public statement, and then, well, fuck, just shoot the pooch. And it wouldn't be your problem, Weber, oh, no, you just took the job. Your friends in the press would spin you as the hero, no doubt. No, it would be my problem."

Weber tried to interject. He wasn't forcing Morris out. He was just seeking advice. But O'Keefe was intent on delivering his message.

"And *then* it would be the president's problem. Some jackass would shout out a question during a photo opportunity with the visiting president of, I don't know, Ecuador, and the president would have to deal with it. It would be another sign of the White House's inability to address disarray and illegality at the CIA, while you, no doubt, would maneuver your way out of it, leaking to your friends that this was about accountability and good management, while we took the shit. Is that a good idea? you ask me. No, thank you."

O'Keefe's face, the torrent released, returned to that placid tapioca.

"I'm not trying to maneuver out of anything," said Weber in a low voice. "That's not my style."

"What a relief," answered O'Keefe.

There was silence as the two men glowered at each other.

"Shit does not flow uphill, Graham."

"It does at the CIA," said Weber.

"That's your problem. And one more thing: We're not entirely defenseless here. If we got wind that you were spinning a version of a

Morris firing that made you look good, at our expense, we would have to respond."

"And how would you respond?" Weber enunciated each word.

"We would tell the truth. We would remind people that this happened during your short watch as director, and that you were asking a subordinate to take the fall."

"Stop threatening me, Tim. I don't want to fire Morris. I want advice."

"Okay, here's my advice. This isn't about Morris. He may be as weird and geeky as they come, but he's not the issue. Think about appearances. Don't make trouble for the president. Manage the CIA, but don't drop a bomb on it."

Weber nodded. He got it. He didn't want to be the shortest-serving CIA director in history.

"Okay, Morris stays. The fact is, I need him. If what he's told me is true, our problems are just beginning."

"No. *Your* problems may be. Not my problems. Not the president's. Are we clear on that?" Even his thin moustache seemed to bristle.

"We're clear," said Weber. "I'll do the right thing."

"I'm sure you will. And if you should by mistake do the wrong thing, well, you have been warned."

Weber's personal life intruded in a way that that was oddly comforting late that afternoon when he returned from the White House. He received a call from the headmaster of the prep school that his sons were attending in New Hampshire. That had been his ex-wife's idea; she thought it would be better if they had "their own place" after she remarried, even if it was an austere institution that celebrated athletics and admission to Ivy League schools above lesser matters. Weber went along; he'd had the boys most of each summer since the divorce, though he suspected that it would be different this year, and every year he remained at the CIA.

The headmaster apologized for disrupting the "director," as he called him throughout the conversation. It didn't seem appropriate to leave a message with Marie, he said. He explained that Weber's older son, David, was "acting out." When queried, the headmaster advised that the boy had been reported smoking weed at an off-campus party, and had been drunk to boot. It was his son's senior year; final college recommendation letters were being prepared. This was *serious*, in other words.

Weber said he would be in New Hampshire that evening; travel was a bit uncertain, he said; he didn't know whether his security men would let him take the last commercial shuttle to Boston, but one way or another he would get there that night.

David was waiting. He was taller than his dad, nearly six feet two inches, and fit from football. When he saw his father walking toward him, the boy burst into tears.

They spent the night at a motel in Concord. The boy was eating himself alive with the stress and loneliness of adolescence. The headmaster seemed to have done his best to convince him that there would be national security consequences for his having smoked pot. Weber laughed and told his son stories about his own mistakes when he was growing up. Weber said he couldn't care less where his son went to college, which made the boy cry again.

"It's hard being a kid, isn't it?" Weber said as they parted the next morning. His son nodded. "Try not to make mistakes, but I'll love you anyway." The boy extended his hand to say goodbye, but Weber hugged him and didn't let go.

12

WASHINGTON

James Morris kept an apartment in Dupont Circle, in a building that had resisted the gentrification that had turned much of the neighborhood into a hipper extension of Georgetown. He had the top floor of a row house, with a little roof garden from which he could see parts of the Washington skyline between the chimneys and façades of neighboring buildings. He liked to visit his roof when he was feeling wired, as a way of calming himself. One of the complications of working for the CIA was that you had to be careful about taking drugs or seeing a psychiatrist if you were feeling out of sorts. But Morris had always managed to keep himself together enough to avoid attracting notice. That was part of how he lived. Every intelligence officer had a secret life; Morris's was just a little more secret than most.

Morris had learned to master the polygraph along the way, as well as his emotions. These "lie detector" sessions were meant to frighten people, but they were easy enough to finesse. Morris had smoothly handled his last polygraph six months before: Ramona Kyle had been his best friend since college. He had mentioned her in his first interview with the agency, and several times since. His visits with her didn't register stress. There were other questions that would be harder now, but his next polygraph probably wouldn't come until the following year, and by then he expected that he would be gone from the agency.

When Morris returned from Germany, he remained closeted in his apartment for a day. He felt secure inside. The windows were barred and the door was triple-locked. He had motion detectors and thermal monitors to make sure that he wasn't disturbed. And he had his computers. He could use these to roam and maneuver, without having to worry that his keystrokes would be monitored and analyzed by a hidden "threat analysis" system of the sort that ran on agency machines. Pownzor wanted his own life. He didn't want to be powned, especially by his workplace.

Morris was having trouble sleeping those first nights back, so he would bring a blanket up to the roof along with a mug of Chinese herbal tea, and let his mind race until it began to exhaust itself. He would stare at the stars, or sometimes imagine them through the clouds, until his eyelids became heavy. What kept Morris awake so late was the burden of his mission. Governments wanted to control the free space of the Internet; hackers wanted to keep it free. It was Morris's destiny to be the man—no, the circuit—in the middle. He knew why people hated the agency as an instrument of repression: They were his people. That was why he could be on both sides, and neither.

The plans and patterns would flash through his mind like bright lights, laser beams of thought, and he would follow the tracers until his eyes were heavy and the light gun in his head stopped firing. In the early morning, two or three, or sometimes not until dawn, he would pick himself up off the mat atop his roof, shivering in his wrap of blankets, and take himself downstairs to his bed.

The second day Morris was back in Washington, he contacted Arthur Peabody, the man Ramona Kyle had recommended. The contact numbers had arrived by mail, in an unmarked envelope. Ten minutes' research revealed that Peabody had retired a decade before as the agency's chief historian. Morris called and introduced himself as an agency employee who wanted to know more about CIA history, and Peabody immediately said, "Oh, yes," as if he had been expecting the call. He invited Morris to come visit that afternoon around cocktail time.

Peabody was a widower who lived alone in a genteel suburb known as Spring Valley, in the far northwest corner of the city. This was a neigh-borhood that had been built for the gentry back in the 1940s and '50s when Washington was still a segregated town. The homes were mostly brick, with big lawns, front and back, and servants' rooms inside to keep a cook or housemaid. From the street, it might have been Richmond or Atlanta, big old houses, screened porches, pools and fountains out back. The houses didn't glisten like the modern ones out in Potomac or McLean. The brick pathways up to the front door were often cracked with age, and the cracks were filled with old green moss. It was the sort of place where wellborn CIA officers had moved when they were young men, and a few of them, such as Arthur Peabody, were still hanging on.

Morris climbed the red walkway and rang the doorbell. It was old, like everything about the house. The bell stuck in the "on" posi-tion, bringing an annoying, repetitive *ding-dong* that only ended when Arthur Peabody opened the door. He stuck his long, thin arm around the corner and fiddled with the button until it stopped.

"This damned thing," grumbled Peabody. "No wonder nobody comes to visit."

Peabody was a relic of the WASP ascendency, a gaunt body, slightly stooped; a long aquiline nose; a high austere forehead, and a face specked with age spots and small scars from surgeries to remove cancerous spots from too much sun on the boat in Maine.

Morris followed the old man through the doorway. The entry hall was dark and musty. To the right was a forbidding study, lined with dark wood shelves that couldn't contain all the volumes. They were stacked two deep on the lower shelves, some books horizontal or upside down. A few of the shelves had just given way, so that books were heaped on top of each other. To the left was an old parlor, whose wallpaper was meant to be gay but was yellowing and peeling with age. Peabody led the way back through a dark dining room to an area that seemed the only place in the house that got any light. This was a breakfast room, facing the back lawn, where an old-fashioned sprinkler was cascading a jet of water.

"Sit down, James," said Peabody. "Can I get you a beverage?"

"Tea, please," said the guest. He looked restrained and studious this afternoon, like a young man visiting his grandfather. The only signs of stress were the deep circles under the eyes, and the inflamed look of the eyes themselves, on red alert.

Peabody padded off to get the tea. He was wearing a worn tweed jacket purchased long ago at J. Press in New Haven, tan chino slacks, baggy at the knees, and lace-up oxfords, one of which was untied. Tortoiseshell reading glasses were low on his nose,

Morris examined the morning newspaper still on the breakfast table, and a copy of the *American Historical Review* on a sideboard. The journal was open to an article: "Sudden Nationhood: Microdynamics of Intercommunal Relations in Bosnia-Herzegovina after World War II." Morris perused it for a few moments and then tossed it aside.

Peabody returned a minute later bearing a silver platter with a teapot and two cups, along with a plate of Walkers English shortbread cookies. The young man helped himself to a cup of tea and one of the sweet biscuits.

"I'm just back from Germany," said Morris. His eyes were fixed on the middle distance, somewhere between the window and the trees beyond. "I'll be heading back overseas soon."

"That's nice," said Peabody. "I'm sure I shouldn't ask what you were doing."

"Let's say I'm opening the curtain on a new play."

Peabody lifted his brows, as if to say: *Aha!* Morris's comment had reminded him of something apposite.

"Open the curtain! I must warn you, Mr. Morris, that this conveys a metaphorical illusion of control."

Morris propped his glasses on the bridge of his nose and leaned toward the old man.

"How so, Mr. Peabody? I'm not tracking."

"The play 'unfolds *inevitably* once the curtain is raised.' I quote Count Metternich in a passage cited by, forgive me, my former doctoral supervisor, Dr. Henry A., you know the rest. Metternich's point was that the play is *already scripted*. Therefore, and I quote, 'The essence of the problem . . . lies in *whether the curtain is to be raised at all.*' That's the thing: You didn't have to raise the curtain, James, but you did, and now everything unfolds as scripted."

"Scripted by whom?"

"I don't know," answered Peabody. "I'm an Episcopalian."

This was nonsense talk, but Morris wanted an answer. His eyes, ringed as they were with fatigue, were alive.

"Seriously, I wonder sometimes who writes the script, not in general, but at the agency. I'm told you know the real story. The 'secret history,' that's what a friend said. And I'd like to know the truth. That's why I'm here."

Peabody's eyes widened. A thin smile crossed his lips. It was as if he had been waiting for someone like Morris to walk into his lair.

"Ramona said I'd like you, and I do, already."

Morris winced a moment at the mention of her name. It was the biggest secret he knew.

"Roger that. I need to understand the agency; not the 'what,' but the 'why.'"

"Oh, yes, I can tell you a bit; quite a lot, actually. But it will surprise you, if you've never heard it. It will make you question the institution where you are employed."

"I've been asking questions since the day I walked in the door. I want answers."

Peabody chortled. His visitor was so eager.

"Well, now, let me get some books, so I can confide these mysteries properly."

Peabody retreated to his study and returned with several volumes whose pages had been marked with yellow stickers. One fat book, nearly six hundred pages, had the bland title *Donovan and the CIA*. A slimmer volume was called *Wild Bill and Intrepid*. They were both written by one Thomas F. Troy.

"Not exactly bedtime reading," said Peabody. "But in their way, they are page-turners. Mr. Troy was my colleague at the agency, if you're wondering. The big book was compiled originally as a secret agency study, but it was declassified some years ago. Troy wrote the second book after he retired. For reasons you will soon understand, the agency has not called attention to them."

"What's controversial? If they're unclassified histories, why would anyone care?"

"Because, my young friend, they suggest to the careful reader that the CIA may have been created by another intelligence service, namely the Secret Intelligence Service of Great Britain, aka MI6."

Morris sat back in his chair. He hadn't known what to expect from Peabody, but certainly not this.

"That's pretty rad," he said.

"Indeed. What I am going to explain is the origin of the species, as it were."

Peabody opened the fat book to page 417 and pushed it across the table to Morris.

"Here," he said. "Read this."

It was a letter, dated April 26, 1941, from William J. Donovan to Frank Knox, secretary of the navy and one of the closest confidants of President Franklin Roosevelt.

"Read it, aloud, please."

Morris studied the first few lines of the letter and then began:

> *Dear Frank:*
>
> *Following your suggestion I am telling you briefly of the instrumentalities through which the British Government gathers its information in foreign countries.*
>
> *I think it should be read with these considerations in mind. Intelligence operations should not be controlled by party exigencies. It is one of the most vital means of national defense. As such it should be headed by someone appointed by the President directly responsible to him and to no one else. It should have a fund solely for the purpose of foreign investigation and the expenditures should be secret and made solely at the discretion of the President . . .*

Peabody took back the book.

"You understand the implications, I trust. It is more than seven months before Pearl Harbor. FDR's man has asked Donovan to research how the Brits run their intelligence service, and Donovan is reporting back the British system so the Americans can . . . well, let's just say it . . . copy it.

"But that's not the official version, mind you," Peabody continued.

"The cover story is that Donovan created the CIA in a sort of clandestine version of the immaculate birth. Allen Dulles described the CIA as, and I quote, 'Bill Donovan's dream.'"

"But the official version is a lie," broke in Morris.

"Indeed. When there was discussion of making the full details public in the 1980s, the CIA's inspector general, Lyman Kirkpatrick, argued it would be 'extremely questionable' and 'shocking indeed.' Here, again, I am indebted to the scholarship of my friend Troy."

"You're saying the Brits wrote the operating system. We would say in geek-speak that they owned the firmware."

"In any speak. It was a controlled operation."

Peabody turned the pages until he found another yellow marker.

"I'll show you another little something. It is a memorandum dated June 27, 1941. The subject is the proper organization of the Office of the Coordinator of Information, which was the predecessor of the Office of Strategic Services.

Peabody opened the marked passage for Morris to see.

"Note the author, please. Commander Ian Fleming, the man who wrote the James Bond novels. As you can see, he goes through the whole order of battle: headquarters; chief of staff, country sections; liaison officers. It's all there, on the SIS model. Our friend Troy found a note from him talking about 'my memorandum to Bill about how to create an American Secret Service' and calling it 'the cornerstone of the future OSS.'

"And there's more, my friend. The Brits were quite pleased with themselves, as well you might imagine. Churchill's office was licking its chops, as if the kingly lion had devoured the innocent and bewildered lamb."

Peabody took the smaller volume, *Wild Bill and Intrepid*, and leafed through the pages until he found the passage he wanted.

"Here's what Churchill himself knew, in black and white, according to his personal office. It is a letter dated September 18, 1941, written by Sir Desmond Morton in the PM's office to Colonel E. I. Stark. Perhaps you would read it to me."

"Out loud?"

Peabody nodded. Morris adjusted his glasses and began reading the words on the page:

Another most secret fact of which the Prime Minister is aware . . . is that to all intents and purposes U.S. Security is being run for them at the President's request by the British. A British officer sits in Washington with Edgar Hoover and General Bill Donovan for this purpose and reports to the President. It is of course essential that fact should not be known in view of the furious uproar it would cause if known to the Isolationists.

"There it is," said Peabody. "Can it be any clearer? They're the hidden hand. Of course they own the CIA. They created it! Read the history, Mr. Morris. It's all there."

Morris looked left and right, as if he feared someone were listening. But it was just the two of them. Two agency hands, having a conversation.

"Why are you telling me this?" asked Morris.

"Because you need to know, first of all. You need to understand why our agency has been such a menace in American life. I searched for the answer my whole career, but it's so obvious, once you grasp it. The CIA is a *foreign implant*. It was created in secret by *another government*. It is a *covert action*. That is a puzzle it took me years to solve and I want you to understand. We all do."

"Who is '*we*'?" asked Morris quietly.

"Like-minded individuals. American patriots. People who believe in liberty. You know one of them, our dear Ramona. But there are many more, unseen. And we are all looking to you, sir."

"Why me? I'm the computer guy."

"Because you can *do* something about it. You can break free of the monstrous secret history that I have narrated. You have the access, and the power. You can strike a blow that nobody else can. This is your moment, if you have the mettle to grasp it."

Morris stood as if to go. But Peabody fixed him with his cunning eyes and shook his head. Morris knew in that instant that it was true, what Ramona Kyle had said. He had to keep going. It was impossible to turn back once he had started down this road. Morris sat back down in his chair across from his host.

"What do you want me to do?" he asked.

Peabody nodded. The thin smile returned.

"Have you ever heard of the Bank for International Settlements?" he asked.

"I know a little," answered Morris. "It's in Switzerland, in Basel, right? It's sort of a central bank for central banks."

"All correct," said Peabody. "But in a deeper sense, it is one of the cornerstones of the Anglo-American plan for the postwar world. It is a surprising fact, perhaps, that FDR wanted to kill the BIS in 1944, because it had done some rather unpleasant business with the Nazis. But the British wouldn't hear of it. They *insisted*. This was to be a symbol of the post-imperial order, the Anglo-American condominium which would control the world of finance, by managing the accounts of every central bank. And so it sits in Basel, a quiet, unobtrusive but unshakable symbol of the permanent order of things."

"And what do you want me to do about the BIS?"

Peabody smiled again, more broadly this time, a grin that stretched nearly ear to ear. He spoke with a vulgarity that was unlikely for his age, but underlined his patrician rebellion.

"We want you to take it down, my boy. We want you to hack it up the ass until its electronic eyes turn brown."

Morris returned to work at the Information Operations Center the next morning. He'd had a fitful sleep, but drove out early to suburban Virginia in his Prius. He buried himself in his vaultlike office at the far end of the operations room, as he always did when he was in Washington. Ariel Weiss stopped by for a brief chat, to go over pending personnel decisions.

In the afternoon, Morris visited Headquarters, at the director's request. It would be the first time he had talked in person with Graham Weber since he'd returned from Germany. Morris was dressed a bit more traditionally than usual, in a collared shirt and a blue blazer. With the addition of a tie, he would have looked like an associate professor of computer science going to meet with the dean. Morris was nervous, wondering if the director was going to fire him. That would complicate things.

Weber greeted Morris in the sitting room of his private dining room, under a portrait of the implacable Richard Helms, whose profile made him look like the last of the Caesars. Tea and cookies, which seemed the essential nourishment of the intelligence service, were promptly delivered.

"You look tired," said Weber.

"I've been working too hard," said Morris. "Too much stress on this German thing. But I've got some leave coming. Maybe I'll take a week. First, I've got some work overseas."

"You're no use to anyone if you get exhausted."

"Yes, sir." Morris adjusted his glasses.

"I've been thinking about what happened in Hamburg," said Weber. "And I've been talking to some people around town."

Morris tensed.

"I appreciate that you offered your resignation, but I'm not going to accept it. The death of that boy wasn't your fault, and I need you for what's ahead. You're the only one who really understands these systems. The others pretend to, but they don't."

Morris blinked. He swallowed hard.

"Thank you, sir."

Weber put up his hand.

"Don't thank me yet. The hard part is just beginning. Have you come up with anything?"

"I just see ripples in the water, so far. We're working some new penetrations of the hacker networks. We're trolling the groups where Biel was active."

"You're doing this under your 'special authority,' I take it."

"Yes, sir. It's the joint program I told you about. I have some new . . . ideas. Things I'm experimenting with."

"Will they get me in trouble?"

Morris laughed. His eyes were pinpricks.

"Heck, no, sir. They're in a good cause. Down with the old, in with the new. That's your mantra, isn't it, Mr. Director?"

Weber studied the young man. He prized himself on his judgment, on his willingness to take the right risks, to do the unconventional thing when it was necessary. That had led him to James Morris, and now he was doubling down on the bet he had made. As a businessman, he knew he should lay off some of that risk, but it was harder in government.

"I can count on you, right? I need strong hearts."

Morris gazed back at him. His head was motionless, but at the last moment before he spoke, there was the slightest tremor.

"Yes, sir. I'm good as gold. We're going to go to the center of this thing and take it down."

Weber smiled. Morris's handshake was firm, too tight a squeeze perhaps, but a show of strength. The director said something genial as he walked Morris to the door. On his way back to his desk, Weber felt oddly not quite as reassured as he had hoped by the conversation. Morris was just fatigued, he told himself. Even computer geniuses had their off days.

13

SILVERTON, COLORADO

From the window of Ramona Kyle's cabin, she could see the old mining town sewn like a cross-stitch into the valley below. The trees on her hillside were shimmering golden red, the leaves swirling down Highway 110 toward the north end of town. In every direction were the jagged teeth of the San Juan Mountains, guarding the western gate of the Rockies. Kyle's cabin was up near the tree line, amid the gray rock that reached almost to the October sky. Nobody with any sense lived here. The highway north from Durango had already been closed once by early snow. In a few weeks, this place would be perfect desolation, populated only by recluses and daredevils.

She was an elfin figure, sitting in a wing chair by the big window, her red hair gathered in a frizzy pony tail, a magazine across her lap. This was her hiding place, an address no one knew, on a county road that even the locals rarely visited. At the San Juan County Courthouse on Greene Street, a few miles below, a deed was registered for the cabin, but it wasn't in her name or traceable to anything she owned. The same was true with her satellite Internet connection, which was her only requirement here, other than the space and silence. Here she could be no one and nowhere.

She thought about James Morris. He was someone and everywhere, enfolded in a world she despised. She had launched him, but she suspected that he was as oblivious of his ultimate purpose as a spinning metal bullet of its target. He took his actions without understanding their consequences. He was innocent, in that way, precious and alone. She wanted to protect him.

A burning log crackled in the fireplace behind her. Kyle rose from her chair and put more wood on the grate, poking at the embers until the flame rose nearly to the damper. Above the fireplace was a Renaissance painting she had bought from a dealer in Florence a year ago, after she had sold her interest in an Italian startup. It was a minor work, from the school of a second-rank painter in Padua, but it appealed to Kyle. It showed the martyrdom of St. Sebastian, the man tied to a tree and pierced with arrows. There was in the martyr's eyes a look of helpless surrender, almost quizzical, not joy but submission. After she bought the painting, she had researched Sebastian's improbable life. His Roman friends were butchered gruesomely, one by one: Zoe, hung by her heels over a fire until she choked; Tranquilinus, stoned to death; Castulus, racked and buried alive; Tiburtus, beheaded. Sebastian refused to flee. A quiver of arrows pierced every limb, but even then he didn't die. He confronted the emperor and spoke out in his agony, taunting Diocletian for his cowardly murder of the Christians, until he was finally beaten into death and silence.

Kyle returned to her chair. The sun had broken through the lowering afternoon sky, illuminating the whole of the town. The outcroppings of Kendall Peak, which rose from the high valley, were bathed in white sunlight, while the dells and crevices fell into a deep shadow of silver black. It would be snowing again soon over Coal Pass and Mola Pass, perhaps closing the two-lane road into Silverton once more. Kyle felt selfish. A person could live and die here with the dignity of a wild animal. She was letting James Morris do the dirty business; requiring it of him, in truth.

Kyle had given up on half-measures. She had concluded over the last several years that America could not change course. The forces of oppression had captured the state so completely that they were the state. The people were the subjects of a tyrannical power that couldn't be reformed or appeased or changed, but only destroyed.

The clouds were darkening over the San Juan range. The sunlight had vanished as quickly as it had come. She picked up the magazine she had been reading. It was *Spectrum*, the journal of the Institute of Electrical and Electronics Engineering. The cover story she had been reading was titled, "Would You Shoot Your Neighbor's Drone?" That was what the world was coming to. Even the geeks were becoming fascists. Kyle put the magazine aside and closed her eyes.

There had been a moment when she had allowed herself to hope. It was a few months ago, when the White House had first floated the name of Graham Weber as the president's choice as the new director of the scandal-plagued Central Intelligence Agency. Weber had a reputation as a skeptic, a man who was connected to the intelligence Leviathan but also critical of it. He had refused to carry out the demand of a National Security Letter that had been delivered to his company by the FBI; Kyle knew the story. Weber claimed that the order was unconstitutional, and he had gotten away with it. James Morris even knew the new director; he had been Weber's guide at a hackers convention a year before, and Morris had wanted to please him, as he did everyone. Kyle had seen it as an opening—a chink in the armor through which she could insert the explosive powder of change. She was pitiless that way; if James Morris or anyone else thought he had a friend inside the heart of the beast, he was a fool.

All that afternoon Kyle ruminated, until the sun set and the sky fell to a last rosy pink in the west above Anvil Mountain. Kyle wondered if there was a last chance that she had missed, a way to subvert the structure without so much collateral damage. Was there a way to communicate to Graham Weber, the CIA director, that he had a choice? The message he needed to hear was that he could still be the man who said no; he could join in the subversion and dismantlement of an unjust system. He had only just entered the gates of the castle; he didn't have to take the side of the defenders. He could be a liberator.

How could she tell Weber that he might still escape the holocaust of surveillance and deception and lies? If the director of the National Security Agency had been given warning that he could dismantle the programs that Edward Snowden later would reveal to the press—terminate them on his own, without the chaotic damage of disclosure—would he have seized the opportunity? If people were given the clear choice to do the right thing, would they take it? Kyle didn't know. Graham Weber was heading toward a catastrophic conclusion, even if he couldn't see it. One person had already died to protect the secret of James Morris's identity, but there would be more. Would Weber see the escape hatch from history?

Kyle thought of what she would say to the CIA director, if she were to communicate anonymously with him. She went to her bookshelf on the other side of the fireplace and took down a volume of British philosophy that she sometimes read to gather her thoughts. She leafed past John Locke and David Hume, until she found the essay *On Liberty*, by John Stuart Mill. It was dark in the room, except for the flicker of the fire. She turned on the table lamp beside her chair and curled up in its creamy light with the book. It was the comfort of truth.

What was the region of liberty? Mill asked. It was "liberty of thought and feeling; absolute freedom of opinion and sentiment on all subjects, practical or speculative, scientific, moral or theological." It required "liberty of tastes and pursuits; of framing the plan of our life to suit our own character; of doing as we like, subject to such consequences as may follow: without impediment from our fellow-creatures, so long as what we do does not harm them, even though they should think our conduct foolish, perverse or wrong."

Liberty could not be divided against itself, or rationed or temporized. "No society in which these liberties are not, on the whole, respected, is free, whatever may be its form of government; and none is completely free in which they do not exist absolute and unqualified." And then Mill's concluding injunction: "A State which dwarfs its men, in order that they may be more docile instruments in its hands even for beneficial purposes—will find that with small men no great thing can really be accomplished." There it was. Could anything be more clearly stated? She would present Graham Weber, this man she had never met but imagined was in some part of himself a kindred spirit, a last opportunity to escape smallness and corruption and un-freedom.

Kyle went to her desk at the back of the cabin, placing a few more logs on the fire as she went. A wolf was howling in the woods below her cabin, a fierce lone cry. She opened her computer and waited for it to come alive, and then she began typing, checking references in her files, and working the text back and forth until it was as concise and direct as she could make it.

Dear Mr. Weber:

I write you this message so that you may save yourself and the Central Intelligence Agency from destruction. You have taken control of a lawless organization that asserts the right to corrupt and destroy others around the world in secrecy. These covert powers are based on the flimsiest legal claims, which themselves violate the U.S. Constitution. You know this, because you yourself refused to obey orders that you knew to be illegal, when you were a private citizen. As a demonstration of my seriousness and bona fides, I cite for you the number of the National Security Letter to which you refused compliance. It was File Number NH-43907, issued subject to Title 18 United States Code, Section 2709. I believe your records will verify the accuracy of this information.

Take the opportunity now to be a leader, in the true and moral sense, by halting the activities of the Central Intelligence Agency that violate the laws of every other nation and treat global citizens as objects for external control by the United States, rather than subjective human beings with their own consciousness and rights and freedoms. Liberty is not divisible, Mr. Weber. It must be for everyone, or it is for no one.

I send you this message as a warning and an opportunity. If you do not reverse course, the process that is now underway will bring down your house around you. The liberating actions of Bradley Manning and Edward Snowden were only a beginning. A global political awakening is taking place in every nation. If the security services are under attack in other countries—China, Ukraine, Russia, Egypt, Syria, Turkey, Britain—do you imagine that the United States can resist? The army is at your gates, even though you don't see it. The Central Intelligence Agency will not survive this challenge. You must decide which side you are on, that of liberty or oppression. The hours left for you to make this choice are ticking away.

Remember the words: "Arise ye prisoners of starvation; Arise

ye wretched of the earth. For justice thunders condemnation: A
better world's in birth. No more tradition's chains shall bind us.
Arise, ye slaves, no more in thrall; the earth shall rise on new
foundations: We have been naught, we shall be all."
   I await some public acknowledgment by you that you intend
to make the necessary reforms. If not, there will be consequences.
   Yours sincerely,
   Anonymous

Ramona Kyle printed out the message, then copied it, then photo-graphed the copy and printed out the picture. She placed the sheet in a sealed envelope marked "Graham Weber, Personal," and put that, in turn, in a larger manila envelope marked "David Weber," which she sent by commercial courier to an associate in California who handled confi-dential financial business for her. At her instruction, he sent the package through several cutouts to the address of a preparatory school in New Hampshire, where it was delivered by a United Parcel Service messenger to the mailbox of David Weber, a senior at the school.

When the young man saw the letter inside marked for Graham Weber, he immediately called his father in Washington. A government official arrived that afternoon and collected the letter, unopened, and carried it to CIA headquarters in Washington, where it was delivered, still unopened, to the agency's director.

Graham Weber read the peculiar text through twice. His first thought was that it was a hoax of some kind, perhaps a scheme hatched by one of his son's fellow students, or more likely, a screwball teacher at the school who was playing out some revolutionary fantasy. But as he read it the second time, the proof of bona fides seemed more difficult to refute. He consulted his own files, and saw that the "file number" that had been referenced, "NH-43907," was accurate. The letter had been sent by the New Haven division of the FBI to a Connecticut subsidiary of his communications company, demanding production of all sub-scriber information pertaining to a particular IP address. To Weber's knowledge, that information had never been made public.

What if the letter was in earnest? What if someone was, indeed,

warning Weber to follow through on his hopes and dreams of reform-
ing the conduct of intelligence activities—or face the consequences?
Weber wanted to dismiss the entirety of the message, but he knew that
one of its arguments was true. Liberty is not divisible. It is not a halfway
condition. It either exists or it doesn't. He knew that another assertion
was largely true, as well: The CIA did assert a right to violate the laws of
all other nations. That, in essence, was its job description.

Weber laid down the letter. He called the personal number of Ruth
Savin, the CIA's general counsel, and asked her to come to his office
immediately. He said he had received a letter that she needed to read,
as soon as possible. She arrived in the director's suite ten minutes later.

"This is crap," said Savin when she had finished reading the letter.
"Don't worry about it."

She was holding the sheet of paper in blue plastic gloves that she had
brought with her, to avoid marking it with fingerprints. She gingerly
took the paper and placed it in a translucent plastic envelope, which she
marked at the top with the date and time, and then initialed and laid
aside. She was flushed, from the urgent summons and the rapid trip to
the director's office. The color in her cheeks complemented the lustrous
black of her hair and the rust red of the tweed jacket she was wearing
over her black dress.

"That's it?" asked Weber. "No further comments?"

"It's well-written crap. I like where it quotes the Internationale at
the end. That's a nice touch."

"Does that mean the author is a Russian? Or some kind of communist?"

"Maybe. Or perhaps the author wants us to think that. It's impossible to know, Mr. Director. How did it get to you, anyway?"

Weber sighed and shook his head. He hated the fact that this breach
had come through his family. It made him feel that his boys were
exposed.

"It was sent to my oldest son at school, delivered this morning by
a UPS courier as part of his regular run. The Office of Security has
already checked on the delivery. They say the sender's address in Boston

is fake. They're pulling the video recording from the location where it was sent, but they don't think they'll get anything useful."

Savin looked at the letter through the plastic envelope.

"The reference number of the National Security Letter, is that accurate?"

"Yup," said Weber. "Precisely right. I checked. How did they get that, anyway? It's supposed to be secret."

"Nothing is secret, really, Mr. Director. It could have come from an employee of your old company. It could have been obtained by one of the privacy groups that has been snooping around for details of these NSLs for years. It could even have come from some disgruntled person at the FBI. There's no way to know. But that doesn't prove anything to me, the fact that somebody got the reference number. That's just bravado. Hacker street cred. I wouldn't take it too seriously."

"You wouldn't? It seems pretty real to me. Someone is warning me that our systems are going to be attacked, just the way the NSA's were by Snowden. They're telling me to make changes at the agency to avoid the damage. Shouldn't I take that seriously?"

Savin studied him: His hair was slightly disheveled; his sleeves were half rolled up his forearms; his open-neck shirt had popped an extra button. He had never looked younger and less like the director of an intelligence agency. He was an outsider, and for the moment he seemed to want to hold on to that status.

"Frankly, no, you should ignore it," she said. "We'll look into all the forensics. The Office of Security will help the FBI try to figure out who sent it. We should probably send a protection detail to your kids' school in Concord, discreetly, at least for a few weeks."

"Okay," said Weber, rolling his hand impatiently. "But what about the content?"

"Honestly, sir, stuff like this arrives in the mail room every day. The whole world thinks the CIA is a bunch of lying criminal bastards, and that we should repent now because it's our last chance. That's the elevator music around here. Usually this stuff gets intercepted by someone else and the director never sees it. This one just got through the net. But it's still crap."

"What if it's true?" asked Weber.

"Meaning what, sir?"

"Don't I have a responsibility to make sure the agency's activities are legal and ethical? I got this job because I made a commitment to the president that I would make changes at the agency and bring it into the twenty-first century. I need to follow through on that."

"Of course, Mr. Director: You do that every day. But can I give you some honest advice as your lawyer?"

"I hate lawyers," muttered Weber. "But yes, certainly I want your advice."

"Your job isn't to protect civil liberties. The president has an Attorney General for that, and the constitution provides for a Congress to pass laws and a Supreme Court to interpret them. Your job is to protect the national security. You have unique powers, working with the president. It's true, what the writer of this letter says. You do have the authority to violate the laws of other countries, under the National Security Act and Executive Order 12333. That's what the CIA does. If you don't put that responsibility first, then you're not doing your job. You have to protect the agency and its people. They're your tools. Sir. With all due respect."

"Including James Morris."

"Yes, Mr. Director. Unless he's done something wrong. You're the commander of this organization. He's one of your troops."

Weber looked out the window. He wasn't sure that he had ever felt the burden of responsibility in quite this way. People often talked in the abstract about the difficulty of striking a balance between liberty and security—but now it was like a knot in his stomach. He could quit. Or he could try to grope his way toward running the agency in a way that met his ethical standards, knowing that if he stayed, the second priority of protecting security would inevitably take precedence over the first, no matter what his conscience said.

"What do you want me to do?" asked Savin.

"Call the Office of Security," said Weber. "Tell them to handle it. Get someone in Concord, but keep them out of sight. I don't want to embarrass my boys."

"And the warnings in the letter?"

"I'll assume they're crap, as you said. I have no other choice, really."

Savin picked up the letter from the director's desk and took it with her as she left the office. Weber sat alone. He put his head in his hands, and then let it fall to the desk, where he rested for several minutes, not exactly praying, because he wasn't a religious man, but reflecting on his mission and asking for help. When he rose and called to Marie for the next appointment, he was in some subtle respects a different man than before.

14

BERLIN

Edward Junot was a short compact man with a shaved head and a stubbly beard. He arrived in Berlin dressed in a black T-shirt and jeans and a black leather jacket, scuffed at the sleeves and elbows from years of use. The T-shirt read RED BULL on the front, and from his eyes, one might guess that he had been speeding for many hours on that drink or some other stimulant. He checked into the Hansel Inn near Nollendorfplatz, a hotel that was so gay-friendly that the manager posted a note saying that it was hetero-friendly.

Before he left to go out, Junot put a stud in his left ear and two in his right. He checked the recording device sewn into the fabric of his leather jacket to make sure it was set at zero, and packed a thumb drive and two cell phones in his pocket.

Junot had been a deep-cover intelligence officer for nearly two years. He had been recruited out of the military, where he had worked as a warrant officer for the Army doing "information operations" in Afghanistan, as they politely put it. His job was to hack enemy websites and, as ordered, attack them—shut them down, insert false information, or insert malware that would track other users. He was so good at that work that he came to the attention of the Kabul station, and he was offered a fast track into the CIA's military transition program.

The CIA recruiter had shown Junot a brochure that said he could make $136,000 annually as a data scientist, just using his computer skills. That was almost as much as Blackwater was paying, with less apparent risk, so he said yes. They sent him home for training—not to Washington but to a facility near Denver that handled interagency officers under nonofficial cover. Six months after that, he first met James Morris, who managed to get him transferred to what he called the "special access unit," which was, and was not, part of the Information Operations Center. From that point, Junot had disappeared into Morris's twilight army.

Junot dressed himself for the Berlin night. He put on his scruffiest black leather boots and a belt with a silver buckle that displayed the skull and crossbones, which he had bought that afternoon in the Hackescher Market in Mitte, where he had been conducting preliminary surveillance. The belt buckle gleamed menacingly, but it was hidden by the black T-shirt hanging loosely over it. For the first time in a while, Junot tucked in his shirt. He was believable as a bad-boy hacker because he was one. Junot liked breaking into computers, making trouble and having rough sex with men or women, he didn't care which so long as he was "top."

The last thing he packed was a paperback copy of the *Illuminatus! Trilogy*, a science fiction series published forty years before that had developed a cult following among German hackers.

Junot left the hotel at eleven p.m., when the Berlin night scene was just finding its legs. He took the tramway from Nollendorfplatz several stations, changed to the underground, rode north a few stations and then changed to another tram that took him to his destination back at Hackescher. Junot descended from the elevated train to the street. It was a pleasant late fall evening, the district crammed with Berliners and foreigners who, to watch them filling the bars, seemed determined to end the evening fall-down drunk.

Junot had a beer in a bar near the market and then made his way east to Morgenthaler Street. At Number 19, he entered an archway into a courtyard that housed a techno bar that was a favorite haunt of Germans who fancied themselves the hacker elite.

People in studs and leathers stood outside the entrance, smoking dope. Inside, the DJ was pumping out repetitive percussion, not at full volume yet because it was only eleven, but flexing his muscles. Junot entered the club and walked to the bar, a dimly lit place with wrought-iron fixtures and an illuminated panel under the rail, crossed with lacy ironwork like a nineteenth-century Art Deco lampshade that gave the bar a look somewhere between Bohemia and Belgravia.

Junot took a stool at a small wooden table and ordered a tequila, and then another. In his line of work, he had learned, intoxication was a kind of cover.

Just before midnight, a man in his late twenties, about Junot's age, entered the bar area. He was tall and slender, with long black hair that fell to his shoulders. He was wearing a black jacket that, despite its tight cut, seemed to hang from his slight body. He was a handsome man, and he caught the eye of the crowd near the bar, men and women both. He was carrying in his hand a copy of *The Eye in the Pyramid*, the first volume of the *Illuminatus! Trilogy*.

Junot slid his book forward on the wooden bar table like a calling card.

"Are you a Discordian, my friend?" said Junot, gesturing toward the book the long-haired visitor was carrying.

The other man nodded. "I am Hagbard Celine himself."

This peculiar exchange of phrases was a recognition code. It would have sounded like gibberish to someone at a nearby table, but the references were unmistakable for anyone who was part of the Illuminatus cult.

Junot and his boss, James Morris, had done their homework: The three novels involved, among their many plots and subplots, the adventures of the Discordians and their hero, Hagbard—who piloted a gold submarine and was an avatar of the true Illuminati who believed in perfect freedom. It was a cult book thanks to a German hacker named Karl Koch, who got caught in the 1980s selling secrets from U.S. military computers and died in a supposed suicide.

Junot ordered a beer for the German and another tequila for himself, with a beer chaser.

"So how's it hanging, Hagbard?"

"It's hanging just fine, mister, what is your name?"

"I don't have a name," said Junot. "Sometimes people call me 'Axel.' On-screen I'm 'Dirtbug,' or 'Snakehead,' or 'Gurulgmaster.' Take your pick."

"I'll call you 'John Dillinger,' maybe." That was the name of another fictional character in the bizarre Illuminatus saga.

"Yeah, that fits. Except my dick is bigger." Junot's voice had the rough edge of someone who was well on the way to being hammered.

"Ho-ho," said the German. He rolled his eyes.

It was nearing midnight and the music was getting louder. The DJ had turned up the bass so that the whole room seemed to vibrate with the music.

"You want to dance?" asked the German.

"No. Gets in the way of my drinking. You go ahead. I'll watch."

The German melded into the crowd of men and women on the floor, losing himself in the layers of sound. Two men tried to dance with him, as did one woman, but he ignored them all. He came back to the table twenty minutes later, trailed by a woman who wanted to buy him a drink. His face was flushed; his long hair was glistening with beads of sweat.

"Let's go outside," said the German. "Too hot and noisy here. I'll come back and dance more later."

"Whatever you say, Hagbard." This was proving easier than Junot had expected.

When they were out in Morgenthaler Street, the night air was beginning to bite. There was a café just down the street, quiet and nearly empty.

"You look cold," said Junot. He pointed to the café door just ahead. "In here."

The American led the way to a quiet table in the back. He brought back two cups of black coffee from the bar.

"So, Mr. Hagbard Celine, they say you can get me inside. That's why I'm here. Not to fuck you, although I can do that, too."

"Ugh," said the German. "Please. And what are you talking about, 'inside'? I don't know anything about you, except that we read the same books."

"Don't mess with me, Hagbard. I promise you that's a mistake. The people who arranged this meeting say you are connected with 'the friends.' That's why I'm here. I always want to make friends. Either that, or I make enemies."

"The friends of what? And listen: I am not afraid of you, Mr. John

Dillinger, whoever you are, whose balls are the size of a hazelnut, I am sure."

The German stuck his chin up.

Junot rubbed the rough stubble of his beard, as if contemplating whether to do something—throw a punch, or perhaps take out a pistol. He was coiled tight, capable of sudden, impulsive action. He squinted at the German, and folded his hands down on the table.

"I must be hard of hearing, because I missed what you just said. So I'm going to ask you again, in a nice, how's-your-mom, American way, whether you know any of the Friends of Cerberus. Because the people who arranged this meeting told me that you did. And they would be unhappy if it turned out that they were wrong and looked stupid, making me look stupid, too."

The young man swallowed hard. He stared at the table and sipped at his coffee. His false courage was gone.

"Yeah, I know someone. We call him Malchik. I don't know what his real name is."

"Is he the real deal?"

"What do you mean? I don't understand real deal. He does not deal drugs."

"That's not what I meant. I meant is he connected to Cerberus. The real Cerberus, or what's left of it, after all the CIA losers and BND assholes have been chucked out. Because we are looking for serious people only."

"I can connect you to Malchik. He is serious. Too serious for me. I will give you an address."

"No way. I want a face-to-face introduction. You come with me. That way, it's your bad if something happens."

The German was scared. He was in a public place, and he could see that the American was half drunk, so for a moment he considered bolting for the door. But what would he do then, and where would he run if the American and his friends came after him?

"What do I get, if I help you?

"Just what you were promised: The cocaine charge will disappear. You'll get your job back at Siemens. Everybody will be happy. I have powerful friends, believe me."

The young man stared at him. His hands were trembling. He had fallen into something he didn't understand, and it was about to eat him up.

"Who are you, Mr. Axel?" he asked. "How did you find me? Are you in the Mafia?"

"Don't ask, Hagbard. Let's just say the ghosts sent me."

From the ashen look on the German's face, it seemed almost that he believed he was in the power of real ghosts, come to life.

"I want to meet Malchik tomorrow," said Junot. "Bring him to C-Base at eighteen hundred. Tell him he'll be meeting a friend of a friend. Can you do that for me? Bring him to C-Base?"

"How do you know about C-Base?"

Junot wagged his finger.

"You forget, Hagbard, I am connected. That's why it's dangerous to make me angry. I'll see you at eighteen hundred with Malchik. You don't get a second chance. Now get the hell out of here, unless you've decided you want to blow me in the bathroom."

The German stood, pale as a bedsheet, and backed toward the door. When he reached the street, he broke into a run, and didn't stop until he reached the Alexanderplatz, a half mile away.

C-Base was ground zero for the Berlin hacker culture. It was located on Rungestrasse in the Mitte district, in an old warehouse that backed onto the Spree River. Just across the river was the old East German television tower, known as the Fernsehturm, topped with a round silver sphere that made it look like the entire structure had landed from outer space. When the Wall came down and Berlin's fledgling hackers wanted a place to gather, they had seized the warehouse and pretended that they were restoring a spaceship that had landed on that spot 3.5 million years ago. It was the sort of innocent Trekkie fantasy that hackers cherished back in the nineties, before they found the dark side. C-Base had survived ever since as a kind of hackers' club.

Junot set himself up that afternoon in a bar on Rungestrasse and waited for his prey to arrive. It was a dead-end street, so he could monitor traffic easily through the window. He ordered a beer, but nursed it.

Germans wandered up and down the street, but Junot saw nothing of interest until just before six p.m., when a tall man on a motorcycle rumbled slowly down the street; in the jump seat behind was the slender man Junot had called Hagbard. The man parked the big Kawasaki and removed his helmet. His hair was tied in a ponytail and he was wearing biker leathers, top and bottom. His eyes were covered by Ray-Bans. He walked into a courtyard marked NO. 20, and entered a door at the back, with Hagbard trailing behind.

Junot waited ten minutes for them to get fidgety, and then walked to the entrance. He looked as fearsome as ever, with his bald head and sawed-off shotgun of a body. He knocked on the entry. The door cracked open; inside was a sign that read NO ALIENS.

"I'm expected," said Junot.

The doorkeeper grunted assent. He led Junot through a makeshift replica of an air lock, with colored lights blinking, and metal knobs and buttons. At the other end of this passageway stood the tall man in leather, flanked by Hagbard.

"Cute," said Junot, gesturing to the light show of the make-believe spaceship entryway.

"Fuck off," said the tall man. He was embarrassed by the kiddie show.

"You must be Mr. Malchik," said Junot. The big man nodded.

Junot proffered his hand, but it wasn't taken.

"I'm Axel," said the American. "Is there somewhere we can talk?"

"There's a bar, but some people in there I don't know. We go down-stairs."

The big man turned to Hagbard.

"Go check. If there's anybody in the library, kick them out."

Hagbard disappeared.

"Follow me," said Malchik. He led Junot past an old Atari game and a stack of discarded twenty-year-old computer hardware. Ahead was a screen topped by a sign that read BIOMETRIC RECOGNITION MACHINE. Junot shook his head.

"What is this shit?

"It doesn't work," said Malchik. "Come on."

The big man descended a winding metal staircase to the basement.

In the first room, mannequins were seated in the stripped-down metal frames of old airplane seats. Nearby, another mannequin, dressed in a fur hat, was installed at an old sewing machine.

They ducked into a smaller room, deep in the basement. Against one wall was a bookshelf, crammed with two kinds of literature: science fiction novels and fat, oversized computer science manuals. Above the shelf, as decoration, was a row of white porcelain urinals that had been nailed to the wall. In the corner of the room were two dilapidated chairs, each losing its stuffing.

"Come, sit," said Malchik, pointing to one of the chairs. He turned to Hagbard, who was hovering anxiously outside the room.

"Get lost," Malchik said to the German youth. He closed the door, took a seat in the other chair and turned to Junot.

"So talk," said the big man. "What do you want?"

"First, I bring you greetings from a mutual friend. I think you know him as Hubert. He arranged for me to come."

"Yeah, I know Hubert. We do some work together. So what? Why you call this meeting?"

"We need some help. You're the only person we know who can deliver."

"Help with what?"

"Zero-day exploits. We're buying."

Malchik laughed. Zero-day exploits, so named because they targeted software flaws that were unknown to the vendor until the first day they were used, were hackers' gold.

"Everyone is buying. You know what someone paid in Thailand last week? Five hundred thousand dollars. For one zero-day exploit."

"We can pay more, on a steady basis. You have the network that can produce. We have the clients. And we're in a hurry."

"What network?" snorted Malchik. "You mean Cerberus? The smart boys of Cerberus Computing Club? Well, I'll tell you something. They are too clean to work for you, whoever you are. They are pure white, those boys. They think Snowden still works for the NSA. They want to mess with government, business, Mafias, anyone who has money. They hack for freedom. Free porn, free sex, free money. I don't know. But they will just laugh if you talk to them. Whoever you are, if you have money, you are the enemy."

"But I'm not going to talk to them, Malchik. You are. They know you. Maybe they're scared of you, maybe they don't like you, maybe they think you want money to pay for pretty women and big motorcycles. But you're one of them. You can get what I need."

The big man shook his head, but he was thinking, calculating in his mind.

"How much?" he said.

"We give you ten million for a steady flow of zero-day exploits. What we want especially are UNIX exploits, or any exploits that will get us into financial databases. Oracle, Unisys, McAfee, RSA, anything you've got. We want random number generators that aren't random. We want to be able to manipulate big databases. You listening?"

"Yeah. I am listening."

"Well, start taking notes, brother."

"I got a good memory."

"Okay, we want networking software that we can beacon. We want anything that's already beaconing inside banks or financial exchanges. We want anything that will get us into SWIFT, even an old zero-day in SWIFT that we can recode. We are especially interested in large international transfers involving central banks. You still tracking this?"

"Oh, yeah," said Malchik. "You got a heavy shopping list, my friend. What you going to do? Break into the Federal Reserve?"

"Something like that. Now here's what we *don't* want: No botnets. We don't give a shit about denial-of-service attacks. No carder bullshit for identity theft. We'll leave that to all your weenie friends in Moscow and Kiev. No code-breaking, password-cracking, none of that. We're fine in that department. We want to get inside large financial institutions. And we need people who can hack in German."

"You pretty big guy," said Malchik.

"Yes, I am. And I want this shit as soon as possible. Day before yesterday."

"Fifty million," said Malchik. "I am not like most hackers. I have expensive tastes." He was smiling, revealing a grille of gold inserts.

"Fuck you. We need to steal the money first. Twenty million."

"Thirty. Not less. I want a G-5, just like in the videos."

"Twenty-five. Money sent to Liechtenstein, Cayman Islands, Nauru, wherever the fuck you want. Not more. Do the deal now, or I walk away."

Junot stuck out his hand.

"Twenty-five million for six months," answered Malchik. "If you like my shit, you'll pay me more. If you don't, okay, bye-bye."

Malchik thrust his hand forward. Both arms from the wrist up seemed to be wrapped in tattoos.

"Deal," said Junot. "We pay in installments. One-third, one-third, one-third, starting tomorrow."

Junot wrote down a Web address with an "onion" in the suffix, which marked it as an account that could only be accessed through an anonymizer known as the "Onion Router." He handed the TOR address to Malchik. The talk back in Denver was that NSA had cracked TOR, but NSA was so swamped with data already, the analysts would never find his tracks.

"Send me the coordinates of where you want the money. And we need to set up how you're going to send your exploits and malware. The Internet Relay Chat boards are all being watched, by everybody. Your techs need to talk to my techs."

"No problem. I send you secure address."

"*Roxxor*," said Junot, using a hacker expression of pleasure.

"Whatever," said Malchik.

Junot looked away for a moment, to ponder something. His eyes turned to the titles on the bookshelf. They were a compendium of the innocent anarchy of the early Web: *The Hitchhiker's Guide to the Galaxy*, the Hobbit books, Robert Heinlein translated into a half dozen languages, a whole row of Philip K. Dick's works in different editions. It was obvious that Malchik had a foot in both worlds, white and black.

"Now that we're business partners, I have one more problem, Mr. Malchik," he said. "I'm wondering if you've heard what happened to a Swiss boy. He worked with some people in the underground. His name was Rudolf Biel."

"I heard about him. He's dead. End of story."

"Yes, but do you know why he was killed?"

Junot was probing, wanting to sample the street whispers, trying to discern who knew what, and how much they would say.

"Maybe I hear some rumors, sure."

"Like what?"

"Like he knew too much about something."

"What something? Come on, Malchik, you don't seem like the shy type."

"You pay for what I know?"

"But I already agreed to pay. You mean pay more?"

"Of course. This is a new thing, so it cost you new money."

Junot wanted information. He nodded.

"What have you got?"

"So here is a hint. We do a lot of business, you understand? We can hack anything we want. It's true. You know this much or you wouldn't come looking for Malchik. Sometimes we even hack governments: the big spies. The ones with three initials. They play us, we play them. Nobody believe it, but this is so. Hubert knows. We have some help, maybe. Who knows why? But yeah, we are inside everything."

"And the Swiss who got killed, Biel, did he know about these code breaks?"

"Who says code breaks? You. Not me. Biel just knew that people were inside these systems. He even had some proofs that he took with him. Some lists, I don't know. People in the underground say so many secrets coming out of America now, unbelievable. Somebody inside is talking. That's what people say. So this Biel got stupid. He went to the Americans. Someone got nervous. Now he's dead. Like I said, end of story."

"You know who killed him? What do you hear on the street when you're out on your big Kawasaki?"

"Come on! You crazy? I don't hear anything. If I do know, then somebody kill me. Fuck off, man. Really."

Junot stepped back. His reconnaissance was done. Malchik either didn't know or wouldn't talk, so it was Junot's turn to plant some information.

"Okay, so I'll tell you what I heard. Big secret, but I want you to know. How about that? It was the Russian hoods. They killed Biel because he was a rat. He was telling the Americans that there were leaks. He was sharing Mafia secrets. So they drilled him."

"That's pretty interesting, Mr. Axel, but you know what? I don't give a shit. We are good hackers. We break into anything. That's what we do. Haxxor forever! But we are not killers. NSA and CIA do that, but not us. If Russian hackers start killing people like Biel, they are just another Mafia."

"My point, precisely," said Junot.

"My friend, you are barking up the wrong pole. We hack to destroy governments. This is so. We work with the Mafias sometimes, yes, it is true. I myself am sometimes one of the hard men, and some of the weak boys in Cerberus, maybe they think I am Mafia, but they are wrong. So you tell Hubert that, yes, it's true we were not happy when Mr. Rudolf Biel decided he want a vacation in America, okay, but we did not pull nobody's trigger. I don't know who did this hit. Nobody does."

Junot rose. He almost had a smile, though it was hard to tell. His face wasn't built for that.

"I don't think that was worth any extra money, do you?" said Junot.

"I tell you nothing so you pay me nothing. Okay. Fair deal."

"I'll tell Hubert," he said. "It's good to be in business. You give us what we want, and you will be a very rich man. Run your network so we can get inside a very big bank, and believe me, twenty-five million is just the beginning."

"Okay. It is a deal, then. I tell you tomorrow where to send money. When the first third arrives, let's say nine million, then we start sending you the zero-day exploits. We got a lot of inventory, believe me. These Cerberus guys are the best hacks in the world."

"One-third is eight-point-three million, and it will be there as soon as you give me the delivery address. And Malchik, you know the first rule of my business?"

Malchik cocked his head. "What's that?" But he knew. He'd seen *Fight Club* a dozen times.

"First rule is, don't tell anyone about my business."

"That's second rule, too, I bet. Okay, I got it."

Junot walked back up the circular metal stairway and through the pretend air lock to the door. Malchik followed behind. Everyone else in the place had scattered. The toy lights were still blinking in the imaginary entryway.

"Let's do this," said Junot. He punched the big man's fist with his own. "And remember what I told you: The Russian Mafia killed that Swiss boy."

Junot walked out into gray glow of early evening. Just over the wall, the waters of the Spree were splashing against the embankment, and a U-Bahn train was clicking toward Yannowitz Bridge Station. The needle of the television tower, once the jewel of the GDR, was twinkling in the East like a monument to a lost civilization.

15

BASEL, SWITZERLAND

Ed Junot tried to look respectable for his trip to Switzerland. He took out his earrings, placed a knit cap over his big bald head and substituted a pair of loafers for his studded black boots; he wore a blue blazer over a white button-down shirt. The costume couldn't change the hard set of his jaw, or the hooded eyes, but it softened the effect. He bought a first-class train ticket for Basel at the gleaming glass-and-steel train station in the Schoeneberg district of Berlin. Waiting for the train to leave, he bought some Mentos candy to suck on, and copy of *Hello!* magazine in German so he could look at the pictures and not appear to be American. It was a long ride, more than seven hours, and he quickly fell asleep. He was awakened in the middle of the trip when someone poked him in the ribs and said, *"Das Schnarchen!"* which he realized must be a reference to his snoring. He muttered, "Fuck off," and went back to sleep.

The train arrived in the late afternoon at the Badischer Bahnhof on the German side of the city, north of the Rhine. Junot walked through passport control into Switzerland and took a taxi to the Basel Hilton, south of the river. He requested a room overlooking the Nauenstrasse. The clerk at the front desk said that most guests preferred to be on the other side of the hotel, away from the road, but Junot said he didn't mind the sound of traffic.

Junot took his bag up to the room and opened the curtains. On the far side of the street, just across from Junot's room, was the nipped, conical shape of the Bank for International Settlements tower, stacked on its foundation like a twenty-story beehive. He unpacked his suitcase and put his meager wardrobe in the closet, and then turned off the lights.

From the bottom of the case, Junot removed a Zeiss spotting scope that he had encased in bubble wrap. He mounted it on a small tripod and placed it atop the desk that faced the window. The lens of the scope was powerful enough that he could read the time on the wall clocks in the offices across the way, and see the expressions on the faces of the bankers who remained in their offices.

Junot opened his computer bag and retrieved a memo from James Morris that he had printed before leaving on the trip. It had the photo, office number, email address and phone numbers of a man named Ernst Lewin, who worked in the tower across the road. His office was on the eighteenth floor, in a room that faced the Nauenstrasse.

Junot focused the scope tighter. He checked the photograph, and then studied the man across the way through the viewer to make sure they were the same. His target, Ernst Lewin, was a tall, thin man, balding, with a prominent nose and black glasses. Lewin was the chief information officer and systems administrator of the Bank for International Settlements. He had "root" access to all of the bank's systems.

From the computer bag, Junot now took a small device that included a focused laser beam transmitter, along with a receiver to capture the returning signal and an interferometer that could convert these signals into sound, and a pair of earphones. This assembly comprised a laser microphone that could hear through distant windows by reading the vibrations caused by the pressure of sound waves against the glass pane. He focused the device on the window of Ernst Lewin until he heard through his earphones the voice of the man calling his wife to say that he would be home soon for dinner.

Junot put the spotting scope and the laser microphone in the closet of his room. He affixed a jam lock to the closet door so that his tools were safe. The tension in his body eased. He was hungry after the long trip and ordered a club sandwich from room service. The sandwich had chicken salad, mixed with mayonnaise, which he disliked, instead of the grilled chicken he had wanted, and the fries were soggy. He ate half the sandwich and put the tray in the hallway.

Junot was restless: After waiting a few minutes to digest the foul meal, he went down to the hotel "fitness room" to work out. The gym had a set of free weights, but they only went up to fifteen kilograms. A woman was using them when he arrived. Junot noisily did push-ups and crunches next to her until she left. The weights were so light that Junot flung them back on the rack. Everything was pissing him off. He went upstairs and showered, and thought about sex while he lathered himself.

He knew he shouldn't go out, but the room felt claustrophobic. He put on a black T-shirt, this one bearing the name of a band called Slip-knot, and put the studs back in his ears. He went downstairs and asked a handsome young bellman where to go in town for music. The young man recommended a club across the river, located in an old military barracks. Junot cruised for a while, looking for someone interesting and submissive, but the music was insipid, just east of ABBA, and his black mood returned. Just before midnight he went back to the hotel and jerked off.

The next morning Junot got up early. He ordered breakfast from room service, and when he had eaten and bathed, he hung the DO NOT DISTURB sign from his doorknob and went to the closet to retrieve his surveillance tools. He placed the spotter and the laser microphone side by side. He focused them on the eighteenth-floor window he had identified the night before, and settled in to wait for Ernst Lewin to arrive for work.

It was 7:30 a.m. when Junot began his watch. An hour later, he heard through his earphones the sound of a door clicking open and then closing shut, and then he saw through the eyepiece the face of Lewin as he took off his jacket, hung it neatly in the closet and settled down at his desk to work.

Junot recorded useful notes through the morning. Lewin's secretary buzzed him at 9:20 to announce Bridget Saundermann had arrived for her 9:30 appointment. Junot made a call to BIS and asked for Miss Saundermann, and was transferred to the office of the deputy information officer. Evidently she worked with other IT staffers at the second

BIS office, a round white stone building at the Aeschenplatz, several hundred yards down the street from the Hilton.

Saundermann entered the room at 9:25 and gave her boss a report on a new trading management system that was being put into beta testing in the trading room. She mentioned several employees who were working on the project, the software vendor who was supplying it, and the bugs that had been found in the networking software that connected the new platform to other parts of the bank's system. They talked about the pressure caused by the recent downturn in Asian financial markets.

Just before 11:00, Junot heard what he had been waiting for. Lewin called someone to confirm his luncheon appointment at 1:00 that afternoon at Maison Verte. Lewin asked for the man by name, Aldo Heubner, and said that it was Mr. Lewin calling. Heubner came on the phone and said that lunch was indeed on as planned, and that he had already booked the table. They spoke in English; that was their shared language, evidently. Junot made notes.

Junot waited a few minutes and then called the restaurant and made a lunch reservation for himself at 12:30. He asked for a table overlooking the river, figuring that Lewin and Heubner would want the same. The maître d'hôtel said he would do his best.

Junot went to his computer and found an Aldo Heubner who worked as a vice president for information systems at a big pharmaceutical company that was headquartered in Basel. So they were fellow IT managers, and social friends, to boot.

Junot listened to a bit more of Lewin's morning routine and made a few more notes, but at 11:45 he changed into his white shirt and blazer and knotted a striped silk tie. He went to his computer bag and removed a final piece of gear he had brought along. It was a miniature shotgun microphone designed to look like a ballpoint pen, with a tiny earpiece to monitor conversations up to fifty feet away. Junot put the pen mike in his breast pocket, checked his tie and headed out the door just before noon.

The restaurant was a mile north of the hotel, on the banks of the Rhine, in the city's grandest old hotel. The main dining room was small and elegant, with crystal chandeliers suspended from the high ceiling, crisp white tablecloths and deep red plush chairs. The room was perfect

for surveillance: good acoustics, low ambient noise, tables well separated but none beyond range.

Junot was one of the first to arrive for lunch and only one table
was taken in the main room overlooking the river. He put twenty Swiss
francs in his palm as he shook the maître d's hand and reminded him of
his request to be seated in the main room. Junot was shown to a table in
the middle of the room, set back from the windows that overlooked the
Rhine, but close enough. He had brought a book to read, along with a
notebook in which to scribble what he overheard. He put the earpiece in
his right ear, away from the door, and studied the menu.

Junot was ordering his meal when Lewin arrived; he was taller and
more gaunt than he had appeared through the scope. With him was a
shorter man with curly hair and a loud voice, who had to be Aldo Heubner. Junot watched them take their seats by the window, perhaps thirty
feet away and in direct line-of-sight range.

He told the waiter, hovering so attentively, that he would have the
lobster medallions to start, and then the pigeon breast with Tasmanian
pepper, and then cheese, and then a champagne parfait for dessert. He
removed the pen microphone from his breast pocket and placed it on
the table, under a newspaper he had brought along.

Lewin and Heubner talked with the pleasure of two friends meeting
in a fine restaurant. They discussed a mutual friend: Roger Friedman,
who worked for UBS; they made plans to see Benjamin Britten's *War
Requiem* oratorio with their wives the following week; Lewin's wife was
named Rachel and Heubner's wife was called Angelique; they discussed
Christmas holiday plans, and the annual dilemma of whether to go ski-
ing in the Alps or fly to the sun in the Caribbean.

Junot feasted on his meal while he listened to the conversation and
made occasional notes. The sound quality was nearly as good as if the
two were sitting at Junot's table. They weren't wildly indiscreet, but they
laid open their personal lives in the way that friends do during a social
encounter.

Lewin and Heubner ate their entrée and main course as they talked,
but they skipped cheese and dessert. They had to get back to work. They
left promptly at 2:30, as Junot was beginning his champagne parfait. He
ate the raspberries but left the rest. He had already eaten enough for a

week. He put his tiny shotgun microphone back in his pocket and gently removed the earpiece, palming it so that even a waiter standing over him wouldn't have seen a thing.

Junot paid the bill. It came to over three hundred francs. He thought how pissed off his Denver handlers would be when the expense account came in. Junot looked at the waiter again as he walked out, thinking how he would like to jump him in the men's room.

The rest was rote work, once Junot had acquired the raw material through "social engineering." When he got back to his room at the Hilton, Junot put the surveillance gear back into his suitcase and set up his laptop computer. Morris had loaded him up like a "script kiddie"—with ready-made hacking tools that he could use once he had set his target and payload. He worked carefully, making sure each step had been completed correctly before he executed anything.

The first step was to steal Aldo Heubner's email address. Junot explored the Internet site of the pharmaceutical company where Heubner worked until he had figured out the basic format for employee email addresses. When Junot had assembled what looked like the right configuration for Heubner, he tested it by using the "email dossier" at a site called centralops.net and found that it was indeed a valid address. He sent Heubner a dummy message at that address, just to make sure. Heubner didn't answer, but the message didn't bounce back.

Now Junot constructed the bait on his digital hook: It was a spoofed message for Ernst Lewin that appeared to be coming from Aldo Heubner's email account, with his normal address visible as the sender. The subject line was *Thanks for lunch*. Below the subject line, the message read:

> *Enjoyed our meal at Maison Verte today. Angelique and I will buy tickets for the Britten oratorio for you and Rachel. And holidays? What about this place at Pointe Milou in St. Barts? Expensive, but let me know what you think. Aldo.*

Below the fictitious Heubner's farewell, there was a live link for a resort called the Hotel Francois in St. Barts. Anyone clicking it would see a dreamy picture of a cabana and blue water, with a menu across the top including "Rooms and Suites," "Bar and Restaurant," "Spa," "Rates, "Services" and "Contact." It would be rude for Lewin not to click on the link, since his friend Huebner had asked for feedback.

The St. Barts resort page was the hook. Encoded with that Web page, so that it would be activated in Lewin's computer as soon as he clicked on the link, was a piece of malware that was a zero-day exploit of the Windows operating system used by the bank's internal computer network.

James Morris had entrusted the zero-day to Junot for this operation. It used a gap in the BIS operating system that would allow installation of malware that would mirror Lewin's account. Once the malware had installed itself, Morris could monitor every keystroke made on Lewin's machine and capture his "root" account passwords that controlled the entire system. Using this root access, Morris could create backdoors and move through the network to discover the usernames and passwords of other "root" administrators. With a few lateral moves, he could alter databases, steal and corrupt data files, create phony accounts and server files and conceal himself by deleting any evidence of the original penetration.

Junot sent the spoofed email message to Ernst Lewin. A few minutes later, to cover his tracks, he sent a message to Heubner from a mock-up of Lewin's address. The subject line read *Christmas holidays*. Below that, the message advised: *Caribbean is too expensive. Let's talk next week at War Requiem about alternatives. Ernst.* If the subject came up, each man would think the other had misunderstood.

Now Junot waited. Forty minutes later he had a text message on his cell phone from a number that James Morris sometimes used. The message read simply: *We're inside.* At a computer terminal on another continent, Morris had registered the beacon confirming that Ernst Lewin had opened the link and installed the custom malware without realizing it. Morris was now able to feed other malware through a backdoor that the initial exploit had opened, and create multiple backdoors to make sure he could remain in Lewin's root account even if the initial penetration was detected later. He could now dump account names, crack passwords and roam through the secret activities of the bank at will.

Why hack the Bank for International Settlements, the clearinghouse for central banks? Junot asked himself that question, though he didn't dare to pose it to his boss. But had he done so, he would have received a simple, if cryptic, answer: Because it's a symbol of everything that has gone wrong since 1945.

16

WASHINGTON

Graham Weber paid an unannounced visit the next morning to the Information Operations Center. He suspected that James Morris had already left town, but he wanted to see the place and meet Morris's deputy, Ariel Weiss, whom Sandra Bock had recommended as a talent worth cultivating. The IOC was located a few miles from Headquarters, in one of those featureless modern office buildings that populate Northern Virginia. It was hidden away from the main highway, in a low-rise shorn of any corporate or other identification. Leafy shrubbery masked the thick electric fencing; a curved driveway hid the guard station that blocked the entrance to the building.

Weber hadn't told anyone he was coming, so the guard was flummoxed when he saw Weber's Escalade and chase car. Jack Fong spoke with the site security chief, and then the two-car motorcade rolled past the lowered steel barrier and into the complex. A few senior officers of the division were gathered in the downstairs lobby when Weber entered the building. They had tumbled out of their offices when the guard announced that the director was on the premises.

It was an odd group, thought Weber as he scanned the bodies that were assembling. They looked barely out of college, most of them, wearing T-shirts and jeans, running shoes or sandals. The best and brightest in the Internet age were not also the best-kempt. They looked unhealthy, to a man or woman: too fat, or too thin; faces puffy or sallow, and not a one of them seemed to have had any exercise in the last month.

"Is James Morris around?" Weber asked the first person who approached him, who identified himself as the IOC's deputy chief for administration.

The administrative officer was a beady-eyed young man in his early thirties, one shirttail exposed. He said he wasn't sure whether Mr. Morris was in or out. He explained that for security reasons Morris never told people where he was.

"That's ridiculous," said Weber. "Call his office."

Morris's personal secretary advised that he was out of the city, on an extended operational trip that he had logged with the deputy director for Science and Technology, to whom he reported.

"I'd like to see Dr. Weiss, then," said Weber. "She's in, right?"

"For sure," said the admin officer, tucking in his shirt as he led the director down the hall to the deputy chief's office. On one wall were posters for Kiss and Megadeth. On another was a banner promoting *Star Wars: Episode VII*. The corridor opened up on a main operations room with several dozen cubicles, each framed with multiple computer screens.

"Green badge?" asked a startled little man with a long beard who nearly bumped into Weber just as he turned the corner into the main work area. He assumed a contractor had entered the building.

"It's the director," said the admin officer. "Mr. Weber."

"Oops," said the gnomish little man. He bowed as if to a royal visitor, and then scurried on.

Weber surveyed the place. It was a strange lair; the room was windowless, to prevent any possibility of remote monitoring. People were dressed informally: there wasn't a necktie or skirt in sight; many wore T-shirts, more than a few in hacker black. Dominating the far wall was the center's crest, with its bald eagle atop the globe of zeroes and ones, its bolt of red digital lightning and its mission statement: STEALTH, KNOWLEDGE, INNOVATION, and its mysterious key, surmounting the emblem.

Was this the new face of the agency? Weber wanted it to be so: No more martinis; better to encourage beer pong after work, for in the twenty-first century, the important targets weren't the heads of intelligence services but their systems administrators—geeky kids like these, who had access to real secrets. This collection of oddballs might be the only way to go after them.

Weber strolled among the cubicles. People were writing code, near as he could tell, bouncing threads of symbols back and forth between the screens on their desks. As he neared the middle of the room, he saw the open door of a glass-walled room. This must be Ariel Weiss's office.

A woman in skinny black jeans and a crisp white shirt walked toward Weber. She was wearing black boots with noticeable heels; her long black hair was tied in a ponytail. She was the only healthy-looking person Weber had seen in the place so far.

She had something more complicated than just pretty in her face; there were layers of beauty, qualities that in another woman might be discordant, but that she held together in a deceptively casual package. Weber wondered at first if she was really the deputy commander of the hacker squad. She didn't look weird or damaged enough.

"Dr. Weiss?" asked Weber, extending his hand as he approached her glass-walled space.

"I'm Ariel," she said. She gestured to the group arrayed around her in their cubicles.

"This is the war room. I can show you around. If we'd known you were coming, we could have put on something special."

Weber shook his head. He was tieless; his jacket was draped over his shoulder and his blue eyes were sparkling. Others might have called him a youthful director, but in this setting, he felt old.

"Another time for the demo," he said. "Right now I want to talk to you."

She motioned him toward her office but he shook his head.

"Let's go back to Headquarters. It's quieter there."

Weiss retrieved her purse from her office and a white cashmere scarf that set off her dark hair. They drove away in his black SUV; she waved goodbye to the administrator, who looked worried that Weiss was leaving the office on an unplanned and unexplained outing.

When Weber got out at the seventh floor, accompanied by the sleek visitor, the security officers milling around the kiosk by the elevator suddenly came to attention. Weber shook his head; he still didn't understand why so many people were necessary for security in a controlled environment. He led Weiss through the anteroom, with its multiple secretaries, into his inner office. The room seemed too big and formal for the kind of conversation he wanted to have.

"Let's go to my dining room," said Weber. "It's much prettier, and just as private." He led her through the sitting room, past the lordly portrait of Helms and into his sunny hideaway in the northeast corner of the building. He told a steward to bring coffee and then leave them alone.

"You really should be talking to Mr. Morris," protested Weiss as she sat down. "He's the one who knows what's going on in IOC. I just keep the wires from getting tangled."

"Nonsense," said Weber. "You know everything. That's what I hear. And I talk to Morris plenty. What I need now are some answers."

"Look, Mr. Director, I'm Pownzor's deputy, but there's a big residual that he keeps in his head. Some questions I can't answer."

Weber poured her some coffee and offered her a chocolate chip cookie.

"Tell me about yourself," said Weber. "We'll get to IOC operations later. You're a woman hacker, right? I thought they mainly came in the male variety."

"We're as rare as rocking horse shit, sir. But we exist."

Weber laughed at the vulgarity.

"That's a new one. So how did you learn the trade, if that's the right way to put it?"

"Simple. I was smarter than the boys. I grew up in Providence, where my mom ran a neighborhood grocery store. I liked to raise hell. So . . . that became hacking."

"I'm a Pittsburgh boy, myself. But I liked to raise hell, too. So do my children, unfortunately."

Weber was relaxing. He didn't often talk about himself.

"Providence is a tough town," he continued. "Mobbed up, people always say. How did a tech genius come out of there?"

"I was the smart kind and also the tough kid. I was good at math, which everyone thought was freaky for a girl, but I also ran track. My senior year, I made money as a waitress in a bar. When I got into MIT, I found out that the way to be a popular kid, if you weren't a preppy, was to be a prankster. At MIT in the 1990s, the best pranks were computer hacks. Still true, I guess."

"What did you do, steal stuff, or what?"

"Have you ever heard of Jack Florey?"

"No. Who's he?"

"Jack Florey was the imaginary name MIT kids used for our pranks. It started freshman year, with this sort of hacker orientation tour, they called it the Orange Tour, organized by people who all said their names were Jack Florey. They took me along, even though I was a girl. We snuck into steam tunnels in the basement and secret passageways under the dome. We went spelunking inside the building walls, silly things like that. My year, 'Jack Florey' hijacked a campus police car, took it apart and reassembled it on top of one of the buildings."

"It sounds like perfect training for being a CIA officer."

Weiss beamed her radiant smile.

"It was, actually! It was like the ops course. Freshman year we turned the MIT dome into R2-D2. A few years later they put a Red Sox logo up there, and then a pirate flag. The idea was that it was good to challenge authority. Computer hacking was just part of that culture. We would break into systems just to show that we could do it. A good hack became known as a 'Jack.' It was a way of being cool, if you were a geek."

"So how did you get from there to working for the, uh, man?"

"You really want to know?"

"Most definitely."

"When I was finishing my doctorate, I decided to become a 'white hat' because I was so scared of what the 'black hats' could do, including me. I got so good at hacking that it frightened me, to be honest."

"What do you mean?"

"The first time I got 'root' on a major airline system, it freaked me out. I found my credit card number on the system. I found all the flights I had taken. I found the routings, and the schedule changes, and the maintenance records. And I realized, if I can do this, any smart geek can. And pretty soon they're going to crack the air-traffic control network and be able to make airplanes fall out of the sky. It was like looking in the mirror and seeing a devil face."

"How did you find your way to the agency?"

"They found me. They're good at that. They go trawling where they know hackers are going to be, at IEEE conventions and hacker meetings. They anonymously sponsor hacking contests and then hire the winners. They find the chat rooms where we hang out online. Pownzor is a genius at that. You should ask him. He was part of the group that pitched me."

"What was the pitch?"

"It was, like, if you want to do cool stuff, and break into whatever system you want, anywhere, and use the best hardware ever made, and get paid for it—oh, yeah, and go after bad guys, too—then come see us. He made it sound like the coolest, most badass job on the planet. I had my doctorate. I didn't want to teach. So here I am."

Weber looked at her skeptically, as if this couldn't be the entire story.

"And that was it?" he asked. "Girl meets agency. Girl likes agency. And they all lived happily ever after?"

She cocked her head. Her boss was asking her to be honest, so she complied.

"I like secrets," she said. "I'm good at finding them out, and I'm good at keeping them. The older I get, the less interested I am in people. They're unreliable. I like *things*. That's why I'm an engineer and not a humanities major, I guess. The happy ending doesn't do much for me."

She was talking fast, the way smart people do, and she was rocking forward as she spoke. When she came to the end of her little story, she looked up at him curiously.

"You're not going to fire me, are you? Because there's a rumor going around that heads are going to roll in the IOC because of some screwup overseas. I thought that was why you wanted to see me."

"Not at all. But I'm curious. Where did you hear about this supposed purge?"

"Pownzor told me there was trouble after he got back from Europe. He wouldn't tell me what he was doing there. He just said that something bad happened and he was getting blamed."

"He didn't tell you where he'd been?"

"No. That's our deal. I make the Information Ops Center work—keep the war room stocked with Doritos and Diet Coke—while he runs off and does his operations. Sometimes he tells me what he's doing, sometimes not. When he left on this Europe trip he didn't say anything, except that he had to go. A week later he was back, looking like shit, talking about how he was going to get fired. Then he took off again yesterday. He runs the world out of the pockets of his cargo pants, if you hadn't noticed."

"I don't really know Morris, but yes, I'm getting that impression."

Weber studied her. She was at once entirely casual and perfectly poised. He thought of himself at her age, fifteen years ago, when he had begun to realize he was really good at running companies and making money. Even on his best days, he hadn't been as focused as Ariel Weiss. He wanted to take her into his confidence; in truth, as isolated as he was, he needed an ally.

"I'm worried about Morris," he said. "He looked exhausted the last time I saw him."

"He is exhausted, Mr. Director. Too much has come down on his head recently. I'm worried that he's drowning."

"I've given him a lot responsibility. I hope he can handle it."

"Pownzor is tough. He gets it done. Maybe it's good for him to get away. He relaxes when he's out of the office. He likes being on his own."

"That's what worries me."

"Why? What did he do?"

"A case went bad. He took control of it, and then it blew up. He offered his resignation, but I told him no, he's still my guy. But he seemed rattled after that, spun up about something. I'm wondering if you noticed anything."

"Pownzor is always a little strange, Mr. Director. That comes with the territory. When you're as smart as he is, you sometimes don't fit."

"But he's okay? Nothing that I should worry about?"

Weiss shrugged.

"I can't answer that, Mr. Director. You have to worry about everything. The one thing I've learned at the agency is that we're all just people, with a lot of issues sometimes."

"Does Morris have issues?"

Weiss opened her hands, palms up. "You're asking me questions I can't answer—probably shouldn't answer. I work for Pownzor. He's my boss. It's not my job to spy on him. Was it his fault, that the case went bad?"

"I don't know yet. But it was on his watch. That's why he offered his resignation. If something goes bad and you're in charge, then you take the fall. People don't get fired enough at the agency. That's why it's mediocre."

"I'm not mediocre."

"I didn't mean you. I meant the organization."

"But, Mr. Director, I *am* the organization, at least the younger part of it. Who do you think is out there? It's people like me. Do you want us to take risks?"

"Of course I do. I want you to take more risks, all of you, a lot more. I want this place to be more aggressive and kick ass."

"Do you want an honest answer, Mr. Director?"

"Yes, damn it. And stop calling me Mr. Director. I keep looking over my shoulder for someone else. Just tell me the truth, and don't worry about it."

"Okay. Then don't hassle Pownzor anymore."

"Why not?"

"Because he's a risk-taker, and everybody knows it. And if people start second-guessing him, then all the people my age are going to say, *Uh-oh. Button up. Slow-roll it or you may get in trouble. The director doesn't like mistakes.* People will go back to the formula for making supergrade."

"What's the formula?"

"If you run lots of operations, you're taking a big career risk; if you run a few operations, it's low-risk; if you run no operations at all, then there's no risk whatsoever of a CEI."

"Career-ending incident?"

"Correct. People are going to say that Pownzor was too aggressive, and that's why he got dinged."

"The slow-roll is the opposite of what I want."

"Then let Pownzor do his thing. He's probably harmless."

"Are you sure?"

"No. But we'll be watching now."

Weber stood up from the lacquered table and walked to the window. All the spaces in the neat rows in the parking areas were filled, as far as he could see. It was a tidy bureaucracy that he ran, but not a very good one. He turned back to Weiss.

"I'm worried about Morris," the director repeated. "I can't shake it. I put a lot of trust in him, but I just wonder . . ."

Weber came back to the table and sat down across from her. She stared at him, not sure what to say. He thought it through one more time, nodded to himself and then spoke to her.

"Will you work for me?"

"I already do. You're the director. Everyone works for you."

"I mean something different. Will you stay in your job, as deputy chief of Information Ops, but also report to me, and sometimes take assignments from me? And not tell Morris, no matter what."

"Be your agent, in other words, inside the IOC? That's what this would be."

"Yes, basically, that's right."

"Wow. That's . . . unusual. Is it legal?"

"Of course it is. I run the organization. If I say I want something, pursuant to the powers the president has given me, then it's legal."

"What happens if Pownzor finds out? He would destroy me."

"I'll take care of you. As you said, I'm the director. I run the place."

She looked him in the eye, studying his handsome, boyish face, trying to make up her mind.

"I mean it," she said. "He would destroy me. I don't just mean move me out of my job. He would wipe me out. Ruin my name and future. He may act like a punk, but he has a lot of friends."

"You have to trust me, Ariel, or don't do it. It's my job to fix what's wrong at the agency, but I need help. You told me you were a risk-taker, so now's the time to go all in. Otherwise, I won't believe all that tough-girl stuff."

"Unfair," she said, smiling. But there was a calculating look in her eye, too.

"What's in it for me?" she asked. "Other than helping you, that is."

"What do you want?" asked Weber. He hadn't expected such a transactional response.

"I'd love to run the IOC someday. Maybe move up to the seventh floor when there's an opening for a deputy or counselor. I'm a good manager."

"You're ambitious," said Weber.

"Of course I am. Princes don't rescue fair damsels for nothing anymore, and vice versa."

"No promises. But you'd be the obvious candidate to succeed Morris, unless I need you elsewhere in senior management."

"Acceptable," she said.

"I'll take that as yes, which is the right choice. For a minute there, I was worried you were just another young careerist."

"I am that, too." She folded her arms across her chest.

"Okay, hotshot, here's your first tasking: I want you to get inside Morris's head: Find out what he does when he's off on operations. There's nothing inappropriate about that. You're his deputy, you're supposed to know what he's doing. You said you like secrets. Okay, time to find out some new ones. Are you comfortable with that?"

"Sure. Like you said, it's my job. But I'm a Company girl, just so you know."

"Good. I'm a Company man now, too. So starting today, I want you to know everything about your boss. Pull his files, rumble his email, anything you can access. If you need help—technical stuff, whatever— just tell me. If you run into walls you can't get through, tell me that, too."

"IOC is all walls. Pownzor has compartments inside his compartments. Nobody sees the big picture except him."

"Well, that's about to change. Gather up the records of Morris's operations over the last two years, all the ones you can find. Look at the operational pattern, and then see what's missing. That will help you know where to look for networks that are off the books."

"Who should I say is requesting all this information?" she asked, arching her eyebrows.

Weber laughed and put his big hand on her shoulder.

"Tell them it's Jack Florey."

She laughed, too. He had been listening to her college stories, after all.

"How should we communicate? If Pownzor is as wired as you think, I need to be careful."

Weber thought a moment. "Back in a minute," he said.

Weber exited his dining room and went back into his office. Weiss stared out the window, thinking of all the CIA directors who had sat here since the 1960s, and the nightmares they had struggled through. Some had been lucky and solved their problems cleanly; most had not. This was the house of broken dreams and ambitions.

Weber returned thirty seconds later with two Nokia cell phones, manufactured circa 2005, and a package containing a string of SIM cards, numbered one through ten.

"This is a clean phone," he said, handing her one of the Nokias. "Every time I call you, toss the SIM card and move to the next one. I have a list of the numbers. I'll have the same rig." He held up the second phone. "Here's my number and a list of the SIM cards I'll be using. Don't let go of these. Sleep with them under your pillow."

He handed her two pieces of paper with the various numbers. She was biting her lip. She closed her eyes for a moment, as if to block a thought.

"Is this hack going to work?" asked Weber. "You're the expert."

"We'll see," she said. "Sometimes at MIT we would talk about 'can't happen' mistakes, which were conditions that theoretically were impossible but had appeared in the system anyway. Like when a file size comes up as negative."

"And what's the outcome, when you get one of these 'can't happen' events?"

"Usually it's a fatal error and the system crashes."

Weber nodded, shook her hand and let her out the door. The secretaries, Marie and Diana, exchanged glances as they watched her go.

17

HAMBURG

K. J. Sandoval, the Hamburg base chief, was still upset about the way her case had been taken away from her by a male superior from another division, and then blown, with no consequences for anyone, near as she could tell. It wasn't fair. Her father had always counseled her with the bromide that in dealing with the Anglo power structure, don't get mad, get even. So after a few days' reflection, she consulted a former Justice Department lawyer in Washington who still had a high-security clearance and specialized in workplace-discrimination cases for people in the intelligence community. The lawyer wasn't sure that Sandoval had a case, but she agreed to write a letter to the Equal Employment Opportunity office, laying out the basics of the complaint, without the highly classified details. The EEO office had a counseling and investigation staff, she said, that tried to resolve cases quickly and quietly.

The key paragraph of the letter read as follows:

Ms. Sandoval has been informed that a matter involving a developmental asset she initially handled was assigned to the Information Operations Center, working with a special compartmented task force. Because she was not asked to join the task force, despite her experience with the case as a designated officer of the National Clandestine Service, Ms. Sandoval believes that she has suffered from unfair and discriminatory action. Ms. Sandoval speaks Level 3 German, and has good liaison contacts in Hamburg and elsewhere in Germany. As her attorney, I request that she be included immediately in the IOC/NCS joint task force. Otherwise, I will make a formal complaint to the Official of Equal Employment Opportunity and request a full fact-finding investigation and resolution.

Agency officials, who had become highly skilled at ass-covering and legal self-protection, recognized immediately that the letter had what they called "flap potential." A copy was sent by the senior EEO compliance officer to the general counsel's office, where it was bumped up to the boss, Ruth Savin. She knew that Graham Weber had made a personal decision to assign the Hamburg case to James Morris, which meant that he would personally be involved in any investigation and arbitration. So Savin made an appointment to see him that afternoon.

"Pain in the neck," said Savin as she handed a copy of the attorney's letter to Graham Weber. A career in the federal government had taught her to regard discrimination claims from civil-service employees in much the same way Supreme Court justices view habeas corpus petitions from condemned prisoners, as a tedious waste of time.

Savin waited opposite Weber while he read the letter. An unlikely smile came over his face. He was looking for new allies, and he saw a chance to recruit another.

"Let's do what she wants," he said. "Have her call me. I'll assign her to work on the case personally, directly for me."

Savin frowned. Her usual legal advice to senior officials was that they keep their distance from prospective plaintiffs, rather than embrace them.

"Are you sure?" she asked. "Cases like this can bite you."

"I need help. She wants to be useful. Sounds like a match to me. Let's call her."

"Now?"

"Why not? Let's see what she can dig up. If she gets anything, we can bring her back here. Meet her away from Headquarters."

"Are you going to tell Morris?"

"No. That's the point. I want someone working this who is *not* Morris."

"You're the boss," she said. Those words were frequently uttered by general counsels, in and out of government, but rarely with equanimity.

Weber had Savin wait with him while Marie dialed Sandoval's secure cell phone in Germany. He wanted a witness. The phone rang. It was after ten p.m. in Germany. Eventually a half-sleepy voice answered, in English.

"This is Haven J. Pullman," said Weber, using the agency pseudonym that he used in correspondence.

There was a pause on the other end, while Sandoval ran through her mental Rolodex of names, cryptonyms and pseudonyms. When she realized who it was, a note of surprise and worry came into her voice.

"How can I help you, sir? Is there a problem?"

"No, no problem. I just read your lawyer's letter to the EEO office. The general counsel showed it to me. I think you're right. I want you to be involved more in this case."

"You do?"

"Yes. We need to do more. But I don't want to put you on the special task force that was assigned to pursue it."

"Why not? I'm well qualified." There was a bite in her response, as she sensed she was getting passed over once again.

"I want you to work directly for me. I'd like a second set of eyes looking at this case. Use your own sources, and follow your own leads. Report to me directly. That's the deal. Don't tell COS Berlin and don't tell EUR Division. This is a private reporting line. Can you do that?"

"Yes, Director," she said, a slight quaver of awe. "Are you sure this is okay, you know, bureaucratically?"

Weber looked at Savin. He smiled.

"The general counsel is with me, and she says it's fine. Isn't that right, Ruth?"

Savin winced, but she didn't say anything.

"What do you want me to look for?" asked Sandoval.

"The obvious questions: I want to know what happened to your guy. And I want to know whether he was telling the truth when he said we had a problem."

"That means I have to get inside the hacker underground," said Sandoval gravely.

"Yes, if possible. Did this Swiss boy give you any leads to work on when you debriefed him?"

"Nothing very good. He talked about the Friends of Cerberus, and the Exchange. I have no idea what they are."

"Find out. Get me some answers. If you have anything good, then get on a plane and fly to Washington. Come right away, no waiting or hand-wringing. Just do it."

"Yes, Director."

"Don't disappoint me. I want a report in a week, and I want to see you right away if you've got something I need to hear."

"What if I get in trouble?"

"Don't. But if something happens, I have your back."

Sandoval was silent for a moment as she considered this profession of loyalty from her supreme leader.

"*Hay más tiempo que vida.* That's something my dad used to tell us."

"What does it mean?" asked Weber.

"'Life is short. Seize the moment.'"

"Smart man. Do what he says. Goodbye."

Weber hung up. Savin looked at him dubiously, but that didn't matter. Now the director had his second back-channel ally—a Spanish-proverb-quoting, semisuccessful, modestly pissed-off, midcareer Mexican-American case officer with a chip on her shoulder and a name that sounded like a hooker's. Perfect.

Kitten Sandoval stayed up much of the night worrying about how to perform the assignment the director had given her. It is often a fact that when we obtain the prize we have been seeking, it feels like a burden. But when she awoke after a few hours' sleep, it was a sunny morning. She pulled the drapes so she could look out over the botanical gardens through the window of her flat. The morning sun was glinting off the artificial lake. Beyond were the pavilions of the Japanese tea gardens, and the orderly grid of plants and pathways of this very German park.

Sandoval made herself a cup of coffee, ate half a sweet bun and threw the rest away so she wouldn't be tempted. When it was nine, she telephoned her most useful friend in Hamburg. His name was Walter Kreiser, the former head of Germany's concatenated *Bundesnachrichtendienst*, or BND, the federal intelligence service.

Sandoval was direct. She asked Kreiser if they could meet for a conversation that very day. He suggested lunch at Die Bank, his favorite brasserie in Neustadt, housed behind the grand façade of a nineteenth-century finance house. But Sandoval said no, this was better discussed in a private place; she asked if she might perhaps come visit him at his apartment in Uhlenhorst, across the lake from the consulate. Kreiser suggested she come at eleven for coffee.

Kreiser was waiting in his apartment, an austere modern German structure of blocks and rectangles, all in white. He was a widower, but his housekeeper kept the place tidy and had set out flowers on the table; she brought a coffee service on a silver platter soon after Sandoval arrived, and then disappeared.

He was a gentle-looking, white-haired man in his early sixties who wore wire-rimmed glasses, a white button-down shirt and rep tie; his every aspect was neat and unobtrusive. He was a product of the early Cold War school of German intelligence officers who had been trained by the British and believed, with their mentors, that intelligence officers should to the extent possible be invisible.

"What a nice surprise," he said, pouring the coffee from the silver pot. "I hope it is nothing bad that brings you to see an old man on a sunny morning."

"I need your help," she said.

He took her hand. He was flattered, but he was not an idiot.

"Don't be silly. The U.S. government wants something. I understand."

Kreiser had taken an interest in Sandoval when she first arrived in Hamburg, not just because she was young and attractive, but because he was unabashedly pro-American and could see that this new arrival needed a mentor who understood Germany. They took to having coffee, and then an occasional dinner. She dressed up when she went to see him and took his arm when they went for a stroll. He reciprocated in his way, buying her presents and taking her to favorite haunts in the old city, telling things about the German scene that she could not otherwise have learned. He liked calling her by her forename.

"So tell me how I can help, my dear Kitten."

"We lost someone, Walter," she replied.

"So I've heard, my dear. I was going to call you, but you saved me the effort. How can I be of help?"

"I don't know. That's the problem. I don't understand what went wrong. The young man who was killed was in my office a few days before he died. He wanted to help us."

"Yes. I heard that, too. You mobilized half of Hamburg and Schleswig-Holstein trying to find him. You Americans do not move quietly."

"But we didn't find anything except a dead body, and a bullet."

"The BfV and the BND are telling the old boys that it was a Russian Mafia hit. They traced the gun, so they are saying, with much congratulating of themselves. Isn't that right?"

"Probably. I don't know, to be honest. That's why I wanted to talk to you. I don't understand where this man was coming from. He was frightened, I can tell you that. He was shaking when he talked to me, but I don't know why."

Kreiser knew Hamburg. He had started his career there and risen to become Hamburg's chief of police before moving to Munich and then Berlin to run the national spy agency. He'd had a good run at the BND, making many friends and few enemies. When he retired, he had come back home to Hamburg, and after so many years of liaison with the CIA, he wanted to keep his hand in, which Langley was only too happy to facilitate. Sandoval had in fact been sent to brief him, which was how they had first met.

"I thought this was being handled by someone else: your Internet specialists. That's what the BND chief told me," he said.

"It is, officially. My visit to you is unofficial. I just want some ground truth about where this Swiss boy was coming from. We need to understand if we are vulnerable."

Kreiser laughed. The smile transformed his face, from its severe and somber lines to something more supple and playful.

"That's a good one, Kitten. You want the old man to help you understand hackers. I am flattered, but I think you need a younger adviser."

Sandoval was too upset to be coy. Kreiser was her best shot, and she didn't want to blow her chance with the director.

"Help me, Walter. You must have contacts in that underground. Certainly your old service does. Germany has more good hackers than anywhere in Europe. Find me someone to talk to, so I won't feel so stupid. Just give me a start."

Kreiser's smile had vanished. His blue eyes narrowed as he reviewed names and cases in his mind.

"These people don't like to talk, you know, especially to your government. They hate the CIA. They live to make difficulty for you."

"Then I'll be someone else, a businesswoman or a professor. Just find me someone who knows this world."

He took her hand.

"They pushed you aside, I gather."

"Yes, and I didn't like it. This is a second chance."

"*Braves mädchen*," said Kreiser.

He rose from the couch and walked to his computer notepad, where he kept his addresses. He scanned it, found what he was looking for and returned.

"I think maybe I have the right person for you. But you will have to be very careful. This one is marked '*Vorsicht!* Handle with care.' He's a German boy, not a boy now, almost thirty. His name is Grulig. He was very helpful to me once, just before I left Berlin. But he's confused. Sometimes I think he has seen a ghost."

Sandoval sat back with a start.

"The Swiss boy had that same look, like he was spooked. What's going on with these people?"

"I cannot say, Miss Kitten." Kreiser poured his guest more coffee.

"This boy can help you," he continued. "But you'll have to go to Berlin. That's where he is. And he'll never meet you in a public place. I'll have to find something else."

Sandoval folded her hands. She was getting to the hard part.

"Don't tell the BND, Walter. Promise me. Keep it off the books. And don't tell anyone at the agency. I'm freelancing. This could get me fired."

He reached out again and placed his big hand over hers.

"My dear, this is a very hot wire that you have touched. If you hold it too tight, you will get burned. You must see where it goes, where it originates, where the power comes from. With that I cannot help you. But I will show you how to start."

Sandoval wanted to be professional. But she could not resist giving the old man a kiss on the cheek.

18

BERLIN

Ms. Kitten Sandoval waited in an austere conference room in a slate-gray office block at the eastern end of the Unter den Linden. The building housed a foundation run by a German finance company for which Walter Kreiser did occasional consulting work. Out the window was the sublime beauty of the Brandenburg Gate, with its Grecian columns topped by the monumental chariot and its four horses hurtling forward through light and dark.

Sandoval was dressed in a black pants suit, carrying a notebook marked "Scylla Security Solutions," which was the name of a proprietary company whose records listed her as a systems analyst. She was wearing glasses and an auburn wig, and at a quick glance she would not be recognized as the woman who worked in the American Consulate in Hamburg. Her papers said she was "Valerie Tennant." She took sips from a glass of mineral water and eventually refilled it from the bottle.

She glanced at her watch. He was late. Walter Kreiser had given her the name of a young man named Stefan Grulig and promised to send him with an escort. Germans were never late. Perhaps Grulig had panicked and refused to come.

Ten more minutes passed, and then there was a knock and the door opened to reveal a young man in a peacoat, wearing a fuzzy turtleneck.

His brown hair was dirty, swept back from his face in the manner of the German actor Klaus Kinski. He looked to be in his late twenties, overweight, baggy-eyed, wondering from the look on his face what he was doing in this gleaming building on the Pariser Platz. Behind him was a thinner man, short hair, ear studs for show, but obviously Kreiser's man, who had been sent along as minder.

"I'm Valerie Tennant," said Sandoval, thrusting a hand toward the young man in the turtleneck. "You must be Mr. Grulig."

The German stood there awkwardly, not sure whether to advance or retreat. Sandoval walked toward him, arm still extended.

"Thank you for coming," she said. She gestured toward the table where she had been sitting. "Please have a seat."

Grulig walked uneasily toward the table. His minder stood by the door. Grulig spoke fluent English, the product of a lifetime on the Internet, but the minder spoke to him in German, saying he would wait downstairs.

"Ich werde jetzt gehen, Stefan, Sie sprechen zu lassen. Ich werde im Erdgeschoss, wenn Sie etwas brauchen. Ich erwarte Sie in über, was, eine Stunde?"

Grulig looked uncomfortable at the thought that his companion was leaving him alone with this strange woman. He shook his head at the mention of an hour with her.

The minder shrugged.

"Whatever," he said in English, and then retreated out the door.

Grulig sat down uneasily at the table across from Sandoval. She put a business card before him. He studied it, but didn't pick it up.

"I work for a computer security firm called Scylla Security Solutions," she said. "We do penetration testing, security consulting, custom software patches. One of our German clients has a problem, and we were told you were the best. We can pay you very well."

Grulig gave a little snort at the notion that she would pay him for his artistry.

"Don't be silly," he said. "If I wanted to be paid for what I know, I could make more in a week than your company earns in a year."

"Perhaps," she said, "but we make more money than you might think. You may not have heard much about us, but we are very successful."

He snorted again. She obviously didn't really understand who he was or what he did.

"If I wanted to sell a zero-day exploit, you know how much I could get? A million dollars, maybe more if it's an iPhone exploit. Do I sell it? No. Why not?"

He studied her, through eyes that were black beads of alienation.

"Because I don't take a shit on the church floor, that's why, and the Internet is my church."

"Wow. Okay, got it. But can I tell you my client's problem? You can decide if you want to help later, when I'm done."

"I don't want to help," he answered flatly. "I am here only because my friend Henning, who is downstairs, asked me as a special favor. And I owe him so many things. But I can tell you now, your problem is not my problem."

Sandoval nodded in agreement, and then went ahead with her pitch anyway, as if she hadn't heard a word.

"My client's problem is that there is a hacker underground in Russia that is hiring people as mercenaries."

Grulig stuck out his tongue.

"Duh," he said. "Everyone knows that."

"Yes, but these mercenaries have gotten so good that my client thinks they can penetrate any network. Even the networks of governments."

He eyed her warily. He had a soft face, now that he was close. He was frightened. That was the look in his eye. Not arrogance, but fear.

"Which government are you talking about?"

She paused as she weighed her answer. He was ready to bolt. She might only have a few more minutes with him. There was no reason not to say it.

"The United States."

He bit his lip, and then rapped the table with his knuckles.

"I knew it."

He pointed to her "Scylla" notebook.

"You work for one of the agencies."

She stared him dead in the eye. There was no answering this question, ever. She pressed ahead.

"My client is interested in an organization called Friends of Cerberus, and another one called the Exchange. You must know about them, or you can help me find out. That's why I wanted to see you."

Grulig swept his stringy hair back from his face. His hands seemed to tremble for a moment. His face, pallid from days and nights staring at computer screens, seemed to have lost any color it had.

"Lady, whoever you are, you are going to get yourself killed, and me, too. These are names that don't exist."

"Yes, but they do. We heard them. And do you know who we heard them from?

Grulig didn't answer, but his eyes showed that he was interested. Scared, yes, but also unable to resist listening to what this American woman was saying.

Sandoval fixed him in the eye again. She could be tough and unyielding in dealing with sources. That was her gift: She looked soft, but she wasn't.

"I'll tell you, Stefan. We heard those names from a Swiss named Rudolf Biel. Do you know who he is?"

Grulig nodded.

"Poor kid," he said.

"Yeah, that's what I think. And I'd like to do something about the people who thought he was so disposable."

Grulig shook his head. But he was in her space now. He could have gotten up and walked away five minutes ago, but not any longer.

"So let me ask you again, Stefan. Can you help me understand this Exchange and the Friends of Cerberus?"

"Who am I talking to?" asked Grulig. There was a slight tremor in his voice. It was as if he had been pulled toward a precipice and forced to look over the edge.

"Just me. I'm an American. That's enough. Nobody from my country knows I'm here. Nobody knows I'm meeting with you, except the man who set it up with your friend Henning, and I'm not telling you who that is. I know this is dangerous. That's why I haven't told any of the people I work with. I just need to know what the *fuck* is going on."

Her profanity seemed to startle him. It was incongruous. He looked at the door. He looked out the window at the Brandenburg Gate, lighter than air for all its immensity, the stone glowing in the morning light. He looked at her and then began to speak, his voice shaky at first, but then steadying.

"You must be very stupid, or very smart, I can't tell which," he said.

"I'm just ordinary, but I'm worried, and I need help."

"Me, too," he answered.

"That's a start. Tell me about Cerberus and the Exchange."

Grulig shook his head at the mention of these names again.

"You don't understand anything, do you?"

"Probably not. So help me out."

"You think this hacker underground is a bunch of criminals. Sleazy guys from Sochi and Kiev who are selling shit and killing people who get in their way. Right?"

"Yes. I guess so. That's true, isn't it?"

"Of course it's true. But who do you think are the buyers in this market? Do you think it's some kind of hacker godfather, who buys up all the exploits and sells them in a thieves' den?"

"I don't know. Tell me. Who are the buyers?"

"The buyers are *governments*. Good governments and bad governments. Sometimes the buyers are companies, so they can fix the vulnerabilities. But more often they are governments that want to use them to get inside networks and systems."

"The U.S. government is a buyer?"

He snorted again, and then laughed out loud.

"You *are* stupid. Of course the U.S. government is a buyer, when it needs to be. But really, that is not the point."

"No? What's the point, then?"

"The point is that the buyers and sellers are inside each other. It's not enough to buy exploits. The governments want to buy the people who create them. There are no more black hats and white hats. It's all the same hat. They're all working together."

"What's the Exchange?"

"A name for something that doesn't have a name."

"Meaning what?"

"It's a market. The boys who pretend to take these systems down are also the ones who help build them back up. They are all traders in the same market. The people who are doing the defense are also doing the offense. You see what I mean? Sometimes they want to give this show a name, so they call it the Exchange, or they call it Carderplanet, or Stuxnet, or Flame. I don't care. They are shitting in my church, all of them. They shit on the altar. I hate them. Do you hear me? I hate them."

She wanted to hug the German, with his fuzzy turtleneck sweater and his dirty hair. Yes, she was beginning to understand.

"It's not enough to hate them," she said. "You have to stop them."

"I cannot. You cannot. They are destroying cyberspace, but it's worse than that. People talk as if 'cyber' were a separate electronic space, but information is the air we breathe. How can they buy and sell the air, these bastards? They are destroying life and freedom. I cannot bear it."

He closed his eyes and swallowed hard. There were no tears, only the sniffling and a nervous cough.

"Who are the Friends of Cerberus?"

"They are liars. Cerberus has no friends."

"Okay, then, what is Cerberus?"

"Cerberus is the dog that guards the gates of hell. Everyone knows that."

"No, really, do you know anything about it? Please."

He smiled, almost sweetly.

"Well, I helped to build it, I should know. Cerberus is the Cerberus Computing Club, here in Berlin, in every German city and town, all over Europe, even in America. It is the home of people who love the Internet, and hate boundaries, and love freedom—and will take action, yes, truly, take action to prevent people from harming our blessed chaos. The Internet took power away from governments and companies, you see, and now these bosses want it back."

"Can I meet Cerberus?"

He laughed, merrily now.

"No. And yes. Who do you think you are talking to?"

"To Cerberus?"

"A part of it. But Cerberus is everywhere. I told you before. How can you meet the air? You breathe it. It's free."

"I need to ask again. It's important. Who are the Friends of Cerberus?"

"They are false friends. It can only be a trick. I have heard the name, but never from someone I trusted. Most of what you hear about Cerberus from the outside is false. Your information is probably a lie, too, I think. But honestly, I don't know."

The sky over Berlin was darkening as the weather changed. A shadow fell across the conference room in the gleaming building on Pariser Platz. The change of light seemed to alter Grulig's mood. He looked at his watch. The nervous look returned to his face. His eyes darted back and forth, as if he felt claustrophobic in the room. She was losing him.

She fixed him in the eye again. She took his hand, but he pulled it away.

"Who killed Rudolf Biel?" she asked. "I need to know. Was it this Exchange Mafia? Or someone else?"

He stood up, shaking his head.

"You, lady, are so crazy and stupid. Didn't you understand anything I said? It is all the same. There isn't a team called Exchange that is fighting a team called, I don't know, USA, or China, or Russian Mafia. When you pull it apart, it's all one team. How can I say who killed him? Don't you get it? It doesn't matter. It's what I told you: There are no black hats and white hats. There are only golden hats, the ones with the money."

"So they can read America's messages, the secret ones from the agencies? I need to know."

"Some messages, maybe. But I am telling you, it is Laocoön: You cannot tell apart the body of the serpent and the arms of the man. The agencies are hungry for exploits, to do their own dirty work. They get inside every system there is, and we never know why. One day they are in Iran, another day in Switzerland, a third day in China. Is there a goal, or is there only this dirty game? I do not know. But it is dangerous."

Grulig moved toward the door. Sandoval reached out and held his arm, but he pulled away.

"Stay," she said. "Let me help you."

He shook his head, the matted hair falling across his eyes.

"No." He walked toward the door. "Do not come with me. Do not follow me. Do not ever contact me again. You got this Swiss boy killed, this Biel. That's what I think. And you will get me killed, too, so good-bye. I never met you. I never talked to you. I will never see you again."

"Please wait. I need help." She almost shouted the words.

"You need to think about what I said, lady. That is all the help from me there is. No more, after that. If you try to come after me, it will be a mistake. I do not make threats. I don't believe in threats, or war, or violence, or flags. But I promise you that if you try to contact me again, or reveal my identity to anyone, I will know. And you will pay a very big price."

With that, he was gone, out the door. Sandoval thought of following him, thought even of making a crash call to Berlin Station in the U.S. Embassy, two hundred yards away on the other side of the Brandenburg Gate. But she had given her word to Grulig that she would protect his anonymity. And there was something else: She had been instructed not to talk to anyone else in the agency except the man at the top.

19

WASHINGTON

The consul general in Hamburg was a middle-aged man, never married, and he didn't like talking about personal matters when he could avoid it. Kitten Sandoval told him the next morning, when she was back from Berlin, that she had a personal medical issue, "women's plumbing," and needed to fly home to see her Washington doctor. He didn't ask any questions. She didn't contact Berlin Station or EUR Division back at Langley, not wanting to be caught later in a lie.

Sandoval caught an early connector flight from Tegel to Munich and flew home to Dulles on Lufthansa. She bought the economy ticket in her true name, and booked herself a room at the Crystal City Marriott. Before she left, she sent an encrypted message to the director's pseudonym account, saying that she would be in Washington that night. She asked him to suggest a location for a secure meeting.

Sandoval watched movies all the way home. She half paid attention as her mind wandered over the events of the past few days. She was in what her father liked to call "*las profundidades del océano*." The deep ocean. The gravity of what she had done made her nervous, but it was also what she had wanted for years: a chance to make a difference, with everyone watching, to be the heroine of the play.

Sandoval had progressed in her career by taking little risks, measured ones. She had come to the CIA by way of Arizona State University, in the usual sort of quiet referral: She had been nearing completion of her master's in global legal studies, hoping to work for the FBI or the DEA, when her dean summoned her one day and said the CIA recruiter was coming to town. He said Sandoval had the right skills: She was bright, conscientious, spoke fluent Spanish as a second-generation immigrant. Her Mexican-born father was a naturalized citizen and Marine Corps veteran who took her to the firing range each weekend. She knew her way around guns, and she had an easy way with people.

The CIA had a lily-white reputation, but Sandoval knew that if they were sending recruiters to ASU, they wanted to give at least the appearance of change. Sandoval went off to the interview, and the first surprise was that the CIA recruiter was a Hispanic woman herself, who had served abroad and seemed to embody the slogan on her promotional brochure about how the National Clandestine Service was "the Ultimate International Career."

In the days after the interview, Sandoval could imagine herself being that woman, having that career and being a soldier like her father, but different. With the encouragement of her dean, she applied to the agency and eventually became a career trainee, on her way to the Clandestine Service. She did a first tour in Managua, where she hadn't liked her boss, and after that an awkward stint with L.A. Division in Washington. She switched to EUR, first in Madrid and then, after six months of German language training, to Hamburg. She had never stepped outside the boundaries in all that time, or felt she needed to.

The events that had begun with the Swiss walk-in, Rudolf Biel, were different. Sandoval had started coloring outside the lines: It was freeform, and although she had recently found a seeming ally in Weber, she knew he wouldn't be able to protect her if things went wrong. He was new and inexperienced; she knew more about the CIA than he did.

A message was waiting on Sandoval's phone when the plane landed at Dulles. The director proposed a meeting at seven-thirty the next morning, and gave the address of Stormhaven Casualty, an insurance office in the flat suburb of Fairlington in Alexandria. Sandoval checked into the Marriott and lay awake in bed for several hours, her mind a white buzz. She took an Ambien and slept a few hours, then awoke a little after four a.m. and couldn't get back to sleep. After she had showered, she put on too much makeup, but that was better than too much fatigue.

Sandoval took a taxi to the address in Alexandria the next morning. She arrived at seven-fifteen, but it took twenty minutes for them to clear her downstairs, so she arrived in the secure second-floor reception area late and embarrassed.

Weber had his feet up on the coffee table of the windowless room they had prepared for the conversation. He popped up from the couch and shook her hand. Sandoval had never met him before. He looked like one of the fraternity boys at ASU, too young for the job.

"I'm sorry I'm late, Mr. Director," she said.

"*¿Qué húbole, güey?*" said Weber.

"Do you speak Spanish?" she asked enthusiastically.

He shook his head.

"The chief of my security detail told me how to say, 'What's up, dude?' Want some coffee?"

She nodded yes, and an aide brought in a huge platter of muffins, donuts, pastries, cookies and fruit, along with a giant coffee urn. The word had gotten around that the director liked snacks. It was enough to feed the EUR Division. Sandoval took some fruit and a cookie.

"Thanks for coming," said Weber. "You're sticking your neck out."

"Yes, sir, I am." She looked away.

"Well, it feels good, doesn't it?"

"I hope so, Mr. Director. I'm a little nervous." She took a drink from the water glass before her.

"Is your name really 'Kitten'?" asked Weber. "That's different."

"I've taken a lot of grief about it, but that's what my parents named me." Her hand was shaking and she spilled a little of her coffee. "Sorry. I am so nervous."

"Take it slow," said Weber. "I have all morning, and this isn't a promotion board."

She adjusted her skirt, took a bite of a grape and then put the plate aside.

"Let's start at the beginning," said Weber. "Tell me about the walk-in, this kid Biel. You're the only one who met him. What was he like?"

"He was frightened, Mr. Director. When he came in off the street, he mentioned two things, specifically, that he wanted to warn you about, face-to-face. He made a point about that."

"Why me? What did he think I could do for him? I had only been director for a week. I was barely on the job yet."

"Maybe that's why he wanted you. He said people were preparing something. I guess he thought you were outside a system he thought had been penetrated."

"But there was nothing in your first cable about a penetration of the agency."

"I was being careful. But when I think back, that's what he was telling me. He knew people had hacked our communications systems. They were inside. That's why he wouldn't stay in one of our safe houses. He thought the information would leak. That's why he wanted to talk to you directly. You weren't contaminated. He'd read about you. He knew you were the new guy."

"What do you think he would have told me, if we'd ever gotten to a meeting?"

"His secrets, I guess. Who the penetration was; how the communications systems had been compromised; what they were planning; why the rush. Whatever he knew, he wanted to tell you. That was his protection: You would take care of the people who were threatening him."

"But I didn't. I picked a 'specialist' to handle it. Another hacker. I thought that was the right thing to do."

Weber took a long drink of his coffee.

"Poor Biel." His voice was a bitter sigh. "I let him down."

Sandoval was startled. She hadn't expected her boss to have taken it personally.

"It was my fault, Mr. Director. Not yours. I should never have let him leave the compound. And then, when Mr. Morris came, I felt a little . . . I don't know . . . intimidated. At first he thought he could find Biel. Then Mr. Morris kept disappearing."

"Where did Morris go?"

"He never said. I thought he had special sources, private operations he couldn't tell me about. He made me feel . . . dumb. Then he got, like, depressed."

She was getting upset again, short of breath.

"Eat some more fruit," said Weber. "Don't worry. You'll be fine."

She took some more grapes, and ate a half dozen, while Weber called for a Diet Coke, bringing forth another huge platter, with cold drinks and finger sandwiches.

"Jesus, no wonder we're having budget problems," said Weber, looking at the array of food. "So tell me why you came today, all of a sudden. Why the crash meeting?"

Sandoval took a deep breath.

"Okay, so to prove his bona fides to me the Swiss boy mentioned the two names I told you about: the Exchange and Friends of Cerberus. I wanted to know more about them, but Morris waved me off, said it wasn't my case. So I didn't do anything until you called me and asked me to help."

"Right. So what did you do?"

"I went to a German friend, Walter Kreiser, who used to run the BND. I asked him to find me someone in the underground. I hope that's okay."

"That was smart. Did Kreiser come up with anything?"

"Yes, indirectly. Through a cutout, he introduced me to a young German hacker, very smart, who traveled in these same circles. His name is Stefan Grulig."

"Did this Grulig know about these hackers, whatever, the Exchange and Friends of Cerberus?"

Sandoval gave him a look somewhere between yes and no.

"That's the strange thing. He said the Exchange and Friends of Cerberus weren't real organizations, they were just names people gave to the underground. He claimed they weren't really criminal groups attacking governments. They were all part of a market, and governments were their customers. He made it sound like they were all in it together. And I thought maybe that's what Biel was trying to tell us. 'We're inside you because we *are* you.' I know that must sound crazy."

Weber shook his head.

"It doesn't sound crazy. What else did he say?"

"He said the U.S. government was hungry for the malware that the hackers in Cerberus Computing Club could produce. Those were the 'friends' Biel was talking about. They wanted to get inside everyone's systems. Grulig didn't say why. He made it sound like our Internet people were no better than hackers. Worse, really. We pay really big bribes, we say in Spanish, '*cañonazo*,' to get this information."

"That's what Morris does," Weber mused, barely mouthing the words. "He buys malware. But why?"

The director took another sip of his Diet Coke as he thought about the pieces of the puzzle.

"Did your source know anything about why Biel was killed?"

"That was the creepiest part. I asked if it was the Russian Mafia and Grulig just laughed, like I didn't understand anything: He said the Russian hacker Mafia and the U.S. government looked like enemies, but really they were the same team. That's when I began to worry."

"Me, too," said the director under his breath, barely audible.

"Is this dangerous, Mr. Weber?"

Weber looked away from her. Lying had become his profession, but he still wasn't very good at it.

"I don't know what this is yet. I'll give you an answer when I find out."

"I'm not backing down."

"Good. I want you back in Germany tomorrow. I don't want anyone to think we know a thing. You have anything else for Mr. Director?"

"Can I ask you something off-line? You don't have to answer."

"Sure. This whole conversation is off-line."

"Was Biel right?" she asked. "Do we have a mole?"

"I don't know." He shook his head. "Maybe it's more like a worm. A piece of code, or a person, it does the same thing. It eats us from inside. Maybe it's someone like Snowden, who thinks he's a hero. I honestly can't say yet. But I'm looking."

"How will you kill the worm?"

The director didn't answer at first, because he didn't know.

"Carefully," he said after a moment. "We need to know how the worm got there. Who helps him? Are there more worms? I don't want to pull out a piece of the worm and leave the rest in there."

"I'm so sorry, Mr. Director."

It wasn't an apology, but an expression of sadness for the weight that this new arrival at the CIA, in his job for less than a month, was now carrying on his shoulders.

Weber told Kitten Sandoval to return to Hamburg and go about her business. He wrote down the password for an email address that he had used to communicate with a confidential business associate in his previous life. He told Sandoval to check that address twice a day and look at anything that had been saved as a draft message, and to respond by leaving another draft. It was a simple trick, but it worked.

Sandoval left in a Red Top taxi that she hailed on the street outside the big sign that read STORMHAVEN.

As Weber was departing Fairlington with his security detail, he asked Oscar the driver to stop at a 7-Eleven on Seminary Road. When a member of the detail tried to follow him in, he told the man to chill out, he needed to use the men's room. He went into the dirty bathroom, locked the door of the stall and pulled out his Nokia. He dialed the number of the identical phone he had given to Ariel Weiss.

"It's Wall-E," he said.

"Hi," Weiss answered. "What's up?"

"I just heard a story that made my hair turn white."

"I think your hair is already turning white."

"I'm serious. The walk-in was right. Hackers are inside our system. They brag about it. We can't leave any electronic footprints, if we can help it."

"RTFM."

"What does that mean?"

"Sorry. 'Read the fucking manual.' As in, 'obviously.'"

Weber smiled. In this anesthetized organization, he felt lucky to have found a live body. He had a plan, and he needed help.

"Did they teach old-fashioned tradecraft when you were at the Farm? The old Moscow rules, 'denied area' procedures?"

"Yes, of course. Dead drops and brush passes. They said we wouldn't need to use them. Our ciphers and crypts were all unbreakable. But I remember."

"I'm out of my league here, obviously, but that's how I want to run this. I'm going to set up a drop we can use on North Glebe Road. I play golf at a country club in the neighborhood, so I can go there without being noticed. There's an underpass that leads to a parking lot. Look for a loose stone at the end of the underpass, on the west side. That's where we'll leave messages. We can use the Nokias, too, but sparingly. Otherwise it's too obvious that it's a closed loop. There's no GPS transmitter on the handset I gave you, but don't use it near your house. You have a house, right?"

"An apartment. I'm single."

"Me, too. That's lucky, because for the next while, you and I are going to be joined at the hip. We are going to live an analog lifestyle. Is there some geeky expression for that?"

"We call it 'deceased.'"

Behind Weber, there was a loud knock. Someone was pounding on the door of the 7-Eleven bathroom.

"I gotta go," he said, ending the call without waiting for her answer.

Weber removed the SIM card and stowed his cell phone. He flushed the SIM down the toilet and washed his hands, and then walked back to his black caravan, which had been waiting patiently for Mr. Director to finish in the bathroom.

When he got back to the office, Weber asked Sandra Bock to summon James Morris back from wherever he was overseas. He told Bock to deliver the message through the Information Operations Center and also through Beasley's retinue at the National Clandestine Service. The flash messages went out; station chiefs in Europe and Asia were asked to make discreet inquiries about the possible whereabouts of the IOC chief. But the aggressive messaging yielded nothing but silence.

Late that day, Bock got a call from a man who said he worked for Mr. Hoffman in the DNI's office. He said that James Morris was on assignment for a joint task force that was run through the NSA. He understood that an effort had been made to contact Mr. Morris, but he couldn't be reached, for the time being. He asked Bock to apologize to Director Weber.

When the conversation ended, Bock phoned the operations room and asked them to see if they could trace the last call. The watch officer said it had come from a number that had been assigned to a freight forwarding company in Denver that had gone out of business.

Bock told her boss what she had learned. He deliberated calling Cyril Hoffman to ask for more information and decided against it. He doubted that Hoffman would tell him the truth.

20

WASHINGTON

Graham Weber had always had a civilian's restrained view about leaks of classified information. He knew how difficult the disclosures made life for the intelligence professionals who were supposed to keep the secrets. But he was never sure that they damaged the nation in the way that the secret-keepers asserted. He'd fought that battle as a businessman when he threatened to close his business if it were forced to keep quiet about actions by the FBI and NSA that he thought were unconstitutional, and he had won that fight, and briefly become a champion for the libertarians. But now he saw the problem from other side of table, and he was frank enough to admit that it looked different.

The leak that rattled Weber most in his first weeks was the disclosure by the British newspaper the *Independent* of a new American program for collecting economic intelligence via the Internet. According to the London newspaper, the CIA had just approved a new program for using automated systems to monitor and analyze new inventions, patents, securities-trading algorithms and foreign-currency movements via Internet data that was available on financial-market platforms such as Bloomberg and Reuters, and in specialized scientific and professional journals. The story said the program had been approved by the new CIA director, Graham Weber, in the first week of his arrival. The inference was that Weber's talk of reform was hypocritical, and that he had in fact approved a significant new extension of CIA economic-monitoring capability.

When he read the story, Weber felt queasy and thought for a moment that he would be physically sick. The leak was disclosing a program he had in fact approved at the end of his first week on the job. It was a new initiative being managed by James Morris and the Information Operations Center, under authorities approved by the agency's most secret panel, known as the Special Activities Review Committee. What frightened Weber was the possibility that the leak had come from one of the people in the small group that had been sitting in his office that first Friday afternoon when he approved the plan.

Ruth Savin called soon after Weber was given a summary of the *Independent* story. The general counsel arrived in his office thirty minutes later and proposed that the inspector general's office immediately begin an investigation, and that they start now with their referral to the Justice Department requesting a criminal investigation.

"How long will all this take?" asked Weber.

"A month to gear up, six weeks at the outside," answered Savin.

"Jesus, that's forever. We have information spilling out of this building into the news media and it takes that long even to start hunting for who leaked it."

"Welcome to the real world, Mr. Director. Leak investigations are sensitive. The president doesn't want to look like he's beating up on the press. He's taken a lot of grief for that already. You can call Mr. O'Keefe and ask him to approve a quicker referral, but I think he'll say no."

"That's okay," said Weber glumly. "I guess on this stuff, where you stand depends on where you sit."

Savin looked at her boss. Already, his ruddy Seattle complexion was turning that pale color that comes from early mornings and late nights and a life spent indoors.

"You want to hear a joke?" she said. "Maybe it will cheer you up."

Weber nodded. He wasn't really in the mood for laughing, but Savin seemed determined.

"Okay, You're at a Jewish wedding . . . how can you tell if it's Orthodox, Reform or Liberal?"

"I give up. How?"

"In an Orthodox wedding, the bride's mother is pregnant. In a Conservative wedding, the bride is pregnant. In a Reform wedding, the rabbi is pregnant. See, that's funny, and you aren't even Jewish."

Weber was chuckling, despite himself.

"You're good," he told his general counsel. "Now go start the leak investigation."

The next day, Marie stuck her head in the door and said that Mr. O'Keefe was calling from the White House. Weber's first thought was that they had decided for real to fire him. But when the national security adviser got on the line, he was polite, solicitous, even. The British foreign secretary and the chancellor of the Exchequer were coming to Washington for a hastily arranged visit. They would be at the White House the next afternoon at two, and the president wanted his new CIA director there. O'Keefe suggested that Weber bring along an analyst to talk about the global economy. The president would be most grateful.

"Let me be honest, Tim," said Weber. "From what I've seen so far, we don't have very good economic intelligence. I wouldn't want to embarrass you or the president. You'd be better off inviting someone from Goldman Sachs."

"Bring someone anyway," said O'Keefe. "It will make the president feel better."

Weber got a call just before he left for the White House the next day from the British Embassy. They patched through a man who introduced himself as Sir John Strachan. He identified himself as the director of the Secret Intelligence Service, modestly, as if Weber might not have known that. He had come over on short notice that morning with the foreign secretary and chancellor, Strachan said, and he was hoping there would be time for a proper chitchat, maybe a "walk in the woods." He made that last proposal sotto voce, as if the two of them were doing something very private.

Weber suggested a venue where they would be able to do just that, and asked his chief of staff, Sandra Bock, to make some hasty arrangements for late that afternoon at the newly useful golf club in Arlington.

Weber brought along to the White House Loomis Braden, the deputy director for intelligence, and Sandra Bock, who knew something about everything. They joined him in the black battlewagon as it made its way down the George Washington Parkway to the Theodore Roosevelt Bridge.

The meeting began at two in the Roosevelt Room on the main floor of the West Wing. O'Keefe had assembled the core national security team: the secretaries of State, Defense and Treasury, along with the attorney general. Aides to these luminaries took the small, straight-backed chairs along the wall, occasionally passing memos and briefing papers to the principals at the big table. The British visitors sat in the middle, across from the president, framed by the Cabinet secretaries. O'Keefe guarded the end of the table, bland and self-effacing.

The president sat at the center of the table under an oil painting of the "Rough Rider" atop his horse. He said so little in Cabinet meetings these days that people were whispering that he suffered from depression. Weber had only met him once since he'd taken the job. The chief executive preferred getting his morning intelligence briefings from O'Keefe. The vice president sat at the other end of the table from O'Keefe, chatting away volubly with his seatmates, in his own world of irrelevance.

Weber's first thought was to sit in the outer rim, next to his aides, under a painting of a Hudson River landscape. But O'Keefe insisted he join the big table with the principals.

The agenda seemed to be mutual reassurance. It was a season when America's superpower status was looking more dubious, and the benefits for Britain of the "special relationship" were being questioned at home. The reaffirmations on both sides were emphatic, but not quite convincing. The foreign secretary and the chancellor both wanted the president to know that even as Britain drew closer to the European Union, its relationship with the United States remained as strong as ever. The Europeans were trying to draw London into tax-equalization schemes, and trade-protectionist policies, and data-sharing regimes, and even intelligence-sharing that would undermine the Anglo-American partnership. But Her Majesty's government would resist whatever pressure was brought to bear, they assured the president.

Behind the foreign secretary sat Strachan, the chief of the SIS. When he arrived he had nodded at Weber and offered a half smile.

The president asked each of his principals around the table to say a few words. When it was Weber's turn, he talked about the challenge of running an intelligence service in an open society, and how much he had learned about the difficulties in his first weeks on the job. O'Keefe at the end of the table made a gesture with his hand that Weber took to mean, *Cut it short,* so the director pitched to Loomis Braden, who talked plausibly for five minutes about the perturbed state of global financial markets.

Then it was O'Keefe's turn to sum up for the American side, and fifteen minutes for the chancellor and foreign secretary to give their final thoughts, and then after ninety minutes the meeting adjourned for "working groups" at several departments and agencies. As Weber listened to the discussion, he found himself wondering if the world of 1945 and its axiomatic policies had meaning any longer, outside of meetings like this.

While the Treasury secretary steered the chancellor through the West Wing lobby and out to waiting journalists' microphones, a small group of national security officials, including Weber, passed through the far door of the lobby into a small hallway and down the narrow stairs that led to the Situation Room.

Weber took one of the black leather swivel chairs that lined the long polished wood table, six on a side. It didn't look like a global command post: there was simple furniture, pale blue wall-to-wall carpeting that might be found in any suburban family room; some video monitors along the wall to display imagery from sensors around the world; a camera pointed at the head of the table where the president sat, for those who might be watching the meeting on video teleconference. Seats had been marked with little name cards, military-style; Weber took a seat on the far side of the table.

O'Keefe stopped by Weber's chair.

"I'll want you to say a little something about the economic surveillance program that was in the *Independent*," O'Keefe whispered. "The Brits are upset."

Weber nodded. So that was the subtext.

The other principals wandered in, a few stopping off at the Navy Mess next door to get coffee or a cookie. Weber noticed that the outsized figure of Cyril Hoffman had entered the room. He was wearing his usual three-piece suit, blue this time, with notched lapels on the vest, and whatever his efforts, he was not inconspicuous. The president didn't pretend to be running the gathering. He simply deferred to O'Keefe.

"Everyone in this room knows what makes the 'special relationship' special," began the national security adviser. "It is the quality of intelligence-sharing across the Atlantic. Our two countries depend on the bonds between the CIA and SIS, the NSA and GCHQ, and the FBI and MI5. Everyone here also knows how hard these partnerships have been hit by the disclosures of the last several years. Our most secret programs have made their way into the press. That is our fault. The chief leakers have been Americans, and as we have repeatedly told our British friends at every level, we are sorry."

There were polite murmurs of thanks and sympathy from the British side. What O'Keefe said was true: From an intelligence standpoint, the disclosures had been calamitous. NSA and GCHQ had been tapping the world's telephone and Internet traffic pretty much at will for the past decade, thanks to programs with code names such as BULLRUN, TEMPORA and STORMBREW that had been among the world's most closely guarded secrets, until one day they weren't. The agencies had officially adopted the ostrich approach on both sides of the Atlantic, insisting that the information was still classified even though it was public knowledge.

"We want to assure our British friends that we will do everything possible to operate in this new space," said O'Keefe. He tapped one end of his pencil moustache as if to make sure that it was still firmly in place.

"Hear hear," said Anthony Fair, his British counterpart from 10 Downing Street. He offered the appropriate assurances about how America could always count on British support, and vice versa, he hoped.

O'Keefe turned to a Navy officer in his dress blues, seated several seats away.

"We'd like Admiral Schumer to give you an update on how the NSA is managing SIGINT operations in the new environment, we hope with continuing British cooperation."

Admiral Lloyd Schumer spent ten minutes reviewing the National Security Agency's efforts to maintain what he kept describing as "lawful activities." He didn't use the code names or offer the wiring-diagram details for this audience. He spoke with a military man's restrained, eyes-forward manner. You wouldn't have known, as he reviewed the collection and cryptological capabilities, that he was, in effect, handling shards of glass from a broken window.

O'Keefe then asked Amy Martin, the deputy attorney general, to brief the British on the current review of legal authorities for surveillance and intelligence collection under the Foreign Intelligence Surveillance Act, as amended. She was crisp and concise, and uninformative. You would have had no idea from her presentation that many of the activities she described were in a kind of legal limbo, pending review by courts, legal advisers and general counsels across the U.S. government. A British legal adviser responded by describing a similar state of uncertainty there, as politicians and Whitehall mandarins tried to decide what the new rules of the game would be.

Finally, O'Keefe turned to Weber, whom he described as "our new colleague."

"I have asked Mr. Weber to say a few words about the program that was revealed in the *Independent*, which I gather came as something of a surprise to you."

Weber didn't talk long. He told them that the agency was continuing its long-standing practice of collecting intelligence through "open source" information on the Internet and some proprietary data it obtained through other means. That was what Ruth Savin had told him to say.

"Although we are collecting economic information, I want to stress that it is not being shared with American companies."

"We thought you didn't do that sort of thing, old boy," said Fair, with icy precision. "We expect that from the French and the Israelis and the Chinese, but not from our American cousins."

"We haven't changed," answered Weber. The British listened impassively, knowing that the gist of the *Independent*'s story was that the American approach had in fact changed, in the scope of collection if not necessarily in the recipients of the information.

"Business is your world, eh?" pressed Fair. "You're coming straight out of the corporate technology side; unusual for a CIA director. So perhaps you can see why we were concerned that this initiative seemed to be one of your, what shall I say, early priorities. First week, I believe."

Weber nodded. He should stop now, before he got in any deeper trouble, but he wanted these people to understand him.

"You should know this program was handed to me when I arrived. Rest assured: I came to the agency to make good changes, not bad ones."

"Well, we're pleased to hear that," said Fair.

The talk moved on. The British still seemed anxious about something. Weber couldn't put his finger on it. The military men discussed new overhead surveillance architecture, whose fruits would be shared with the Brits, and forward defense against cyber-enemies. It was a bloodless conversation until John Strachan spoke up.

"Here's the thing," began the MI6 chief. "We are facing an intelligence threat now that is unprecedented, really. These leakers and whistleblowers would be easier to control if they were paid agents of foreign intelligence services, but unfortunately, for the most part, they are not. That does not, however, make them any less dangerous to our common enterprise."

Hoffman had been doodling before, but now he spoke up.

"I assure you that we share your concern, John. These liberty addicts are driving us crazy. Timothy has already apologized that we let several of them wander into the sanctum sanctorum. But what do we do about it? How do we pursue an adversary that is, as it proclaims, anonymous and self-perpetuating?"

"We penetrate them," continued Strachan quietly. "Get inside these hacker cults and turn them upside down."

"A lovely thought," said Hoffman. "But I'm afraid that Mr. O'Keefe and his lawyers have concluded that would be illegal."

"Pity," said Strachan.

"Isn't it," said Hoffman with a pursed smile.

Weber was silent. This wasn't his world yet, really. But he knew from what Sandra Bock had told him that Hoffman was attempting to do precisely what he had told the British, in this large gathering, could not be done.

As he was leaving the meeting, Weber stopped by to introduce himself properly to Strachan and hand him an index card with the address for their private rendezvous later that afternoon.

21

WASHINGTON

John Strachan out of the office was like a summer drink, a Pimm's Cup, say, or a good gin and tonic with a slice of cucumber: pleasant to taste, but with a bite, too. He was a thin man, light on his feet, dressed in suits that could only be made to measure. He'd spent a career overseas for the Secret Intelligence Service, mostly in Africa and South Asia, and he had the facility for languages that seems to come naturally in the British service as part of its postcolonial lineage. When Strachan made an observation about the growth of Baloch nationalism in Quetta, or Tamil unrest in Andhra Pradesh, you could be fairly sure that he had seen it with his own eyes, and perhaps conversed about it with a principal agent in his native language.

Strachan had asked for a walk in the woods, and that was precisely what he got. Sandra Bock had called the club steward in Arlington to say that Mr. Weber wanted to take a stroll around five, hopefully after the last foursome had finished for the day but when there was still enough light to see. The steward wanted to be helpful. The CIA was nearby; he didn't inquire further about the purpose of the meeting.

Strachan rolled up to the white-pillared clubhouse on Glebe Road in an embassy sedan and was met by a member of Weber's protection detail. The director was around the other side on the back porch, sitting in a white Adirondack chair and admiring the view. Immediately below was the eighteenth green, with its approach flanked by two other fairways, left and right. In the distance was the Gothic bulk of the National Cathedral, and to the east, downriver, was the obelisk of the Washington monument, slender as a candlestick in the distance. The light was fading; the last foursome had finished and made its way into the clubhouse.

"Jolly nice spot," said Strachan, approaching his host. He was dressed in brown oxfords with thick rubber soles, a chesterfield coat with a velvet collar, and was a carrying a walking stick.

"Let's take that walk," said Weber, bounding up from his chair. He was dressed in the style that is usually called "business casual."

The director skirted the eighteenth green, circumambulating a large bunker, and headed down the hill into the fairway, toward a topiary hedge three hundred yards away that spelled out the initials of the club's name. Jack Fong and the security detail had gone ahead, and agents were installed in the woods or by the water hazards; a lone bodyguard trailed behind.

"I'll come right to the point," said Strachan when they were a hundred yards from the clubhouse. "We're nervous about something."

"Why? Your delegation was smothered in kisses all afternoon. America loves you. People even apologized."

"That was quite a show, and you're right, it was tickety-boo. No. I'm thinking about something rather more private. Perhaps we should walk on a bit, eh?"

They were approaching a small pond at the turn of the dogleg on the long eighteenth fairway. Geese were floating silently in the thin light of late afternoon. At the approach of the two men, the birds took wing, beating their way off the surface of the pond and toward the setting sun over the crest of the hill. Except for a brace of security men thirty yards off, they were quite alone.

"What's worrying you, John? I'm the new boy, but I'll try to help however I can."

"No polite way to say it: We're worried that you have a leak."

Weber laughed. He didn't mean to, but it just came out.

"I'm sorry, but everybody has a leak! It's a condition of life nowadays. I've even noticed some SIS material showing up in the press, if I'm not mistaken. I promise you, I take it seriously. Please don't think that because I'm an outsider I don't value secrecy."

"I know that, of course I do. And I'm not talking about Snowden and his progeny. We'll survive all that. It's just that we hear this chatter. From what we gather, you're rooting around for some sort of penetration of the agency, electronic or otherwise, we don't know. But it makes us nervous."

"That's our business, John. But why should it worry you? We're on it; we'll handle it."

"Well, that's just the thing. It worries us, either way. If you have a problem, then we have a problem, because we're joined all over, really; the blood-brain barrier is dissolved with us. But if you *don't* have a problem, then we want you to stop rumbling around. It frightens your foreign chums."

There was a somber set to his jaw, but a twinkle in his eye, too.

"I'm not sure I follow you, John. There's something you're not telling me."

"Of course there is. Always, forever, must be. And you doubtless want me to divulge it."

"I'm no spy. But I never had a business partner in my life I didn't trust."

Strachan nodded. That was the thing about Weber. He might not know much about intelligence, but he was demonstrably a man who understood how the world worked, and had created tens of billions of dollars in value for people in the process.

"So I will be blunt," said Strachan. "You have a young chap who is your chief boffin, Internet wizard. His name is Morris. Brilliant fellow, everyone says. From what we hear, he's the one you've set out as cat among the pigeons. Trying to find where your leak might be. But the problem is, he also makes us nervous."

"How so? As you say, he's an uncommonly clever fellow. He could even be a Brit, he's so smart."

"I suppose I had that coming. Why does Morris make us nervous? Well, he didn't, for a long time. We thought he was the best thing since the fork-split muffin. We allowed him to wander rather freely in the UK. Still do. He has multiple identities, runs something or other, very black, that's part of the great joint venture between 'the cousins.' We don't ask questions. We gave him free run, but then, as I say, we began to get nervous."

Weber walked on for a while, ambling with Strachan toward the short rough and past a big sand trap, matted by rain, rakes askew nearby on the grass. Weber didn't know what to say, so he didn't say anything at first.

"What is it about Morris?" asked Weber eventually. "Why the anxiety?"

"He's an unguided missile, from what we can tell. He seems to have a hunting license to do what he pleases, and he has that halo that comes from having worked in the White House. He has odd friends, too, who don't particularly esteem Her Majesty's government and the traditional order of things. Morris just seems, how shall I put this? Separate."

Weber had deep questions of his own about Morris, but hearing this criticism of him from a foreigner, he felt oddly protective.

"I want my people to be iconoclastic, challenge the old ways. We need more of that, probably, not less."

As Weber walked, he kicked at a clod of grass and dirt, a divot that nobody had bothered to replace. It exploded in a small shower of dust and flutters of grass.

Strachan looked at him skeptically, as if he were trying to appraise him for membership in a social club.

"Well, it's more than that, you see. We know you lost a potential defector in Germany the other week, the fellow ended up revolverized, from what we hear. I'm not asking you to say anything, old boy, just noting for the record that we have our sources. And the thing that bothers us, really, is that you sent Morris to bat, and he's been bowled in the first over. Not good. Quite bad, actually."

Weber had stopped dead in his tracks, near a ball-washing machine at the eighteenth tee.

"I'll take care of Morris, John. He does some very secret work, not all of which is run by the agency. But I am aware of his quirks and difficulties. He an ex-mathematician, quiet type: Nerd, we say. I have my eye on him."

"You're not getting my point about Morris, old boy. We think he's not to be trusted."

Weber's eyes froze into a dark icy blue. The color drained from his cheeks. He didn't like having the head of a foreign intelligence service make accusations about one of his senior aides, especially when he had been having private worries about the man himself.

"That's my call, not yours. Until further notice, you can assume that James Morris directs our Information Operations Center and that he has my confidence. If that changes for any reason, I'll let you know."

"Oh, dear, I fear I have offended you," said Strachan. "I didn't mean to do that, certainly not in our first real meeting. I just wanted you to know that we were a bit concerned, your man bumping around in the dark looking for a mole, and us not knowing what was going on. Made us feel . . . unloved."

"I'll look into it," said Weber. He had reached the eighteenth tee and crossed over a little bridge to the ninth tee, which took them back up the hill by another direction.

"I'd be so grateful."

They were heading sharply uphill now. Strachan dug his walking stick into the ground, to help himself along.

To clear the air, they talked about other matters of mutual interest, especially Iran. The British had a source they had managed to keep alive for a decade inside the Iranian nuclear establishment, even as American and Israeli networks were being rolled up. Weber admired that operational skill; that raw ability to look someone in the eye and tell a lie, which seemed to come so naturally to the British, and to the Iranians, too, for that matter.

They had a glass of whiskey in the club bar before Strachan announced that it was time to go or he would miss his return flight. He rose from his barstool, gave Weber a cousinly pat on the back, turned on his heel and marched out the door, saying he would call his embassy car. Weber had already told his security detail to have an extra car waiting, so with only a little protestation, the SIS chief bundled into the back of the limousine, scraping the mud off his shoes with his walking stick.

Weber waved goodbye until Strachan's car had turned the bend on Glebe Road, and then went back into the bar and had another scotch while his security men stood post.

Weber tried to put the last few hours together in his mind. The British were worried about the special relationship and wanting to caulk the seams; they were anxious about the historic signals-intelligence partnership between the United States and the UK, and trying to shore up the edges of that, too. They were reeling, as was America, from the disclosure of so many secrets. And they were particularly concerned, it seemed, about James Morris, and what they regarded as his threat to Anglo-American comity.

What Weber had to decide was whether the conversations of these last few hours made him more worried about Morris or Strachan. He pondered anew the question that had led him to remove the Donovan statue from the lobby on his first day . . . the worry that the CIA might be constrained by the looping coils of its historic partnership with British intelligence, which was a symbol of the larger problem of being anchored to a past that didn't fit the present.

There is a Gresham's Law of consciousness: New ideas devalue old ones. Weber had to decide which theory of the case made sense, and then defend it against mental challenge. The new idea that Morris could be a leaker and a mole trumped the old idea that he was an iconoclast and change agent. But how to act on it?

When Weber got back to the office, he called Beasley and said he wanted to review the Information Operations Center's activities abroad. James Morris might have special authority to conduct undercover operations abroad. But intelligence activities in every country overseas came under the purview of the chiefs of station, who reported to the CIA director. If Morris's people were moving from country to country, Weber wanted them stopped at the borders until their identities could be checked with the local CIA stations. In Britain, the London station chief, Susan Amato, should use her liaison relationships to have the British put a watch on anyone who was thought to be an IOC operations officer.

Beasley, who had been itching to get control of Morris's black operations for many months, promised the director that it would be taken care of. Weber sent another personal cable to Morris, ordering him home for the second time and threatening him with dismissal and possible prosecution if he refused. There was no response.

22

GRANTCHESTER, ENGLAND

James Morris did not have a relaxed side: The hurricane lamp of his consciousness was always alight. So even in the emerald postcard of rural England, Morris felt restless. As lunchtime approached, he wanted to escape out the window of his office, into the meadows of Grantchester and the city beyond. Of all Morris's hideaways and false fronts, this operation in a village just south of Cambridge was his favorite creation. The sign over the door read FUDAN–EAST ANGLIA RESEARCH CENTRE, and the employees were a mix of Britons and Chinese. But this was Morris's place, funded mostly with black money from his joint operation with NSA. And it was truly secret, even from the Brits.

Morris's computer messages were stacking up in multiple accounts. He needed to concentrate on his business, especially now when it was so tangled. But there was the problem of getting Ed Junot back into England. The chief of station in Grosvenor Square had somehow discovered Junot's operational alias, and was demanding that the UK Border Authority prevent him from entering the country. That was bad enough, but the German security service had also cracked his alias identity and had put out a BOLO notice for his true name, as well.

Morris usually found it galvanizing to solve problems that eluded other people. He knew that if he could focus, he would jump into the electrons and find some invisible way to route Junot back to Britain through a clean entry point. But in his restless fever, he couldn't get a fix on it just now.

Morris was stressed; though he would never admit it, the plain fact was that there was too much baggage stacked on his wagon: He was recruiting a European hacker network as he had promised Cyril Hoffman; he was supposed to be pursuing the murder of the Swiss walk-in, as he had pledged to Graham Weber; and most importantly and deviously, he was pursuing the separate agenda that was demanded by his dearest friend, Ramona Kyle—and the big idea her friends had developed for shaking the institution at the center of global finance. It wasn't simply that these goals were in conflict. They were violently unstable, like volatile chemicals that might explode if they were mixed. They came together in Morris's mind only, which was why he occasionally felt that his head was about to detonate.

The secret was to use the tools, people and front companies that had been created for one set of objectives to serve another. That was the simple truth about secret work. Because it was so hidden from outside observers, it was easy to misdirect. That was what Snowden had understood, burrowing away in the NSA's archives. Once you had the keys to the castle you could go in any room and take what you liked.

"Rebalancing" was a word that soothed Morris. That was all he wanted to do, really. Whatever people might say later, he was trying to put matters back in a proper balance after a sixty-year misalignment. Morris tried once more to concentrate, but his mind kept wandering, whirring with thoughts of being somewhere else, not in charge. He willed himself to focus on the gray business of zeroes and ones on the screen before him, but it didn't work.

He rose from his desk and walked down the hall to the office of Dr. Emmanuel Li, the director of the institute. He knew that he looked a mess, in the disguise he'd been wearing since he got to Britain. Before entering Li's office, he tried to tidy himself up, patting down the hair of his wig, adjusting the odd, oversized eyeglasses that Denver had given him as part of this ensemble and pulling up his pants so they weren't hanging on the narrow ledge of his buttocks.

Dr. Li was a fastidious man himself, with a buzz cut and round spectacles. He understood the reality of Morris's secret primacy at the institute but chafed at it, too. Morris stuck his head in the door.

"I'm going out for an hour or two," said Morris. "Lunch break. If anyone calls, I'm not here."

Dr. Li made a polite, false laugh.

"But Mr. Morris, you are always 'not here,' even when you are here."

"Then tell them I'm here. I don't care. But I'm going out for a while. Stretch my brain."

"This part of the body is not easy to stretch. It gets exercise when it does nothing. When it is stretched, it becomes tight."

"Well, thanks for that, Dr. Li," said Morris, muttering, barely under his breath, "Fuck me."

Morris walked down the rear stairwell, avoiding the main entry and the reception desk, and out into the crisp midmorning. It was late fall, not quite winter, but the sun was low in the sky, casting deep shadows even at noontime. The grass was a rich moist green, thick like peat. The turf was protected by a little chain and a sign advising people to keep off, but Morris walked over it and down the dewy meadow toward the Cam.

A few punters were out on the water. Morris watched their long poles cut the surface. The ones who knew the technique sent their narrow boats forward like a shot. The novices jerked and quivered and held the pole so long it looked as if the boat might skitter away and leave them clinging to the lance for dear life, dangling above the water.

Morris took out a secure cell phone, on which he had disabled the GPS locater. He saw so many messages from Headquarters and from his various outposts it was wearying just to scroll through them. He had two other phones with him, also GPS-free, with different aliases and entirely different networks of contacts, but he didn't bother to look at them. They would only add to the buzz in his head. Everybody wanted him and nobody could find him, which was normally the way he liked it. But today was different. His pantomime of control was wearying. Today he wanted someone to control him.

He took the third phone, in an identity that had been stolen for him a year ago, and dialed a number in Cambridge. A human being never answered this number; the phone only took messages. Morris asked for Beatrix and said he would be there in thirty minutes. It cost money to have this privilege of access, like having a jet idling on the runway. But money was the least of Morris's problems.

Morris walked the muddy footpath though Grantchester Meadows toward Cambridge. He was really buzzing now, a tickle of excitement softening his limbs. When he passed a petrol station, he ducked into the men's room and removed his wig and glasses and put them in his pack.

The walkers from Cambridge were trooping toward him on the lunchtime jaunt they liked to call the "Grantchester Grind." Morris slipped past them, through the cattle gates and turnstiles along the public way, dipping toward the black muck along the Cam.

The swans were out at the Granta Pub and floating indolently in Mill Pond. Their beaks coiled into their necks in a sinuous curve. They were filthy creatures, for such beauties, like ballet dancers with a thousand-dollar-a-day habit. They seemed so graceful afloat, but up close they were ugly, unpleasant birds.

Beatrix was waiting in a modern apartment just past Market Square, near the Lion House shopping arcade. She had the lights dimmed when Morris arrived. She'd had a little time to prepare, at least. It was awful when she had to get the place ready while he waited and his desire melted. Morris heard the slap of a gloved hand. The door opened. She was dressed in black leather, corsets and studs girding her body; her bosom was armored in a black brassiere. Morris fell to his knees.

By two-thirty, James Morris was back at the research center, sending a volley of messages to subordinates on several continents and in several aliases. It helped that he was lit now like a Halloween lantern, and that the anxiety had drained from his body, so that it was pliable again and his mind could think.

Weiss had been messaging from Headquarters, asking where he was. She needed to answer some inquiries from the comptroller, which had required opening some restricted electronic files, using authority she had in Morris's absence but rarely used. Morris passed over her communications, as he had for a week. Weiss was the bookkeeper. Morris barely registered her activities most of the time. He liked to call her a "fire-and-forget missile," but in practice this mostly meant "forget."

Morris had meetings scheduled at the end of the afternoon with two prospective "fellows" of the institute. He was like a team manager before the trading deadline, trying to get all the right players in place. His research budget was elastic; he could hire as many world-class hackers as he could find, to do whatever he instructed. Here in England, he had the incomparably opaque Dr. Li to handle arrangements. Prospective candidates might suspect they would be working for China; perhaps a few thought the real sponsor might be GCHQ in Cheltenham. But it was a rare person who saw the American hand.

The first of these final crash recruits was an Israeli electrical engineer named Yoav Shimansky. He had dropped out of Cambridge a year ago after winning a graduate fellowship, gotten into debt feeding a drug habit and had begun hacking for profit about a year ago.

Morris had begun inquiring about the Israeli after one of his operatives had noticed some artful coding in a hack on numbered accounts at a Swiss private bank. They traced the code back to an IP address in Russia, which in turn linked to one in Israel, which connected finally to the real author of the code in the UK, who turned out to be Shimansky. He had other interesting qualifications: He had served in the Israeli military, which meant that he knew his way around classified systems, and he had visa problems in the UK, which meant that he was vulnerable.

The Israeli candidate was waiting in an interview room on the first floor. Dr. Li's secretary knocked on Morris's door and told him it was time, past time, and that Dr. Li had already gone downstairs to meet the visitor. Morris didn't hear at first; he was listening to a club mix on Spotify; a DJ named Oliver repeated over and over the words: "The night is on my mind." When the administrator from downstairs rapped on his door, he removed his earbuds. He put his cell phones in the safe, adjusted his wig in the mirror to make sure it fit, put on his goggle-eyed glasses and descended the stairs. He was not an imposing physical presence, in or out of disguise, which gave him an anonymity he had always used to advantage.

Shimansky sat at a table, with a computer screen and keyboard in front of him. Li sat across from him, facing another screen that displayed the same information. The Israeli was scrawny from his drug habit, and had deep circles under his eyes and an unhealthy brackish pallor from spending too much time indoors. He was fidgety in his seat, while Li sat still as a statue.

Morris was rubbing at his nose when he arrived. He took the empty seat next to Li.

"I'm Hubert Birkman," he said, extending his hand. "I'm the principal engineer. I used to work for Hubang Networks here in the UK. Then I came to the center." Morris spoke with a mid-Atlantic accent, somewhere between Britain and America.

"I'm Yoav," said the Israeli. "Unemployed."

"We know your work. That's why Dr. Li and I wanted you to come see us today. We do penetration testing at FEARC. We need to get inside our clients' systems, to show them their vulnerabilities and help them make corrections. We're looking for people who know how to hack, basically, but aren't crazy."

"I heard all that, thank you very much," responded the Israeli. He spoke from deep in the throat, every word heavy with phlegm, so that he sounded sardonic even when his statements were straightforward.

"Our biggest clients are in the financial sector," said Morris. "Large banks, some hedge funds, even some central banks."

"Okay, sure, whatever. I don't mind."

"We'd like to see what you can do," said Morris. "That's our drill when we interview potential fellows. We want to see you penetrate a system, to make sure you have the technical skills. I assume Dr. Li explained all that."

Shimansky nodded dubiously.

"I told your Chinese boss I would break into the Bank Gstaad. That's my demo tape, except it's not a tape, it's happening on-screen. I prepare some of it before, but still: You watch, whatever you want. But I have to ask, you are not a cop, right?"

"We have nothing to do with law enforcement in the United Kingdom or any other country. We are a research institute only, with close links to our funders in Asia, of course." He nodded to Dr. Li at his side.

"We will share only with our clients whatever you do for us as a research fellow. Including what you show us today. All that will be in the contract, along with the nondisclosure agreement."

"How much you pay?"

"Sorry. You go first."

Shimansky shrugged.

"You have the money. I need the job."

"So log in." Morris pointed to the computer. "Today, your username is 'fellow' and the password is 'guest.'"

Shimansky logged himself into the center's system, which immediately displayed a Mozilla browser.

"Go ahead," said Morris. "Walk us through it."

"Okay. So first I go to TOR. You want me to do that, to hide where I am, unless you are crazy."

"Use TOR, of course," said Morris, nodding. How quaint that the Israeli trusted the "Onion Router" as an anonymizer. Its triple layers had been peeled back by the NSA, but hackers still swore by it.

"So I pick my target, Mr. Dieter Kohler, a vice president of Bank Gstaad. I do some research on him already, so I know that he is a big traveler, uses all the travel sites and airline sites. So I do 'man-in-the-middle attack,'" when he thinks he goes to buy airline ticket, giving them his information, he is really going to me, to my proxy server. Here, I show you how the capture worked, on my site."

Shimansky's fingers tapped at the keys, and the screen displayed his own Internet site. Then up on the screen came a display that looked exactly like the website of Sitzmark Airlines, a charter company that arranged helicopter ski trips.

"So a week ago Mr. Dieter Kohler goes to Sitzmark Airlines to make charter reservation for this winter. I know he will do this because he did it last year and the year before that; always in October, okay. But when he goes to Sitzmark, thinking it is a trusted site, he really goes to my proxy, which I take from cache."

As the Israeli typed on the computer, his wan face seemed to come alive. It was like the thrill of any sport; when the player was in the zone, he gave up conscious control to preconscious intuition.

Morris has been following the display closely, but now he broke in.

"How did you get the certificate, so Kohler's computer would think your dummy was a trusted site? Even this little airline would have Transport Layer Security, right?"

"Of course they have TLS. I have to spoof that. So, I show you. I get certificate from Trustnode. Not direct, but someone I know, he buys one, then gives to an Israeli friend, who gives to another Israeli friend, who gives to me."

The screen image changed to a screenshot for the certificate authority's Verisign certificate.

"Nice," said Morris.

"Now Kohler makes his reservation. He types in all his information, credit card, everything else, thinking this is TLS-protected, but he doesn't know it's me. I show you."

Shimansky brought up more screenshots that showed the capture of Kohler's basic data, name, address, credit card number, security code.

"So you went phishing, without phishing."

"You got it, Mr. Birkman. I have all his information. And also, because I own the proxy server, I know the IP address that Herr Kohler is coming from. He shouldn't be using his company computer to make his personal ski reservations, but, you know, he is like most people, so he does."

"Got it," said Morris.

"I even ask Kohler for a password for the charter flight reservation. Because I know maybe he uses the same password multiple times. People shouldn't, but they do."

"People are stupid," said Morris, with a wink that was barely visible behind his oversized glasses. He had already decided to hire the Israeli kid, but he wanted to see the rest of his demo.

"Yes, this is a useful and true fact, Mr. Birkman. So now I have his password, too. His bank is small, so it doesn't use two-factor authentication, but only static passwords for remote access. And it has stupid employees, who use the same password everywhere. So what do I do now? I go to the Bank Gstaad site and pretend that I am him."

Shimansky typed some more, and the monitor displayed the Bank Gstaad employee's screen, in real time. The Israeli typed in the username and password he had stolen from Kohler, and he was in the system, seeing a display of the bank's proprietary information.

"I am lucky. I see what the bank vice president sees. Here, I show you, these are the numbered accounts that Herr Kohler manages."

A series of numbers came up on the screen, followed by some large amounts in Swiss francs. All were over ten million; some were over one hundred million.

"But there is a problem," said the Israeli in a sly voice. "I know the numbers, but I do not know who they belong to. How do I fix that?"

"You tell me," said Morris.

"Easy. The URL of the bank's public website is gstaadbank.com.ch. Here it is."

Shimansky typed in the firm's Web address and the monitor displayed the client-friendly interface of its website, with the white of the Alps and the blue sky as a background behind the basic information.

"So the bank's customers come to this site all the time, to check their accounts. They shouldn't do it, I know, but they do. Okay, so I use a cache version of the real Gstaad site to build a proxy that looks just the same, exactly the same, except that the URL of mine is one letter off. So the address of my dummy site is gstasdbank.com.ch. Here is what it looks like."

He typed in *gstasdbank.com.ch*, one mistyped letter, an *s* instead of an *a*, an easy mistake to make, and sure enough, up came a site that looked identical to the one before. Like the real site, it asked clients to register the usernames and passwords to get information about their accounts.

"God bless 'fat fingers,'" said Morris.

"Yes, and I can tell you, Mr. Birkman, that rich people's fingers are pretty fat. So when they go to the Gstaad site, sometimes they mean to hit that second *a* but they miss it and hit the *s* that is next to it. And so they are at my site, and not the bank's. Here, like I show you."

On the monitors was a screenshot of a customer's completed sign-in, with username and password typed to access the site.

"When they go to look at their money, the site crashes, what a pain this is, so maybe they go back again, but this time, they hit the right letters, the *a* and not the *s*, and they are back at Bank Gstaad for real, but it's okay for me, because I have their username and password, and also, I have their IP address."

The Israeli displayed the IP address information for the Bank Gstaad customer he had most recently hacked.

"So if I do a little detective work on this IP address, I can see that it belongs to Mr. Alireza Najafi-pur, who does his commercial banking through Dubai . . ."

Shimansky typed some commands, and the screen displayed the IP address of a Dubai branch of a global commercial bank.

". . . but who really lives in Tehran."

The Israeli typed again, and now the screen displayed the image of a simple commercial website written mostly in Farsi, but an English-language address visible in the upper left-hand corner that showed the firm in question was a food-distributing company based at 3 Dr. Bahonar Street, off Bahonar Square, in the Niavaran district of Tehran.

"So now I know something, eh?" said Shimansky.

"Yes, you do," agreed Morris.

"But you see, this is really only the beginning of how I can make mischief. Because I can inject SQL into the system of the bank and the accounts of the users, too. And then I really begin to know some things."

A few more clicks on the keyboard, and Shimansky showed the rudiments of an attack using Structured Query Language that is injected into a database and then can read, write, delete or modify data stored there.

"So this is what I do," said the Israeli. "And you just watched me do it, so you know this is no bullshit. If your clients need, what, protection against this, okay, I am ready."

"Roger that," said Morris. "We'd like to offer you a fellowship. No bullshit."

"So now I ask again, how much, please."

"That depends. Our research fellowships begin at a hundred fifty thousand dollars annually. With bonuses, that can go higher. This is for exclusive work. No freelancing."

"I can make this much at a bank. No way. I stay unemployed, I make more money."

"Maybe, but you have visa problems."

"You solve them?"

"Of course. Our institute has many friends here in the UK."

"Okay, very nice, but a hundred fifty thousand still is not enough. Sorry."

"Let me ask you a question that might affect how much we can offer you. Did you ever work for Unit 8200 when you were in the Israeli army?"

"What are you? An Israeli spy?"

"Maybe," said Morris. "But answer my question. Were you in 8200? Did you do any cyber-work when you were in the army?"

"Sure. Of course I did. What you think they would do with some-one like me? Turn me into a paratrooper? I have trouble taking a walk on the beach in Tel Aviv with my shirt off, too many people laugh at me."

"I won't ask you what you did for 8200, but I take it you know your way around classified cyber."

"Who's asking? China?"

"No, me. Hubert Birkman."

"Yeah, sure. I know my way around lots of things."

Morris wrote a number down on a piece of paper and passed it to Dr. Li, who had been silent throughout the interview. The Chinese man pursed his lips.

"Could you excuse us for a minute?" said Morris, motioning for Dr. Li to join him in the hall. The Israeli resumed fidgeting.

Morris returned thirty seconds later, with the Chinese man who was his nominal boss.

"Dr. Li has authorized me to make an unusual offer to you. We are prepared to pay two hundred fifty thousand as an annual research stipend, plus full use of the computer lab here, plus bonuses for any unusual penetration work, such as zero-day exploits, to reflect the value they would have in the marketplace. Plus we will take care of your visa problem, and find you housing here in the Cambridge area. How does that sound?"

"Pretty fucking great, actually."

The Israeli was finally smiling, dropping his cynical ex-junkie hacker pose as he contemplated all that money and, for once, a hassle-free lifestyle.

"We need you to start work right away, and we want to focus you on large banks; very large banks. Are you cool with that?"

"Why not?" he said, trying to sound unimpressed.

"Okay," said Morris, shaking Shimansky's hand. "We have a deal. You ready to sign the contract and nondisclosure agreement?"

"Whatever," said the Israeli.

Morris pushed a four-page agreement across the desk. It was marked with the letterhead *One World*, which was one of the cover names Morris was using for his project. Dr. Li got up and left the room.

"Initial each page at the bottom and sign the last page where the red sticker is," said Morris coolly.

Shimansky began reading the document.

"Don't try," said Morris. "It's all legal bullshit. You won't understand it, believe me, and I don't have time. Just initial and sign."

The Israeli shrugged. He signed as instructed and pushed the paper back to Morris.

The young American's face and posture changed. The slouch was gone, and so was his lackadaisical manner.

"Welcome to my world, Mr. Shimansky. This is a legally binding document in the United Kingdom and everywhere else that has a legal system. It says that if there are any disputes, they will be arbitrated by a mediator of our choosing. It also includes a nondisclosure agreement that holds you responsible, with unlimited liability for damages, if any warranties are breached. If you say or do anything we feel violates this contract, we can take you to court."

"What kind of agreement is that?" asked Shimansky.

"My kind, your kind, it doesn't matter, because you just signed it."

The Israeli glowered at Morris. He didn't like to be manipulated so crassly.

"So I can leave," he said.

"Try it," said Morris. "Be my guest."

Shimansky rose and opened the door of the interview room. An armed guard was standing in the hallway. The Israeli tried to pass but the guard pushed him back into the room and down into the chair he had just vacated.

"We're going to be friends, honest," said Morris. "You'll like the work. But don't try that again."

"What *is* the work?" asked the Israeli. "And please, Mr. Birkman, no more bullshit about your clients."

Morris smiled. He took off his wig, which was itchy, revealing his short brush of hair.

"I'm glad you asked that, Yoav. How would you like to hack a bank with me and some of my pals: the biggest goddamn bank in the world? How would you like to take money out of one account and put it into another? How would you like to make debtors become solvent at the push of an 'enter' key? Does that appeal to your sense of mischief? *Nu?*"

The Israeli cocked his head. What hacker wouldn't want a challenge like that? It was like asking a bank robber if he wanted to take down Fort Knox.

"You pay me, like you said, and I'm in."

"Attaboy. I knew I would like you. So let me explain a few things about what we have in mind."

Morris laid out his scheme. Even Yoav Shimansky, a man who made it a point never to show his emotions, could not help but be impressed.

23

CAMBRIDGE, ENGLAND

James Morris had vanished. He wasn't answering his phones and he was ignoring all electronic messages. His location was concealed from his CIA colleagues, and even from the staff who worked for him in the joint NSA cover office in Denver. He had given his contact information in East Anglia to only one person. So Morris knew that it could only be that very particular friend who left an unsigned letter for him with the receptionist downstairs at the Fudan–East Anglia Research Centre. The note read: *Meet me at 5:00 at The Silver Locket.* The handwriting was distinctive, small letters, sharply formed, branching like spindly roots.

When Morris received the note, it was nearly four-thirty. He told Dr. Li to delay the last interview; he needed to take a walk and would be back as soon as he could. It was dusk when Morris set out, and in the low light the fields were plush green and the furrows and hedgerows a deep velvet. He walked quickly toward the pub on the outskirts of the little town. Morris passed the memorial to Rupert Brooke, the World War I poet who had made the village modestly famous. Morris didn't care about poetry. The only poems he could remember liking had been generated by an AI program he'd created when he was at Stanford: You typed in the theme, say *love*, and the names of the characters, the setting and a metric scheme, and out came a poem.

Morris went into the Silver Locket and asked the barman for a pint of lager. It took a few moments before his eyes adjusted to the light. Then he saw Ramona Kyle, sitting at a table in the corner. She was drinking a glass of fruit juice. Morris sat down beside her. She was wearing a wool sweater with a crew neck, the kind that teenage boys wear in prep school. Her red curls were tied in a tight ponytail. She closed her eyes and formed a kiss with her lips, without touching him. He smiled.

"Hey, you," he said. "What's up?"

"I was in England seeing some people, and I got worried about you. I thought you might be lonely."

"Me? No way. I hate people. I like being alone."

Kyle smiled. She looked to the other tables. The pub was beginning to fill with people coming in after work.

"That's my man," she murmured. She put a finger to her lips for quiet.

"Seriously," he whispered, "why did you come? I'm okay. Nobody knows I'm here. I want to keep it that way."

"The truth?"

"Always."

"I was afraid you might be getting cold feet. I wanted to check your temperature."

"I'm chill. I'm recruiting my last engineers now. This is going to be the hack of the century. Don't be nervous about me, K. I'm all in."

"Good. You have to move soon. The heat is on the *Independent* again after that story. Eventually it will be on you."

Morris's face lost what little color it had. He licked his lips, which had suddenly gone dry. He leaned toward her and spoke in her ear.

"Did you plant that?"

"Don't ask," she said. "That's our deal."

He took his beer and drained the glass.

"I don't care anymore. Let's blow it all up."

"Shhh!" she said, her finger to her lips again. "You need to be careful, Jimmy."

"I am. That's why I'm here. You're the one who broke security."

"There's someone I want you to meet," she said, very quietly now. "That's the other reason I came."

"I'm not meeting people now."

"He's over there." She looked across the lounge to a muscular young man in a blue blazer and a purple and white college scarf. Morris followed her eyes. The other man looked like a Cambridge undergraduate, almost. He nodded. He'd seen Ramona before, in a desolate park in Maryland.

"His name is Roger. At least that's his work name. When I get up, he's going to come over here and introduce himself."

"What if I don't want to meet him? I told you, I don't like people."

"Not an option. But you'll appreciate him. He can help."

Ramona Kyle finished the last of her fruit juice and donned a raincoat over her sweater. She leaned toward Morris.

"I am so proud of you," she said. "Most people do nothing. You're doing everything."

She walked away. The front of the bar was full now; she disappeared into a knot of people before she reached the door.

The young man in the scarf came over and sat down next to Morris, where Ramona had been. Someone watching them would have guessed it was a gay pickup. He was carrying a paperback book on "Scala," a new high-level programming language.

"How are you doing, man?" he began. There was a slight accent in his voice. Morris couldn't place it, but it was east of Germany. "I'm Roger. Can I buy you a beer?"

"I have to go," said Morris. "I have an appointment."

"No problem, man." He put his hand on Morris's knee. Morris was startled, but he didn't move.

"When you get up to go, take the book with you."

"I have plenty to read," said Morris.

"Take the book," whispered the man. "It has some information that will be helpful for you. It also has the time and place of our next meeting."

Roger stared into Morris's eyes. He was a powerful person, handsome, but more than that. He had an operative's way of subtly establishing rapport and control at once,

Morris removed the man's hand from his leg and stood up. "I'll think about it," he said. He turned and walked toward the door. Under his arm was the Scala book.

———————

Dr. Li was waiting just inside the door when Morris returned to the office. He was looking at his watch. It was after six. The five-thirty appointment had already arrived, with annoying punctuality. Morris muttered an apology. He went upstairs and locked Roger's book in his safe. He wanted to lock himself away, too, but it was too late for that. The time for deliberating or holding back had passed, he wasn't sure when, but the opportunity to withdraw was gone. Now he had to execute.

The last appointment was a Chinese research student named Bo Guafeng. Dr. Li had found him through a friend who was a fellow of Girton College, where Bo was a research student. Dr. Li learned that he was from Wuhan in the interior, which probably meant that he wasn't from a rich family and needed money. He was proficient in computer science, and he had something of a reputation as a hacker. Within the Chinese student community, he was known as a rebel who wore his hair long and dressed in a leather jacket.

Can be controlled, wrote Dr. Li on the margin of the young man's résumé.

Morris nodded. He was trying to pay attention, but he was distracted.

Young Mr. Bo was wearing a black gabardine suit with his hair trussed in a ponytail. From the moment he shook Morris's hand, it was obvious that he was trying hard to appear to be a diligent student, as opposed to his natural demeanor of mildly antisocial rebellion. That was precisely the wrong strategy to adopt for a meeting with Morris, but there was no way for the Chinese student to know that, and enough bits of maladapted behavior showed through to make him a believable hacker.

As before, the applicant was seated at a computer keyboard, in front of a screen, with a companion monitor facing the interviewers. This time Morris let Dr. Li do most of the talking. He was tired, and he wanted his Chinese colleague to have "face" with Bo, in the event that he was hired. Dr. Li began with a largely fictitious description of the activities of the Fudan–East Anglia Research Centre. Dr. Li was an excellent liar, whatever his other limits.

Morris introduced himself as a former employee of Hubang Networks' subsidiary in Britain that marketed their routers and other hardware to European clients. This identity was backstopped, in case Bo bothered to check. The spurious Chinese connection would reassure Bo that he would not be courting prosecution by the Public Security Bureau when he returned home.

Morris gave a rote description of the particular fellowship position they were looking to fill. Bo looked at him intently, evidently curious about this American who seemed so well connected with Chinese information technology.

"We need a shopper," said Morris, "someone who can research the things that might be dangerous to our clients—so that they can take defensive measures. You understand, Mr. Bo?"

"Oh, yes, Mr. Birkman," he said eagerly. "Dr. Li told me what you want. I am ready to show my skills."

"We are waiting," said Dr. Li, gesturing to the keyboard. "You take us on a shopping trip."

Dr. Li gave him the guest username and password, and Bo opened his browser. He looked up and saw that they were waiting for him to display his hacking expertise.

"First, I think we must open TOR account for Onion links."

Bo typed quickly and the browser interface for torproject.org appeared on the monitors.

"I think now we would like to go to TOR Hidden Service Directory. We will see what they have there."

He looked at a sheet he had brought along and typed a sixteen-letter address, starting with *dppm* and continuing with a string of seemingly random letters. This opened a browser screen that displayed service providers that were running TOR, too, so that the connection was double-blind; triple-encrypted.

"Okay, easy stuff," said Dr. Li.

"Now I think maybe you want to look at what people can buy from the Russian carders, which could harm your clients."

The Chinese research student looked again at his crib sheet and typed another sixteen-letter string, this time beginning *wihw*, and up came a price list. For one hundred credit cards, the price today was $5,000. This was a competitive market. There was so much identity theft these days that prices were falling.

"Not bad," said Dr. Li. He was stingy with his praise.

"I will look now at stolen PayPal accounts."

This time the young man typed a shorter address, starting with *ivu4*, and in an instant the current market in PayPal money online was displayed.

"Maybe it is U.S. user account information that is a problem for your clients. These names are Social Security numbers, DOBs, which is the date of the birth, and the address and phone number, of course."

Another glance at the sheet and few more keystrokes, here beginning *jppc*, and he was once again inside an online warehouse of data, with identities priced by the thousands this time.

"Better," said Dr. Li.

"And now, finally, I will take you to Silk Road, famous online market, where you can see many more services that can be harmful, even drugs, you will see, very dangerous even to be here online."

This time Bo typed in an http address that began with *silkroad*, which did indeed take them to a marketplace of illicit goods and services that could be acquired online. It required a username and password, and then a PIN number, all of which he executed flawlessly. Obviously, he had been to these places before.

"Acceptable," said Dr. Li.

Li looked toward Morris, who passed him a note with one word, *mule*, dashed on the paper. Li nodded.

"Is there anything else you would like me to perform?" asked the student.

"No, Mr. Bo. Mr. Birkman and I can see that you are a diligent man. Do you have any questions?"

"Well, let me think . . ." Bo knew that you are always supposed to ask a question in an interview, but he was stumped for a moment. Then a query occurred to him.

"Are you connected to Fudan University in Shanghai?" He looked at Morris, then at Dr. Li. Both were silent for a moment while they considered what lie to tell, for in truth they had no connection whatsoever. The American spoke up.

"We work with some of the best Fudan faculty. Not with the university itself, of course, but with some of their top computer science people."

"Thank you very much." Bo seemed relieved at the thought that there would be Chinese academics along for the ride, whatever this vehicle was.

Dr. Li looked again at Morris, who rolled his hand in a gesture that said, *Let's get on with it.*

"We can offer you work here," said Dr. Li. "We pay rather well, I think."

Bo Guafeng could not suppress a quick smile. It was the first unrehearsed gesture of the interview.

Morris handed over another One World contract. He repeated the ritual of the nondisclosure agreement, this time not quite as aggressively as with the Israeli. He wanted to get the details finished so he could hand the Chinese kid off to Dr. Li. He didn't have to elaborate the legal details. He could tell from the look on the Chinese man's face that he already knew that Morris "owned" him, had owned him from the moment he walked in the door.

"We are going to need you to do some traveling for us. Do you like to travel, Mr. Bo?"

"Oh, yes," said the Chinese student. "I like travel."

"Good. Because we're going to send you to Switzerland. You have your passport, right, no visa problems, no difficulty getting in and out of Britain?"

"My passport is fine, Mr. Birkman. What do you want me to do in Switzerland?"

Morris shook his head. He was tired. He'd had too much sex and too much anxiety, and now one too many conversations with people who were irrelevant to him, except as tools in his kit.

"Tomorrow," said Morris. "Dr. Li and I will explain it all to you tomorrow. But tonight we want you to stay here with us at the institute.

We have a bedroom upstairs, where some of the other fellows will be staying, too. We can send someone to Girton to get anything you need tonight. How does that sound?"

"I don't know," said the Chinese.

Morris's voice was sharper now. This was not the time to challenge him, not when he needed to crash.

"I'm sorry, I must not have heard you right, Mr. Bo. Did you say, 'I don't know'? That's the wrong answer. The right answer is, 'Thank you very much, Mr. Birkman. Yes, I would be happy to stay here with you and Dr. Li.'"

The Chinese nodded. Morris called for Dr. Li and the guard to get the kid out of the way so he could sleep.

Before he went to bed, Morris opened the Scala manual that Roger had given him. Stuck between several pages in the middle were an index card and a stapled list of information that ran several sheets.

Morris studied the list. It showed the usernames and passwords of the systems administrators of several dozen central banks around the world, along with their routing codes and SWIFT addresses for depositing payments or making withdrawals. It was a carefully chosen list: Some of the banks represented countries that were very rich, and others were from impoverished nations where people lived on several hundred dollars a year. Included with the information for each bank was the account number and administrator password for its treasury account at the Bank for International Settlements. It was information that could only come through an intelligence service, but Morris knew that it wasn't one associated with the United States.

He put the stapled list in his safe. It was a sublimely useful document, in the way that Ramona Kyle knew it would be.

Morris looked at the index card, which was the other item tucked into the computer book. It listed an address in London and a time and date less than a week hence. Morris told himself that he would stay away from this meeting; he would use this "Roger's" material, wherever it came from, but he would keep his distance from the man himself.

24

MILTON KEYNES, ENGLAND

Edward Junot traveled to England by cargo container. It was fitted with a bed, a reclining chair for reading and listening to music on his headphones, a store of food and drink, a chemical toilet and, at Junot's particular request, a set of free weights. It resembled an isolation cell in a high-security prison, except that the ventilation was worse. Junot had protested that he would rather swim across the North Sea, but his handler in Denver said he had no choice; this was the most secure route back to England, where the boss was waiting for him. His identity had been blown, and the authorities had him on watch lists at the regular air and sea border crossings. If Junot didn't like his travel arrangements he could complain to Hubert Birkman personally on arrival.

Junot sat in the crate in Rotterdam for two days before it was loaded onto a container vessel bound for Britain. He could hear the noise of the port, day and night: the trucks and trains arriving with their cargoes, the cranes loading them in great stacks onboard the container vessels; the hulking ships steaming out of the water maze of the port. He heard the pelting of rain on the crate and the creak of the metal frame as it rattled in the wind. The intense sounds made it seem like living in an iron lung. He could hear everything but see nothing. For Junot, compact and heavily muscled, the only release was to work the weights, curling the heavy pods toward him with arms taut as metal cable.

On the third day his carton was loaded onto its mother ship. He could feel the pincers of the crane tighten around the steel frame and imagined the metal crate floating through space, a wingless flying box, and being lowered toward its stack on the boat.

The container hit the deck with a hard thump. Junot heard the shouts of the ship's crew, voices spattering out English, Greek, Tagalog and a half dozen more languages. The crew moved in ordered chaos as the ship cast off its lines and headed out of port, chugging slowly at first, guided by a pilot and nudged along by tugs, and then faster with the ship's wake breaking at the bow and washing astern in a continuous waterfall. They steamed free of port and into the North Sea, where the roll of the ocean waves settled into a regular rhythm.

The voyage itself took less than twenty-four hours, passing from Rotterdam across the North Sea toward the Humber Estuary. Junot's handler had told him that his container would be off-loaded in Grimsby, an ancient port at the southern mouth of the Humber. The larger port of Hull farther upstream was too busy; too much cargo and too many watchers. Better to land in the secondary anchorage.

Junot heard the shouts near his container while the vessel was still out in the rolling swell. His crate and a few others were readied for this first stop on the big ship's voyage. The ship slowed, banking its engines and reversing its propeller and then eased forward toward the quay. From onshore came the shouts of the dockside crew, in the thick knotted dialect of north England. The boat slowed to an idling drift; when the lines were secure, the vessel jerked backward and then forward, before it came still. The giant crablike claws of the dockside crane grabbed Junot's metal box and cranked it ashore, where it landed with a thud.

Outside, beyond Junot's view, the afternoon was a cool cerulean blue, the color compacted in the low light of the northern latitude. The vessel that had brought him from Rotterdam was docked just inside the lock that guarded the quay, past an old brick lighthouse ten stories high that had guided the passage up the North Sea for several centuries. Now that Junot knew he was on land, he felt claustrophobic in the box. He had arrived but remained trapped inside his metal container.

The crate sat on the dock many hours more: Inside, Junot gorged on what was left of his larder; he defecated in the chemical toilet whose stink now filled the metal box.

Night had fallen, bringing a sharp drop in temperature when the truck arrived to load Junot's container for the last leg of his journey. A smaller crane lifted the box; he heard the dockhand joke in his thick Geordie accent that the cargo had so little weight it must be a drug haul. They loaded it onto another pallet, this time the bed of a sixteen-wheeler, and let it sit awhile longer until Junot finally heard the cab door swing shut, and the engine spark, and a few moments later the freight truck was winding its way down the docks, and then picking up speed as it reached the open highway.

Junot made another meal, and opened another beer. He was tired of the music he had brought along, so put aside the earphones and listened to the whistle of the wind and the whirr of the road and felt that peculiar sense of pressure on his body as the airflow bowed the metal box.

The truck rumbled south through the night along the motorway, past the smells and noises of industrial cities whose lights were barely visible through cracks in the metal shell. The truck's rhythmic sway on its fat tires produced a low hum that lulled Junot to sleep in his reclining chair, making him forget even the rank smell inside his box.

Junot awoke when he heard someone pounding on the heavy lock on his door, and then banging the metal levers that sealed his container. He roused himself, gave his bearded face a slap and pulled up his trousers.

"Is this the Denver cargo?" called out a familiar voice, thin but insistent. There was a pause and then he repeated the phrase: "Is this the Denver cargo, goddamn it?" Junot had forgotten the recognition code.

Junot pounded three times on the metal frame, paused and then banged twice more. He repeated a second time this encrypted drumming; three beats, then two. The man outside swore as he struggled with the steel bars that fastened the crate, and then the metal door swung open wide.

"Jesus! It smells like shit in there," said James Morris, peering into the dark vault.

"Fuck you," said Junot, emerging unsteadily from the crate and walking down the metal cargo ramp. "You put me in here, you prick. It's like being buried alive. Try it yourself next time, Pownzor."

Junot was rubbing his eyes. His legs were wobbly. He stood in the unloading bay of a warehouse. The driver had vanished. From the angle of the sun, it appeared to be early morning. He hadn't recognized Morris at first with his wig.

"Where the fuck are we?" asked Junot.

"Milton Keynes," answered Morris.

"Who's he?"

"It's not a person, it's a place. Milton Keynes is north of London. It's near Wolverton, if that's any help. Denver picked it because nobody would care what arrived here."

"Well, thanks for that." Junot looked back at the container and shook his head. "Fucking nightmare, this was, for a trip that should take an hour in an airplane. What's going on? Why are you shipping me around in a box?"

"You are very hot, my friend. Headquarters has put out a detain-on-sight order on you. You'll have to disappear for a while."

"What do they know?"

"Don't worry about it. It will all blow over. Meanwhile, take a shower so I don't have to smell you anymore. Then we'll talk."

Morris led Junot to an old Vauxhall station wagon. They drove a few miles west to a bed-and-breakfast overlooking a well-mown green lawn. Junot disappeared for a scrub in the bath. He lay down on the bed after he had toweled off and was going to take a few minutes' rest, but he quickly fell asleep and was awakened an hour later by Morris pounding on the door.

"Get up. We need to talk," said Morris. He was animated, even jocular, in directing a member of his secret staff.

Junot dressed quickly and followed his boss down to the Vauxhall in the parking lot. He had shaved his scalp and face while taking his bath, so his head looked once again like a slick and durable piece of cement. He had put in his ear studs, too.

They drove a few hundred yards down a small road to a pub called the Ostrich. Morris had already made arrangements with the owner and they were shown to a private room. The publican assured Mr. Birkman that nobody would disturb his business luncheon.

"Will you tell me what the fuck is going on?" asked Junot when he was seated at the little table and provided with a pint of pale ale.

"Don't talk so loud," said Morris in a low voice. "You're hot because I'm hot, and people have figured out that you work for me. They can't find me, so they're going after you."

"Which people are we talking about?"

"Headquarters. The London station chief has put you at the top of her personal shit list. She has alerted Five and Scotland Yard and the tooth fairy. That's why we could not bring you back in business class. Sorry."

"Susan Amato is a worthless analyst piece of shit," said Junot. "What's she doing as a station chief, anyway? Let alone making me travel in a goddamned outhouse?"

Junot's face was red. He was a choleric man, and when he was angry he had the menacing, pansexual presence of a man who would fuck or shoot anything in his way.

"Calm down," said Morris. "Susan Amato is history. Focus on the mission."

"Which mission? Hacking central banks? Or recruiting dipshits in Berlin?"

"Don't be an asshole," said Morris. "Drink your beer. Chill out."

"Okay," said Junot, taking a breath. "I'm just an enlisted man. What's next, Lieutenant?"

"We're almost there. That's why I brought you home, so we could talk. And I'm sorry about the transportation, really. It was the safest way, under the circumstances. But I'm sure it was unpleasant, and I apologize."

Morris was leaning in toward his colleague. His voice changed when he wanted something, as if a can of lubricant had been poured into the crankshaft.

"Thank you." Junot's fingers, which had been clenched on the table in tight fists, slowly uncurled.

"Let's start with Berlin. How did the recruiting trip go?"

"Aces all the way."

"Who did you pitch?"

"The guy's name is Malchik. Actually, that's his handle. You want all the details? I gave them to Denver already. He checks out."

"Yes, of course I want the details."

"His real name is Misha Popov. He lives in Germany, but he's a Russian hood. He is a serious fucking hacker. I mean it. He's got a network that's the best."

Morris shook his head. "Impossible. I've already got the best."

"I'm telling you, this guy Malchick scared me, and I'm the guy who scares other people."

Morris shrugged. "What does he have?"

"Zero-day exploits stacked up like a deck of poker chips, that's what. Plus, he has the little goonies who are going to keep cranking them out—the Cerberus Club kids, who hate big business and secrecy so much they can penetrate every bank and intelligence service and pussy parlor on the planet. And thanks to Malchik, they are unwittingly passing it to us."

"How much did he cost?"

"Twenty-five million U.S., for six months. In three installments. Wired to his account in Vaduz."

Morris sat back in his chair and shook his head. "For a hacker? He'll gag on it," he said.

"Quality costs money."

"We've never paid anybody that much."

"Pownzor, don't worry, man. If he delivers, he's worth it. If he doesn't deliver, I'll shoot him. Money-back guarantee." He pointed his finger toward Morris and pulled down his thumb like the firing hammer of a revolver.

"That's reassuring. And keep your voice down, please, especially when you are talking about shooting someone."

Junot leaned toward his boss and spoke in his ear.

"Thank me, Pownzor. Please say, *You did a good fucking job in Germany, Ed. Thanks a lot.*"

Morris backed away and shook his head.

"You want my hand on your dick? Forget it. What about Switzerland?"

"Basel is cool. Nice buildings."

"That's not what I'm asking."

"The river is beautiful, too."

"Cut the crap. Is it all wired down?"

"Food is surprisingly good."

"Fuck off, Junot. The BIS platform is ready, correct?"

"Of course it is. You saw all the lights blinking, all the beacons in place. It's phat. We own the systems administrator. What more do you need?"

"We need the database administrator. I'll dox her, too, to be safe. I just want to make sure you got out without leaving any traces."

"Clean as a Swiss asshole."

"They're going to come looking for you."

"So what? They'll find a club sandwich on room service and a four-course meal that cost a month's salary, but that's it. No traces."

Junot bobbed his big rock-hard head contentedly. Morris shrugged, which was his version of approval.

Morris was hungry. He rose and found the barman, who delivered two cottage pies and two more pints of ale.

Junot attacked the food with the ferocity of a man who hadn't had a proper meal in four days. Morris ate eccentrically, as he did everything; he skimmed off the mashed potatoes on top but left the layer of ground beef on the bottom, teasing the residue with his fork so that its surface was rippled in waves.

"Don't play with your food. That's what my mother said," said Junot when he had finished every morsel of his own cottage pie.

"Well, my mother told your mother to piss off, because her son was going to Stanford, whether he ate his hamburger or not."

Junot laughed. "I love you, boss." The chiseled bald man reached out to give him a kiss, but Morris backed away.

"You pervert," said Morris. "We need to talk about tasking your asset, and then I am out of here."

"Tasking? These are geeks, man. Let the IOC take care of them."

"We're staying away from Headquarters. Weber wants me fired, and then arrested."

"Don't pick a fight with the boss, Pownzor. Bad idea."

"I don't need Weber. My authorities are direct."

"What does that mean? 'Direct' from where?"

Morris cleared his throat.

"The top."

Junot looked at Morris skeptically.

"And the director's not in that loop?"

"Not always. You may hear gossip from your Blackwater buddies about how I'm under a cloud. Forget that. I have all the authorities I need."

Junot nodded. Loyalty was his code. But it had to be reciprocal.

"What about my money?" Junot asked.

"Denver wires it every month to the accommodation address in Warsaw, just like you wanted. But why Poland? It sounds insecure. Are you fucking someone there?"

Junot winked. "The money doesn't stay there. It goes to an account in the Caymans."

Morris rapped Junot's bald head with his knuckles. "You're not as stupid as you look," he said.

"I'm your bitch, Pownzor. Now what do you want me to tell Malchik?"

"Tell him Hubert needs to get inside big financial databases. We want exploits that will crack Linux, SWIFT, Oracle, all the trading platforms. We're going after hashed data, so we'll need to crack the hashes in real time. We need this stuff yesterday. No bullshit. He should deliver now or he can kiss the money goodbye."

"What if he asks what we're using all his exploits and hash crackers for?"

"Tell him to fuck off. We are paying him twenty-five million to deliver product, not to ask questions. If he gets too curious, it's time for your money-back guarantee."

"You are a hard dude, man."

"No, I'm not. I'm just smart."

Morris and Junot left the pub separately. Junot returned to the bed-and-breakfast, where he stayed for another day before moving on to a new safe house Morris had rented for him in the East End of London. Morris spent the afternoon on a local field trip that was the real reason he had told Denver to route Junot to Milton Keynes.

A few miles to the east of the "new town" stood a modest country house in the village of Bletchley, perhaps forty-five miles north of London, near the main railroad line that connected the capital with the north. The name of this country estate was Bletchley Park, and it was here that British cryptologists had managed to crack German "Enigma" encryption machines and read Germany's most secret messages during World War II.

The mansion house stood at the foot of a broad lawn. It was a plain house, of red brick and white clapboard, thrown up in the 1880s by a financier from London. A white cupola crowned the roof, but the rest of the structure was undistinguished by any architectural adornment. The temporary huts where the code-breakers had worked were gone. The country house still stood, its physical ordinariness a counter-monument to the brainpower that had been assembled here.

James Morris strolled the grounds where Alan Turing and the other misfit geniuses of their day had labored against the barbarians and done work that, quite literally, had saved civilization. Morris thought, immodestly but with his whole heart, that he was involved in a similar endeavor.

25

BRISTOL, ENGLAND

James Morris worked like a man who knew he was running out of time. Grantchester was too hot now: He relocated his command post to Bristol, in the West Country. It was easy to disappear, if you knew how to vacuum your electronic exhaust. From Bristol he directed the network that he had assembled. He provided each member the same template of operations: Penetrate your target with malware that finds a hole in the code; exploit through "social engineering" the human weaknesses that allow you to gain control of a systems administrator or database administrator. He stopped communicating even with the covert clearinghouse in Denver, lest they understand what he was really doing.

Morris chose Bristol for the same reason he had chosen Cambridge: It had a university that excelled in mathematics and computer science. So many amateur hackers were online that Morris could mask his own digital tracks. He took an apartment along the Queens Road, near the university, and filled it with servers and screens. He lived on caffeine in various forms and a new favorite food, Ramen noodles, which he consumed day and night.

Morris had five principal operatives: Edward Junot in East London, his gofer and enforcer; Emmanuel Li, the Chinese director of his "institute," who had left Grantchester for a new hideaway; Misha Popov, the Russian tough guy in Berlin, known by his handle "Malchik," who ran a string of unwitting German hackers; Yoav Shimansky, the Israeli who had served with the IDF's Unit 8200; and the Chinese graduate student Bo Guafeng, who tapped into his hacker connections back home. Morris had other people in other networks: hackers picked up from the semi-anarchist libertarian groups that flourished at the margins of the cyber-world. But he used them now mostly for chaff, to distract and deceive.

Morris gave each member of his core group a basic toolkit. They had an updated version of the attack suite known as Metasploit, beloved by "white hat" penetration testers and "black hat" hackers who wanted to take systems down. When Morris's team members had gained access to a system, they could steal its files by typing *download*; insert files by typing *upload*; or create a keylogger that recorded every touch of the target's finger, simply by typing *keyscsan_start*. The tools were all pre-configured: *hashdump* stole the Windows hashes that were supposedly protecting passwords and data; *timestop* changed the recorded times when files had been created or altered. Morris's team could disable security systems, add backdoors and encode malware into .exe files that were nearly undetectable.

"It's too easy," Morris liked to say. And it was.

But Metasploit was only the start. Morris provided his operatives with newer, fancier tools that could surmount controls that had been created to deal with Metasploit. At times they'd use older tools like Back Orifice, a pun on Microsoft's BackOffice software for servers, which could control computers running the Windows operating system. They had ProRat, another Windows tool that allowed insertion of backdoor Trojan horses, aka RATs, or remote access tools, which could infect all the computers on the same local area network. They had Sub7, yet another remote access tool. It was like a medicine cabinet stocked with poison pills.

Morris liked to hack his own team members, to keep them nimble (and convince himself that the Pownzor hadn't lost his touch). But it was also a way of sharing the ideology that Morris had believed since his youth, even as he had gone to work for the U.S. government. He was an advocate for freedom. Like so many other hackers and whistleblowers, he imagined that the United States had been hijacked by evil bureaucrats; his experience at the CIA had only deepened that suspicion. The United

States had inherited the imperial mission of Great Britain, without real-izing it. The British had created the CIA as the operational arm of this post-imperial regime, with Americans toddling along behind. Morris was determined to break that chain. He had imagined two months ago that the new CIA director, Graham Weber, might be an ally. But that was folly. Weber was caught in the ooze and muck.

Ground zero for Morris was the Bank for International Settlements in Basel. Over the past weeks, he had been studying this financial epi-center. He gathered books from online sellers, using several dummy accounts. The BIS in Morris's mind had become the hub to which all the spokes of command were connected. It provided the world's central banks with liquidity, it bought and sold their gold and other instruments that were part of the international repository of financial reserves. It set the capital standards that were the global financial system's measure of international health. It was the umpire and scorekeeper: It maintained the records attesting which institutions were healthy with adequate reserves and which were dangerously undercapitalized. If it was hacked, he could be a digital Robin Hood, taking money from rich countries and giving it to poor ones.

Morris believed that by disrupting the BIS he was restoring the state of nature: Malchik, Yoav, Bo and the rest regularly found their screens going dark and then coming alight again with the messages about One World, and the reign of Internet freedom that would follow the end of the old order of 1945. He sent the fastidious Dr. Emmanuel Li pictures of kitty cats and sunsets and people holding hands, with the message: *Keep them Free: One World*. He thought Li would be reassured by these images of life as a Coca-Cola commercial.

From his apartment on Queen's Road, Morris would look down onto the Bristol docks to the Avon River that flowed west into the Bristol Channel. By day, it was an ugly industrial vista. But by night, under the lights, the old bridges and wharves took on a soft lemony glow. Morris would sit on his deck after a day of coding, and watch the lights refract and dilate with the beat of his heart. He took the edge off with a shot of brandy and then retreated to bed, where he read himself to sleep with his monographs about the BIS.

The more Morris read about the "Tower of Basel," as one book called it, the more he saw the BIS as a compendium of all the mistakes and conspiracies of the twentieth century. The bank had been created in 1930 to manage the flow of German reparations payments, and its profits were supposed to go to Germany. In the 1930s, it came to be seen as a financial backstop for the Nazis. The Allies seemed united in wanting to liquidate the BIS after World War II, but bizarrely the British had insisted on rescuing it during the 1944 Bretton Woods negotiations—to the point that John Maynard Keynes threatened to walk out of the conference if an American plan for defunding should be approved. Keynes was so agitated about the BIS issues that observers feared he'd suffered a heart attack. The Allies finally agreed that the BIS should be "liquidated at the earliest possible moment," which Keynes interpreted as, "Not very early!"

And on it rolled, for seven decades: Until James Morris was instructed to shatter this symbol of Anglo-American tutelage.

Morris used the BIS routing codes and account numbers he had received from Roger to tailor his attack. These codes and passwords made it easier to program the Robin Hood part of his scheme, moving funds from account to account. He had his team develop a string of backups, in case the BIS plan wasn't enough. This second tier included commercial banks in London and Manchester whose software supported the Bank of England's reserve management; the London stock exchange; a hedge fund in London and a private-equity fund in Edinburgh. But these were fallbacks.

To prepare his attack, Morris and his researchers had gathered a basket of exploits that could penetrate all the major systems used by financial institutions: They targeted the "Corebank" and "Alltel" software of Fidelity Information Systems; Oracle's "Banking Platform" and "Flexcube" software; the Swiss-based Temenos "T24" system; the Indian-owned Infosys "Finacle" suite; the London-based Misys "Bank-Fusion Universal" system; and the German "SAP for Banking." These software platforms shared a common unintended feature: They all were targets for a determined assault.

Morris admonished the members of his network to pay special attention to backup systems: Where were they? How could they be

accessed? How was the mirrored data from the main institution transferred to the backup center? How frequently was it backed up? Morris
had prepared for this as well, studying the leading software vendors that
provided data protection and backup services for the financial industry.

Morris had cunningly dissected the world of global finance. His
target in Basel touched, at one or two degrees of separation, nearly every
institution around the world. A shock wave transmitted through these
institutions would create not just a disruption, but something more. The
financial system was like a snowflake: so intricate in its fractal patterns,
but so fragile.

Morris was shopping for milk and cereal and fruit juice at the Tesco near
his apartment when he noticed someone was following him. It wasn't
fancy clandestine surveillance, with teams of people in relay and layers
of coverage, but just one person. He was compact and well dressed, with
the muscular build of a soldier. He was wearing a blue peacoat and sucking on a piece of hard candy.

It was only when Morris caught his intense eyes that he realized it
was the same man who had approached him in the pub before he had
quit Grantchester, the man Ramona Kyle had introduced as Roger. He
had given Morris an index card with the time and place for a meeting
in London, but Morris had let it pass two days before. Now, somehow,
Roger had found his new command post.

The man followed Morris through the checkout at the market and
then down the street to a café, where Morris had planned to get an
almond-flavored latte before he went back to work in his lodgings over
Queens Road. When Morris sat down, the man took the table next to
him. When he got up to move, the man simply walked over to Morris's
table and took the closest chair.

Morris's face was impassive, but he was frightened. This was the
first sign of surveillance he'd seen; the first indication that anyone knew
where he was since he left Cambridge. He played dumb.

"Do I know you?" asked Morris, peering through his spectacles at
the young man in the peacoat.

"I'm Roger," said the young man, extending his hand. "You missed our meeting."

The cowl of a foreign accent shrouded his voice. It could be Russian, Polish, Romanian; somewhere east of the Danube. He didn't make any attempt to cover it this time.

"I don't do meetings," said Morris. He grabbed his package and rose from the table and began moving away. But Roger was quicker. He pushed one of the light café chairs so that it was blocking Morris's preferred exit path, and with the other hand pulled Morris's bag of groceries away from him and slung it over his shoulder.

"I'll walk with you," said Roger. "Don't worry, I'm alone."

"I don't want to talk to anyone. Go away or I will call the police."

Roger smiled. "Really? I don't think you will call the police. No games, please. I will talk, and you listen, okay?"

Morris shook his head. He headed the opposite direction from his flat, down toward the quayside along the river.

"You have a chance to be a great man, Mr. Morris, do you know that?" Keeping up, pace for pace.

"Fuck off," said Morris.

"Not so loud," said Roger. "And I mean it. You can be the man who changes history: The one who stands up for liberty, who says no to the police state. People will tell stories about you and sing songs. Maybe you will not be appreciated back home in America, but in the world you will be a hero. Yes. But you need help."

"From you? Forget it. And anyway, I don't know what you're talking about. I'm an American graduate student."

"Okay, fine. Whatever you say. But think of Brother Snowden. He was all alone, just like you. He did not have a pot to piss in. Everyone abandoned him. But then he had friends. Yes, Russian friends. I am not embarrassed to say it. We are the home of the hacker, the true home. We are the friend of WikiLeaks and Anonymous. We are the new generation. It is like the 1930s. The gods are dead. There is a new world coming. We are the helpers, the facilitators."

Morris stopped. The sun was glinting off the canal in the distance. They were alone, out of earshot of anyone on the streets.

"Who are you?" Morris demanded. "And don't give me that 'Roger' shit. Where did you get that information about the BIS?"

"Specialists provided it. People who share your cause."

"You *don't* share my cause. You're a Russian intelligence officer. What else could you be? What I don't understand is why my friend Ramona wanted to introduce us."

"Your friend Ramona is wise. She is a realist. She knows that you are part of a great movement, but it needs help. You are taking on a super-power. You need friends."

"Not Russian friends! Are you kidding me? Russia is a police state."

"Look, James, you do not have the luxury to make such fine distinctions. There is a great struggle going on in the world, between the arrogant power of the American and British services and the yearning of the world to escape. It is light and dark. You cannot debate who is pure enough to be your friend. I am sorry. That is selfish. You must win, and we are the only people who are strong enough to help you."

The Russian talked with a cold passion, like a man who believed that he had history on his side. The NKVD agent handlers who recruited the Cambridge Five in the 1930s must have spoken with the same seductive, dominating voice. The world was at a crossroads; a principled person had to choose sides.

Morris was shaking his head.

"Peddle it somewhere else, my friend."

But the Russian was undeterred. He was a good officer, or he had the true faith, or maybe a combination.

"I mean it! You should come in from the cold, like Snowden did. The raid you are planning on the BIS is fine, but it is nothing compared to what you could do with us. We can create a League of Internet Freedom. Putin, he will be gone. All those people in Moscow with their whores and diamond rings and Mercedes, they are finished. The trench coat boys from the special services will be gone, too. All gone! This is the time for us, people like you and me. What do you say?"

Morris shook his head. This Russian would destroy him. How was he going to get rid of him? He thought about his weapons. He had only one, really, which was to self-destruct.

"Look, Roger, or whatever your name is, I don't know who you think

I am, or what I'm planning to do. But I will tell you one thing. If I ever see you again, I will abort my mission. I won't explain, but let me say that from your perspective, that would be very stupid."

"Strike a blow for freedom," said Roger.

Morris pushed his glasses back on his nose and stood up straight. He was half a head taller than the Russian.

"Yes," said Morris. "I may just do that. But alone."

"I have more information for you. More codes and addresses."

"I don't want it. Go away. I mean it."

Morris walked quickly along the banks of the Avon, his shoes clattering on the cobblestones. He stopped when he reached the gates of a lock and looked back, but he couldn't glimpse the Russian. They could see him, evidently, but Morris decided that it didn't matter, so long as they didn't get in the way.

26

WASHINGTON

Dr. Ariel Weiss put a hand-lettered notice on her door that read CONSULT THE DOCUMENTATION. That was a geek-speak way of saying, *Solve it yourself,* to the young officers of the Information Operations Center who were accustomed to wandering by her desk and asking her advice. In every office, there's someone to whom people turn when they have problems, and Weiss had become that person since she'd come to work for James Morris, who had the people skills of a mollusk. But Weiss's life was more complicated now, and she no longer had time to be anyone's big sister.

Weber had given her the assignment of turning her boss's operations upside down—to pull at the threads of Morris's cloak until the fabric gave way. But her search had proven far more difficult than she had expected. Ed Junot's cover identity had crumpled in Germany, but now he had disappeared again, and Weiss didn't know where to look for him. She suspected that Morris must have secret help from somewhere else in the government, or somewhere outside, or perhaps both. But his movements were too well hidden.

Weiss had been staring at her twin computer screens for several hours, searching for traces of Morris's movements, and she needed a rest. She opened her door and stepped out into the indoor cavern that was the operations room of her center.

The floor was laid out like a Silicon Valley start-up or a Google research lab—the sort of places where her colleagues had worked before joining the agency. At the far end of the room was an open refreshment area with free food and drinks; stockpiles of caffeine to keep the code writers humming. These were Weiss's people more than Morris's. They were loyal, attentive and needy: a community of hyper-intelligent people who had decided to invest their brainpower on behalf of their country, rather than with big corporations. They wanted a psychic return, if not a financial one.

Weiss was dressed in her usual uniform of black tapered slacks, a close-fitting white cotton shirt and the tailored leather jacket she'd bought the day Morris made her his deputy. She left her office heading for the free food. She wanted something hot and something cold, a coffee and a Diet Coke, and maybe something sweet, and then she would go back to cracking the massively encrypted code that was James Morris.

Alvin Crump, the leader of one of the Iran cyber-teams, saw Weiss leave the office with her head down, lost in thought. His desk was in her path. He rolled out his chair so she would trip over him if she didn't stop.

"Hey, Dr. Weiss, 'sup?" he asked.

Weiss's eyes opened wide as if waking from a trance. She came to an abrupt stop in front of Crump's desk.

"The usual," she said. "Lots of subroutines, but no compiler. How about you, Crump? Have you located the Supreme Leader's opium connection yet?"

"Working on it," said the young man. He ran electronic operations against leadership figures in Tehran, using bits of malware and trapdoors installed so widely that the Iranians must wonder if the computer bugs flowed in with the electricity and water. Weiss's reference to the opium dealer was a joke, but just barely. Crump's team had tracked every movement of the top Iranian leaders for so long they might have written the ayatollahs' personal calendars.

Weiss started off toward the coffee bar, but Crump was still in her way.

"Is everything okay?" asked the software engineer. "You're scaring us a little, honestly. We've never seen you work so hard. Your door is always closed, and the screens are turned so nobody can see what you're working on. Are we going to war or something?"

Weiss laughed, but she could see the concern on Crump's face. People from nearby cubicles were listening, too. Weiss made these people think that what they did was cool and sexy. When she was preoccupied, so were they. She turned to Crump and the half dozen others nearby who were craning toward her.

"I'm sorry I've been such a poop the last few days. I'm crashing on something for Pownzor, and you all know how crazy he can get. But everything's cool. If there was any trouble, he'd be back here to micromanage it, right?"

"We're beginning to wonder if Pownzor really exists," said Crump. "Has he been fired?"

"Of course not!" she said, waving her hand dismissively. "Whatever made you think that?"

"Gossip. It's all over the building."

Weiss deflected the query with another brush of her hand.

"That's all bullshit. Would I still be here, if Pownzor was in trouble? Answer: No. So everyone chill, please."

"If you say so," said Crump. He looked relieved. So did the others who were near enough to hear the conversation, many of whom were already sending messages to their colleagues on the chat screen. Dr. Weiss said everything was fine, so it must be true. This might be an organization of professional liars, but Weiss was seen by her colleagues as someone who never lied.

She got her coffee and Coke—real, not diet—and took two cookies, one oatmeal and one chocolate chip with macadamia nuts. It was as many calories as she normally ate in a day, but she needed energy in a hurry.

When Weiss returned to her office, she printed out copies of the budget items she had been studying all morning on-screen. Weber had asked her for a picture and she would give him one: She laid out the sheets on her desk like pieces of a jigsaw puzzle and began to look for the straight edges that formed a border. She needed to find patterns in the data that could tell a story of what Morris was doing.

It took Weiss many long hours, but eventually she found symmetry in Morris's movements, once she stripped away the random noise. He always traveled overseas in alias; she could show that because she had access to his real-name credit card accounts. They were never used when he was away. That meant that the overseas trips were undeclared to the local intelligence services, who knew Morris by his true name. Whatever platforms Morris used overseas weren't part of the IOC's regular structure. Weiss could show that because she reviewed all the IOC's official foreign basing and travel expenditures and signed off on them once a quarter for the inspector general.

There was another recurring feature, so predictable that it was a marker. At some point every six weeks or so, Morris traveled to Denver, sometimes only for a few hours. Weiss knew about the trips because she had access to Morris's IOC calendar, to coordinate his Washington schedule. She could see the repeated notations: "DEN," which was the airport code for Denver International Airport. She never saw the bills, which weren't handled in the IOC's regular accounting channel. That meant Morris must have a different compartmented spending authority, separate from his regular line. They were off-budget trips, in other words. It was as if Morris were visiting a second information ops center, except that the organization didn't have an official presence in Denver.

Overlaying one anomaly on top of the other, Weiss could hypothesize a larger shape: Morris was running a separate network of agents and operations overseas, and he was coordinating these activities through a covert base in Denver. She'd heard talk over the last year about joint operations with the NSA, but they were never discussed. Perhaps that's what the Denver office was about. It was a plausible structure for his operations, but it didn't explain what he was doing.

To fill in the picture, Weiss needed evidence of how Morris's off-book operation had been spending money. At first that seemed impossible: How could she assess the budget of a compartmented program to which she didn't have access? But after a day of spinning her wheels, Weiss had an idea. Even if she wasn't authorized to enter this black area, she still might be able to observe what was going in and out.

Weiss needed to tell the story in a way that Graham Weber would understand. She spent another few days assembling her jigsaw pieces. They came in the form of budget authorization numbers. Morris had given her passwords to request operational funds from the comptroller in his absence. He would give her the numerical code of the item for payment, and she would make the formal request to release funds. It saved him time, and allowed a continuous flow of funds when he was traveling.

But as Weiss went deeper into Morris's password-protected accounts, she saw that not all of the fund requests went to the numbered budget accounts that were controlled by the CIA. Some went to unspecified "interagency" accounts whose provenance was unknown to Weiss. She went through the painstaking work of examining every payment request that had passed through any of Morris's password accounts and checked them against line accounts for IOC's official activities. When she had finished her culling, she had identified five payment requests outside CIA internal controls.

The rogue payments varied in size, from a few hundred thousand dollars up to a recent authorization for $8.3 million that Weiss had submitted a week or so back. Who was receiving these funds? She didn't have official access to that information, but Weiss had been a hacker long enough to understand the subtle ways to trick people into revealing secrets, through techniques that were politely known as "social engineering."

Late in the afternoon, Weiss called the executive director's office, which handled daily management of the agency and also liaison with other parts of the intelligence community. She asked for Rosamund Burke, a budget officer who normally supervised her IOC accounts. She called in the afternoon, in the expectation that Burke wouldn't want to hassle with procedures and red tape late in the day.

"Hi, Rosie. It's Ariel. I need a favor."

"Just ask," said Burke, who was part of the old-girls' mafia that was increasingly powerful in the agency.

"I need something. My boss is traveling again and he wanted me to chase something down."

"That man is a whirling dervish. Is he married?"

"Pownzor? No way. He can't stay put."

"What do you need, girl?"

"He wants me to double-check some items we sent up for payment. He thinks he may have miscoded some of them."

"Typical. Which ones are they?"

Ariel ran through the five numbered accounts from the off-budget group. She added three more normal payment orders to mask her intent. When Weiss had finished the list, Burke read it back to make sure she had the digits right.

"Are these all yours?" she asked. It was a normal question, not a suspicious query.

Weiss wondered whether to bluff. No, she thought. The best lies are the ones coated in truth.

"They're a mix," she answered. "Some are IOC accounts and others are ones Morris is running separately, where he asks me to handle the paperwork. Protect me. I don't want to get him in trouble. He's worried we're paying the wrong people."

"He's a little ragged around the edges, isn't he, your boss? Not the first. What do you need?"

"Payment information: Where the money goes."

"You want to do this off-line, by phone?"

"That's what Morris wants. He doesn't want a paper trail, in case he screwed up."

"This is way off-line, dearie. Some of those budget accounts are run through the DNI's office. I get cc'd with a payment notification, but I'm not supposed to circulate them even on the seventh floor."

"Right, Morris mentioned something about that," Weiss lied.

"Okay. This call didn't happen. And if there's any question, you're going to need to call Hazel Philby in the DNI comptroller's office."

"Sorry for the hassle. I just don't want my boss to get in trouble for late payments."

"Okay. Here goes nothing. I don't have true names for recipients, obviously. Crypts only."

"I don't even need the crypts. I just want to confirm the payments."

Burke punched the most recent payment order number into her computer and then read out the detail.

"FJBULLET is the latest. That was requested last week. He's German, from that digraph. Eight-point-three million dollars, payable immediately to an account in Liechtenstein. That one says 'EJ' in parenthesis, after the crypt."

"Uh-huh." Her voice was flat, but the initials got her attention.

"You need the account number?"

"No, that's okay."

"Next, SMTOUGH, two hundred fifty pounds sterling, payable to an estate agent in Cambridge, Keith Aubrey, for property that's listed as 'Grantchester.' I assume that's in England, with those place names and that digraph, but you never know. That one says in parenthesis, 'Li.' Got that?"

"Yes, that checks out."

Burke read through three payment orders that were for regular IOC operations. With these, Weiss already knew all the details: One was to pay agents inside a Russian computer security firm, another was to pay contractors in Atlanta who were working on offensive cyber-tools, a third was a onetime recruitment bonus for a systems administrator in Cairo who had been pitched by an IOC officer seconded to the Near East Division.

Weiss listened attentively to each one, even though the information was useless to her purpose. Eventually, Burke hit on several more of Morris's mystery accounts.

"We've got LCPLUM, must be Chinese if it's 'LC,' six million dollars to a numbered account in Macao. That one also has 'Li' in parenthesis. Got that?"

"Yes. What else?"

"Two more on the list you gave me. I have BELOVELY, that's Poland if memory serves, for one-point-five million euros, payable to an account in the Caymans, okay? That one says 'EJ,' too. And I have MJCRISP, which I think is Israel, though we don't see that one much, and it's for two hundred fifty thousand dollars, payable to an account in London, fancy that, and it has 'Li' again, in parens. Is that everything you need?"

"Yes, that's the lot. You're a superstar, Rosie."

"It's true, I am. I have to hustle or I'll miss my ride. Like I said, you need to check this with Hazel Philby. But don't let on you know they're DNI interagency operations."

"Got it. I'll check with Morris as soon as he's back. He's the only one who'll know. Maybe you could give me that bank account number in the Caymans."

"Sure, dearie, but then I seriously have to go. The Caymans routing number is 2108746, repeat that, 2108746. The account number is 57173646, repeating 57173646. Have we got all that?"

"Yes. Sorry to be such a pain. It's just that things pile up when the boss is away, and Morris is always away."

"Ciao, ciao."

Weiss hung up the phone and took a deep breath. She was a better liar than she might appear. She studied the notes she had taken while Burke was talking. She had five data points; that should be enough to deduce something about Morris's hidden operation that would satisfy the director's curiosity.

She stared at the cryptonyms and the amounts. It was easy enough to make some guesses. FJBULLET must be a Germany-based agent, and a very expensive one. His information was good enough that Morris was willing to pay top dollar. SMTOUGH sounded like a safe house operation in Britain, though the rent was so large it sounded more like an office than a flat. LCPLUM was for someone in China, probably an agent or a small network, and someone who couldn't come out to the West and needed the money in Macao. BELOVELY was an asset operating in Poland, or at least getting his mail there, who was hiding his money in the Caribbean. And MJCRISP was apparently an Israeli living in England and wanting access to the money, as if it were an overt salary.

The intriguing items were the letters in parentheses, "EJ" and "Li." They had to be the work names of Morris's case officers. Li could be anybody; it seemed like every other Chinese had that surname. But Weiss knew from her earlier digging that one of Weber's key assets was a former military officer named Edward Junot.

She sent a flash cable to the London station and asked them to check "Li" and the name of the estate agent, Keith Aubrey, and the Grantchester address. They came back in less than an hour with an ID for Dr. Emmanuel Li and an address for his research institute. Weiss cabled back and asked the station to rumble the location. They sent someone to knock on the door that night. The Grantchester office was empty, and the mail was piled up behind the slot.

Weiss decided she had enough to go back to Weber. She could

show that Morris was running operations in Europe and Asia that were outside the CIA's control. If he had authority to recruit and pay these agents, Weiss had never seen anything on the books. The authority must reside in another compartment, controlled by the director of National Intelligence.

Weiss put a new SIM card into her Nokia and texted Weber's phone: *Meet at 2200 at your drop. Trick or treat.*

Late that afternoon, Marie delivered the last tray of that day's classified paperwork for the director. These were several cables from stations overseas, two intelligence reports requiring approval before dissemination downtown and a draft National Intelligence Estimate on the situation in Syria. She brought the collection of documents into the office and laid it on the director's desk.

Weber was on the phone. He was talking to Ruth Savin about an inspector general's report that had to be delivered soon to the congressional intelligence committees. There were permissions for permissions these days, and reviews of reviews.

When Weber finished with Savin, he turned to the tray of classified material. He read the cables quickly, and penciled notes in the margins that he would share later with Sandra Bock. He leafed through the intelligence reports and signed his initials on the cover page. The Syria NIE he reviewed more carefully, especially the executive summary at the beginning. Peter Pingray, the retiring deputy director whose last day was Friday, had already signed off on it. It was a revision of an earlier draft that Loomis Braden had rejected because it didn't note the agency's warnings about Al-Qaeda's presence in northeast Syria. A footnote had been added.

Weber was about to replace the draft NIE in the basket when a plain white envelope tumbled out. It seemed to have been caught in the back pages of the lengthy intelligence assessment.

Weber took the white envelope in his hands. It had no mark of origin or return address. On the front was printed his name, *Graham Weber*, in black type. Weber opened the envelope and removed a single sheet of paper inside. He had the unsettling feeling that he was repeating an identical moment in time. He opened the folded paper and read the words:

> *The traitor appears not a traitor; he speaks in accents familiar to his victims, and he wears their face and their arguments, he appeals to the baseness that lies deep in the hearts of all men. He rots the soul of a nation, he works secretly and unknown in the night to undermine the pillars of the city, he infects the body politic so that it can no longer resist. A murderer is less to fear. The traitor is the plague.*
>
> —Marcus Tullius Cicero

YOU ARE LOOKING IN THE WRONG PLACE.

Weber was unsettled. He put the sheet back in the envelope and put it on his desk. The boyish face was pale. Sweat beaded on his forehead. He buzzed Marie and asked her to come in from the anteroom. She thought at first that he was just calling for her to remove the classified paperwork, and began to reach for the tray, but he stopped her.

Weber held up the white envelope with his name typed on it.

"This fell out of the draft NIE. It's addressed to me. Do you have any idea how it got there?"

Marie examined the envelope. The director didn't ask her to open it, so she left the flap closed. Then she examined the intelligence estimate, ruffled the pages and shook it to see if anything else was caught inside, and then quickly examined the other documents that had been in the tray. She could see that the director was upset.

"I don't know where this could have come from, Mr. Director. I sorted the papers before I put them in your tray. If this fell out of the NIE, it must have been there when it arrived at my desk. That's the only thing I can think of."

Weber patted his forehead with a tissue. He didn't care if his secretary saw him sweating. She was one of the few people in this building he had grown to trust.

"Where do the NIEs come from, Marie, before they come to this office? Who originates them?"

"Well, they're prepared by the National Intelligence Council, which collects views from all the agencies. They come through the deputy, Mr. Pingray, to you. He doesn't read much these days. Ms. Bock can explain it better than me."

"No, you're doing fine, Marie. Where does the National Intelligence Council paperwork come from?"

"It's part of the Office of the Director of National Intelligence, sir, over at Liberty Crossing."

"So they work for Mr. Hoffman, the people who put these things together? And the paperwork would start with Mr. Hoffman's organization, is that right?"

"Yes, Mr. Director. I can take this envelope and walk it back. We can ask for forensics on it, too. See if there are any prints or DNA. Would that help? I can call the Office of Security now."

Weber thought a moment.

"Maybe later, Marie. I'll hold on to it for now. It's probably nothing: Just a practical joke. There are a lot of cutups around here, right?"

"Yes, sir," she said, taking the tray.

Weber stared out the window. He had wanted to manage a creative, dynamic organization like a business, and what he had encountered instead was a Rubik's Cube of interlocking conspiracy. Was he looking in the wrong place? The disturbing fact was: He didn't know. He had to think carefully about each of the strands of thread that had passed through his hands in these few short weeks, and decide whether he could see a pattern.

Early that afternoon, before her planned rendezvous with Graham Weber, Ariel Weiss went shopping at the Whole Foods Market on Leesburg Pike in Tysons Corner. She had run out of skim milk, Greek yogurt, breakfast cereal and fruit, which were the things she most liked to eat. She had been taking her time, browsing in the crowded aisles of the market, when she glimpsed someone she recognized. His name was Dan Aronson. They had dated for nearly a year when she first joined the agency. Back then, he had worked for the CIA's Directorate of Science and Technology, but eighteen months ago he had moved over to the

Office of the Director of National Intelligence to supervise compartmented technology projects.

Weiss didn't want to see him. Ex-boyfriends were dead wires for her. She had initially been drawn to Aronson partly for the same reason she liked the CIA. She enjoyed the cult of secrets, and he was an initiate. But the claustrophobia of the clandestine world had gradually choked their relationship. They knew too much, in too small a space: They couldn't talk about it, and they couldn't not talk about it. Eventually Weiss had a secret that she really couldn't tell Aronson, which was that she was seeing someone else. He found out soon enough. When people have been intimate, they can smell betrayal. Weiss turned her cart away from the yogurt case and Dan Aronson and headed the other way.

Aronson caught up with her in the next aisle. He pretended that it was a random encounter. He proposed that they have an espresso in the Whole Foods coffee bar. Weiss protested that she had to finish her shopping and get home; she had a date later that evening. But Aronson wouldn't be put off. They rolled their carts past the fruit and the cut flowers, and into the little café.

Aronson tried to make small talk when they sat down, telling her how well she looked and asking after mutual friends, but Weiss cut him off. It was too much of a coincidence, running into him this way after nearly two years, and she had learned not to believe in coincidences.

"What's this about, Dan? You're making me uncomfortable."

"So . . . I heard people talking about you in the office this afternoon," he said. "I thought you should know."

"You mean someone told you to come find me and have a talk."

"Yes, basically. People told me you were poking around some files that are off-limits, and that you might get in trouble. You can't do that anymore, Ariel. Even if you have Top Secret Codeword clearance, if you start making 'anomalous requests' these days, the alarm bells start ringing."

So that was it: After talking to Weiss that afternoon, Rosamund Burke had immediately called her friend Hazel Philby in the DNI's office to report the conversation, and Aronson had been summoned to chase down his ex-flame. So much for loyalty among the old-girls' network.

"Did you follow me here?" asked Weiss.

"Not exactly. Someone else did. I was nearby, at Liberty Crossing, so they told me to come find you."

Weiss shook her head. "Wow, that's creepy."

"Sorry. This wasn't the way I wanted us to meet again."

"Screw that," said Weiss. "What's the message you're supposed to deliver?"

"It's not a message. It's an invitation. You should come see Director Hoffman, as soon as possible. It's a personal request from him."

"I'll have to clear it with my boss, Mr. Weber."

"Don't do that," said Aronson. "That's part of the DNI's request. He wants to keep this private. He said that, otherwise, he'll have to tell Security about your unauthorized request to the comptroller. That's a serious violation."

Weiss gave him a contemptuous look.

"What a little shit you've become. I'm disappointed."

Aronson ignored her remark. He had the opaque look of an intelligence officer whose every thought was compartmented and censored.

"What should I tell Mr. Hoffman?" he asked.

Weiss thought a moment. It was her own boss, Graham Weber, who had asked her to chase down the information about Morris. But she wasn't about to pick a fight with Cyril Hoffman. That was career suicide.

"Tell Mr. Hoffman that I'll call his office tomorrow and request an appointment."

Weiss walked away from Aronson, leaving him in his seat and her shopping cart in the café. She felt sick, and didn't want to eat the food she had picked out, or stand in line with the scores of secret-keepers who shopped here at Tysons, or remain in this place one instant longer.

27

WASHINGTON

Ariel Weiss arrived early that night for her ten p.m. meeting with Graham Weber. She stood at the exit of the concrete underpass that ran beneath North Glebe Road in Arlington. She had returned home from Whole Foods several hours before to change clothes and steady her nerves. She put on a black dress at first, and then changed into skinny jeans. She finished a bottle of wine that was left over from the previous weekend's date with a case officer from the Near East Division she had unwisely invited home.

The wine had relaxed her, just enough. She knew how to lie. She had gotten caught doing something that she wasn't supposed to do, and now she was being squeezed. She was keeping secrets within secrets, but that was her life. She responded as she always did, by willing herself into the appearance of calm, putting on her makeup and making herself attractive and unreadable. People have different kinds of addictions. For Weiss, it was the pleasure of a double life. She didn't feel anxious as she waited for Weber to arrive. Ambiguity was a comfort zone.

She looked at her watch. It was nine forty-five. She had the occupational habit of always arriving early for appointments. She nestled among the parked cars, looking for any movement. The art of concealment was one of her few professional weaknesses: She was too attractive. A recruiter had actually warned her that this might be a problem for her as a case officer. If she approached a male "developmental" at a cocktail party, the prospective agent would imagine she was hitting on him. She had found a part of the Clandestine Service where she could be truly invisible—sitting behind the screen, ugly as sin as far as anyone knew, important because of the code she wrote and the operations she managed.

Weber was approaching. She heard the distinctive click of leather heels, and the thin notes of someone whistling "On the Street Where You Live" from *My Fair Lady*. She looked for the director's security guards, but didn't see them or the armored Cadillac. He passed by where she was hidden and then stopped; he made the sound that used to be called a "wolf whistle." She eased herself between the cars and approached him from behind. He hadn't changed from work. His face was worn.

"Going my way?" she said in a low voice. She was wearing black boots against the night chill and a long black cashmere sweater over her jeans.

"You move like an elephant," answered Weber. "I heard you coming from halfway across the lot."

"Bullshit," she whispered. "Where are we, anyway?"

"I play golf at the club across the road." He mimicked a golf swing as he led her out of the parking lot into the darkness of the adjoining alley.

"Are you any good?"

"Yes. I'm good at everything except running the CIA. Let's take a walk before my minders come find me."

Weber turned left onto Rock Spring. He seemed to relax when they were a few paces into the suburban street: Tall evergreens and stone walls shielded the properties. His mind echoed with the injunction he had read a few hours before: *You are looking in the wrong place.* But what was the right place? He slowed his pace and turned to Weiss.

"What have you got on Morris? I need to sort this out before the White House decides to de-appoint me."

"I've found his network, but not him. I don't know where he is. I need more time."

"What have you got?"

"I can document that Morris is running his own string of agents outside the agency. They're in Europe, England and China, from what I've seen. He seems to have a second operations center that he runs out of Denver, to do things overseas that are too sensitive for the regular IOC."

"Who pays for it, if it's not on our books?"

"The director of National Intelligence."

"Can you prove that?"

"No. But I know it. It's probably run with NSA money."

Weber closed his eyes a moment. He saw Cyril Hoffman's connection with Morris, but he didn't understand it.

"Why would Hoffman do that? Why take the trouble?"

"Isn't that obvious, Mr. Director?"

"Not to me."

"Morris is doing things that wouldn't be approved by normal channels. So it's run through the DNI."

"This isn't about Morris, is it?" said Weber, half to himself. "We're 'looking in the wrong place.' Maybe Morris is under someone else's control. Maybe the Pownzor got powned, and we just don't realize it. What about that?"

Ariel Weiss looked at him skeptically.

"Another country is using him? Is that what you mean?"

"Maybe." Weber nodded. "Or perhaps there's someone else who's the real mole, who's guiding Morris. What foreign service would know enough to run something like that?"

Weiss took a long moment to scroll through her mental map.

"It's a short list. The handlers would need technical mastery of cyber. It could be the Russians; Morris probably has Russian contacts in his German network. It could be the Israelis; one of his new recruits was an Israeli. It could be China; he just ordered a payment of ten million dollars to Macao, and he has a guy named Li who's helping him. And he spends a lot of time in Britain, so put that on the list, too."

"Israel, Russia, China, Britain. That's the champions' league in terms of cyber, right? So, in theory, Morris could be playing with any of them."

"Affirmative," she said.

The two had reached the corner of Old Dominion Drive, a busy street with cars passing regularly. Weber led her to a smaller access road about five feet below the highway. He took her hand as he pulled her across the street. She let it drop quickly when they reached the far corner.

"Who's this man Li?" he asked.

"He's a Chinese émigré who works in a lab outside Cambridge that Morris set up on his black budget. It's empty now. I asked London station to check. They've scattered. London pulled traces on the Chinese man today. His full name is Dr. Emmanuel Li. He's listed as the director of the Fudan–East Anglia Research Centre. I also found footprints of a guy named Junot, who's on Pownzor's black payroll. He's the guy we BOLO'd."

"Jeez, lady, you got a lot!"

Weiss raised a finger, not quite pointing it at Weber, but cautioning him.

"I had to stick my neck out to get all this. I hope it's not going to get cut off."

"Do you want to tell me how you got it?"

Weiss pondered the request.

"Probably not," she said. "At least, not yet."

"You're keeping things from me."

"Yup. It's for your own protection. And mine."

"I'm going to need to know soon. Understood?"

She nodded.

"Why haven't we found Junot?"

"Because Pownzor is smart. He uses cutouts for cutouts. I think Junot is getting paid through Poland, routed to the Caymans. Morris is using him to recruit people in Germany. He just signed off on an eight-million-dollar payoff to an agent in Germany, payable through Liechtenstein. I ran the traces, and I think the German agent is actually Russian."

"Is Hoffman protecting Junot, too?"

Weiss shrugged.

"How should I know? That's way above my pay grade."

"This is weird," said Weber.

"Everything is weird, but what in particular?"

"Here's a description of our mystery man: He's in a very sensitive position at the CIA, and is also in contact with Israelis, Russians, Chinese and Brits. He has old friends at the White House. And he is funded covertly by the director of National Intelligence. Who is this man?"

"James Morris."

"Correct. And the question is: Who is he really working for?"

"Maybe it's just for himself," she said.

"Or maybe he has an ally."

Weber's radio crackled from inside his pocket.

"Damn it," he said. "My security detail is looking for me. They'll turn on the searchlights thirty seconds from now. You head back the way you came and I'll walk back to my club."

Weiss was looking up at Weber. There was a flicker in her eye, of uncertainty. Was she playing a double game now, or a triple game? It was hard to tell the difference.

"Are you going to talk to Cyril Hoffman?" she asked.

"I don't know. I need to think about it. Let's keep this to ourselves for now."

She looked at him calmly. Her eyes were warm and sympathetic.

"Of course, Mr. Director."

"Does the DNI's office know we're asking questions about Morris?"

"Not from me. But they're going to find out."

Weber shook his head. The rumble of his armored Escalade was audible a few dozen yards away.

"Jesus Christ," he said, shaking his head.

"Are you okay?" she asked.

His radio was buzzing again.

"Of course I'm okay. I just need people I can trust. I hope that includes you."

She nodded. The SUV was approaching. He turned toward the car. She reached for his elbow, to say a last word.

"Be careful, sir. You're the CIA director. This isn't a company, it's the government. You speak for ten thousand people. You can't make mistakes."

He looked at his watch as the SUV door clicked open a dozen yards away.

"I have to get home," he said. "My boys are visiting D.C. But I get it: You're right that I can't make mistakes. I won't."

On her lips were the words, *I hope not*. But she watched him in silence as he strode toward the big black car.

Weiss wondered as she walked away whether she was cheating on Weber, just as she had done with Morris. It couldn't be helped. She had learned over her years of intra-agency dating that the reasons people were drawn into CIA careers also made them unsuitable partners, almost by definition: They were good liars; they knew how to conceal their feelings; they knew how to do bad things and get up the next morning and do them again.

Weiss was one of them. Weber wasn't. She wanted him to succeed, but she wasn't ready to bet her career on it.

Weber's sons were waiting for him at the Watergate when he got home. The security detail had let them in, and the housekeeper had made them some food. They were watching football on Weber's immense television in the living room. When he opened the door, they jumped up almost like cadets coming to attention.

"Who's winning?" asked Weber.

"Washington," said Josh, his younger son, who at sixteen was nearly as tall as his brother David.

"I don't believe it," said Weber. "Washington always loses."

Weber picked up the remote control and clicked off the set.

"Sorry, boys, but we need to talk," he said.

They both nodded, now serious and silent.

They had come to visit because David had decided he wanted to leave school and join the military. His younger brother had convinced him to visit their father before he did anything stupid. It was fall of David's senior year. People don't leave then unless they're about to get kicked out or it's a suicide dive.

"So you want to drop out," said Weber. "Why?"

"I'm wasting my time, Dad. The pot thing last month was an example. I'm afraid I won't get into a good college."

Weber waved his hand and clucked his tongue.

"I don't care about that," he said.

"I want to join the Marines," said David.

Weber didn't answer for a few seconds.

"That's a good thing to do," he said eventually. "But not if you're running away from something. Are you?"

David looked at the floor.

"Yeah, I guess. I just don't think I'm doing much in school. I'm wasting your money. I want to be doing something real."

"I get that," said Weber. "But think about it. If you want to withdraw this semester, I'll call the headmaster and work it out. I'm sure he'll say okay. Go get a job. Work construction. Join a ski patrol for the winter. I don't care. But don't join the Marines unless you're sure that's what you want to do. The military is no joke. It's stupid to get killed because you couldn't decide what else to do. If you still want to be a Marine in six months, I'm for it."

"You are?" David was surprised. He had expected parental anger or disappointment, but not support.

Weber turned to his younger son, who had been watching apprehensively.

"What do you think, Josh?"

"Uh, I guess I agree with you. I'm worried about David in the Marines. I'm worried about you at the CIA. This is all scary. Are you okay, Daddy? You look kind of tired."

"I'm fine. Exhausted, but fine. This job is like *Homeland*, for real. I can't tell you about it. But, well, do you ever feel as if everyone around you is lying?"

"Yeah, all the time," said David.

"Me, too," echoed the younger boy, rolling his eyes.

Weber laughed.

"So what do you do about it, boys, when everybody's lying?"

Josh looked at David, who answered for both of them.

"I tell them to fuck off. Not out loud, but in my head."

"I'll try that," said Weber. He walked to the kitchen and got a beer from the refrigerator.

"What are we going to do this summer, Daddy?" called out Josh.

"That's a long way off. Don't you want to be with your mom?"

"Uh, no," said Josh. David shook his head. "We want to do something cool with you. We never see you anymore."

"I'll take it under advisement," said Weber.

"What does that mean?" asked David.

Weber looked at his oldest son and smiled. "Don't join the Marines yet. Think about it for six months. Promise?"

David nodded. "Promise," he said.

"Then the sky's the limit. Tell me where you want to go on vacation and we're there."

"Come on, Dad," said Josh. "You always say that."

"This time I mean it," said Weber. He took a swig from his beer and put his arms around his sons.

28

FORT MEADE, MARYLAND

Cyril Hoffman paid regular visits to the National Security Agency. It was one of the sixteen intelligence organizations under his supervision that were, as he liked to say, the arrows in his quiver. Hoffman managed the community with a light hand. To run the agencies, he tried to pick good people who understood the technologies of surveillance and collection and then, generally, left them alone. Graham Weber was the rare agency chief he hadn't personally chosen, but that couldn't be helped. The CIA was always a special child: needy, accident-prone, easily wounded. Hoffman had felt sorry for Weber the day he was appointed, but that empathetic feeling had given way in the weeks since to something closer to antipathy.

Hoffman's trip to the "Fort" on this day had been requested by Admiral Lloyd Schumer, the NSA director. Schumer wanted Hoffman to hear personally about some new information that he had collected, which he didn't think was appropriate for community-wide dissemination. Schumer had volunteered to come to Liberty Crossing but said it would be easier to talk at the NSA. Hoffman agreed. He felt like getting out of the office anyway. The DNI's Lincoln Navigator was prepared for the trip, along with an identical vehicle that accompanied the first as backup and chase car.

Hoffman was dressed formally, as always for work. Today it was charcoal gray, with chalk stripes, a handsome suit his tailor had made on his last trip to Hong Kong. To the links of his gold watch chain he had recently added his Phi Beta Kappa key, which he had found in a drawer and decided made an attractive pendant. On his head was a stiff-brimmed gray homburg hat that he had acquired at Borsalino in Rome.

He relished the long drive for a chance to listen to music on his digital player. After some thought, he selected a Philip Glass opera titled *Akhnaten*, which, although famously difficult, was one of Hoffman's favorites. The opera had vocal passages in the ancient languages of Akkadian, Biblical Hebrew, and the Egyptian of the *Book of the Dead*. Hoffman hummed and occasionally sang along with Akhnaten's arias in an eerily high countertenor voice that startled even the driver, who was familiar with Hoffman's eccentricities.

The Lincoln Navigator proceeded to Fort Meade via the Beltway, whose entrance was a few hundred yards from the front door of Hoffman's office. They circumnavigated the Washington suburbs in a loop that crossed the Potomac and skirted the Maryland suburbs, and then they headed north on I-95 until they reached Route 32 East, which then turned into the aptly named Canine Road and the NSA's well-guarded gate. Hoffman was waved through the barrier and the vehicle turned toward an office building that resembled an opaque black cube. To the right was a low-rise building of the sort you might see on any military base; Fort Meade was a military installation, after all, with soldiers in uniform lumbering between buildings.

Admiral Schumer met Hoffman at the entrance to the black monolith of the NSA headquarters and navigated the peculiar front reception area. The entryway confirmed that the NSA had something to hide: Rather than a straight path through the lobby, the corridor veered left, and then made a ninety-degree right angle, before opening to the inner hallway. This maze-like entrance had been created to check any straight passage for beams or waves, in or out.

The admiral was wearing his service dress blues, tidy and compact, decked with ribbons; he presented a contrast with Hoffman's flamboyant garb. He showed Hoffman several new entries on the black marble wall engraved with the names of more than 150 NSA personnel who had died on duty. Above the long list was the code under which the agency had operated: THEY SERVED IN SILENCE. That reputation for discretion had been shattered by the recent hemorrhage of disclosures, but the NSA was officially in denial. It still treated all its documents as top secret, even the ones that had been published in the newspapers.

Hoffman was still humming quietly to himself; he stopped when the admiral beckoned him toward the elevator. Some of the people streaming past in the corridor were dressed in jeans and T-shirts. The NSA had concluded over the last decade that if it was to survive as a cryptological service, it needed to go geek. The problem was that free minds wanted free spaces, too.

The Admiral's office was ostentatiously bland. He had a modest desk, with three computer screens behind, and three telephones. The one nearest his chair was for quick, secure communications; it had red buttons so the admiral could call his counterparts at other agencies instantly: There was a button for the CIA director, another for the chairman of the Joint Chiefs, a third for the national security adviser and so on. A second telephone connected with the public telephone network and switching; a third, marked STE, was used for secure encrypted calls. Schumer had pictures of his kids, too, lined up amid the top-secret hardware.

The admiral gestured for Hoffman to sit at his glass-top conference table, facing a window whose blinds were perpetually drawn. Coffee was served; aides disappeared, leaving the two of them alone.

"So nice to escape my office, Lloyd," said Hoffman. "How's life at the Fort?"

"We're surviving. It's hard for the older employees. They spent a lifetime protecting secrets that get blown in a few weeks. They're depressed. But the younger ones adapt. Applications are up again. That's something. If we lose the smart kids, we'll be dead."

"Which one will be the next ambitious malcontent who decides he can save the world by exposing the wiring diagram?"

"I worry about that every day. But we should see the next Snowden coming. We can monitor everything a person does now. I get a report every day listing any employee who has requested anything out of the ordinary. You need a buddy along when you download anything, FTP anything, practically when you go to the toilet. We'll see the dangerous ones. Knock on wood." He rapped the glass-topped conference table.

"I wish other agencies were as tightly buttoned," said Hoffman. "We have a new CIA director who thinks it's time to open the windows and doors and let the sun shine in. And he has some people working for him, I'm afraid, who think it's fine to request files on programs they're not cleared for. Not my choice, but there you are. I reassure myself that the way Weber is going, he'll never last."

Schumer nodded noncommittally. He wasn't about to criticize a fellow agency director.

"So what's on your mind?" asked Hoffman. "Other than locking the doors and windows?"

"Something is bothering me. I'll be frank with you."

"You'd better be. Otherwise I'll send you back to submarine duty."

"We've been picking up some things the analysts don't understand," said Schumer. "First, we're getting signs of new malware in some of the circuits we monitor. We're seeing some of the European hacker networks go dark, we don't know why. We're registering new activity in China and Russia that connects with some IP addresses that we try to monitor in Britain even though we told GCHQ we wouldn't. We think something is up."

Hoffman stared at the admiral.

"So?" he said. "What's the actionable item here? I'm hearing noise, not signal."

"Well, that's the problem, Cyril. It is mostly noise. But to the extent there's a central locus, we think it's an agency officer from the Information Operations Center."

"James Morris," said Hoffman.

"Yes, sir." Schumer nodded. "We know Morris has some special authorities from your office, so we don't want to get in the way. And we gather that Director Weber has found him useful. But there is something you need to know. The analysts gave it to me several days ago, but I asked them to double-check so I could be sure before I told you."

"Well, what is it, man? Go on."

"James Morris has been in contact with a Russian from the SVR in Britain. We're able to decrypt their traffic again. They've had two meetings with him and the Russian case officer claimed in a cable to Moscow that he has delivered information to Morris."

Hoffman was fiddling with his tie as he listened.

"Are you sure about this? Morris is many things, but I wouldn't have thought he was a traitor."

"Yes, sir. As I said, I didn't want to tell you until the agents had double-checked. But we decrypted the case officer's reports about a meeting with a special source, and then we were able to decrypt a special message to SVR headquarters at Yasenevo that gave the agent's true name. It's James Morris."

"Do we know where Morris is?"

"No, sir. The Russian officer met him in a small town near Cambridge, but he's not there anymore. He's not showing up on any digital track we have."

"What is Morris *doing*?" muttered Hoffman. "Has he gone completely off his rocker? He has been polygraphed more times over the years than I have. How did they get to him?"

"Judging from what we were able to decrypt, the Russians seem to be running him through some sort of free-the-Internet cover. It's like WikiLeaks, but more high-minded. They have some prominent supporters. Professors, tech gurus, people like that. It seems to have roots at Stanford, and in Silicon Valley. Sorry about that."

"Good Lord Jesus, protect us. Do the British know?"

"No, sir, not so far as we can tell."

"Well, don't tell them. Let's sort this out on the home front."

"Yes, sir."

Hoffman flicked at the lapels of his jacket. He adjusted the crease in his trousers. He was thinking.

"James Morris is a Weber project," said Hoffman. "He wanted some younger, creative people to take more responsibility at the agency, and he sent Morris out on a very sensitive operation. He gave him a hunting license. The problem is that Morris is swimming in a pond with the rest of the fish, including Russian fish. And they all pee in the same water, which gets pumped back into our tanks."

"I'm not sure I follow the fish part," said Schumer, "but I get your point."

Hoffman was nodding, in agreement with himself.

"The question I find myself wondering about," Hoffman continued, "is why Graham Weber lets this young gentleman, Mr. Morris, wander so freely. We don't really know all that much about Weber. He is not of our world, is he? He's a businessman. He got rich making deals and cutting corners. That's what people do in business."

"I'm out of my lane now, Cyril."

"Sorry, old boy. I'm thinking out loud. I shouldn't draw you into it."

"There's one more thing I wanted to warn you about," said Schumer. "I mentioned at the beginning that some new malware is surfacing in Europe, which my analysts linked to Morris. The problem is, some of them think it's a prelude to a coordinated cyber-attack."

"By Morris?"

"That's what the analysts think. So you have to tell me: If this is Title Fifty covert action and it's none of my Title Ten military business, just say so and we'll stay out of the way. We just don't want to let something slip inside the air gap at CIA that could contaminate other systems."

Hoffman took off his glasses. He took the tie from beneath his vest and rubbed the lenses of his spectacles. Then he stuffed the tie back under the vest. The glasses were more smudged than before.

"It's not any Title Fifty operation I approved. Let me pursue it, for now. Morris is Weber's man. If he has allowed this young man to fall into perdition, he needs to answer for it. If Weber should prove to have a shorter than expected tenure at CIA, well, so be it. I think he already has a good pension."

"Perhaps I should send Director Weber a report on the foreign activity connected to his networks? He needs to know about that, doesn't he? Just to be safe."

"Oh, yes, of course. Russian links, Chinese, all that. Quite right," said Hoffman. "Send him a report about the foreign contacts with Morris. Mention something about the malware, too. Copy me. That way we can't be blamed later for not giving a warning. Meanwhile, I'll jump on this Morris business. We need to find him first, and then turn him inside out. I may need help from other agencies, FBI, whatever. Don't you worry."

Schumer closed up the folder on the conference table. He had planned to give it to Hoffman, but he said he would redo it and send a new, briefer version to both directors, Hoffman and Weber.

"Hold off a day on that, would you? I need to get started on Morris before there are too many ripples in the water."

"Certainly, Mr. Hoffman. It's a relief, reading you into this. I was worried, I can tell you."

"Of course you were," said Hoffman, nodding gently. "It's quite serious."

Hoffman, never a man to be ruffled by events, wanted a tour before he got back into his enormous black car, so Schumer walked him through some of the secret spaces in the black cube of the NSA's headquarters. The surveillance tools were still mostly in place, Snowden notwithstanding, allowing the analysts to dial into metadata and content around the world, so long as they had the proper legal stamps on their requests.

Hoffman was surprised, making his tour, to see just how young and freewheeling the NSA workforce was. They did their recruiting now at hacker conferences and a dozen other less visible honeypots for the smart and mischievous.

As he was on his way out, Hoffman saw a young man in a T-shirt that said DEF CON XX. That triggered something in his mind. The young Swiss man who had wanted to defect, who had come in from the underground to warn that the agency was penetrated—he had been wearing a shirt with that same logo. Hoffman had seen it on the video recording of his initial handling by the base chief in Hamburg, which had been circulated by Earl Beasley.

Hoffman always played a long game. But he suspected that, in this case, the decisive innings were nearer than he might have thought. One the way home, he listened to another of Philip Glass's operas, *The Making of the Representative for Planet 8*, and thought about the puzzle that was taking shape.

When Hoffman returned to the office, he was told that Dr. Ariel Weiss from the CIA's Information Operations Center had telephoned, requesting an appointment. He told his secretary to call Weiss back immediately and suggest that she stop by Liberty Crossing late that afternoon at six p.m., if possible. He asked the secretary to advise Weiss that this would be a private meeting, at the personal request of the director of National Intelligence, not to be shared with any of her colleagues at the CIA.

Weiss's office was near the ODNI complex, so it was easy enough for her to slip away and make the short journey to Hoffman's headquarters. She was cleared quickly through the lobby and escorted upstairs to a capacious suite. When she arrived, the director of National Intelligence was sitting at a round table, away from his desk, going over some papers.

His secretary rapped on the door. Hoffman looked up over the top of his glasses. His eyes widened. He'd never met Ariel Weiss before. She had dressed up for Hoffman, exchanging her usual trousers and white shirt for a gray suit with a pencil skirt and fitted jacket. Her demeanor was cool and composed, as ever.

"The alcove, please," Hoffman told his secretary. She led Weiss into a small adjoining room, windowless and lined with bookshelves, which Hoffman used for personal or especially sensitive meetings.

Hoffman followed a few moments later and closed the door. He removed his suit jacket, so that he was wearing his pin-striped vest, decorated with its sparkling gold chain. The room had a drinks cabinet and a bucket of ice. Hoffman hung his jacket neatly in a closet and walked to the bar.

"Too early for whiskey? I think not."

He poured himself a half glass of the amber liquid and sprayed in a jet of seltzer water from a crystal bottle. He added two cubes of ice.

"And you?" he asked.

"The same," said Weiss. "Neat."

"Good start," said Hoffman. "There's hope."

They sat down across from each other in brown leather chairs separated by a cherrywood table. The little room danced with the flickering yellow-blue flame from a fake fireplace against the near wall. It was almost cozy in this small room.

"Cheers," said Hoffman, raising his glass and taking a sip. Weiss put the glass to her lips, let the taste of the whiskey moisten the tip of her tongue and then set it down.

"Do you enjoy your job, Dr. Weiss?"

"Yes, sir, I like it a lot."

"Is it your expectation to remain with the agency a long time?"

"I don't know. As long as the work is challenging, yes, I think so."

"And do you aspire to higher management? People tell me that you're ambitious."

"I like the job I have," she answered cautiously. "But if something attractive came along, of course I would be interested."

"I see. Well, that's good. But it behooves an ambitious person, especially, to be careful and follow the rules."

"I know that, Mr. Hoffman. I try not to violate the rules."

"Oh, really? Because I gather from a member of my staff, Ms. Hazel Philby, that you were making unauthorized inquiries yesterday about some DNI payment accounts that are strictly compartmented. That's a violation of the classified-material handling rules, where I come from."

"I did nothing wrong, sir. I was investigating activities by personnel from the Information Operations Center at the request of senior CIA management. I was following the rules, not breaking them."

"I'm not sure that a disciplinary panel would agree with you, Dr. Weiss. In fact, I am rather certain they would find you at fault, in a way that might put your security clearance and continued employment at the agency at risk. But let's put that aside for the moment."

Weiss was shaking her head.

"I can't let that stand, Mr. Hoffman. You are accusing me of something. I need to respond."

Hoffman raised his hand.

"Enough. I said we would return to this later. I want to talk about something else. How much do you know about the activities of James Morris? I gather that's what you were poking your nose into so deviously. What have you found out?"

"Morris is the problem you should be worrying about. He's running a secret network with Russians, Chinese and Israelis. He's totally outside CIA control. From what I picked up, his authority and funding come from your office, Mr. Hoffman. The ODNI supports his clandestine operations out of Denver."

"Have you told Graham Weber that?"

"Of course I have. He's my boss."

"But Dr. Weiss, I am also your boss. And I am telling you that whatever authority I may have given to Morris, which is none of your business, it does not include working with Russians, Chinese and Israelis. That is freelancing. And in my opinion, it's a result of your esteemed 'boss' giving Morris too much authority. This ball is on Weber's racquet, not mine."

"I'll leave the turf question to you, sir," said Weiss coolly. "But based on what I've seen, someone had better take action quickly. Because I think Pownzor Morris is about to do something very crazy and dangerous. It's just a hunch. But since you asked me about him, that's what I think."

She picked up her glass again, and this time she took a healthy swallow of whiskey.

Hoffman snorted, but it was impossible to know whether it was in appreciation of the young woman's resolve or in anger. He stirred his drink with his index finger.

"What do you know about Morris's contact with the Russians?" asked Hoffman. "You said you found evidence he has links with them. What about it?"

"I don't know much. He's forming a little army of hackers. I think one of them is a Russian. But there are also Chinese and Israelis. I don't know what they're planning. Do you?"

"Of course not! I told you, Morris is freelancing. I have talked to the people in Denver who, according to your sources, are his facilitators. Well, they know nothing. He went off-line a week ago."

Weiss studied him. Was it possible that Cyril Hoffman, the master of the secret world, was getting flustered?

"You have a problem, Mr. Hoffman," she said.

"No, Weber has a problem. I am trying to resolve it. What do you know about Morris's contacts with the civil liberties crowd?"

"Not much. He's a hacker, so he's been hanging around with those people since college. We all have. It goes with the territory."

"Could he get sucked into some WikiLeaks thing? Some Snowden thing? Is that possible?"

"Anything's possible, Mr. Hoffman. Pownzor is a very private guy. There's a lot going on inside him that I never know about. I think he sees his old friends from college and graduate school, but he never talks about it."

"Jesus, Mary and Joseph," said Hoffman. It was his version of a curse. "This is going to be complicated."

"What are you going to do, Mr. Hoffman?"

Hoffman pondered her question. He took a long drink of his whiskey and soda.

"I will take discreet action. That is a personal specialty, if you didn't know. I have contacts. The Russians are not immune to reason. They can be persuaded. So can almost everyone. Am I right, Dr. Weiss?"

"Most people can be persuaded. But I'm not sure about James Morris. I've worked for him for two years, and I've never convinced him to do anything he wasn't already planning."

Hoffman smiled. It was an eerie look that came suddenly across his face, and then vanished.

"Well, there it is! If Mr. Morris cannot be persuaded, then we may have to let him blow himself up. Self-destruct. Poof! And then we're all rid of a problem. We are, and maybe the Russians, too."

Hoffman smiled again. His eyes were twinkling as he peered over the top of his glasses at Weiss.

"I have no idea what you're talking about, Mr. Hoffman."

"That's a relief. I feared I was becoming transparent. Now then, what about you? I hope you will agree that you are in something of a compromised position, Dr. Weiss. If I contact the Office of Security at the agency and request a formal investigation of your conduct—of your trickery, let us be frank about it—in convincing the CIA comptroller's office to divulge classified material inappropriately, I am almost certain that you would be suspended from your job. I would insist on it, actually. I am a victim in this matter."

"I would protest to Director Weber, my superior. I was conducting legitimate inquiries on the agency's behalf."

"Bosh! Weber can't save you. He's too new. He's too inexperienced. He's dangerous, in my opinion. His silly nonsense about 'rebalancing' and 'restarting,' all of that is just so much fluff. He is upsetting the order of things. I would be surprised if he can save himself when all this is over. But he certainly can't save you."

Weiss didn't answer. She understood the deal Hoffman was proposing: Her silence and compliant behavior in exchange for keeping her job. She didn't want to respond. Hoffman studied her, waiting for an answer, and then he decided that her silence was enough.

"Very well. I will assume that we comprehend each other. I hold the future of your career in my hand. You are a bright and talented person, obviously, and I would very much like not to injure you. Indeed, I would like to *help* you. But in return, I expect you to act in accordance with my wishes and requests. Otherwise, you will very quickly find yourself out of a job. Is that clear?"

Still, she didn't answer.

Hoffman rose, and shook her hand.

"A doughty lass, but not a stupid one, I hope."

He reached for a buzzer, and the secretary returned and escorted Ariel Weiss out of the office and back down to the lobby.

29

BATH, ENGLAND

The antiquarian bookseller on Pierrepont Street in Bath had served many eccentric customers, but few with the relentless obscurantist curiosity of James Morris. He had slipped into Bath from nearby Bristol to satisfy a few personal needs, of which book browsing was only one. He had earlier paid a visit to a woman who had been referred to him, in the strictest confidence, by the incandescent Beatrix. Now, in the afterglow, he was indulging another passion at a celebrated local bookseller. The establishment occupied a fine old listed stone building near the Avon River, a mile below the crescents that surmounted the city. The bookseller's office had carved arches over the windows and a handsome gabled roof. Inside were the incunabula of the book world: ancient tomes in glass cases; tools used for printing and binding; and what looked like acres of old books.

Morris approached the wizened bookseller at the desk. The man was wearing an apron, and had metal garters on his sleeves to keep his cuffs from encumbering his hand movements. He might have been working in identical costume when this establishment was founded in the nineteenth century. Morris, in contrast, was wearing a black leather motorcycle jacket and cargo pants, which hung from his waist as if from a wire coat hanger.

"I'm looking for an old book about finance," said Morris. "It's called

The Bank for International Settlements at Work. It was published in 1933, when the bank was three years old. Does that ring any bells?"

"We have no bells here, sir. We are a bookseller. Let me consult the catalogue." He pulled out several metal drawers and examined index cards with meticulous notations.

"Lucky you," he said dubiously. "We appear to have a copy. The book is by Eleanor Lansing Dulles. It was published by Macmillan, in 1932, actually. Let me bring it out."

The bookseller disappeared into the stacks and returned with a dusty volume, running to more than six hundred pages. He handed it gently to Morris.

Morris opened the book to the title page and scanned the three pages of the preface. He closed the book and looked at the bookseller with genuine astonishment.

"Teraflop! Eleanor Lansing Dulles was the sister of John Foster Dulles and Allen Dulles. Can you believe that? She thanks her brother John Foster in the preface. It's true! It *is* a conspiracy."

"I beg your pardon?" The bookseller wasn't used to emotion in his workplace.

"Never mind. I have another request. Do you have a 1903 French monograph called *Essai sur l'Histoire Financière de la Turquie?*"

Morris had been assembling a small library on Ottoman financial history; this was another of his private obsessions. He liked to see the hand of the British, encouraging the bubble and then puncturing when it suited their interests. It was part of Morris's new obsesssion with the idea of a hidden British hand that had directed every turn of the wheel from the nineteenth century into the twenty-first.

The shop owner advised him curtly that the shop didn't carry foreign books. He glowered at the intruding customer.

Morris retreated toward the shelves carrying his bulky BIS history. He found a collection of books about intelligence. He surveyed the meticulous Cold War histories that Christopher Andrew had compiled from the Russian defectors Gordievsky and Mitrokhin. The Cold War bored him. Morris was about to walk away when he saw a fat book in a plain red cover called *MI6: The History of the Secret Intelligence Service.* It was nearly nine hundred pages, as big and heavy as a stack of bricks.

Morris returned to the register with the bulky history of British intelligence on top of his BIS tome. The bookseller appraised him. This was a peculiar reader.

Morris paid cash for his books and was on the way out the door when he stopped and turned back toward the cash desk. His face was alive suddenly, with a mixture of shame and excitement.

"Do you possibly have a book called *Justine*?" asked Morris. "It's translated from the French."

The bookseller paused. There was a twinkle of recognition in his eye. "By the marquis?" he asked.

Morris nodded. The heat was rising under his skin, reddening his cheeks.

"Ah! Alas, it's out of print; very rare. We do get occasional inquiries from collectors. It's a bit of a cult item, that one. If you'd like to give me your card, perhaps I could have one of them contact you."

The bookseller waited conspiratorially. Morris's pleasure at the prospect of purchasing the book turned instantly to panic at the fear of discovery. He turned suddenly and made for the door, clutching his two volumes. Out the door, he turned right and walked up the street toward the river and the tourist destinations along its banks.

Morris was safe. He found a wooden bench set back from the Avon looking upriver toward the parabolic banks of the stone weir that stretched nearly across its width. Beyond was a covered bridge, perfectly formed in imitation of the Rialto Bridge in Venice. Morris was lost in time. He unwrapped his new acquisitions and held them in his hands. He spent his life with the digital representations of words but took particular pleasure in the physical object that is a printed book.

He opened the Dulles book on the BIS and leafed through the pages. It was written in the confident certitudes of rising American empire. The old world was faltering. America was its rescuer and protector. It needed multilateral institutions like the BIS to mask its hand and lend an idealistic sheen to its activities.

Morris came upon a passage near the end of the book that conveyed this illusion of higher, unselfish purpose that was so characteristic of the Dulles brothers in their global machinations and now, he saw, of their sister, too:

A frequent criticism of the Bank which cannot be ignored was that it was too much concerned in profit making . . . For a while, it seemed as if the Management were motivated by a desire to impress the business man and commercial banker with the ability to conduct B.I.S. affairs on a sound commercial basis, rather than with the desire to demonstrate its importance as a public service organization.

Who was Sister Eleanor kidding? The BIS wasn't a philanthropic organization. It was the lynchpin of global capitalism.

A few pages later, still on his bench above the Avon, Morris came upon a passage that gave him the shivers. The words might have been written directly to him, from more than eight decades ago. He read them as an injunction, a seal on his mission:

The Bank is likely to be put to many severe tests and to perform large services in the years to come. The liquidation of this new effort in financial collaboration is extremely improbable. The lines are, nevertheless, still uncertain. It is possible to project the curve based on past actions a little way into the future, but it is not possible to predict the influences, political and economic, which may shift its direction.

Here was Morris, the liquidator. The future, so long delayed, was about to arrive.

Morris picked up his books and began strolling again toward a small hotel on Walcot Street where he had left his bags. He meandered past a throng of people gathered around the Pump Room, which since Georgian times had housed the Roman baths that made the city famous.

The square was thick with students and tourists jostling past each other, but Morris was oblivious. An effetely dressed man in his forties brushed Morris's wrist, hoping to get his attention. The flirtation was annoying. Morris turned and headed back the other way, toward the Avon and the refuge of his hotel.

Head down, clutching his books, living inside his head, Morris trod down Cheap Street toward the river again. People were gathering in the pubs and restaurants. He followed the curve of an old byway and took a last look at the Avon. A cool early November wind was rippling the water and flapping the banners that hung from some of the riverside buildings.

It was like the 1930s. What was required was a jolt, a catastrophic moment that caused people to see there was no foundation, and the empire would fall.

He had his detonation charges in place now: He had wired the bank at the center of the other banks. With its disorder, the insolvency of the entire system would be revealed. He would rearrange the bankers' world according to rules of human justice, not inherited supremacy. For he could control the numbers; they were recorded in zeroes and ones, like everything else. They were not immutable facts but representations that could be altered.

Morris scuttled away from the river. There were too many people about; it was time to be sheltering himself. He walked up Walcot Street until he came to the beige brick façade of a small hotel. The desk clerk knew him as Mr. Bjork, traveling on a Finnish passport.

Morris went up to his room and ate ice cream, which was the only thing that seemed palatable. He opened the fat history of MI6, which he had been saving as a kind of treat for when he was in private, and began scanning the chapters.

MI6 had claimed to open its archives for this "official history," but the amazing, audacious fact was that there was nothing there. The book went on, page after numbing page, citing agent code names and operational meetings—and the table talk of the various grandees who had been given the title "C" and run the service. But there were few real secrets or revelations . . . for the simple reason that a conspiratorial organization cannot produce a history. It commits nothing of importance to paper. It is like an epic poem, recited from generation to generation but never written down.

Would a British historian of MI6 ever write that they had created the CIA in their own image to protect the remnants of empire when Britain itself could no longer afford the upkeep? Of course not. Would they say that they had taken a democratic nation, born in a revolution against

Britain and its aristocracy, and welded to it an intelligence service populated by the very Anglophile aristocrats that American democracy had meant to destroy? Dulles and McCloy, Helms and McCone—these names might have come out of Burke's Peerage.

Morris found pages that hinted at the truth, however obliquely. He read the text of a December 1940 letter from Sir Stewart Menzies, "C" himself, introducing "Wild Bill" Donovan to Churchill:

> *Donovan has a controlling influence over Knox, strong influence on Stimson, friendly influence [on] Hill and President. A Catholic, Irish American descent, Republican holding confidence of Democrats, with an exceptional war record, places him in an unique position to advance our aims here.*

It was obvious what they had done, if you understood the story. They couldn't avoid leaving footprints. Yet the tracks were just dusty and covered enough that the ruse had held, then and now. Morris leafed a few pages further and found a message from Victor Cavendish-Bentinck, rejecting a proposal that Churchill personally embrace Donovan's secret role and warning:

> *If message ever became known it would expose Colonel Donovan to the imputation of being a British agent instead of the splendid free-lance that he is.*

Ha! "Splendid free-lance," indeed! But Morris had penetrated the code and seen this story for what it was. His friend Ramona had been clever to send him to a professional historian like Arthur Peabody, who could point the way. But an engineer like James Morris, unschooled in the "humanities," could follow the wiring diagram. And then, with luck, he could rewire the grid.

Morris fell asleep for a few hours with his book open; he dreamed of his afternoon with Beatrix's friend. He cried out in the dream, and he worried for a moment that people in the neighboring rooms would hear and make inquiries. But the hallway was quiet and empty. Morris lay awake for a time, and then took a pill. He would be gone from Bath the next morning, his journey almost done.

Morris took the 8:04 train to Paddington Street Station the next morning. He was late; he didn't care: It was a form of power to make other people wait. The train compartment smelled of cigarettes even though smoking had been forbidden on the British railways for years. He found a window seat at the end of a car, beating an older woman to it. He gazed at his reflection in the glass, barely recognizing himself, and then peered through the panes at the fields beyond the tracks. Vaporous puffs of condensation hung over the grass and shrubs but they vanished in the heat of the rising sun and the approaching city.

Morris looked at the immense scroll of unanswered messages on his three phones; the world was nipping at his heels, no matter what disguise he wore or proprietary business he used as his cover. He had managed to elude them, but that couldn't last much longer.

At Paddington Station, Morris descended from the train carriage and joined the rivulet of travelers who were heading to work. He rolled his suitcase behind him; on his back was a pack with his computer and other electronic gear. The rest of his kit he had destroyed. It was just 9:20, still time to pretend that you weren't late. Commuters jostled Morris every few yards until he was safely out of the station and walking down Sussex Gardens toward Hyde Park. He maneuvered his angular body among shorter, chunkier pedestrians marching toward their offices. He had forgotten to eat breakfast that day, as most mornings.

He crossed Bayswater Road and entered the park gates near the ornate Italian Gardens. He checked his watch. It was nearly 9:40, and he was certainly late. What of it?

Morris rolled his bag noisily past the Baroque fountains and onto an asphalt path that bounded the kidney-shaped pond that stretched nearly the length of the park: Boys were playing soccer on the grass, even on a school-day morning; in the distance, wealthy women on horseback were taking a morning ride in the park, as they had for centuries in this impermeably sealed island nation. Morris strolled toward a wooden bench that looked across a stand of shrubbery to the pond. He looked at his watch again, but only for show.

Waiting on the bench was a young man dressed in a swish Burberry raincoat. He was perhaps thirty and looked like a young merchant banker, newly hired by one of the old-line firms but restless, not sure he belonged. He removed a Benson & Hedges cigarette from a gold pack and stuck it to the flame of a lighter engraved with the seal of the Bank of England.

Morris sat down on the bench beside him. Even in his haggard, furtive form there remained something seductive and charismatic about Morris. He was like a romantic poet in his haunted, passionate affect. He was hungry for self-destruction. Beads of cold sweat formed below the hairline of his wig. He leaned his bag against the bench and removed his backpack.

"You're late," said the man. "That's regarded as poor form in your trade, I believe."

"I overslept," said Morris. That was the truth. He had thought of catching the 7:21 train, so that he could make his appointment with ease. But he had been in a deep, drugged sleep, and when the alarm had sounded he had pushed the snooze button.

"I have what you asked for," said the young man. He held his cigarette between his thumb and forefinger. He removed a thin beige legal folder and laid it on the bench.

Morris looked at the skinny folder.

"There's not much of it," he said.

"It's too hard. Everything is password-protected. They've had the cleverest people working on it for years. All I have is a few routing numbers and IP addresses. It's too difficult to get all the way in."

Morris stared at him, and then smiled.

"I don't have to get in. That's the *point*. You don't have to get into the water to drain the pool."

"Whatever, mate," said the Englishman. He had the modern upperclass style of affecting a workingman's diction.

Morris looked at the arid Englishman. He felt like a febrile animal, sweating from every pore, next to this dry relic of empire. Morris was subhuman in every respect except one: He was smart.

"Get lost," said Morris. "Go back to your bank and its creamy parlors. The check is in the mail."

"You're a nasty one," hissed the young Englishman. "But the pay is good, ain't it?"

The young banker stood and buttoned his raincoat and adjusted his silk-lined paisley scarf. He left the beige folder on the bench and ambled off.

Morris held the brown envelope from the bank on his lap. He could look at it later. It was only rows and numbers, hieroglyphics, incomprehensible to most people. The structures on which people put their faith and credit were so many digits. Towing his baggage, he rolled off to a nearby hotel on Bayswater Road, where he ordered breakfast and began to read the modest but useful dossier from the Bank of England.

Morris was finishing the last of his eggs, scooping up the yolks with the crust of his bread, when he saw a most unwelcome visitor settle into the restaurant. He was wearing a different jacket than the peacoat he had worn several days ago in Bristol. Now it was a blue blazer with a tie, Mayfair-style.

But it was the same Russian man, the one who had called himself Roger. Morris wanted to escape back into the street. He called for the bill. It wouldn't do to get arrested for skipping on a breakfast check. But the Russian was already seated beside him.

"Going somewhere?" asked Roger, looking at the suitcase and backpack.

"Maybe," said Morris. He didn't look up from his day-old copy of the *Financial Times*.

"Have you reconsidered?" asked Roger.

"I don't know what you're talking about."

"This is your destiny," said the Russian. "You cannot escape destiny. I told you before: There is a new world waiting to be born." He softly hummed a chorus from *Les Misérables*.

Morris threw down his napkin. "This is ridiculous. I don't want Russia's help."

"But you have our help anyway. We are always there, like Anonymous. We see you, even when you don't see us."

"I'm gone," said Morris, standing up from his breakfast table. The Russian gently raised a hand.

"Ramona says hello. She misses you. But it's too difficult now. She's gone somewhere else, to Venezuela, to wait."

"Fuck off."

"They know about you back home, my friend. You are not safe anymore. You need protection. That is our specialty. What, do you want to end up in an airport transit lounge? No, you need help."

"I'm out of here, I mean it. I don't need anyone's help. If you try to stop me this time, I will go to the police, I swear. You *need* me to keep functioning. I don't need you for anything. It's all done. You don't matter. I don't even matter."

Morris walked out of the hotel restaurant. The Russian followed but Morris went straight to a policeman outside the restaurant along Bayswater Road, just as he had promised. The Russian vanished.

Morris asked the policeman for directions to London Heathrow via the underground. The encounter with the Russian had clarified something he had known already: It was time to go home, immediately.

Morris walked down the busy road to the Lancaster Gate underground station. Black taxis were queued nearby, but Morris waved them off. He changed trains twice, to make sure, but he doubted anyone was following him—and he didn't really care. It was too late.

In Morris's backpack, he carried the implements of another identity, which he had brought with him from Bristol for emergencies. There was a new tablet computer, with a new IP address, new credit cards, a new cell phone and, most usefully, a new passport and a disguise that matched the passport photograph. Morris started up the new computer and, using the newly minted credit-card identity, made a reservation for a flight late that afternoon.

30

WASHINGTON

Admiral Lloyd Schumer called the CIA director to alert him that he was sending a report for his eyes only. Weber read it as soon as it arrived, while the courier waited outside. It was a brief analytical report describing evidence that James Morris and other CIA personnel who worked for him had been in unauthorized contact with foreign nationals from China, Russia, Israel and Britain. The report cited the NSA's forward network-monitoring of malware that might be used by Morris, and the analysts' assessment that an attack was likely.

The report was written in careful, noncommittal language, but the inference was clear: A foreign intelligence service might have access to the CIA's secret networks, through Morris or some other channel. The report also cited an earlier CIA defector report from Hamburg, never confirmed, about a possible hostile penetration of the agency's systems.

Weber's throat was dry. He had trouble swallowing for a moment. He took a drink from the jug of water on the credenza. There was nothing in the report that he hadn't already suspected, based on what Ariel Weiss had discovered. But it was a jolt seeing it typed on a page and bound in the top-secret folder of another agency. He felt the vulnerability of an automobile driver who sees another vehicle veering toward him as if in slow motion. The driver sees the crash coming with perfect vision, a frame at a time, but he cannot stop it.

On his desk Weber had taped the words of the oath of office he had taken a few weeks before. The language was dry and archaic, but he took the words seriously and looked down at them occasionally as a reminder of what mattered: He had solemnly sworn to support and defend the Constitution of the United States against all enemies, foreign and domestic. He had taken that obligation freely, without any mental reservation or purpose of evasion; and he had promised to faithfully discharge the duties of his office.

And now, he thought, so help me God, I am failing. He sensed enemies, foreign and domestic, but he couldn't touch them. He wanted to defend the Constitution, but he wasn't sure what that meant.

Beside the copy of the oath Weber had taped the three rules Sandra Bock had given him after he arrived as director: *Always have a plan. Always be the first to move. Always seek cover and escape the fire zone.* He was violating all three injunctions. This wasn't his world. The CIA wasn't his enterprise. His movements in this job were not intuitive and natural. They were guesses, rather than instincts.

Weber had only one colleague he trusted, and her only partially, a young woman with abundant intelligence and ambition but limited experience. He suspected the motives of most everyone else around him; even his chief of staff Sandra Bock was an agency loyalist who would work easily enough for another director when he was gone. But he had asked Ariel Weiss to be his person and work secretly for him. He needed to talk with her now, and he couldn't wait for another elaborate exchange of signals and a meeting in a suburban parking lot.

Instead of sending a circuitous message, Weber decided to invite Weiss through the front door. He summoned Bock and told her that with James Morris still unreachable, whereabouts unknown, he needed to see the deputy director of the Information Operations Center immediately.

Dr. Weiss appeared in the director's office an hour later. She was carrying a red folder that contained summaries of the IOC's current activities along with some new research on Morris.

Weiss hadn't had time to dress up for the sudden visit to the seventh floor. She wore her casual IOC outfit: black jeans, white shirt, short tailored jacket, long black hair pulled up in a bun that revealed her graceful neck. Weber still found Weiss's physical presence disorienting.

"Take a seat, Deputy Chief," said Weber. "We need to talk."

He opened his desk drawer and removed a plastic device that looked like a radio–alarm clock. He set it down on the coffee table facing the couch where Weiss had taken a seat. He flipped a switch, and from the device came the sound of surf on a beach: the gentle cascade of the wave rolling inshore and the pebbly wash of its retreat. Weber turned up the volume until it was loud enough to cover their voices.

"It's called a Sound Soother," he said. "It's supposed to help you fall asleep. Never travel without one."

"Are you kidding me? You think you might be bugged in your own office?"

"The walls have ears," he said, smiling, under the sound of the waves. "People have been playing games with me from the first day I took this job. Around here, even the shadows cast shadows."

She appraised him. He wasn't Superman, certainly, but he was tough. He was making bets without knowing the outcome.

"You're a gamer," she said. "You don't scare easily."

"I'm stubborn. I received a report this morning from the NSA. They're seeing the same foreign tracks around Morris that you did. They're wondering if there's someone inside the agency with a foreign connection."

"How can I help?" That, at least, was not an offer she had made to Hoffman.

Weber ran his hands through his hair. It was too long. Since becoming CIA director, he hadn't found time to get a haircut.

"I'll draw you a chart. You're an engineer. You people always like charts."

Weber went to his desk and retrieved a pad of paper. When he returned to the couch, he drew a circle, and around its circumference he wrote five names: *Timothy O'Keefe*; *Cyril Hoffman*; *Earl Beasley*; *Ruth Savin*; and *Graham Weber*.

"These are the five members of a committee that nobody is supposed to know about. The members call it the Special Activities Review

Committee. The committee, how should I put this? It authorizes things in the name of the president that would probably be illegal, if anyone outside this circle knew about them."

Weiss studied the list. She pointed to one of the five names.

"Ruth Savin is the CIA general counsel. How can it be illegal if she's a member of the group?"

"That's precisely what she would say if anyone ever raised questions. She has legal opinions saying that the impermissible is permissible. That's what this committee is all about. I decided my first week here I can live with that. The president is the president. The Constitution says he can order whatever he wants through his representative on this committee, who is O'Keefe. So for constitutional reasons, I'm removing the commander-in-chief's man from my list of suspects. I'll remove myself, too, unless you object."

Weiss laughed. "You're the only honest one in the bunch."

Weber crossed out O'Keefe's name and his own from the chart.

"Let's suppose," continued Weber, "that someone on this committee is working for another government. My first job as CIA director is to identify that person and stop him, or her."

Weiss shook her head.

"You're looking for trouble, Mr. Director," she responded. "Don't complicate things. The bad guy here is Morris."

"That's what it looks like. But if there's one thing I've begun to learn around here, it's that you shouldn't assume the obvious. It could be any of them. We don't have a 'mole.' That's Cold War talk. We have a big fat worm that's eating us from the inside out. It's hiding now, waiting for me to make a mistake and get fired, so it can go back to work. But it's here. There's a ghost in the machine. I can feel it."

She gave him a look that mixed fear and something else, between sympathy and pity.

"I'm sorry for you, Graham." She had never used his first name before, so the word had a kind of intimacy. "What are you going to do about it?"

"We stress the system, to see who gets nervous. I am going to hit my fellow committee members. Scare the hell out of them, probe for the areas that would make them vulnerable to foreign manipulation: debts, personal connections, past activities. And then we see if they sweat. It's like what the Office of Security does around here, hooking people up to the box—except without a box."

"I can sweat their computer systems, too," said Weiss. "Have you ever heard of 'digital hydrosis'? If you stress a system hard, it perspires."

"The things I don't know . . . How do computers sweat?"

"Malware has tells. When you interrogate the system, it can't help but reveal inconsistencies like latency and other stuff when it's under the control of an outside attacker."

"Sorry, but that is unintelligible to me."

"Easy explanation?"

"That's the only kind I'll understand."

"Okay: If an attacker is controlling a system remotely, their interaction is slower than a user interfacing through a local mouse and keyboard—because it has to route through the global network. That's latency. And automated software accessing content on a network is going to do so in set intervals, where a human browsing would be at random intervals. That's another tell. Lastly, everything that executes on a computer has a unique digital fingerprint which can be hashed into a unique identifier that can't be changed or spoofed."

"So make the machines sweat. Scare the crap out of them."

"I'll try. But you make me nervous with your sound machine. I don't want to get fired. I want to get promoted."

"Your request is logged." Weber was trying to make a joke of it.

"That's not good enough. I'm risking everything. I need a promise."

"The only person who can fire you is me, and I trust you."

Weiss studied him. She understood him so little. Perhaps it was the businessman side of him, that he had so few edges or corners. His life was smooth. It didn't have tracks.

"How do I know that I can trust you?" she asked. "Some people warn me that I shouldn't. They think I'm making a mistake. They think you'll never last here."

"Do you believe them?"

Weiss thought about her conversation with Hoffman, the warning from her ex-boyfriend Aronson, the gossip among friends, the occasional shots across her bow from rivals within the building. These dangers were in the air, but the man across from her was real.

"I don't know. I want to believe that you can deliver. This place will be a mess if you fail."

"Then make a bet on me," he said. "You'll come out a winner."

"Don't make promises you can't keep, Graham," she said.

"I don't."

"Let me ask you something, since we're being honest. Do you have a private life?"

"Not really. Not since I took this job."

"Well, here's some unsolicited advice. Be careful. There are a lot of people in this building who don't like you. When the secretaries see me walking into your office, they roll their eyes. And outside, it's even worse. The DNI hates you. It's an open secret around town. You need to be careful. You're not from this neighborhood. If I'm the only friend you have, that's not enough."

Weber nodded. She stood and walked toward the door. He was going to call her back, but he knew that every word she had said was true. He did need to be careful. But he was going to run this all the way down to the end—find out who the traitor was and catch him in the act.

When Ariel Weiss left his office, Weber told Jack Fong, the head of his security detail, that he was going for a walk. He went to his desk and removed his Nokia trash phone and several one-time SIM cards; from another drawer, he took the encrypted BlackBerry that had his personal contacts. He took the elevator downstairs, accompanied as always. His security chief pressed the button for the garage level, thinking that they were taking the vehicle, but Weber punched "Lobby."

As he walked through the marble court, a few employees nodded but only one came up to shake his hand. The electric atmosphere of his first days had gone. People understood that the agency was in some kind of difficulty, even though they didn't know what it was. The rumors were flying that Weber might be leaving after a month on the job.

When he was outside, in the slight chill of early November, Weber stopped a moment and told the chief of his detail that just this once he thought he could manage by himself. He was only going a few hundred yards. When the chief protested, Weber told him it was an order. He descended the steps and walked across the VIP parking lot to the main road that circled the Headquarters complex. He headed right and walked just past the drive that led to his private garage.

Weber stopped and sat down on a bench. He took out his Nokia and made three calls, each to a senior national security official he had met through the Intelligence Advisory Board and an earlier tour on the Defense Policy Board. One now held a senior position in the National Security Agency; the second worked in the Office of the Secretary of Defense; the third was in the National Security Branch of the FBI. Each had access to the most secret counterintelligence information in the government.

Weber hoped that he had established a personal relationship with each one that was strong enough to carry the weight he was about to impose. But he wouldn't know for sure until his private network was in action.

Weber began by asking each one if they would promise not to reveal what he was about to tell them, regardless of other commitments they might have. Each agreed, reluctantly. Weber then explained that he was beginning a very secret counterintelligence investigation and would need help. He would be examining three senior intelligence officials. He explained the specifics of what he would be looking for: names, actions, reference points. He asked each of the three to report anything relevant to him personally, after leaving a coded message in Stratford Park off Old Dominion Drive in Arlington.

"I need to see who runs where, after I squeeze them," he told each of his accomplices. "If they contact foreigners, I want to know."

Before each new call, he changed the SIM card in the phone. When he was done, he walked back to find his security chief pacing by the front door.

31

WASHINGTON

Graham Weber began his stress tests the next day, after meeting his senior staff to review classified testimony he planned to give the next week to the Senate Intelligence Committee. He asked Ruth Savin to stay behind after the session. The other aides filed out of the big office, and Marie closed the door after them, leaving Weber alone with the agency's top lawyer. She was a handsome woman, all her features fused into a hard, dark jewel: the lustrous jet-black hair that maintained its perpetual youthful color; the intelligent face that kept its smile even when she was demolishing a bureaucratic opponent; the lithe body of a former dancer. Savin was tough, about big things and little things: She had personally demanded that Weber's predecessor, the unlamented Ted Jankowski, provide yoga classes for women who didn't want to sweat in the agency gym with the men and their barbells. And she got what she wanted.

"Is everything okay?" asked Savin when they were alone.

Weber shook his head.

"Everything's a mess," he said. "But you're going to help me fix it, whether you want to or not."

Weber motioned for her to sit down on the couch, and pushed his chair closer so that the setting would seem more intimate. He didn't know much about the CIA's lawyers, except that the operations officers resented them. The operators had started buying legal insurance in the 1990s, as colleagues began facing criminal prosecution for doing what they had been assured was legal and necessary. They complained that the lawyers had you coming and going: One set told you what you could do; then another set took you to court for following the guidance that was retrospectively deemed to have been incorrect. Their inevitable answer when officers complained about changes in the rules was: Get a lawyer.

"You don't trust me, do you?" she asked.

"Honestly, no. In business, I always looked at the general counsel's office as a necessary evil. But right now I need you. So I guess I have to trust you."

Savin shrugged. "Better to be needed than loved. That's what my mother said when I told her I would never get married. But then I got married. So I know it's better to be both, needed and loved."

Weber nodded in appreciation of her sardonic self-assessment. She was a likable woman under the hard exterior.

"I have a delicate problem," he said. "I need a smart lawyer's advice."

"But you couldn't get that, so you asked me. Okay, what's the problem?"

He paused and took a deep breath, knowing the offense he was about to deliver, and then pressed ahead with his ploy:

"We have some new reporting that Mossad has a high-level source within the U.S. government, maybe within the agency."

Savin nodded. Her face betrayed no emotion.

"How can I help?" she asked.

"I think I'll need to polygraph senior staff within the agency, without telling them what I'm after. Is that legal?"

"Sure, you're the director. You can do whatever you want with the Office of Security. But shouldn't you ask the Bureau to do this if it's an espionage case?"

"I don't trust them. They may be penetrated, too. That would just tip off the Israelis to shut down their operation."

Savin fixed him with a level look. She had a professional placidity, but she was a hard nut of a woman.

"Are you sure about this? Who's your source?"

"I can't tell you that. It's a personal contact, usually reliable."

"Foreign national?"

"Meaning what?"

"Does he have an ax to grind? Does he have 'Jew spies' on the brain?"

"I can't really tell you much, except that I don't think he's crazy. It's a serious charge. My instinct is that I need to check it out. Maybe I should ignore it. That would sure be easier, politically. You're my lawyer. What do you think?"

She squinted at him. Was he trying to trap her?

"Pursue it, Mr. Director. But be careful. I think maybe you're being diddled."

"What smells wrong to you, Ruth?"

"I think this is an old rumor coming back at you. For years after the Pollard case, people at the Bureau thought there was another high-level Israeli penetration at the NSC, or maybe the CIA. There was an electronic intercept that seemed to show the Israelis had information that could only have come from the highest level. The suspicion was that it was a Jewish-American with top-secret codeword clearances. They even had a name for this supposed Mossad mole: He was 'Source Mega.' Very dramatic."

"But it was bullshit?"

"Who knows? So far as anyone could tell, it was crap. The Bureau chased it for years. They went after AIPAC, Jewish national security staffers, the congressional committees, people at the agency. They came up dry. But they never proved there wasn't an Israeli mole, either, so the story lives on."

She studied him once more, then continued in a lower, slower voice.

"They even went after me. I was staff director of the Senate Intelligence Committee before I came to the agency. My boss was in trouble with the Senate Ethics Committee; he was about to get censured. The Bureau claimed I tried to call in some favors with the Israelis to help him out."

Weber nodded. "I heard rumors about that."

"Everybody did. That's the first thing anybody knows about me around here: That I was a suspected Israeli spy. And they turned up some pretty damning material, everybody thought."

Now it was Weber's turn to be wary. Why was she telling him all this? Was it to make clear that she was innocent, or to deflect him with a show of openness? He didn't know.

"What did they have?" asked Weber.

"Special intelligence, meaning wiretaps. They had a longtime Mossad agent under surveillance. They picked up a call between him and me. In the call, I supposedly asked him if he knew anyone who could help out the senator. I reminded him that the senator was a longtime friend of Israel. He said he would see what he could do. They had it all on tape. The Bureau tried to squeeze me with it, hoping they could find Mega."

"But the wiretap was phony?"

"No. It was all true. I said all those things. And even worse, the Mossad man made some calls, and the senator's ethics problem eventually went away. So they thought they had a real case. They took it to a grand jury."

"But you weren't indicted?"

She looked at him fiercely and pounded the table with her small fist.

"Hell, no. I'm not an Israeli spy. I'm a loyal, patriotic American. I have two sons who served in the U.S. Army in Iraq. I made a mistake in calling that man and asking for his help. I didn't know that he worked for Mossad, but that's no excuse. The point is, I never gave classified information to anyone. Period. How do you think I got this job as the agency's general counsel? How do you think I passed polygraph exams for ten years here? Do you think the Jewish conspiracy fixed that, too?"

Weber studied her. He had made her sweat.

"I didn't accuse you of anything, Ruth."

"Sorry, I was over the line. You may be a know-it-all from Seattle. But you're not an anti-Semite."

Weber laughed, despite the tension of the moment.

"What happened to Mega?" he asked.

"How do I know? Maybe he never existed. Maybe he's still out there. I have no idea. But I am telling you all this—at some personal risk, I would note, and without benefit of counsel—because I don't want you to chase an old rumor if that's all it is. You have enough problems already. Don't add to them if you don't have to."

"Is that a threat, Ruth?"

"No, it's just friendly advice, Graham. From someone who is truly your friend. I hated Jankowski and what he did. I blame myself for not blowing the whistle on him sooner. I want you to succeed. But I want you to be careful."

Weber nodded. She was the kind of ally he needed.

"Someone is fucking with us, Ruth."

"Meaning what?"

"Someone is reading our mail. It's the most dangerous thing that could happen to the agency. There are only a few services that could even think about getting inside our defenses."

"And the Israelis have the capability." She didn't say it as a question, but as a statement of fact.

Weber nodded. "That's why I have to make sure there's no Mossad penetration inside the agency: Because we've got company, from somewhere."

Savin looked at him, unsmiling and, for a long moment, unblinking.

"I'll help you in every way I can, Mr. Director."

She shook his hand.

"Thank you," said Weber. "I want you to do one more thing for me: Don't talk to anyone about this, not a soul. I'll think carefully about what you've told me. But for now, I don't want anyone else to know. I don't want to muddy the water. No talk, no movement, no alert. If Congress asks why they weren't informed earlier, that's my problem, understood? Can you promise me that?"

"Yes, sir," she said, again fixing him with that lawyer's gaze that was intimate and removed at the same time.

When Savin had left, Weber closed the door and sat down in the big red leather armchair. He shut his eyes and made his own mental notations. Ruth Savin was believable: She had said many things that would cast suspicion on a guilty person but an innocent wouldn't fear. He believed her when she professed her loyalty to the United States, but sometimes life was more complicated than that.

Of one thing he was confident: She had given him a promise that she would not disclose what he had told her to anyone else, nor would she take any action that might alert people to Weber's investigation. If she violated that pledge, Weber's three invisible friends in the national security bureaucracy would detect her actions, and Weber would know.

32

WASHINGTON

The second name on Graham Weber's stress-test list was Earl "Black Jack" Beasley, the chief of the Clandestine Service. Beasley was born to be a cardplayer or a spy; it had been his good luck to be both. He might have been a child of the East, in the sense that he lied so easily and believably that it was very hard even for a polygraph to register deception.

Beasley was in fact a son of the Bronx: His father had been a doorman in a building on Fifth Avenue, one of the first black men to crack the Irish Mafia's hold on those plum blue-collar jobs. The old man was always perfectly dressed and punctual. One of the tenants took an interest in him and his family; Beasley got a spot in a fancy private school, then a scholarship to Princeton. One day the prodigal son skipped class and took his handsome face and photographic memory into a casino in Atlantic City, and began the life that many of his colleagues described with the shorthand the "black James Bond."

But Black Jack Beasley was much more interesting and complicated than that double-barreled stereotype. He had traveled to the most extreme limits of risk without blinking. Weber wasn't sure he could make Beasley sweat. People said the chief of the Clandestine Service was like Smokey Robinson, the lead singer of Smokey and the Miracles, in that people had never, ever seen him perspire, even under the hottest stage lights.

Weber had been wary of Beasley as a figure of the old guard. He had been appointed to head the Clandestine Service by Jankowski, and there were rumors that Beasley had known about Jankowski's skimming of money, and perhaps more. The FBI director gave Weber a private briefing the first week, and he mentioned the Beasley rumors: He explained that when the first whiff of Jankowski's activities was in the air, Beasley had made an "operational" trip to Cyprus to see the station chief. The FBI suspected that Beasley had gone there to retrieve his own money and stash it somewhere safer, before the scandal began to shake the walls, but they could never prove it.

Beasley had been the subject of another investigation that was recorded in the files. During the early days in Iraq in 2004, there had been a diversion of operational funds: The agency at the time was bribing tribal leaders in Anbar Province with stacks of hundred-dollar bills that were air-freighted into Al-Bilad on wooden pallets. It was a covert-action program with loose controls—handwritten receipts, often in wobbly Arabic script. One of the agency's most trusted Iraqi agents reported to the station chief in Baghdad that tribal leaders were paying kickbacks to his chief of operations, who at that time was one Earl Beasley.

The inspector general launched an investigation. But it hit a wall after they polygraphed Beasley. He passed the lie-detector test on all the key questions. And after that, the Iraqi informant clammed up. When the Near East Division chief confronted Beasley about the missing money, Beasley called him a racist. Jankowski wanted him in Iraq, so they let him stay on. And in truth, he was a brilliant operator, first to last. He had shot his way through Al-Qaeda checkpoints more than once when Iraqis saw the black face in civilian clothes and assumed, correctly, that he must be a CIA officer. Beasley was a gunner.

Beasley had Russian friends. That was also on paper. He had been recruiting Russian agents on his first assignment to London in the 1990s, after the Berlin Wall came down. Moscow was the Wild West. People were looting everything that wasn't bolted to the floor, and some of what was, and then bringing the cash to London.

Beasley's technique was to troll for recruitment prospects in casinos. He was Mr. Lucky: He would dress up in his tuxedo, handsome as a movie star, and go to the craps table and start throwing money around. The big fish always gravitated to him; he was the best floor show in the casino. Always some of the high rollers were Russian. Beasley would lose a hundred thousand dollars with them, or win it, it didn't matter; and then he and the Russians would get drunk. Before the sun came up, they would begin spilling their stories and Beasley would have them. He'd unwind them for a week, and then move on to the next casino.

In 1993, Beasley had recorded more annual recruitments than any case officer in CIA history. Corridor talk had it that some of the money stuck to Beasley's fingers; that he and the Russian oligarchs shared secret bankers. That was part of the Cyprus rumor, back when the Jankowski scandal began throwing off smoke. But Beasley was too good; or possibly he was actually honest. He was such an artist that you couldn't rule out the possibility that he was innocent.

Weber knew that he needed leverage on Beasley, or Black Jack would float away once again.

When Weber got home the night after meeting with Ruth Savin, he put another SIM card in the Nokia and called a very particular friend. Walter Ives was the deputy chief of the Criminal Division at the Justice Department, who had responsibility for national security cases. He had been in that section since he'd left law school in the 1980s. Weber knew him because they had been classmates in college. Weber had been a lacrosse jock; the rough, portly Ives had been the team manager. Weber had made only a handful of good friends in college, but Ives was one of them.

Ives handled all the sensitive matters for Justice: the espionage cases, the surveillance and warrant applications; the prosecutions of intelligence officers that had to be dropped because the information was too sensitive to reveal. He was bald, with a large belly and the demeanor of a career civil servant: He bought his suits at Jos. A. Bank. He lived simply in a house in Silver Spring that was the nicest he could afford on his Justice Department salary. His compensation was that if there was one man in government who was trusted with all the secrets, it was Walter Ives.

Weber called Ives at home and asked to meet that night at a bar on G Street behind the FBI building where they used to go drinking when Weber came to D.C. for visits early in his business career. Ives didn't ask why; he hadn't seen Weber since he had taken the CIA job, but he knew he wouldn't be calling if it wasn't important.

The bar was a dingy old Irish pub that had survived in seedy decay even as the surrounding neighborhood became chic. This was once a place where broken Justice Department lawyers and FBI agents used to spend the afternoons pretending they were out doing casework, before the invention of the cell phone made such subterfuge impossible.

Ives shambled in. He was wearing a denim work jacket and a pair of trousers held up by suspenders, which made his stomach look round as a medicine ball. He wore thick glasses, and he looked from a distance like he might have wandered in from a homeless shelter. Weber looked ten years younger than his classmate.

When Ives sat down in the booth across from Weber, he smiled contentedly. He liked the fact that Weber, whom he had always regarded as a straight shooter, had become CIA director. Ives regarded misuse of government office as an outrage.

Weber ordered a whiskey; his guest requested a 7UP. That was another thing about Ives: He liked to hang out in bars, but he didn't drink.

"You're handling the Jankowski prosecution, correct?" asked Weber, after they had shared pleasantries.

"Jankowski is a jerk. That guy has driven his last Mercedes convertible, if I have anything to do with it." Ives still spoke with a New York accent, a vestige of his boyhood in Queens.

"Is he going down?"

Ives nodded. "He'll plead out. I have fifty counts of wire fraud before I even get started with conspiracy. A jury would eat him alive."

"I need a favor," said Weber.

"I don't do favors."

"Then this isn't a favor. It's a matter of national security."

"That's different," said Ives. "What do you need?"

"What have you got on Black Jack Beasley? Do you have enough to charge him in the Jankowski investigation?"

"Probably not. He's smarter than Jankowski."

"Is he cooperating?"

"A little. He says he doesn't know anything big, but he has given me some names and dates. He and his lawyer act like they're my best friends. Listening to them, you'd think Beasley was working for Common Cause."

"What's the best you've got on him? Not necessarily that you could prove in court, but that you feel in your gut."

"I have to be careful, pal. Even with you. What you're asking is a no-no. The judge would crucify me."

"What about the Russian connection?" pressed Weber. "It's in the files at the agency. Some of it, at least: The gambling relationships. The Cyprus accounts."

"Shit, if you have that already, why do you need me?"

"Because it's old, and people already know it, and Beasley's already made up a story to cover it. I need something new."

"Christ, Graham. What did he do to you? Bang your girlfriend?"

"I don't have a girlfriend," muttered Weber. "Give me a break."

"Sorry," he said. "What do you need it for?"

"I need Beasley's help on something big. But I've got to make sure he's not working for somebody else. I need to bust his balls and see what he does."

"You think he's working for the Russians? Shit, wire him up to the box. Don't waste your time asking me. Grill him yourself."

"It won't work with Beasley. The machine can't read him. That's what people tell me, people who've been through this with him before. It's not lying that moves the needle with him, it's telling the truth."

Ives sighed, like a man resigned to do the right thing despite the rules.

"Okay, I'll give you something you can use. This isn't grand jury information, technically."

"Whatever you say. I'm listening."

"Jankowski tried to use Russian contacts to hide his money. We think he got the contacts' names from Beasley."

"Jesus, Walter, that's pretty good. You got any details I can work with?"

"Some. You're right about Cyprus. That's where it started. Beasley knew a lawyer there who had handled money for him once. He was the Goldman Sachs of money laundering, this guy. He had connections everywhere. He knew how to set up trustee accounts that had no traces. No name behind the number; just a law firm. The firm would place money in different locations: a hundred million here; fifty million there; two hundred million a third place. Never so much that people got really suspicious. And you know where this magical law firm was based?"

"New York City."

"Close enough. Stamford, Connecticut. And what do you suppose they would say, whenever we made inquiries?"

"Attorney-client privilege."

"You got it: A lawyer in the States has ironclad protection. Honestly, Graham, the Cayman Islands can't touch America when it comes to money laundering. Jankowski had already used cutouts before it got to the lawyer anyway, thanks to Beasley's man in Cyprus. The Cypriot banker would collect the money for Jankowski, then distribute it to trusts, all of which had power of attorney that resided in the vicinity of Stamford, Connecticut. Nice, huh?"

"Sweet. How did you crack it?"

"The Foreign Intelligence Surveillance Act is a great piece of legislation. That's all I have to say on that subject."

"So Beasley gave Jankowski the name of Mr. Fixit in Cyprus?"

"Correct."

"What else do you have on him? I need to really scare the shit out of him, Walter."

"I have one more thing. We did turn up a Russian connection. His name is Boris Sokolov. He used to be mobbed up with the scariest people in Russia and Ukraine. Then he got so rich he went straight, more or less, and moved to London. He's in the software business, in addition to every other business you can imagine. I think he was one of Beasley's agents once upon a time. Black Jack clammed up when I ran the name by him: National security matter, can't discuss it. I pushed him; I mean, look, my clearances are higher than Beasley's, for Christ's sake. But his lawyer asked to talk to the judge in camera, and we dropped it."

"What's the Sokolov connection to Jankowski?"

Ives leaned toward Weber across the table in the little booth, so that their heads were nearly touching.

"I can't prove this. But I think Sokolov is an agency asset, right? He's also wired into the SVR, probably handling money for people in the Kremlin. This is a guy who doesn't make enemies. So Jankowski and Company must have had contact with him as a source, right? But he's also investing with Jankowski through one of those numbered accounts. That I can prove. They have investments in a Russian database company that NSA doesn't like. I know that, too."

"Are you going to take it to the grand jury?"

"Nope. The AG decided it was a reach. That's how delicate it was, it went all the way to him. Don't ask me if the White House was involved, because I don't know. But the bottom line is we decided to let it rest. I told Beasley's lawyer that his client wasn't a target a month ago. Very hush-hush; even Ruth Savin doesn't know about the case. There. That's everything you need to know, which I told you only because I got a special legal waiver from the deputy assistant attorney general for national security."

"Which is you."

"Correct." Ives finished the rest of his 7UP. "I have to go. I'd like to flatter myself by thinking that my wife is worrying that I'm off with another woman, but she probably just thinks I'm lost."

Ives turned to go and then stopped.

"It's nice to see you, Graham. I'm worried about you. The word is that you've got some serious headaches."

Weber shrugged. "Just doing my job, like you."

"You want some advice?"

"From you? Always."

"Find yourself a nice girl. That's what my wife would tell you. This shit will chew you up, if you're all alone."

Weber smiled, for the first time that night. "I'll think about it," he said.

33

WASHINGTON

The next morning Weber walked down the hall to Earl Beasley's office and stuck his head in the door. It wasn't exactly a cold call. He'd had Marie phone ahead to make sure the esteemed head of the National Clandestine Service was in residence. Beasley popped up from his desk when the director arrived, feigning surprise. They had done reciprocal reconnaissance: Beasley had been alerted by his secretary, an African-American woman in her fifties who had been his personal assistant for nearly a decade.

Beasley was dressed immaculately, as always, in one of his Turnbull & Asser shirts, blue stripes against a white collar and cuffs that set off the cocoa brown of his skin. His cuff links were ribbed strands of gold, from Tiffany's. The belt was the subtly patterned skin of an alligator, as were the shoes. His suit fit every line of his body, made to measure by his tailor in Hong Kong, who he always claimed had been Richard Nixon's tailor, too.

Weber looked trim, but more weathered than a month before; he was still affecting the casual, tieless look, but it was less convincing now, and the workforce had stopped emulating him.

"How's the living legend?" asked Weber.

"Pretty fucking good, actually. How 'bout you, Mr. Director? You staying out of trouble?"

"The opposite. I'm stepping in it, with both feet."

"That's what people say, but I tell them: Do not bet against a billionaire. Bad mistake."

"I'm touched."

Weber approached Beasley and lowered his voice. "I need to talk to you. Outside the glue factory. What are you doing tonight?"

"Besides banging my new girlfriend? Nothing."

"Well, come out with me. We'll take my ride."

"Are you sure? You know what folks think when they see a good-looking black man in an Escalade."

Weber laughed. "Someday you're going to have to stop this race-baiting shit."

"But not yet. I'll see you at seven-thirty. I know you never leave the office before then, because my soul sister Diana reports to me. Actually, that's a lie. Marie tells me. But I want you to be paranoid that the brothers and sisters are watching every move."

"I'm doing fine in the paranoia department, thanks. See you at seven-thirty."

Beasley arrived at the appointed hour. He had just spent ninety minutes in the gym. Weber, in contrast, had been in meetings almost constantly. That was the surprise about running a big agency: It was entirely pyramidal, like a big American corporation in the 1950s. The director was required to make decisions all day long, every day, to take all the strands of this enormous secret bureaucracy and hold them tight in his hands as if he held the reins of a team of thousands of horses.

They took the elevator down together to the basement. Weber said something to the impassive Fong, the head of his security detail, out of Beasley's hearing, and the chief relayed it to the driver of the big Cadillac SUV.

Beasley got in the backseat next to Weber.

"I hate these fucking cars," said Beasley. "They're for pimps and hos. Why don't you get something dignified, like a Lexus or a Range Rover? Even a Ford Expedition would be better than this thing, which says: *I'm your bitch, Mr. President. I'm coming right over.*"

"Shut up, Black Jack," Weber said, trying not to laugh. He looked at the driver, who was also suppressing a smile. "Let's get out of here."

They motored out of the garage and turned left onto the circumferential road, which took them to the George Washington Parkway and then over the Roosevelt Bridge. Both men were silent most of the way: Weber had his eyes closed, resting after the unbroken attentiveness of his day. Beasley checked personal messages on his BlackBerry. He was divorced again, for the second time, and it was said around the office that he was with a different beautiful woman every night.

The Escalade crossed the bridge and made its way up Eighteenth Street. Just past M Street it made a left into a side street, and then left again into a service alley.

"Where we going, Mr. Director?"

"You'll see. My surprise."

The car pulled to a stop in an alleyway behind M Street, facing the back doors of the bars and restaurants that lined the 1800 block. The sign next to where the Escalade had stopped read LUCKY LADIES. Weber got out and headed toward the door of the establishment. Beasley stepped down from the SUV and turned to his boss.

"Are you taking me to a titty bar?" he asked.

"Looks like it," said Weber. "What's the matter? Are you afraid of white girls?"

"Shit," said Beasley, shaking his head and following behind.

They went up a narrow staircase into a dark room that was illuminated only by the spotlight on the dancer, who had already stripped down to her G-string. Weber eased his body into a booth in the back, almost invisible to the other customers. Beasley sat down next to him, adjusting his jacket and trousers so as not to get them wrinkled.

"You are a crazy nigger," said Beasley.

"Thanks. What are you drinking?" A waitress had appeared as soon as they were seated. Weber ordered a Macallan, neat, and Beasley asked for the same, with ice and a finger of soda. The dancer jiggled and jived under the lights. She was impossibly top-heavy, with a payload suited for a sixteen-wheeler on top of a Volkswagen body. Drunken men close to her were applauding and putting money in her garter. The drinks arrived. Weber clinked his glass against Beasley's and took a long swallow.

"I'm told case officers used to bring agents here," said Weber. "That was back before the world had gone hard core. Now I guess it's tough to impress people with a pair of tits."

"Isn't that the truth? I would have brought agents here, too, back in the day, but people would have thought I was a coke dealer."

"Good cover for an Exeter man, I would have thought."

"I went to Andover, asshole." Beasley was sensitive about his prep school background, which contrasted with his superfly image. Weber had that advantage over Beasley. He was a middle-class boy from Pittsburgh. The closest he had gotten to a prep school was working as a bouncer at a junior prom at Shady Side Academy.

The dancer wiggled toward their booth. She bent low over Beasley, nearly brushing her snow-white breasts against his black face. People in the bar couldn't see very well, but some of them were hooting. Weber put twenty dollars in her garter and nodded for her to move on.

"That was exciting," said Beasley. "Were those big things for real?"

"Of course not," said Weber. "God doesn't make them that size. Drink up. We're leaving."

"You mean I don't get to stay for a lap dance? I was just getting to like it here."

"Sorry, this stop was to confuse my bodyguards. They're out front scanning the customers. Meanwhile, we're going around the corner to an apartment where we can talk."

"Wow. You must work for the CIA."

"I'm learning."

Weber left forty dollars on the table. He levered his frame out of the booth and descended the back stairs, Beasley following behind. The big Escalade had disappeared. Weber led them down the alleyway a few dozen paces and then right, to the back entrance of a red brick apartment building.

Weber rapped on the service door; evidently he was expected, for it was opened quickly by a man in janitor's overalls, who led them up a set of stairs to an apartment on the second floor. It was provisioned like a proper safe house, with an array of food and liquor spread out on the countertop bar that separated the living room from the kitchen.

They started again with two more scotches and took seats across from each other at the dinner table. Weber was beginning to look relaxed, finally. Beasley, however, still unsure of the reason for this unlikely night out on the town, seemed to be getting more anxious. Beasley leaned toward his host.

"Okay, Graham, I call. Why did you bring a hardworking man like me out on a school night, when you know I should be at home calling my momma?"

"Like I told you this morning, I need to talk to you. There's trouble in River City and you and I need to get straight about it in a hurry."

Beasley threw up his hands in mock protest. "What did I do? Always blame the black man."

Weber brought his fist down on the table with a clunk that rattled the glasses.

"Cut the crap. Tonight you and I are going to be serious, for once. I need some answers."

"Okay, got the serious part. I'll put on my Princeton face, if that will make you feel better."

"Don't put on any face, just level with me. Otherwise you are going to be in a world of pain. I mean it."

Beasley sat back, surprised by the bluntness of Weber's words and demeanor. Weber could be a hard man when he needed to get someone's attention. Beasley eyed him, less playful now. He was off his game, not sure where Weber was heading.

"What's this about? Is it that Morris thing? Because I don't know anything about where he is or what he does. The little prick hides everything from me."

"Listen to me," said Weber. "The worst thing that could happen to an intelligence agency is happening to us. Someone has gotten inside the house and monkeyed with the wiring. I thought at first that it was just Morris, but now I'm not so sure. What I'm seeing could only have been done by another intelligence service."

"Who you looking at?" asked Beasley. He had emptied his glass quickly and was staring at it, wishing there were more.

"The Russians," said Weber. He paused and studied his companion's face. Beasley was too good a player to show any obvious reaction.

He was staring back at Weber. That was a peculiarity, perhaps. It was a statement that should elicit a reaction.

"You think?" said Beasley after a few seconds.

"The Russians have the tradecraft in cyber, for sure. They have the motive, which is that they still live and breathe for the chance to run a penetration against us. They have all of Snowden's goodies in their kit now. And maybe they have an old friend in the agency, to whom they could turn for help."

Weber said the last few words slowly and quietly, so that the implicit message would be clear.

"What the *fuck* is that supposed to mean?" responded Beasley.

"Tell me about Boris Sokolov. And keep your voice down, or we can go down to Pennsylvania Avenue and do this at FBI headquarters."

"Who's Boris Sokolov? What the hell is this? I should be calling my lawyer, instead of playing twenty questions with you."

"I would definitely advise you not to call your lawyer, unless you want to turn this into an espionage case. In that event, I'll have you arrested tonight, and we'll do this the way lawyers do. So let me ask you again, politely, what do you know about Boris Sokolov?"

Beasley studied him, guessing at the cards in Weber's hand and calculating the odds.

"He used to work for me, as you obviously already know. I developed him in London when I was working the Russian account. There isn't a 201 on him because he wasn't that kind of asset. This was a matter of 'rapport,' shall we say."

"Meaning you stole money together?"

"Boris stole a shitload of money. He is a world-class thief, in addition to being a very good source of information. Me, I was a public servant. I've already been through all this shit with the Justice Department, as you doubtless also know. If they had a case, they would bring it. But they don't, and they admitted as much to my lawyer. So in my universe, that makes it official: I didn't steal a goddamn thing. Next question."

"Same one: Tell me about Boris Sokolov. Is he still working for the Russian service?"

"Fuck, yeah, part-time. Sure he is. That's why he's so valuable. He's inside their shit. But he knows that if he doesn't do what we tell him, we'll rat him out to the Brits and he can move to Murmansk."

"And you're still talking to him?"

"Occasionally. When I need something. He knows every dirty Russian on the planet. He's like a who's who of assholes. I get information from him that I can feed to my field officers. They do the rest. That's what the chief of the Clandestine Service does, by the way. I know you're new around here."

Weber ignored the shot. He wanted to unwind what was in Beasley's head, not fight with him.

"Let's see if I've got this right: You have maintained contact for years with an SVR asset, but you never recorded him as a CIA asset. Now, someone looking at that would probably say: *If Sokolov wasn't working for the agency, then Earl Beasley must have been working for the Russians.* Or am I missing something?"

Beasley shook his head. "You're scaring me, Graham. You must be in a heap of trouble, to be throwing a shitball like this at me. But since you made the charge, I'll answer it. No, I wasn't an SVR agent. Not now or ever. Pull it back, or I am calling my lawyer. And you can arrest my ass whenever you want. I'm not scared of you. You're fucking desperate."

"Why did you put Ted Jankowski in touch with Sokolov?"

"Say what?"

Beasley got up and walked to the bar, where he poured himself another whiskey.

"Let me rephrase the question," said Weber. "Why did you help Jankowski hide his money, using Sokolov and your fixer in Cyprus?"

"This is that same Justice Department bullshit. I told you they dropped it."

"But this is me asking. Why did you put them in touch?"

Beasley thought a moment. He could try to brazen it out, but it seemed possible that Weber wasn't bluffing about having him arrested, which would set in motion a process that would be very hard to control, and almost certainly ruinous to his career. Beasley answered with a practiced calm.

"Jankowski wanted to know people who were good at hiding money.

I didn't ask why, but I could guess. So I gave him the two best names I had. I didn't ask what he did with the information and he didn't tell me."

"Is that the truth?" pressed Weber. He had always thought that human beings were better at detecting lies than machines.

"Yes, it is," answered Beasley. He didn't say, *Fuck, yes*, or *You're goddamned right*, or offer any other embellishment. He just affirmed that it was a truthful statement. Weber decided to believe him.

"Okay," said Weber. "Charge withdrawn. Tell me something else, since this is truth or consequences. Did the Russians have a handle on Jankowski? Did he help them get inside the agency?"

Beasley paused before answering.

"I don't know. I've wondered that myself. The SVR would have burned him, for sure, if the president hadn't fired him. But I never saw any sign that he was on the hook to the Russians, and I was looking."

Weber nodded. He decided to believe that, too. He had one more question, which hadn't formed in his mind until that moment.

"Why did the president wait so long to fire Jankowski? A lot of people suspected he was stealing money. It was an open secret, but the president didn't do anything back then. What changed?"

"You want my guess? Because it's no more than that."

"Yes, absolutely."

"Cyril Hoffman liked Jankowski. He told the president he would manage the problem. When Hoffman decided Jankowski was going down, it was lights out."

Weber closed his eyes, trying to figure out in the flickering dark of his mind how these pieces fit together. His eyelids felt heavy from fatigue, as if weights were pulling them down tight. Beasley saw the drained look on his boss's face and reached out his hand.

"Hey, you okay, Mr. Director?"

Weber sighed and opened his eyes. It was oddly reassuring to see Beasley across from him, his perfect tie wrinkled, his white collar beginning to sag from perspiration.

"I have a favor to ask, now that I've run you through the wringer," said Weber.

"What's that, boss man?"

"It's very sensitive. If anyone ever asks about this conversation, I'll deny it happened."

"Okay. Got it. Mutually assured destruction."

"This is no joke, as you'll see. It involves Hoffman. I want you to pull anything you may have in your files on his overseas investments."

"Say what? Have you lost your mind?"

"No. The opposite. I know there was an investigation a few years ago about Hoffman's ties with some Chinese high-tech companies, through a Pakistani friend of his who used to be head of the ISI. It was briefed to the Intelligence Advisory Board when I was a member. I want some paper on that."

"Shu-wee!" said Beasley. "That could get me fired."

"Yeah, but so could all this other shit we've been talking about. I need it quick, like tomorrow morning. You need to go in and out. Get one of your secretaries to do it, so you don't leave any traces. Can you do that?"

"What's in it for me?"

"Survival," said Weber, "and a continued prosperous future."

Beasley appraised the director. It was true what he'd said: He was learning.

"You are a tough motherfucker, aren't you?"

"Yes, I am," said Weber. "Let's go home."

They exited the apartment by the back stairs, but this time Weber made for the bright lights of Eighteenth Street and turned the corner at M, back toward Lucky Ladies. Two burly men were standing outside the entrance, scanning pedestrians on the sidewalk. When they saw the director coming toward them, they jumped. The Escalade was parked down the block, and a few moments later it was rolling toward them.

"I'm your nigger," whispered Beasley as they stepped toward the car. "You can count on me."

Weber spoke into his ear.

"You're my colleague. And it's a fact: I am counting on you."

34

WASHINGTON

Graham Weber considered how to approach Cyril Hoffman, a man who for all his eccentricity was an intimidating presence. Hoffman had been balancing the equities of the spy agencies, Congress and the White House for so long that it had become intuitive. In this dexterity, it was sometimes said that he had taken on the characteristics of the Pakistani or Jordanian intelligence chiefs with whom he had dealt for so long, but that was an injustice: Hoffman was a tidy, cultivated gentleman, not a Third World secret policeman. He always had a notion of where he wanted to end up, even if it was not usually apparent to others. He had been appointed director of National Intelligence for the simple reason that he was the country's best manager of the craft. He was good at solving other people's problems and then receding back into his world of opera and rare books.

Weber by comparison was a Washington amateur. That made it hard for him to find an angle of approach, a need or vulnerability on Hoffman's part that he could turn to advantage. But Weber sought his own leverage in the financial records he had requested from Beasley.

Weber was pondering how to initiate the conversation. But as it happened, Hoffman approached Weber.

The intelligence director called Weber on the secure phone from his office in Liberty Crossing, a few miles west of CIA Headquarters.

He proposed that the two of them should go on an "outing" together. There was so much to discuss, he said, and the office didn't seem like the right place.

"I suggest that we go boating," ventured Hoffman. He explained that he kept a small sailboat at a marina on the Potomac, just south of the airport. He proposed a nautical rendezvous that afternoon, if Weber could clear his schedule: It was a clear day with fair winds; high tide was at three, so they should meet at the marina at two-thirty, sharp.

Weber apologized that he was due at the White House that afternoon for an NSC meeting. But Hoffman said cheerily not to worry about that, the meeting had been canceled. When Weber's secretary Marie called the Situation Room a minute after he hung up with Hoffman, she was told that the meeting had just been postponed because some of the principals couldn't be present.

The two intelligence chiefs arrived at the Washington Marina within a minute of each other. They made an improbable sight for the handful of people at the landing that early November afternoon. The two shiny black SUVs pulled up to the gray face of the boathouse; the security details had already staked out the wooden dock. Overhead was the roar of a Delta jet coming in to land at the airport a half mile away across the shallow bay. A young couple who were pedaling their bicycles along the Potomac bike path stopped to watch; they were shooed along by one of the security men.

Hoffman descended from the open door of a Lincoln Navigator, a car even more grotesquely large than Weber's Cadillac Escalade. He was wearing boat shoes and a pair of faded cranberry-red pants. For a top-coat, he wore a jacket embroidered with the DNI's logo on the left breast and his name, *Cyril*, in script on the right. Atop his head was a sun-bleached cap that had the word (REDACTED), in parentheses, stitched above the brim.

Weber was wearing the outfit he had put on that morning for work. In deference to Hoffman he had worn a tie, but when he saw his host's boating costume, he took it off and put it in his jacket pocket. Hoffman had Weber on the back foot already; Weber wondered if the director of

National Intelligence had discovered his recent discussions with Ruth Savin and Earl Beasley and was attempting a preemptive strike. But the CIA director was not entirely defenseless; he'd had a productive morning with Beasley, before Hoffman's call.

Hoffman's sailboat was already rigged and moored to the dock, its sails flapping in the wind. A man in jeans and sneakers stood by the forestay, holding the boat steady. Under his jacket was the bulge of a weapon.

"My yacht," said Hoffman, gesturing toward the small craft. It was a nineteen-foot fiberglass sloop, from a class known as the "Flying Scot," as simple a boat as you could find. On its stern was painted its name, (REDACTED), along with its home port, WASHINGTON, D.C.

Hoffman stepped gingerly into the vessel and assured himself that everything was shipshape before inviting Weber to join him. His round gut bowed the blue shell of his windbreaker, but he moved with surprising agility. Weber clambered aboard with less finesse, and the little boat dipped sharply when he stepped in. The security man in sneakers steadied the craft while Weber boarded, holding the side stay to keep it from rocking. Weber settled into place along the port railing.

"Do you know how to work the jib?" asked Hoffman.

"Nope," answered Weber. "They didn't have a yacht club in Pittsburgh."

"I can manage it," said Hoffman contentedly. He reached around Weber and trimmed the jib, pulling the sheet through a wooden jam cleat.

"Cast off," he told his aide on the dock, who undid the bowline and laid it on the foredeck. Hoffman trimmed the flapping mainsail until it was taut and gently filled with wind. He pulled the tiller toward him and the little boat glided off on a puff, while Hoffman hummed to himself.

Weber was sitting on the leeward side, his weight tipping the boat toward the water as it slipped away from the dock.

"Move, please," said Hoffman, gesturing to the windward side. Weber transferred his frame to the other side of the cockpit, and the craft immediately righted itself and gurgled forward. Another plane was just overhead, casting a large shadow on the water and ruffling the sails with the exhaust of its engines.

"Isn't this just . . . ripping?" asked Hoffman, gazing with pleasure at the wide expanse of the Potomac. Weber nodded dutifully, though his face betrayed discomfort. He pulled his cashmere blazer tight against the breeze.

"There's a Top-Sider jacket in the hold," said Hoffman. "Put it on. You'll feel much more comfortable."

Weber reached under the deck for the windbreaker. His movements rocked the boat and he had to grab for the railing to steady himself. When he put on the yellow slicker, he stopped shivering.

The boat was churning along, making for the wooden breakwater that skirted the western edge of the harbor. Hoffman adjusted the jib and checked to make sure that the centerboard was properly lowered. Then he turned to Weber, taking off his (REDACTED) cap so that the bill didn't obscure his view of his companion.

"Comfortable?" asked Hoffman.

"More or less."

"Good, because I need to discuss something uncomfortable. Sorry to drag you out on the water, but I couldn't think of a more secure place to have a conversation."

"I figured."

"You're in trouble," said the DNI.

"I know," answered Weber.

Hoffman continued as if he hadn't heard the response.

"Your problems come in different shapes and sizes. The biggest is James Morris. He's on the wind, you can't find him and there is every reason to believe he is up to serious mischief. I believe the NSA director sent you a little something summarizing his concerns about young Morris and his misadventures."

"It scared the hell out of me," said Weber.

"As well it should. How much do you know about Morris?"

"A little," said Weber. "I'm digging for more. What can you tell me?"

"Two things that might be useful. First, he is, forgive the term, a pervert."

"What's that supposed to mean?"

They were nearing the breakwater. Hoffman eyed the sail. He reached past Weber for the jib sheet and pulled it out of the cleat so that it fluttered for a moment in the wind.

"Ready about," said Hoffman. He pushed the tiller away from his rotund form, announcing at the same moment, "Hard a' lee."

The mainsail swung amidships as the boat turned into the wind. Hoffman pulled in the jib sheet on the starboard side and cleated it, motioning at the same time for Weber to transfer his bulk to windward. This ballet took less than five seconds and the boat was skimming off on the other tack. Hoffman moved with economy; even with a touch of grace. He studied the sails and the sky, seemingly lost in the rigging of his little boat.

"You were saying," pressed Weber. "How is Morris a pervert?"

Hoffman blinked, paused and blinked again.

"Let us say he has peculiar sexual tastes. Far be it from me to question another person's personal behavior and interests. Live and let live, says I. The problem with Mr. Morris is that he 'acts out,' in a way that exposes him and the agency to danger."

"He 'acts out' what?" asked Weber.

Hoffman answered clinically, through pursed lips, as he enumerated the behavior.

"Bondage, discipline, sadism, masochism, bestiality, coprophilia, urophilia, acrotomophilia. A full spectrum of deviant activity, I would say."

"How do you know?"

"Because he's sloppy. He allows himself to be known. That is the part that is not forgivable. The rest, piff, what do I care? But he is beginning to raise eyebrows."

"Not at the agency. This is the first I've heard of any of it. The book on him is that he's a weird, smart kid who knows a lot about hacking."

"He is all that: a useful fellow in most respects. But he is also a deviant. That is rather common in the hacker underground, or so I am told. They have been poached in pornography, these hackers. That is part of the cult. Obtaining illegal or extreme imagery is a rite of initiation."

"Is that so?" said Weber vaguely. He felt stupid and wished, even more than before, that he wasn't captive on this little vessel with a skipper who resembled Humpty Dumpty in boat shoes.

Hoffman gently wagged a finger toward Weber.

"Your problem, if I may say so, is that you consort with other high-minded individuals like yourself, who couldn't conceive of such activities and thus tend to overlook the evidence. But you might ask that nice young woman Ariel Weiss, whom you've been consulting. I'll bet she has her suspicions about what Morris does after dark."

"How do you know about her?"

"Please, Graham. I don't want to seem boastful. But there is very little that I don't know. Every intelligence agency in the nation reports to me, and there are few people in senior positions who don't owe me a favor of one sort or another. Dr. Weiss is an ambitious young woman. Of course I know her."

Weber was silent, pondering what Hoffman had just told him, and also the puzzling question of why he had chosen to share this information now.

The little boat had made its way to the middle of the broad river. Ahead lay Bolling Air Force Base and its neat rows of military housing. To the west, upriver, was the compact epicenter of national government: Congress, the civilian agencies, the White House, the monuments and museums, all arranged symmetrically as if the federal establishment were a formal garden. The president was weak, it was universally believed; the Congress was enfeebled by partisan divisions; it was as if the balance wheel had broken and the real work of the government had stopped, but the garden remained immaculate.

"I think . . ." began Hoffman, without finishing the sentence. His attention was absorbed by the boat. He tacked again so that they were heading upstream, and then he steered farther off the wind, easing the main and jib sheets so that the sails were extended. The little craft gained speed as it sailed on a broad reach toward Hains Point.

Weber was impatient. He didn't give a damn about sailboats. He was running an intelligence agency that had been penetrated, by whom or for what purpose he didn't understand, and meanwhile he was trapped in a confined space barely large enough for two big men, while his host discussed sexual practices using obscure Latin words.

"You said you had two things to tell me about Morris. What's the other?"

"Ah, yes," said Hoffman, coming back into focus. "It seems that Morris is uncommonly friendly with the Chinese."

"Are we talking sex again?" asked Weber, though on this subject he actually knew more than he was letting on.

"No, we are talking business. Morris has a surprising range of Chinese contacts in the information technology area. I believe some of them trace back to his youth. He spent two years in China after graduating from Stanford. Were you aware of that?"

"Yes, actually. I know Morris did some programming for Hubang Networks back then, among others. He has been running an off-the-books research center in Cambridge with a Chinese partner, too. People tell me that it gets its money from a black account in the DNI's office. Fancy that!"

"Clever you." Hoffman took his hand off the tiller and clapped his hands. "But don't you find this Chinese connection worrying?"

"Everything about Morris worries me."

"NSA thinks he is in regular contact with some of the corporate fronts the PLA uses for its cyberwar operations. Not just Hubang, but Golden Sunrise Technology in Shanghai, and Sinatron Systems in Guangzhou. Very bad actors, those two, the NSA says. They want me to blow the whistle on him. Cut him off. And they have some disturbing information about Russian contacts, as well, that I won't bore you with now."

"But you're not sure it's time to pounce yet," said Weber. "You want to watch and wait, and see what else Morris is up to. Am I right?"

"That is our modus operandi in counterespionage cases, as you will discover. We are not policemen but intelligence officers, so we would always prefer to let things play out longer and see where they lead. But with Morris, I am beginning to wonder. Perhaps it is time, as the FBI likes to say, to 'pull the trigger.'"

"Take him down, Cyril. Be my guest, if you can find him. It's going to be one hell of a scandal when it comes out: a CIA officer with links to the Russians and Chinese. And what's more, he was working on secret, undisclosed programs for the director of National Intelligence. I may get my wish and bring the house down, after all."

"There are other ways to pull the trigger, Graham. We can let the unfortunate Morris autodestruct, as it were. He can play out whatever fantasy he's working on, and destroy himself in the process."

"You're the master," said Weber, pulling back the strands of hair that were blowing in the wind. "But here's what's puzzling me. I'm asking myself: Why does Mr. Hoffman have a hard-on for Morris all of a sudden? Two weeks ago when I asked for advice you had the mumbles."

"'Hard-on' is not a term in my professional vocabulary," said Hoffman primly. "Nor is 'mumbles.' But I am inclining toward the view that we should take action against Morris soon. This is a man capable of doing serious damage."

Weber eyed Hoffman. The two of them were confined in such a tiny area, it was as if they were on top of each other. The sloop rocked in the big wake of a passing powerboat. Weber leaned back against the bulkhead for balance.

"You don't have to convince me that Morris is trouble," said Weber. "But the funny thing is, he's not the only person who has close ties with the Chinese and the Russians."

Weber let his words sit in the air for the moment. Hoffman fiddled with the jib sheet.

"Whatever do you mean?" asked Hoffman.

"Well, take yourself: As director of National Intelligence, you're the top dog. But people tell me you met six months ago with the chief technology officer of Hubang Networks. And I'm told you even have some investments with Chinese technology companies that are held for you by a trustee in Islamabad. A former general named Mohammed Malik. Do I have that right? And I learned something interesting today about the Jankowski case. Did you know that he didn't keep all the money he skimmed? No, apparently he had a partner in the intelligence community who shared the loot. They did it through a common contact in the SVR."

"Well, aren't you a sly fellow," said Hoffman. His eyes narrowed till they were small slits on that big round face. "You've been spying on your Uncle Cyril. That's unfriendly, where I come from. Not what you'd expect from a shipmate."

"Due diligence," said Weber.

Hoffman studied the younger man. There was a new coldness in his manner, as if a switch had flipped. He had regarded Weber with mistrust before, but now it was something closer to open hostility.

"If you bother to check," said Hoffman, "you'll find that all my investments have been disclosed to the White House counsel's office."

"I have checked," said Weber. "There's no record of the Pakistani trust or its Chinese holdings. And the DNI secretariat hasn't logged any of your meetings with the man from Hubang, or with the chief technology officer of Yabo Systems. As for the Russians, I gather the information has all been given to the grand jury. The prosecutors just aren't sure what to do with it yet."

"Are you threatening me?"

"Not at all, skipper. I just wanted you to know that I've been doing my homework."

Hoffman stared ahead at the approach of Hains Point, still a hundred yards distant, and looked up at the darkening sky.

"Prepare to jibe," he said curtly. "That means lower your head, or the boom will take a divot out of it."

Weber dropped as low as he could in the small boat. Hoffman called, "Jibe ho!" and pulled the tiller toward him. The wind caught the mainsail and it whipped sharply across the beam, just missing Weber.

"I think it's time to return home, don't you?" said Hoffman mildly. "It's getting late."

"I was just starting to enjoy myself. But whatever you say."

Hoffman steered the boat on a close reach back toward home. The wind was dying as the light fell, and they were making slower progress downstream than they had before, even with the gentle push of the tide and the river current.

"You surprise me, Graham," said Hoffman.

"Why is that? Because I don't roll over and let people pat my tummy?"

"That's part of it, yes. It turns out you are a resourceful fellow. But I was thinking more of the fact that you appear to have no clear idea of what you are dealing with. You have insinuations, but not a plan."

"Don't be so sure, Cyril. But speak. Enlighten me."

"I think I've said enough already. Too much, probably, but never mind. Time's up. The creditors have called their notes. Bankruptcy looms. Isn't that what your business friends would say, eh, Graham?"

Hoffman took a cell phone from the inside pocket of his blue jacket, just under the stitching that read *Cyril*, and placed a call to his aides at the marina.

"We need a tow," he said into the phone. "Send the launch."

He put the phone away. Within thirty seconds they could see a twin-engine powerboat moving out of the harbor and toward them at high speed. Several minutes later, the Coast Guard launch was alongside, and a uniformed sailor was attaching the towrope to the bow cleat of *(Redacted)*.

Hoffman sat impassively in the stern. The bow of the sailboat lifted as the towrope took hold, and then the powerboat surged forward, pulling its cargo in its wake. The sailboat's stern was so low that the water churned just behind Hoffman's ample bottom, spraying his cranberry-red trousers.

Weber studied him, measuring the man: Hoffman had been prepared to sacrifice James Morris with an indifference bordering on ruthlessness, but what was he trying to protect in the process? The DNI chief had alleged that Morris was a tool of Chinese intelligence, and perhaps the Russians too, but the very directness of his ploy made that allegation suspect. Hoffman obviously knew more about Morris than he was willing to share.

And what of Hoffman's own links abroad? The intelligence director had bristled at Weber's mention of his dealings with the Chinese and Russians, but that touched only a corner of Hoffman's global network. Weber was gathering the elements of a complex story, but Hoffman was right: He didn't sufficiently understand what he was dealing with. Yet, watching Hoffman's angry, sullen actions, Weber had reason to hope that he would soon know more. Everyone made mistakes eventually, even Cyril Hoffman.

Hoffman was silent. He had said his piece, and heard more than he had expected in return, and now his boating foray was over. Hoffman looked at his watch. The silence continued until the little boat reached the landing.

In Hamburg that day, K. J. Sandoval, still toiling as a consular officer on the Alsterufer, received an anonymous letter addressed to her work name Valerie Tennant. Inside was a picture that had been taken from a screen grab of a posting in a password-protected chat room. The page displayed a caption with the German words *Ein Held*. A hero. Below the words was a picture of a man Sandoval immediately recognized.

It was the thin, elusive but unmistakable face of James Morris. Sandoval knew who had sent the photograph. It was from Stefan Grulig, the German hacker who hated the idea of people shitting in his Internet church. His message was that comrades in the hacker underground, for whatever reason, regarded Morris as a champion of their cause. Grulig didn't have to sign his name to the message; he was the only person who knew the Tennant identity.

Sandoval scanned the photo and sent the encrypted file to the pseudonym account of Graham Weber at Headquarters.

When Weber saw the photograph, it confirmed his deepest worry about Morris. The spark that he had seen so many months ago in Las Vegas—the passion that had made the young man such a creative intelligence officer—had burned through his loyalty oath.

Weber called Beasley and asked him to work with the London station to utilize the surveillance network deployed by British police to find James Morris, urgently, now, and to have him arrested if he could be located. The British were said to have four million hidden cameras in place. That surveillance network could do almost anything, except see through disguises.

Weber made one more request of Beasley. He asked him to immediately promote Kitten Sandoval one grade, to GS-14, and to begin looking for an opening as station chief for which she would be the first candidate, director's orders.

35

SAINT-BRIEUC, FRANCE

Cyril Hoffman had never found a truly "neutral" meeting place during the Cold War, for all that people talked about Vienna or Istanbul or Berlin or Hong Kong. Those were simply divided cities that straddled the fault line. The closest he had come to a free zone during his decades as an intelligence officer was France. It was the French need to conceal secrets that made the country a discreet rendezvous point. Their business elite was interwoven with a kind of corruption that people expected in Lebanon, perhaps, but not at the center of Europe. To enter this forbidden France, it was necessary to have a French host who was part of the "*réseaux*," the networks of power and corruption. And Hoffman had discovered this space early in his career.

Hoffman required a meeting place because he needed to do a deal: He had concluded that he had no choice but to seek a devil's bargain with the Russian intelligence officers who had attached themselves to James Morris. He had pulled more information from Admiral Schumer at NSA and his counterpart at the FBI, and it was evident what the Russians were doing with Morris: They were riding the new ideological wave of anti-secrecy. It was absurd, given that Russia was a police state internally, but no more so than the Russian ability to raise the idealistic banner of global anti-capitalism in the 1930s. The Chinese might have a hand in Morris's machinations, but they were irrelevant to Hoffman, except for their future propaganda value. No, it was the Russian card that Hoffman needed to play, in a safe location.

Hoffman contacted his friend Camille de Monceau, who had for many years run a covert-action wing of the French DGSE from its tidy, modern headquarters on the Boulevard Mortier in the northeast of Paris. He did so indirectly, using as an intermediary a French journalist they both had known for many years. A sanitized telephone contact was quickly arranged, and Hoffman made his request. He told the French officer that he needed his help in organizing an urgent meeting, in France, with Mikhail Serdukov, the deputy director of the Russian external intelligence service, the Sluzhba Vneshney Razvedki, known simply as the SVR.

"He will ask what it concerns, *cher ami*," said de Monceau.

"Tell him it's about James Morris, and that it will be mutually beneficial. That should be enough. I would like to meet him in twenty-four hours, at a safe house in Brittany. If he agrees, we can meet in Paris and I'll take him there."

"Who runs the safe house?" asked the Frenchman.

"I do, personally. It doesn't belong to any service, just to *ton oncle*, Cyril. You'll never find it, so don't try."

Word came back immediately from Moscow that the Russian, who in addition to his other jobs ran counterintelligence against the West, would be pleased to meet his old friend Mr. Hoffman.

That left Hoffman very little time to prepare, and one essential task. He had his secretary call Dr. Ariel Weiss at her office at the Information Operations Center. It was a blind call, at Hoffman's request, from a nongovernment number.

"This is your mentor and protector," said Hoffman. "I said I might need to ask for your assistance. Well, now I do."

It took Weiss a moment to realize who was calling. When she understood it was Hoffman, she wanted to hang up, but knew that would be unwise.

"What do you need, Mr. H? As you know, I only respond to authorized requests."

There was a wisp of a smile behind her voice. She sensed that Hoffman was now the one in need.

"This request is authorized by *me*, damn it. I need whatever dossier you have gathered on Morris's overseas activities: names of his operatives, dates of payments, operational plans; whatever you've got."

"Why can't you get it yourself? That stuff all ends up in your shop."

"Because I can't. I am not doing what I'm doing, if you follow me. I am trying to straighten this business out, in a way that will not advertise itself. It would be very much in your interest to help me. And obviously, the corollary is true: It would be very damaging to refuse."

"Got it. But I have a request of my own. You have to tell me what you're using the information for. Otherwise, it violates normal tasking orders. I'm not allowed to give it to you."

Her tone was proper, but sly, too. She was using the community's own rules and procedures against its nominal boss.

"I'll think about it. Meet me at the Lebanese Taverna in Tysons Galleria in an hour, with whatever information you've assembled. I have a plane to catch."

"Meet my request or no material," insisted Weiss.

"Don't press your luck. Just be there in an hour."

Weiss collected the material about James Morris that she had gathered on her hunting expedition, including the final cache of materials she had obtained by stealth from Hoffman's own agency. She included the additional, corroborating material that the London station had pulled together about Morris's associates. She packaged it all together in the proper, security-coded folders, marked it for dissemination to the director of National Intelligence, and headed downstairs to the security officer. She showed him the classified materials and the routing order, as she was required to do, and then walked to the parking lot and her BMW convertible.

The drive to Tysons took less than five minutes. She parked near Macy's, a hundred yards from the restaurant entrance, and sat in the car until ten minutes before the appointed hour.

Weiss was waiting at a table upstairs when Hoffman arrived, his tie askew, his Phi Beta Kappa key dangling awkwardly on its chain. He had the not-quite-shipshape look that sailors refer to as "flying pennants."

"I know. I'm a mess. Don't tell me," said Hoffman, usually so fastidious. "Too much to do. Too little time. Did you bring what I asked?"

Weiss pointed to the bag near her on the banquette of the booth.

"Of course. But I need to know what you're going to do with it. Otherwise, as I told you on the phone, I don't have authority to give it to you."

She smiled primly. Hoffman rolled his eyes.

"I am going to use it to help young Mr. Morris blow himself up. I told you that before."

"But who's helping you? You said you're going on a trip. Who will you see?"

Hoffman shook his head.

"I can't tell you that."

She looked at the old man's eyes, which were worn with the stress of the last few days. She was not a bluffer, usually, but in this case she thought it was a reasonable bet.

"Obviously it's the Russians," she said. "They're the only ones who can stop these people. They could have stopped Snowden, but they didn't. Now you want them to help you detonate Morris."

Hoffman looked at her. His face was impassive. He began to hum, an atonal passage from *Nixon in China* by John Adams.

"I'll take that as a yes," said Weiss, smiling. "You're meeting unofficially with the Russians."

Hoffman took the bag and lifted it over the table. It was demeaning to have to ask for things. He didn't like it. He cleared his throat.

"I need you to do something else, please, Dr. Weiss. While I applaud your enthusiasm for wheedling information out of people, you seem to have forgotten that in this matter I have the leverage. You are a midlevel manager who has committed a firing offense, while I am director of a large government agency."

"So?"

"So I am going to require that you do something in a week or so, to bring this matter to a close. It may be distasteful to you, but it will allow you to keep your job. Nay, to advance further up the ladder."

"What is it?"

Hoffman smiled, feeling he had momentarily regained a little of his dignity by making another, unspecified threat.

"We'll save the details for later. It's just something that has to be done, that's all."

Hoffman stood, holding the bag that contained the modest trove of information that Weiss had brought for him.

"Sorry to be impolite. Not like me, really. But I am due at Landmark Aviation at Dulles." He looked at his watch. "Indeed, I am late."

Hoffman bustled off. It was too early to drink, but Weiss ordered a beer, just so she could sit and think a few moments by herself before going back to work.

Hoffman flew through the night in a Gulfstream jet, unmarked except for its tail number. He landed at Le Bourget, the airport nearest the center of Paris used by corporate aviation. Camille de Monceau, his friend from the DGSE, met him at the plane. With him was a man in a fedora hat and sunglasses, who embraced Hoffman and gave him a kiss on each cheek. The two clambered aboard, while Hoffman's plane refueled after the transatlantic voyage. When the petrol hoses were pulled away, the Gulfstream took off for the short flight west to St. Malo–Dinard, which was the closest usable field to Hoffman's destination.

It wasn't until they were in the air that de Monceau's guest, Mikhail Serdukov, removed his hat. He was a restrained, well-groomed Russian man, not at all in the old image of the KGB. He was well toned from the gym, dressed in a good Italian suit. He and Hoffman talked only occasionally, remembering meals in Helsinki and Beirut and Islamabad. Their French host gossiped about people they knew in common in the global intelligence fraternity: this Jordanian intelligence chief who had been blackmailed by his mistress; that Georgian who had been caught abusing prisoners and forced into early retirement.

When they landed, a deep blue French Citroën limousine took Hoffman and Serdukov the rest of the way to Saint-Brieuc. They left de Monceau behind, to watch the plane, as it were. Two well-armed Ravens from the Air Force's global security staff were there, as well, to protect Hoffman's communications gear.

The Citroën deposited Hoffman and his Russian friend at a beach house above the rocky coast at Saint-Brieuc. The November air was chilly, but a low sun was bright in the sky. Hoffman carried a briefcase. He led the Russian into the house. It appeared, from the outside, to be a derelict seaside cottage, built perhaps in the 1930s and then left as a relic of that time, shingles worn and paint peeling. But the door was open, and inside the place was warm and well lit.

Hoffman offered the Russian a seat in one of two big wicker chairs that were placed by the window and looked out over the sea. The windows had been cleaned, too, and there was a perfect view of the waves battering the rugged cliffs of the Brittany coast.

"Let me tell you a little story before we get down to business," said Hoffman. "Would you mind that? It might put us at ease."

"I always like your stories, Cyril. They make me forget what I am doing."

"Not in this case, my dear Mikhail. Not at all. I want to sharpen your appreciation."

"It is normal, then," said Serdukov. That was every Russian's favorite word, "normal," probably because they had experienced so little of it in their lives.

"I want to tell you how I came to acquire this house," said Hoffman. "That's a secret all itself, isn't it? And it will help you to understand what I am going to propose to you in a few moments. Does that sound reasonable?"

"Of course, Cyril. A lifetime tells me that you are reasonable."

There was a bottle of whiskey on the windowsill. Hoffman poured a glass for himself and a glass for his Russian guest.

"Well, then, here it is: I acquired this house from a Frenchwoman who, I dare say, was one of the great spies of World War II. Had it not been for her, it is possible that neither of our governments would exist; indeed, the entirety of our world would be different. For you see, my French friend, I will call her 'Juliette,' stole one of the greatest secrets of the war—the fact that the Nazis had nearly perfected their V-1 and V-2 rocket bombs. God knows how, but she managed to coax it out of some German officers, who must not have wanted Hitler to win the war.

"That is what our forebears did, yours and mine: They stole the secrets that won the war."

"Very interesting, of course, Cyril. But you are not a history professor, not me, either. And you are not in the beachfront real estate business, I don't think. So really, I do not understand."

"You are so impatient. That is not Russian of you. You must let the story unfold. But I will continue: The reason my friend Juliette sold me this house was that it was of great sentimental value to her, but it was also unbearable for her to look at. And the reason is that it was from this very spot that she was supposed to be rescued by the British and brought to London to be debriefed in more detail about the rocket bombs. There was a rubber boat that was supposed to pick her up, just out there."

Hoffman pointed through the window to a place just past the surf, in the lee of a rocky cove.

"Can you see it? Well, the British boat was there, all right, and Juliette was ready to scramble aboard to safety. But someone had ratted her out to the Germans. Betrayed her! Sold her for nothing, this courageous woman. And she was arrested here, right here, in this town, by the Gestapo."

"Remarkable woman. We had many like her, in Stalingrad and Saint Petersburg. We try to remember them, but it is hard now. The country they died for, the Soviet Union, does not exist. You took it from us. That makes me sad, I am sorry. What became of your friend Juliette?"

"Well, you see, Mikhail, that's why I wanted to tell you the story! She was taken by the Nazis into Germany. She spent a year in concentration camps. Ravensbrück. Törgau. Königsberg. The worst. She was starved, beaten, tortured. I needn't tell you the details. But you see, here is the miraculous fact: Through all that year of nightmare and death, she never told the Germans the secret that she had betrayed to the British. Not a word. She was silent. They didn't realize she had shopped their most advanced technology and allowed the British to combat the weapon that could have altered the outcome of the war."

Hoffman sat back in his chair. He drank from his whiskey. He pointed out to the spot in the cove and said again, "Right there."

"Why do you tell me this story, Cyril? If this is the prelude, what is the music?"

Hoffman handed Mikhail Serdukov the briefcase he had brought along. Inside were redacted versions of the documents that Ariel Weiss had given him, which he had prepared on the flight over.

"We have a problem," said Hoffman, "you and me and all the people who are heirs to the world that my friend Juliette created for us. The problem is that people from a younger generation, who do not understand what spying and sacrifice are all about, are trying to tear our world apart. They think that because technology connects everyone now, the world is open and there are no secrets. You and I know better than that. We know that without secrets, we will lose the very things we are trying to protect."

"This is about James Morris," said Serdukov.

"Indeed it is. I know that you are a professional, Mikhail, so I will not insist on a tedious rendition of the evidence that your people have been in contact with Morris, or that they have helped him leak classified information. Or indeed, if I am not mistaken, that your service killed a young man in Hamburg who had learned of Morris's penetration of the agency and was trying to alert us."

Serdukov put his hands up in protest, but Hoffman waved him off.

"Please, Mikhail. I made no allegations. And may I remind you: *Qui s'excuse, s'accuse.* No, the point I want to make is this: We have an interest in making Mr. James Morris and his little network of do-gooders disappear. I think you know where he is planning to strike. Well, so do I. NSA picked it up yesterday. He is planning to attack that atavistic symbol of global finance, the Bank for International Settlements."

Serdukov shrugged.

"What of it?" he said.

"My sentiments, exactly. I can even see some benefit for our respective governments. But the point is, Morris's other mischief must stop. I can find a way to blame his BIS stunt on others. But not if your colleagues continue to behave irresponsibly."

"What 'others' were you thinking of?" asked Serdukov.

"The Chinese. They are convenient for both of us. You will see, if you go through the documentation I've brought along, that young Morris has been rather promiscuous in his foreign contacts. Not the sort of thing a reliable agent would do."

Serdukov smiled, despite himself.

"Not at all," said the Russian. "An unreliable man, from what you say."

"Quite so. I knew that you were a man of reason. Always did, from the first time we met, what, twenty years ago."

"Thirty," said Serdukov. "How do you want to do this . . . business?"

"Ah, my dear fellow, leave that to Cyril. I just wanted to make sure that we were partners in this matter. And that it would stay buried within the ocean of oceans."

Serdukov looked at the coast, assaulted by waves, rocks becoming sand.

"Yes," said the Russian. "I think that is possible."

Hoffman shook his hand and poured him another drink. They took a little walk along the coast to stretch their legs, but they didn't tarry. They had done their business and it was time for them both to get home. Serdukov entered the blue Citroën, carrying the briefcase that Hoffman had given him, and headed back to Paris by car.

Hoffman waved goodbye, standing by the limousine window as if he were bidding farewell to a family member after an afternoon at their seaside compound. Another car arrived soon for Hoffman and returned him to the small, windswept airport at St. Malo–Dinard, where the engines of his Gulfstream were already whining.

The French host, Camille de Monceau, bade Hoffman farewell on the tarmac. The American, cleared by a special permission from the French air-traffic authority, flew directly back to Washington, arcing out across the English Channel and the Irish Sea. De Monceau returned by helicopter to Paris, where he was back at his desk before dusk.

36

WASHINGTON

As it happened, James Morris flew back to Washington via Paris. It was time to come home: All his software and hardware were in place; he needed only to hit the "execute" button. His new identity was solid, but he hadn't wanted to face the extra layers of security at Heathrow for a U.S.-bound flight. So he made arrangements with one of Beatrix's friends in Paris and stayed overnight in her establishment. He was spoiling himself: He knew that the alarm bells were ringing in Washington and that the game was up. But at least he could get home: His clandestine identities and special authorities remained intact. And he had the one real advantage that the spy always possesses, which was that he knew what he planned to do, and others didn't.

When Morris's plane landed at Dulles, he took a taxi to his apartment in Dupont Circle. It was cold and musty when he opened the door. The mail was piled up on the floor just inside his front door. Why did they even have mail anymore? Morris took off the wig and oversized glasses. He put the extra passports and credit cards and cell phones in the safe that was bolted into his closet. He took a shower to wash off the grit of the plane. He scrubbed his body with the flannel cloth until it hurt. When he emerged, wrapped in a towel, he cleared the steam from the mirror and looked at his face. He was thinner than when he had left. He could see the bones in his cheeks and the knobby cleft in his chin. In his eyes, he saw deep fatigue; it was an exhaustion that couldn't be erased by a hundred years of sleep. As tired as he was, his face looked flushed, as if his brain were too hot for his skin. He felt for his penis; it was limp and unwired.

Morris dressed, but he stayed in his apartment. He ordered groceries from Peapod. For dinner, he was too tired to make anything, so he ordered takeout from a Thai restaurant in the neighborhood. The smell of garlic filled his apartment. He opened a window to clear the air and threw the food away, uneaten. He took a slice of bread from the bag of groceries, and then another. He had the feeling that his body was an encumbrance; it was a chore feeding it. He went to sleep for a while; when he woke up in the predawn, he took a pill, but it didn't work.

Graham Weber summoned Ariel Weiss to his office. Weber was restless now, ready to pounce. His visit two days before with Hoffman had made him hungry. Marie knocked to announce the arrival of Miss Weiss. He looked at his face in the mirror over the credenza and saw that there was still color on his cheeks from two days before.

"Somebody's been in the sun," said Weiss when Marie had closed the door. She removed the black overcoat and red cashmere scarf she had worn against the afternoon chill and handed them to Weber, who hung them in his closet. She took a seat across from Weber's desk. She had two folders in her hand.

"Where have you been, anyway?" she asked, studying the unlikely November sunburn. "Tell me it's the Bahamas."

"On the Potomac," said Weber. "The director of National Intelligence invited me to go sailing."

"Cyril Hoffman? That old man? I can't imagine him in anything but an easy chair."

Weiss didn't mention the fact that she had recently seen Hoffman herself, and that she knew he had traveled urgently overseas to see a Russian. Concealment quickly becomes a habit.

"Hoffman is a man of many talents," said Weber. "He wanted to tell me confidentially that James Morris is working for the Chinese. Or at least that's what he claimed. You never know what's really inside Hoffman's head."

"You can ask Morris yourself, Graham. He's coming home today. In fact, he should have arrived at the airport from Paris a few hours ago."

"This is my day for surprises. How do you know that?"

"Because he told me so. He sent me a message, copying you and Beasley and Ruth Savin."

"An open email? That doesn't sound like Morris."

"He's in from the cold. He sent the message to our public addresses. Maybe he posted it on Facebook, too."

Weber stared up at the ceiling for a moment and then tilted back toward her. His eyes sparkled with the light of a man who thinks he has solved a puzzle.

"Morris is the fall guy. He's gotten a summons home from Control. It's a one-way ticket. He has become expendable. Whoever was running him doesn't need him. That's it!"

She looked at him with her head cocked, as if he had misspoken.

"But I thought Morris was the mastermind. How can he become the chump?"

"Morris is a dazzling performer, but he is not the ringmaster."

"I'm processing that, Mr. Director. 'Recalculating route,' as my GPS system is always telling me. Meanwhile, I have some new morsels for you."

Weiss handed the first file to Weber.

"Morris definitely has friends in China," she said. "Hoffman is right about that. I have the documentation."

Weber examined the file. It listed the employees of the Fudan–East Anglia Research Centre, along with more traces Weiss had run on Dr. Emmanuel Li and his intelligence activities on China's behalf, under a different alias.

Weber closed the file. He stared out the window, across the bare treetops.

"The Chinese are all over Morris," he said. "That's the line Hoffman was selling. But we don't see them doing anything. If it's an operation, what's the point?"

"Maybe Morris is a sleeper."

"Morris? Are you kidding? He's too noisy. That was another thing Hoffman wanted to tell me, by the way. He said Morris likes kinky sex. Is that true?"

"How should I know? Morris is my supervisor. I don't ask who he sleeps with."

"Hoffman claimed that extreme sex is part of the hacker culture, although for Hoffman any kind of sex is probably extreme. He said I should ask you."

"Thanks for that." She was blushing.

"As a technical expert on hackers," Weber said gently, "help me out."

"Well . . . it's certainly true that hackers get interested in weird stuff. 'If something exists, there's pornography of it.' That's one of the rules of the Internet. I'm sure Pownzor has seen plenty of bizarre material, and maybe he likes some of it. 'Nothing is sacred.' That's another rule of the Internet. But Pownzor is good at what he does. He wouldn't get caught unless Mr. Hoffman was looking very hard."

"Sorry, that was probably none of my business," said Weber, embarrassed now. "What else have you got for me, besides the fact that your boss is back and that he has Chinese friends?"

"We picked up something strange at the Information Operations Center. We're not sure why, but a new beacon started flashing this week inside the Bank for International Settlements. I phoned the NSA and they've been monitoring the same thing. I'm sure Hoffman knows about it."

"So what is this beacon telling you?"

"Probably that someone is getting ready to do a hack. They are moving the pieces in place for something. But we don't know what it is."

"Morris knows," said Weber.

"Go ask him, Graham. He'll probably be back in the office tomorrow. You can go over and surprise him. I'll message you when he's there."

"Morris may not realize it, but he has hit the wall," said Weber. "He's finished. He'll end up in prison."

"Okay, boss," she said. She wondered if Weber could pull it off. He kept surprising her, but she suspected he didn't understand how many enemies he had.

The next morning, after Weber had received his intelligence briefing from Loomis Braden and reviewed the overnight cables with Sandra Bock, there was a knock on the door. Marie said that the deputy chief of the Information Operations Center had called and left a message that the director, Mr. Morris, had returned to the office.

Weber summoned the security detail and made the short drive to the office park where the IOC was hidden away. It was ten, well past starting time for most government workers, but a few young people in T-shirts were still arriving.

Weber passed through the security gate downstairs and walked into the big operations room in the center of the building, where Weiss and Morris had their offices. Many younger employees were at their desks, working their two screens, jumping in and out of classified chat rooms. Their faces had the awkwardness of abnormally smart people whose talents had blossomed through antisocial behavior.

An Asian-American woman looked up from her screens as Weber was passing and was startled, as if she had just seen a celebrity.

"Oh, my god, Mr. Director," she said. "What are you doing here?"

Weber put his finger to his lips. "Shhh," he said. "It's a surprise visit."

He continued walking, past the glass-enclosed space where Ariel Weiss worked. She was at her machines, but she looked up at Weber and smiled.

A few dozen more paces, and Weber arrived at the metal door at the far end of the atrium that guarded James Morris's office. It had two electronic locks and an intercom to call inside. Where the rest of the center had the open feel of a communal workspace, this was a closed zone: a secure compartment within a top-secret facility.

Weber knocked three times on the door, harder with each rap. There was no answer. Next, he pressed the intercom buzzer. There was no answer to that, either, at first, but he kept his finger on the button until he got a response.

"Go away. I'm not seeing anyone," said a voice through the speaker.

Weber pressed the intercom buzzer again, and held his finger down for a full twenty seconds until the voice returned.

"Stop bothering me, damn it. Who the hell is this?"

Weber leaned toward the speaker. He spoke quietly so the rest of the office wouldn't hear him.

"This is your boss, Graham Weber. Open up, now, or I'll blow the fucking door off its hinges."

There was a pause of about twenty seconds, and then a buzz and the door opened. As Weber entered the inner office, he could hear the metallic teeth of a shredder. The door closed behind him, and there was a soft whirr as the locks automatically rebolted the door.

Morris approached Weber. His hair was longer than last time, cropped at different angles. Under his eyes were deep circles, beyond fatigue. He was wearing a black T-shirt and a short black jacket that barely reached his waist. He had lost so much weight that his body seemed to have too much skin; the wrists looked fragile enough to break. On his feet were a pair of black Chuck Taylor sneakers with yellow laces. Only his fingers, long and delicate, looked undamaged.

"You look like hell," said Weber.

"I just got home," said Morris. "I've been traveling for a while. I was going to call."

"But you didn't. So I came myself."

Morris bit his lip. His usual bland self-assurance was gone.

"Are you going to fire me?"

"Yes. And arrest you, too. Can you give me any reason not to?"

"No. Please do. Get me out of here. Honestly. I hate this place."

"What's wrong, James? You look like you've seen a ghost. Tell me."

"I can't." His eyes had lost their spark.

"Okay," said Weber. "Then I'll tell you."

The director spoke in the direct, assertive tone he had used in a thousand business meetings.

"You're in deep shit, my friend. The Chinese own you. Maybe the Russians, too. Your sexual fetishes are common gossip. You're trying to pull off a big hack at the BIS, thinking nobody's watching, but you're sloppy and you're about to get caught. So I would say, yes, you're in very deep shit. And the only person who can get you out is Graham Weber. But you have to level with me."

Morris shook his head and uttered a thin, nasally laugh, almost a snicker.

"You sound like the CIA director."

"I am the CIA director, Morris, and you are going down unless you start telling me the truth."

Weber pounded the desk as he spoke. The sound reverberated in the small, enclosed office. Morris was startled for a moment, but then looked away.

"I believed in you, at first," said Morris. "I thought you wanted to change things. But you don't. You want to keep them the same. I feel sorry for you. They'll destroy you."

The director pointed a finger at Morris.

"Save it for your prison memoirs. You piss me off. And you know what? I am an ornery son of a bitch when I get angry. I may not know everything, but I know more than you think I do. And I promise you, you will regret not taking my offer of help."

Morris shrugged. "I'd love your help, really. But it wouldn't do me any good. You can't do anything for me, Mr. Director. You're the anvil, not the hammer."

"Who's running this show? I'll bet you don't even know yourself."

"Ask Mr. Hoffman."

"I already did," said Weber. "He said that you're going down. He's going to burn you on China and on your sex games."

Morris shrugged again.

"I don't think so," he said. "But you should ask yourself why he threw me up as the bait. Why now?"

"Good question. What's the answer?"

"Hoffman thinks you're stupid. He thinks you'll go for the sizzle and forget about the steak."

Weber reached into his coat pocket and removed one of his Nokia "burner" phones and handed it to Morris, along with a slip of paper with his number written on it.

"Call me," said Weber. "It's off-line. You don't have much time. You may not want my help now, but you will soon. Either that or you're dumber than everyone has been telling me."

Morris looked at him skeptically, but he took the phone.

Weber exited the big bolted door and marched across the operations room, drawing more stares. The lights were on in Ariel Weiss's office along the side wall, but she wasn't visible through the windows. That was just as well: Weber needed time alone. The big black car was waiting, its engine idling. Weber told Oscar the driver to put the flashing lights on and get back to Langley in a hurry.

It was a frosty day, the first hint of winter in the air. From Weber's office on the seventh floor, he could see the dry leaves billowing in little whirlwinds, and fluttering across the entrance to the Headquarters building.

Weber dialed the cell number of his friend Walter Ives at the Justice Department. He asked if there had been any changes in the Jankowski case, including any new evidence about Earl Beasley, the chief of the Clandestine Service. The case was still on track, Ives said. The letter to Beasley's attorney informing him that he wasn't a target still stood. But there was one interesting development: Beasley's attorney had called the day before to set up a meeting the following week, where he said his client might have some new information that would further implicate Jankowski.

"How sweet," said Weber. Beasley was gift-wrapping his cooperation. The evening at Lucky Ladies and the conversation afterward had accomplished that much, at least.

"One more thing, Walter," said the CIA director slowly. "We are conducting an espionage investigation of one of our employees. His name is James Morris, and we think he has been leaking information with help from the Russians. I'm going to ask Ruth Savin to make a quick criminal referral to Justice. You should have it in a day. Get the Bureau to arrest him."

"So you found your mole," said Ives. "It's real."

"I think so."

"I'm sorry," said Ives.

"Yeah. Pretty bad." Weber rang off.

Weber had to finish ruling out his other suspects. He next called the three people he had chosen as his hidden scouts: The first was an Army brigadier general who worked as the deputy chief of the Central Security Service at the NSA. Weber asked him for the results of the project he had described a week ago: Had the NSA picked up any signals, through telephone or Internet messages, which would connect Ruth Savin to anyone on the watch list of known Israeli intelligence officers or agents in the United States?

"She's clean," said the Army brigadier general. "If someone's in contact with her, they're using a carrier pigeon."

Weber had never really doubted Savin. The swirl of Israeli influence in Washington touched everything and anyone connected with politics; it was the most successful political-action program in history. But once Savin had come to work at the CIA, she had only one overriding loyalty. People who impugned her were ignorant, or anti-Semitic, or both.

Next Weber asked the brigadier general about Earl Beasley, the chief of the Clandestine Service. Had Beasley been in contact with any Russian asset—an FSB or SVR officer, an agent of influence, a facilitator or banker? Again, the answer was no, but the general noted one interesting development: Beasley had asked NSA for any information on a Russian moneyman named Boris Sokolov; he was looking specifically for derogatory information involving Sokolov's contacts with Ted Jankowski.

Of course Beasley was gathering incriminating information; that was the gift for Walter Ives that Beasley was assembling for delivery by his lawyer. Beasley was a player; he was betting with the house this time, and laying on some extra insurance.

Weber called his second contact, who handled intelligence liaison in the Office of the Secretary of Defense. This man saw all the sensitive paper that zinged around the E-Ring. Weber asked him the same questions: Had he seen any monitoring or other data that mentioned either the CIA general counsel or the chief of the Clandestine Service? Here again, the slate was clean.

Weber polled his last counselor, the one who worked in the FBI's National Security Branch and had the most sensitive information of all. He had been looking all week for anything that might implicate Ruth Savin or Earl Beasley. The Bureau had informants and wire surveillance in so many places: It was like shaking a tree; if something was stuck up in the branches, it was bound to come loose and fall to the ground. But again, from the FBI contact, there was nothing.

Weber was satisfied that his two colleagues were clean: Ruth Savin, whatever her actions when she was a staffer on the Hill, had no discernible contact with Israeli intelligence; Earl Beasley might have a truck-load of dirty laundry from Russian mobsters and spies, but he wasn't working for them.

Weber asked the FBI man a last question that was so delicate he had refrained from querying his other two informants. Had anything passed across the screen of the FBI National Security Branch that suggested any unusual activities or contacts with foreign governments by the director of National Intelligence, Cyril Hoffman?

The FBI deputy director coughed awkwardly. He fumbled for words.

"That's my boss, sir," he said quietly.

"I know," said Weber. "But I need the truth. If you've seen anything, I want to know it."

The FBI director paused a long moment. Then he asked Graham Weber to meet him, alone, at the tennis courts in East Potomac Park at four that afternoon.

At Weber's insistence, they went in Jack Fong's own car, a Chevy Blazer. Fong left him at the entrance to East Potomac Park. The FBI man was standing next to the bubble that covered the tennis courts in winter. He looked cold and uncomfortable. He motioned for Weber to follow him to a space behind the bubble where they wouldn't be seen.

They talked for less than fifteen minutes, and then the FBI man returned to his office atop the FBI fortress on Pennsylvania Avenue. Weber went back to the CIA and told Marie that he had been out shopping. He rattled around the office late that afternoon and into the night, wondering what he should do with the information that he had obtained about unauthorized travel.

37

WASHINGTON

Graham Weber was not the first to move, violating a cardinal rule that Sandra Bock had given him when he arrived. The morning after his visit with Morris, he arose at his usual hour of five in his apartment at the Watergate. It was a gray monochrome outside, with a white chop in the water that made the river blend with the overcast sky. He had slept badly, in fitful interludes through the night. Weber wearily put on his sweats and sneakers and descended to the street and the jogging path along the river. He went downriver to Hains Point and back, paced by younger men and women who pranced by him with their bottoms wrapped in spandex.

When he had showered and shaved and eaten a quick breakfast, it was nearly six. The big black car was waiting down on Virginia Avenue. Weber came out the door and walked to the curb, where the driver was holding open the door. Oscar had been deployed in Iraq and Afghanistan and had had a decade of stress. He liked having a job where the biggest thing he had to worry about most days was a traffic jam.

They set off for Headquarters. Oscar varied the route slightly each day in recognition of Weber's status as a high-value target. One day they might take the Whitehurst Freeway down to Key Bridge, another day they would make a U-turn on Virginia Avenue and take the Roosevelt Bridge. This morning Oscar turned left onto Rock Creek Parkway and up the ramp past the monumental statues onto the broad span of the Memorial Bridge, framed on either side by the gray churn of the Potomac. Weber was reading the *New York Times*; the lead story was about the latest turn of the ceaseless European financial crisis. The British pound had come under heavy pressure the last several days, joining the eurozone in misery.

Weber's car was about two-thirds of the way across the bridge when the engine stopped. It wasn't a sputter or a cough that suggested fuel or carburation problems but a sudden loss of all power. The motor went silent; the running lights inside the car were extinguished; there was the sound of a battery alarm as the airbags deactivated. Jack Fong, the security man riding shotgun next to Oscar, cradled his automatic rifle on his lap as he reported a Mayday alert on the emergency communications frequency.

"What's wrong?" asked Weber.

"I don't know, sir," shouted Oscar. He was struggling to control the car. The power steering had disappeared, along with the power brakes. Every electrical system in the car had become disabled simultaneously.

"Head for the circle," shouted Fong, pointing toward the grass beyond the embankment at the far end of the bridge. The car coasted toward it as Oscar shouted out the window to warn other cars away.

"Get down, sir," the security chief told Weber. Military training had taken over and he was treating this like a combat operation in downtown Kabul.

Oscar managed to bring the big car to a stop by riding it up on the grassy circle at the far end of the bridge; as the grass slowed the vehicle, he applied the emergency brake. The chase car swerved and followed the lead vehicle up onto the traffic circle. The two security men jumped out and formed a perimeter around Weber's wounded car. Two cars that had been dented by the Escalade after it lost control had also pulled over.

"We have to get you out of here, Director," said Fong. He was calling for help when his radio went dead. He tried swapping out the battery with a fresh one—it made no difference. Fong's face turned red like a stoplight changing color.

"Is the backup car safe?" he shouted to the driver of the second vehicle.

"I think so," said the driver.

Fong looked to Oscar, who shook his head. He didn't trust the chase car. If the lead vehicle had been hit, the backup was vulnerable. Weber was standing outside the car by now, trying to dial a number on his cell phone, when the security chief urged him toward the vehicle with a ferocious, protective shout.

"Sir! We are under attack. I want you inside and on the seat, now, please."

The security chief tried to get on top of Weber and shield his body, but the director wanted freedom of movement, above all now, and he wasn't having it.

"Back off, Fong," he shouted. "Let me call the watch room and find out what's going on."

Weber dialed the number on his BlackBerry. He was just starting the conversation, explaining where they were, just over Memorial Bridge on the Virginia side, when the phone went dead.

"Oh, Christ," muttered Weber. "I know what this is."

Fong was pushing him down again, and this time Weber didn't resist. The security chief made the director lie flat on the seat while he assumed a firing position above him. Oscar and the two men from the chase car chambered their weapons and formed a tighter perimeter around Weber's Escalade.

Five minutes later there was a wail of sirens and a kaleidoscope of flashing lights as a Federal Protective Service emergency response team arrived in three cars. They were joined by two cars each from the Park Police and the Secret Service, who had picked up the emergency calls, along with a D.C. ambulance that had followed the parade. Officers rushed toward Weber, weapons drawn.

"We need you out of here now, sir," said Fong, eying the gathering fleet of cars and onlookers. He pushed Weber toward the lead FPS vehicle, an armored Chevy Suburban. A second member of Weber's detail evicted the FPS man who had been sitting in the front passenger seat and took a firing position.

"Move, now, to CIA Headquarters."

The Suburban roared off from the circle and up the George Washington Parkway, the muzzles of two automatic weapons just visible over the bottoms of its front and rear right windows. Weber's communications were still down, so Fong took the driver's cell phone and reached the Office of Security command post. Weber gestured for Fong to hand him the phone.

"What the hell is going on?" asked Weber.

"We don't know, sir, except you're under attack. Every system we have on you is down."

"Has anyone else in the government been hit? White House, or DOD?"

"Negative, sir. We just checked. Everything else is up. You look like the only target."

"This is a diversion," said Weber.

"We're not calling it that way, sir. This is a Tier One red alert. Whoever is going after you is punching every button. We have to get you locked down at Langley now. We want you to use an alternative office on the fourth floor until we've run this to ground."

The watch officer asked to speak to the head of Weber's detail, and he handed the phone over to Fong, who grimaced as he listened to the situation report. He turned to Weber.

"Sir, you need to be out of sight," he said. "Right now."

"Too late for that," said Weber.

"I'm serious, Mr. Director. I have to order you to lower your head so it is not visible through any of the windows."

Weber did what Fong asked. They were all following procedure.

The Chevy was traveling nearly eighty miles an hour up the parkway that hugged the ridgeline above the southern bank of the Potomac; its siren was wailing so loud that frightened drivers veered their cars onto the bare shoulder to get out of the way.

As the SUV neared the agency, it made a power turn onto the ramp that curved up toward the CIA front entrance. The metal barrier lowered just in time to let the screaming car through. They raced past the bubble and the main entrance and veered right, into the driveway into the underground garage. The driver relaxed only when the metal gate closed behind them.

A welcoming committee from the Office of Security was there to meet them, including Marcia Klein, the deputy director who ran Support.

"What's the story, Marcia?" asked Weber, sitting up straight again in his seat.

"We don't know," said Klein. "My guys are taking apart your car now, looking for disabling devices. They're still working it. We asked the Bureau for help five minutes ago. I hope that's okay."

"This is a cyber-attack," said Weber. "It's an inside job. It has to be. They got into the electronic system in my car and shut everything off. They did the same thing with the comms."

Klein nodded and then shrugged feebly. She was embarrassed to have so little information.

"We really don't know, sir."

"Well, I do. It's cyber, and you won't find anything. They're too good for that."

"Maybe, Mr. Director, but right now we have to get you to a safe room. We have one predesignated on the fourth floor. Nothing gets in or out without our say-so. We pipe all the systems in separately, air, water, power, and every wire into the room is clean."

Weber shook his head.

"That's just where they want me," he muttered. "Isolated and inoperative."

"Sir?" asked Klein. She was prodding the director to move toward his private elevator now. It was pointless to resist. They were trying to protect him, even if they didn't know what, why or how.

"I know you're just doing your job, Marcia, but I'm telling you, this is an inside job. You're doing just what they want."

"Yes, sir," she answered.

They entered the small elevator with Klein in front and the omnipresent Jack Fong following up behind. Klein pushed "4," and with a slight jerk of the cables the director's private elevator began to rumble upward in its shaft.

Between the second and third floors, the elevator came to a sudden stop and the lights inside the cab went out.

"What in God's name just happened?" exclaimed Weber.

"Get down, sir," said Fong, in the absurd momentary belief that lower in the elevator cab would be safer. Fong began to draw his weapon but Klein stopped his hand.

"Not here," she said.

Klein had a flashlight in her pocket and she shone it on the controls, looking for the alarm bell. She pushed it but no bell rang. She took the emergency phone from its cradle but it was dead.

"This isn't funny anymore," said Weber.

"Roger that," said Klein. She took her own communications device from her pocket, which fortunately was able to transmit and receive in the metal housing of the elevator.

"We have a Code Red in the director's private elevator," she said into the phone.

Weber could hear the anxious squawk of the voice on the other end, a watch officer who apparently thought the agency was under attack.

"Slow down and listen to me," said Klein. "The elevator cab just stopped between floors two and three. Send an emergency team to get us out now. I mean right now."

"How do we get in?" asked the watch officer on the other end of Klein's phone. They were on speakerphone, and you could hear the shouts of confusion in the background.

"Force the doors above and below," said Klein." When you get into the shaft, come down the elevator cable. Bring the emergency fire team. They've practiced this. Call them, right now, while I'm waiting."

"Fire team is already here, Ms. Klein," said a voice through the speakerphone.

"Good. So remember: There's a trapdoor above the cab, but bring along a blowtorch to burn through, just in case. And I'm serious when I say move it. Whoever stopped this elevator could crash it. It's on you."

"You mean that, about crashing the elevator?" asked Weber in the dark of the small cab.

"Roger that," repeated Klein. "I have to assume right now that some- one is trying to kill you."

"They just want me out of the way," said Weber.

"Maybe permanently, sir."

Already they could hear the rescue teams banging on the door above and below, squeezing a crowbar to force the metal doors open. When the doors banged open, the alarms went off on two and three both, creating a din. Somebody shut off the alarm on the second floor, but the one above kept beeping annoyingly.

It was getting stuffy in the little cab, as they waited for the rescuers to make their way to the box and cut them free.

"It stinks in here," said Weber.

They heard a thump on the roof as one the rescuers put his feet down, and they could feel the cab sway slightly from the weight of the additional body.

The fireman pulled at the trapdoor, and specks of paint fell on them from above. The rescuer tugged some more, and still it didn't give, and ten seconds later they heard the hiss of a blowtorch. After a few more seconds, a blue-white flame seared through the metal. The rescuer tugged again at the trapdoor, and this time it opened.

The intense beam of a floodlight spotted above the third floor illuminated the cab as if it were the inside of a microwave oven.

"Get the boss out of here, now," shouted Klein up through the newly opened hole.

A rope dangled through the opening. It had a webbed seat attached.

"Step into the harness, please, Mr. Director," said Klein.

Weber put his legs through the webbing as instructed, and Klein called for the rope to be lifted. It was an awkward fit through the escape door at the top, and they had to push and pull him, top and bottom, to get him through. But finally his form was winched up the half floor to the open elevator door on three. Arms reached out to pull the director into the open doorway and help him remove the harness.

"That was exciting," said Weber deadpan, as someone handed him a glass of water. He was still dressed in the suit he had put on for work, but it had become dusty in the ascent through the elevator shaft, and his tie was askew.

Security officers were hustling him down the hall now.

"What's the rush?" said Weber, trying to slow the pace. "I need to freshen up."

"We've got to get you out of the building now, sir," said a man Weber recognized as Klein's deputy. "Someone is trying to kill you."

"I doubt that very much," said Weber, shaking his head. But he wasn't about to convince the agency security people, whose worst nightmare was coming true.

They were almost to the stairwell. Weber turned to the leader of the group.

"Is this necessary?" Weber asked. "I need to be someplace where I can monitor things."

"We can't risk that, Mr. Director. We've got to get you to a secure remote location, immediately. That's orders."

"Whose orders?" Weber asked as they prodded him down a stairwell. Nobody answered.

Weber was between armed men, above and below him on the steps. They moved as if they expected a firefight around every turn of the stairwell. They exited through an emergency door just to the right of the main entrance and out into the sunlight. One of Weber's escorts pointed to a large vehicle parked just below in the VIP lot.

"That's your car, Mr. Director," he said, leading Weber toward the armored limousine. It looked like one of the backup presidential limousines, heavy enough to resist an antitank missile.

Klein, the deputy director for Support, had made it outside now and was standing near the vehicle. A ring of men in paramilitary gear surrounded the lot. Weber had never seen their uniforms before. They weren't from Ground Branch or any of the agency security details Weber had ever seen.

"Where is the secure location you're taking me to?" asked Weber. "Does it have communications?"

"I don't know, sir. They are going to disclose the destination when we're en route, for security."

"We could be heading for Oregon," said Weber.

Klein didn't laugh, nor did any of her colleagues. This was their business, and for them, professionalism meant operating autonomous of the person they were protecting.

"Empty your pockets, please, Director."

"Why?" asked Weber. "All I've got is my wallet and some personal communications gear."

"Keep the wallet," said Klein, "but we need to leave any communications devices with the techs, so they can make sure you're not carrying any GPS trackers or bugs so someone could find you in the secure remote location."

"Is this necessary?" asked Weber.

Klein nodded, and Weber understood. The security director was doing her job.

The door of the armored limousine was opened. It was as thick and heavy as the door of a bank vault. A paramilitary officer stood next to the open door, weapon at the ready. Weber looked at the officer's unusual uniform, searching for some marking.

Weber finally saw on his shoulder a small patch that read ODNI.

"Who ordered this operation?" Weber repeated his question. "I want an answer, goddamn it, or I'm not leaving."

This time, through fear or pity, Klein responded.

"Director Hoffman at ODNI is the command authority, reporting to the White House," she said. "They just want to make sure you're safe."

"Of course they do," said Weber.

They were in the car now, and the door slammed closed. The vehicle surged out of the parking lot, down the access road and toward the parkway. No sirens this time; just high-speed driving, with motorcycle outriders fore and aft.

When the car turned onto the Beltway and then up Route 270, Weber guessed that they were heading for a destination in the woods near Camp David, and that it might be a while before he had any normal communications again.

38

BASEL, SWITZERLAND

The attack in Basel began about the same time that Weber's car lost power on the Memorial Bridge. It was invisible, like a puff of frost in the almost-winter air of November in Switzerland. The team leader was Ed Junot, who knew the target best. He commanded the small group that James Morris had recruited, plus two paramilitary officers who had been assigned to Morris's covert Denver base several months before. Their tasking orders said that they'd been detailed to a Title 50 unit that was under the command of the Office of the Director of National Intelligence, on authority of the National Security Council. That meant the operation, though it involved military officers, was also a covert operation whose existence was a secret of state and could be denied if it were ever discovered. By law, it didn't happen.

Junot set up his Basel command post in a suite at the Hotel Metropol, a block west of the main office of the Bank for International Settlements on Nauenstrasse. It was an uncomplicated modern hotel. He had another new identity now, after his others had been blown. He didn't look like a roustabout anymore, but like a businessman. With a good haircut and a well-tailored suit, a tattooed anarchist could look like a vice president for sales. The night he arrived, Junot did five hundred sit-ups in his room. Then he watched *Despicable Me 2* on the hotel video.

The four other members of Junot's team slipped into Basel and checked into different hotels around town. They brought their own computers and other gear. Junot had taken a room with a balcony, on which he placed an antenna that could download a secure Internet signal from a satellite overhead.

The team included a retired Special Forces warrant officer named Mike Rubin, who had learned bank operating systems during a stint with a Joint Special Operations Command task force that worked on terrorist financing. He was one of the two specialists who had been sent in from the Denver base on Morris's orders. He was a man like Junot: an underemployed ex-trigger-puller out to make some money as a paramilitary contractor, no questions asked or answered.

Rubin's first task was to review how the bank backed up its trading records and files. It took only an hour to establish that the backup files were managed by Bridget Saundermann, the deputy chief financial officer, who was based at the bank's secondary offices in a round stone building up the street from the ziggurat-shaped main headquarters building. The backup data was transferred to a second network of servers for archiving, and then encrypted for permanent storage in the BIS's "cloud" servers, located at a server farm in Zurich.

"They're sloppy," said Rubin. He explained to Junot that the data was only backed up once every thirty minutes, rather than continuously, and that there were multiple points of access and interference with the data set.

At noon Basel time, Junot gave his team the "go" signal. Their first assignment was to seize control of the Treasury functions that maintained the BIS balance sheet. The bank's assets were denominated in "special drawing rights," or SDRs, a basket of currencies of the major financial nations. At the hour when Junot issued the "go" order, the BIS balance sheet totaled 213.5 billion SDRs, including 35.9 billion in gold and gold loans; 53.5 billion in Treasury bills; 46.2 billion in securities purchased under trading agreements; and 77.9 billion in non-U.S. government and other securities. This was meant to be the world's financial nest egg.

An instant after noon, the Treasury system crashed, halting monitoring and updating of these accounts. At roughly the same moment, also on Junot's order, the BIS trading system, which handled global clearing of central bank transfers and other international accounts, also crashed. Junot's team was able to monitor frantic efforts within the BIS and its IT Department to restore these functions.

Morris's genius was evident in the sabotage of the system's recovery efforts, as much as the attack itself. The efforts to reboot the system failed, due to inconsistent readings of the time clocks and other logic functions of the main system. This was also thanks to malware that Morris had custom-written for Junot's team; it was inserted in the initial attack: Basic logic rules and parameters had been altered so that the systems stacked on top couldn't function.

Morris had inserted other tricks: The system software that was supposed to generate random numbers to support encryption and password generation began to generate autocorrelated numbers; the time clocks that supported operations were no longer in sync. Some clocks had been changed, but it was impossible initially to identify which ones. System components recording different time signatures couldn't communicate. Another logic bomb corrupted the operating system rules for mathematical operations, so that, in effect, 1 plus 1 no longer reliably generated the number 2.

The scramble to deal with the data crisis was complicated by the fact that Ernst Lewin, the systems administrator, Bridget Saundermann, his deputy, and several dozen other top members of the Information Technology Department had been locked out of their accounts and couldn't get access to the system. The security consultants who were scrambled in Zurich, London and Palo Alto were also locked out.

In the precious initial minutes that BIS systems were incapacitated, Junot's team introduced a series of changes in the basic Treasury and trading accounts. The amount of gold recorded as being held in reserve shrank by nearly three billion SDRs; the volume of loans advanced to central banks increased by two billion. All other balance sheet items were also subtly adjusted. As the BIS balances were reduced, sums were automatically transferred to the accounts of Third World nations that were part of the BIS system. The software erased any sign that these transfers had been made. It was like a magic trick. Money disappeared from one pocket and reappeared in another.

The trading system was similarly affected. By changing logic rules within the system, it was no longer possible to clear trades. Data that was meant to be sent to the back office for resolution was instead bounced back to the counterparties, creating confusion in central banks across the world. In this confusion, more redistribution of wealth was accomplished. The amounts were small on the scale of global commerce, but large for some of the African, Asian and Latin American beneficiaries.

The central banks, suddenly unable to reconcile their sums and balance accounts, tried desperately to get in touch with the BIS by electronic message, then by phone. But the VOIP telephone system also went dead; it relied on digital routing that could be corrupted by whoever held the "root" authority of the systems administrator. Bloomberg terminals continued for the first several minutes to send BIS data and allow messaging, but these, too, soon went down.

Junot's team attacked the BIS backup facilities at the data center simultaneously with the main attack. These backups were essentially vast databases, organized with computer rules that weren't very different from the rules about columns and rows that were used in normal Excel data tables and spreadsheets. As the rules were changed, the integrity of the backup data tables dissolved. The reserve data was no longer internally consistent, nor did it match the first-level data in the system itself.

Junot delivered a final payload that had been prepared by Morris and attached to an .exe file that could be pushed through one of the backdoors. It included a special piece of code that automatically transferred a specified percentage amount from the transactions of the Bank of England into the accounts of the central banks of its former colonies in Africa. In the code was inserted a string, easy enough to find later, that identified this piece of malware as "*imperialismtax.*"

"Nothing but net," said Mike Rubin to Ed Junot when they were done. That was a bit of NSA jargon, the slogan of the Data Network Technologies group, in addition to basketball slang. It meant the same thing: Clean, in and out.

The burp in the financial markets began about ten minutes after the attack. It started with broker-dealers who were conducting trades or swaps with the BIS trading desk. A dozen or so were in the middle of taking orders to buy or sell securities when the chat room on the screen went black, the message system crashed and the electronic addresses for BIS traders came up blank. The broker-dealers tried for several minutes to establish contact with their BIS clients and, when that failed, they began lighting up the global grid with increasingly anxious queries about what was happening at the Bank for International Settlements.

The dealers messaged their biggest clients first: the major money center banks; the biggest hedge funds and private equity funds. Nobody knew what was going on, but uncertainty in a major financial institution is a "sell" signal, no matter what the reason. By 12:15 Basel time, Bloomberg and Reuters had both moved bulletins saying that the Bank for International Settlements computer system had failed. The selling started within five minutes after the initial crash at noon, but once the Bloomberg and Reuters stories moved, they triggered a global cascade of fear and major selling on all exchanges and markets that were open.

By 12:20, the German DAX index was down 6 percent; the French CAC 40 was down 9 percent. The FTSE in Britain was off just 4 percent, but selling pressure was building. After-hours markets in Asia that traded derivatives showed a fall in futures prices for the Nikkei average in Japan and the Hang Seng in Hong Kong; these futures were falling even faster than the European averages. U.S. markets had several hours before they opened, but futures trading for NYSE and NASDAQ stocks was also sharply negative. The only markets that didn't seem affected were those of the poorer emerging economies of the Third World. There, for reasons the market analysts couldn't understand, there was buying pressure, rather than selling.

At 12:40, after two phone calls with a bewildered BIS management in Basel, the European Central Bank joined the Bank of England in requesting that market authorities suspend trading on all European exchanges until the discrepancies at the BIS could be reconciled. The suspension was expected to be brief, until the BIS's backup systems could take over and begin clearing and reconciling trades again.

The Federal Reserve, in a statement issued at 12:40 Basel time, said that although U.S. markets weren't yet directly affected, the Fed was prepared to extend liquidity to European central banks in unlimited supply until the BIS problems were resolved.

Regulators and central banks still had about three hours before the real crunch time arrived with the 9:30 a.m. opening of the New York Stock Exchange and NASDAQ.

The president was called at 6:30 a.m. by the Treasury secretary, Anthony Glass. He reported a major computer attack on the Bank for International Settlements, of unknown origins. He explained that the chairman of the Federal Reserve was preparing to issue a statement aimed at stabilizing the markets, and that he was talking with the governors of the Bank of England and the European Central Bank about further steps. A coordinated rescue plan of some kind would have to be devised before the 9:30 a.m. NYSE opening bell.

"Do whatever it takes," the president told his Treasury secretary. He left it to Glass to decide how this hortatory statement should be carried out. Timothy O'Keefe, the national security adviser, called Glass five minutes later to say the president wanted an American-led rescue plan, if it came to that.

The BIS, the central bank of central banks, was all but inoperative for more than an hour. When the computer system finally went back up, the logic bombs and other malware festering in the system caused it to crash once again, and for the rest of that day and into the next, all of its Treasury, trading and clearing functions were unstable. The world's leading computer security experts were on airplanes by late that afternoon, flying to Zurich and then to Basel to help with the forensics.

The investigation would come later. The immediate issue was how to halt the decline in most global financial markets, which had accelerated after the European Central Bank and Bank of England statements halting trading. The interruption had simply increased selling pressure in other markets that weren't included in the suspension. Those markets received such intense order flow that they weren't able to handle normal processing and clearing. At 1:15 the Dubai Financial Market and NASDAQ Dubai both suspended trading.

Television and print reporters began to gather outside the BIS headquarters around 12:30; their satellite trucks were visible outside the main building on Nauenstrasse and also the secondary offices, where the IT staff was based, at Aeschenplatz. The doors were locked, and no BIS spokesman was prepared to issue any statement at a time when the nature and origins of the computer crash were still unclear. The lack of official comment fed rumor and speculation by reporters, who were talking to their sources at commercial banks in Zurich and London and passing along what amounted to gossip.

Bloomberg tried to enforce some discipline in separating fact and rumor. But since there was no hard fact to report, the news media coverage served to increase market anxiety without offering any path or timetable for resolution.

Financial crises always converge on Washington. If the center holds, then the periphery begins to relax and order returns—with U.S. dominance reinforced. Indeed, if someone had been worried about the waning power of the United States, and had wanted to give the creaky post-1945 order a shot of hormones, that someone would have welcomed the opportunity to piggyback on the crisis caused by a bizarre team of hackers whose identities were at first unknown to the world.

The process of recovery began even as the crisis was still a jumble of inchoate signals and crashing systems. At 1:15 p.m. Basel time, and 7:15 a.m. in Washington, the chairman of the Federal Reserve, Michael Vander, met in the Situation Room at the White House with Treasury Secretary Glass. Teleconference lines were opened with the heads of the European Central Bank and the Bank of England.

The meeting had just started when a large figure walked into the room, carrying a cup of tea that he had brought from the Navy Mess, along with a powdered sugar donut. Unlike most of the dour faces in the room, he had a placid, almost genial demeanor. Despite the early morning hour, he was dressed immaculately in a three-piece gray flannel suit. He was humming a tune from the musical *Sweeney Todd*, the story of a malevolent barber who bakes the flesh of his victims into meat pies.

The well-dressed gentleman who was humming this incongruous tune was the director of National Intelligence, Cyril Hoffman.

"What a dangerous world we live in," whispered Hoffman to the national security adviser, Timothy O'Keefe, who had also just arrived. Hoffman was smiling.

"Where's Director Weber?" asked Glass, the Treasury secretary. "We could use his financial brain this morning, in addition to the spook stuff."

"Weber is under protection. We have a report that his automobile has been disabled. Security is taking care of it. We'll keep him safe."

"Indeed," said O'Keefe. He nodded for the Treasury secretary to begin.

"We see two possibilities," began Glass. "The first is a rescue plan led by the United States and supported by all sixty central banks that are members of the BIS. That group would include China, Russia, India, Turkey, Brazil, Saudi Arabia and so on down the list until you get to Bosnia and Herzegovina. The advantages are obvious. This list includes every financial power of any consequence in the system."

"What . . . are . . . the . . . uh . . . disadvantages?" asked Michael Vander, the Fed chairman. He had a disconcerting habit of pausing between almost every word, as if summoning an extra volt of brainpower.

"It might take too long. It's almost eight a.m. now. The New York markets open in ninety minutes. Unless we have something ready to go, we're going to have to follow Europe and suspend trading."

Hoffman cleared his throat. He leaned toward the conference table so that his vest was touching the mahogany. He was wearing a jeweled tie pin that morning in the shape of a rooster.

"A word, Mr. Secretary, if I might. Off-line, please."

The feed to the video monitors was temporarily muted. The British and European guests suddenly found themselves looking at a test pattern and listening to static.

"An important disadvantage with Option A is the problem of attribution," Hoffman admonished the group.

"I don't follow that," said Glass.

"Plainly put, the question is: Who done it? We don't know at this point, but I have an initial report from Admiral Schumer at the NSA that the malware in the BIS attack had a Chinese signature."

"That's worrisome," said Glass. He looked toward O'Keefe, who nodded assent.

"Quite," said Hoffman. "And one word more, Mr. Secretary. A number of the countries on the BIS list of partners would give us security concerns."

Hoffman handed the secretary a list of the top sixty partners, on which he had circled China, India and France. Glass gave the paper to O'Keefe, and then to the Fed chairman.

"What about Russia?" asked Glass. "Shouldn't they be on the bad-guys list?"

"I think not," said Hoffman. "They give us heartburn, but I don't think they pose any cyber-threat to financial markets."

Glass shrugged. "You're the intelligence expert," he said.

"Speaking *strictly* from an intelligence standpoint," said Hoffman, "I would be happiest if the United States was acting on its own. We could get support from reliable friends, Britain, Germany, perhaps even Russia for a little breadth. That way: No baggage, no haggling, no hands in the till. But obviously, the decision is up to you gentlemen."

"So is that Plan B?" broke in the Fed chairman. He was looking at the clock on the wall, and then at his watch, for emphasis. "Plan A seems to be in . . . uh . . . liquidation, and the markets are quite, quite . . . volatile."

Everyone looked at Glass. The Treasury secretary took a drink of coffee, made a nervous cough and announced the policy he thought the president had wanted from the beginning.

"Plan B is us, a U.S. rescue. Are we comfortable with that? We would propose temporary American aid and governance, backed by some sort of committee that includes Britain Germany, Russia, whatever."

Glass looked to the Fed chairman and O'Keefe, who both nodded. Hoffman had the palms of his hands together on the table, as if in prayer. He nodded, too.

"You might call the Russian Embassy," said Hoffman. "Tell them we'd like them on board on this one."

Everyone nodded or shrugged. They wanted to get moving. A Treasury aide scurried off to call the Russian economic attaché, who, as Hoffman well knew, was a representative of the SVR.

"Turn the teleconference monitor back on," said Glass. The screens came alive again, from London and Frankfurt.

"We want to propose an American rescue, backed by a financial coalition of the willing." Glass looked at his watch. "We propose to launch it in another hour, at nine a.m., Washington time. The Fed and the Treasury would guarantee liquidity, and we would convene a transitional supervisory structure for governance of the bank. We'll bring in some partners: I suggest the British, Germans and Russians, for a start."

"What does 'governance' mean, in legal terms?" asked the chancellor of the exchequer on the screen. He had been a barrister before taking his post in the cabinet.

"Governance means that we run it until we hand it back to the BIS board. The bank will have to go into some version of receivership, at least briefly. The receivers will have responsibility for auditing the books, certifying the reliability of the computer systems, overseeing the investigation of what happened."

The chancellor nodded. "Under the circumstances, I think that's the best we can do. Do you have the paperwork ready?"

"Most of it," said Glass. "The NSC staff has been working on this since six."

Glass turned toward the Frankfurt monitor. "What does Europe think?" he asked.

"The ECB has no authority to take a position, independent of the EU member nations," said the European Central Bank representative apologetically. "But we are glad that Germany will be included in the transitional governance structure."

"Well then, I think we have a deal," said the British minister, taking his teacup and dipping it toward the video camera.

The governor of the Bank of England, a distinguished economic historian from Oxford who had said very little during this discussion of law and policy, now spoke up. She had a smile that was like a Roman circus mask. She was famous, other than as the first woman governor of the bank, as a biographer of John Maynard Keynes.

"How ironic that America is rescuing the BIS. We have come full circle, rather," she said.

"How so?" asked the chancellor, whose dubious expression was captured on another camera.

"Henry Morgenthau, FDR's Treasury secretary, wanted to kill the Bank for International Settlements at the time of Bretton Woods. He thought it had been some kind of Nazi clearinghouse, which was not altogether wrong. Keynes had to stop him. Did you know that?"

"No," said Glass. At the same instant, the Fed chairman, never unmanned in a duel about economic history, said, "Yes."

"Yes, indeed, it was Lord Keynes to the rescue," she continued. "The BIS was dissolved, then undissolved by joint British-American cooperation. And now we're back where we started. It's 1945 again."

"With the Russians along, for good measure," said Hoffman, speaking sotto voce, in a comment that was not picked up by the audio-video monitor.

A barely audible humming sound had started up again. It was the director of National Intelligence. As the others were talking, he had gathered up his things and was now slipping away from the Situation Room while the other members of the group worked out the details. It was a reestablishment of the proper order of things, in Hoffman's mind. The stakeholders in the status quo, America and Britain, had even managed to get a rope around a sometimes mischievous Russia. He headed out the door to his limousine, and the senior officials barely noticed that he had left.

Hoffman placed a call on his way back to Liberty Crossing. He called the deputy chief of the Information Operations Center and reminded her that she had made him a promise.

39

WASHINGTON

Graham Weber began plotting his moves from the moment he was bundled into the limousine at Langley and moved involuntarily toward his "secure undisclosed location." He had seen parts of this catastrophe coming toward him, not all of it, but enough to arrange his own strategy for accomplishing the duty to which he had sworn an oath, to protect the nation from enemies foreign and domestic. What he couldn't know was how completely Cyril Hoffman had sought to paint the story in colors of his own choosing. Hoffman had composed the crime scene like a still life; the artifacts were arranged; the human elements were assessed and deployed. Hoffman was an artist, in his way. He flattered himself that even a businessman such as Graham Weber could appreciate his eye for detail and nuance. Hoffman, in truth, had thought of almost everything.

The fingerprints were there, waiting to be discovered by competent forensic sleuths. The attackers who hacked the Bank for International Settlements had taken elaborate precautions to hide themselves, but in a digital world where every keystroke lives forever somewhere, they hadn't been careful enough. That was what the mandarins of the cyberworld advised reporters: Just be patient; the details will emerge.

It took several days for the first account of the investigation to leak. The *New York Times* carried a story saying that the attackers had used tools that were identical to those used by Unit 61398 of the People's Liberation Army based in Shanghai, which had figured in previous cyber-reporting by the newspaper. The Chinese strenuously denied the story, issuing an unusual on-the-record statement from the commander of the PLA himself. But people took the denial with a grain of salt. The *Times* story said that the investigation was being conducted by the NSA's Cyber Command and the director of National Intelligence, at the special request of the president and the secretary of the Treasury.

The *Wall Street Journal* countered with an exclusive of its own, saying that some of the malware that had corrupted the arithmetic functions and time clocks of the BIS was similar to malware used by Chinese cyber-warriors when they had crippled foreign search-engine portals and social-networking sites. These tools had surfaced in other Chinese attacks against targets around the world. The *Journal* leak had more information about the attackers' methodology, based on what they described as sources familiar with the NSA investigation.

When rogue CIA officer James Morris was identified a few days later as an organizer of the attacks, the story exploded into a meta-scandal. Five days after the Basel incident, the *Journal*, *Times* and *Washington Post* were each briefed separately by the White House on an investigation that had been launched by the CIA inspector general. The investigation was focusing on a criminal plot by Morris, director of the Information Operations Center.

Each newspaper's account carried the essential fact that Morris had operated out of a Chinese-owned front company in Britain called the Fudan–East Anglia Research Centre. The White House sources said Morris and his agents had been recruited to attack the Bank for International Settlements as part of a Chinese campaign to identify and control key parts of the financial infrastructure in Europe, in what the officials said, not for quotation, was "preparation of the battlefield."

Morris was a perfect villain. His personality emerged in baroque detail after the Senate and House Intelligence Committees were briefed on the inspector general's investigation. Somehow, the newspapers were able to obtain photographs of him and publish his true name, despite the Intelligence Identities Protection Act that was supposed to prevent such disclosures. He looked like the image of bad behavior: the pale skin; the feverish eyes; the tall, stick-thin body; the black-frame glasses on the end of his long nose. It was the look of unwholesomeness. Truly, he looked like a man who would inhabit the darker sections of a European city rather than an American official.

The CIA announced that it had made a criminal referral to the Justice Department about Morris's activities, based on evidence gathered by a whistleblower who had worked as his deputy. She was not further described. The news media waited for Morris's arrest, but the FBI announced twenty-four hours after the first story naming him that he appeared to have fled the country, using the cyber-skills that allowed him to transcend the normal borders and boundaries.

The FBI alerted Interpol and every intelligence and security service abroad with which it had liaison, and gave them details of Morris's multiple identities. There were reported sightings in Bucharest, Moscow and Bangkok, but they all proved to be false leads. The hacker king who had taken down the Bank for International Settlements allegedly on behalf of his Chinese patrons (and perhaps others unnamed) appeared to have vanished into the digital mist.

Graham Weber returned from his "secure undisclosed location" after a week, when the FBI and the director of National Intelligence made a formal determination that he was no longer in danger. His hideaway had been in Bunker Hill, West Virginia, near Camp David and the old archipelago of evacuation sites that had been prepared to receive officials in the event of a nuclear attack during the Cold War. Guards had watched him night and day for those seven days, keeping him inside a fenced perimeter that was patrolled by guard dogs and armed security personnel from the Office of the Director of National Intelligence. All of Weber's communications devices had been confiscated when they put him in the armored limousine at the CIA. His strenuous efforts ever since to contact the world outside the secure undisclosed location had all been rebuffed. But he had time to think, which had always been his most potent weapon.

The afternoon of Weber's departure, the CIA had issued a statement, first to its employees and then to the public. The announcement disclosed what anyone who had witnessed the early morning scene on Memorial Bridge would have suspected—which was that an attempt had been made to disable the director's armored vehicle. The statement said that for his own protection, the director had been moved to a remote, well-guarded location.

On a sunny mid-November morning in West Virginia, one of Weber's guards gave him a copy of the statement to read.

"This is a lie," said Weber, pointing his finger at the guard. "I've been kidnapped."

Weber said that he wanted to talk to the president or the secretary of defense or the chairman of the Senate Intelligence Committee. When his jailer didn't respond, he began to shout and put up such a ruckus that the guard had to retreat toward the door, and when Weber came after him, the guard restrained him physically.

The chief of the guard detail came running from the control room after watching the pandemonium on closed-circuit television.

"I'm sorry, Mr. Director," said the chief guard as he helped Weber to his feet. "This is for your own protection."

"Fuck you," said Weber.

Weber tried cooperation after that, thinking that rapport might be more effective than resistance. Weber was an innately charming person; he had built his career on the ability to achieve rapport with business colleagues. But every time he began to make friends with one of his guards, that person was transferred out of the facility. Each of his three escape attempts was quickly foiled, and after the first, Weber was given food that he was convinced was drugged to make him sedated and pliable. Weber tried not to eat, but self-starvation was not within his kit of survival skills. His movements within his "cabin" were monitored by cameras in every room; when Weber knocked out a camera lens, it was quickly replaced.

When Weber concluded that there was no escape, he focused all the more on his plans for revenge. He knew nothing about details of the attack on the Bank for International Settlements, but he had suspected that it was coming—and that an essential part of the plan had been to make sure that he was out of the way. The question was which way the pieces would fall. He knew that he would need help from someone he trusted, and he thought often of Ariel Weiss. Sometimes he dreamed about her.

The agency workforce had been perturbed but not altogether displeased by the sudden disappearance of their new director, a man whom many officers still regarded as a visitor rather than one of their own. There was a view, expressed quietly in the soft-lit halls of Headquarters, that perhaps this was a blessing. Weber had been pounding on too many doors. He thought he could run the place like a business, but of course that was a mistake. The CIA had its own rules.

It was rumored, also, that Weber had given special authority to James Morris, who senior officers now claimed to have mistrusted all along. Thank goodness for Mr. Hoffman, up the road, who was viewed more than ever as the godfather.

Whatever they thought about Weber, CIA employees were frightened by the vulnerability of their workplace. Everyone had heard what had happened in the director's private elevator, minutes after the incapacitation of his car: If cyber-attackers could compromise these highly protected zones, they could do anything. The CIA was supposed to be protected by an "air gap," which meant that it wasn't vulnerable to such attacks, in theory. But the electronic moat obviously had been penetrated.

CIA employees are gossips, especially when they feel that their interests are at risk. The agency had kept a lid on the fiasco with the director's elevator, but with multiple investigations under way, the details were going to surface. So a story emerged, with enough detail to be credible.

James Morris was the threatening presence "inside the air gap." Many readers missed, in the first-day accounts of his role in the Basel attack, that as part of the plot Morris had conducted a cyber-attack on his boss, CIA Director Graham Weber, crippling his car and even striking at him within CIA Headquarters. The newspaper reports initially didn't give details, but the juicy parts leaked, including the disabled elevator stuck between floors.

Graham Weber was escorted back to his apartment at the Watergate seven days after he had left. He was a spark plug ready to fire, after the week of solitude. The doorman had kept the newspapers for him. He quickly scanned the headlines, with mounting astonishment as he saw the events that had taken place since his forced evacuation, and the explanations that had begun to surface.

Weber put the papers aside and called Ariel Weiss, using the last of his Nokia burner phones and SIM cards. He had been waiting a week to talk to her. She didn't answer the first call, and he didn't leave a message, but she called back five minutes later.

"Oh, my god, are you safe?" she said. Her voice sounded as if she were choking back tears.

"They kidnapped me, Ariel. They put me in a car and held me incommunicado."

"I know," she said, her voice still brimming with emotion. "You're a hero."

"What are you talking about?" he asked.

"Haven't you read the papers? They've exposed Morris. He was working for the Chinese, just as you thought. He attacked the biggest bank in the world. You were the only one who tried to stop him."

"That's the cover story."

"It's the truth, Graham. Where are you? You must come see me. We need to talk."

"Is it safe? Shouldn't we be careful? Meet at the same place as before."

"Let's meet for a victory drink. I told you, you're a hero. Morris is finished. I've spent the last three days with the inspector general. I'm testifying before the grand jury tomorrow."

"What have you been telling them?"

"How you saved the agency. How you were the only one who understood what a threat Morris was. How I helped track down the information for you. What we found, about the Chinese."

"That's great," said Weber. "But it wasn't just Morris."

"I need to see you. Meet me in an hour. I'll be in the bar downstairs at the Watergate Hotel."

She caught him by surprise, even though he was waiting for her. He was sitting at the bar when he saw her reflected image in the mirror, and he almost didn't recognize her. Walking toward him was not the hacker girl, the CIA technical wizard, but a woman who knew how beautiful she was. The tight black sheath revealed the body usually hidden under a white cotton shirt.

Ariel Weiss put her arms around Weber and kissed him on the cheek. She was wearing perfume, for the first time in his memory.

"That's a nice welcome," he said. "I should get kidnapped more often."

"Don't joke! Morris tried to kill you. Now you're safe."

"Somebody tried to get me out of the way, but I doubt it was Morris. And whoever it was, they didn't want to kill me."

"How do you know that?"

"It's not that hard to kill someone. If they'd wanted to, I'd be dead." She ordered a glass of champagne and took his arm.

"I love heroes who say they're not heroic."

"Thanks," said Weber. He liked to be flattered as much as any man, but the past week had been so frustrating that even compliments sounded off-key.

"I need your help, Ariel. This is a big ball of lies. You're the only person I can trust. We need to go over Morris's papers, and your files, too. Everything we can."

She shook her head, and took a long sip of her champagne.

"The damn lawyers got there first. They came in three days ago and sealed everything in Morris's office and mine. We're locked out of everything except current operational accounts."

Weber was puzzled.

"Why are they doing that now? Now is when we need to go back and see what Morris was doing, and who he was really working for."

"You'll have to ask the inspector general, Graham. He has all the files, and from what I hear, he's sending them over to the Justice Department as fast as he can to put together the legal case against Morris."

"What's the rush?" asked Weber. "Morris had plenty of friends before, in the White House, at Liberty Crossing, everywhere. Now he's the universal scapegoat. People are missing the point."

She took his hand and looked him in the eye. She wanted to reason with him, to help him understand.

"The whole world is angry about what Morris did at the Bank for International Settlements. They're scared that the Chinese, and god knows who else, could take down the markets. They need to understand how it happened. The U.S. and British governments are trying to clean up the mess, and we can help them. We know the story: You and I do. We tracked Morris to his front company in Cambridge and we pulled out the details of his operation, the people he was recruiting, the whole thing. We have to tell people what we know. Don't you see, Graham?"

Weber shook his head. He saw red lights blinking.

"This is a scam. Morris had help. He's the fall guy, maybe, but he's not the one who put this in motion. Cyril Hoffman admitted to me on his boat that Morris was expendable. And if we're talking about working with the Chinese, Hoffman has more investments in Shanghai than Morris could ever dream about. He said so, on that goofy sailing trip. And what about the Russians? How did they just disappear?"

"I want to help you make this go away, Graham," she said.

He ordered another scotch. The first one had gone to his head; he had eaten so little during his forced relocation that his stomach was empty. He told the bartender to put more ice in his whiskey, as if that would make a difference. She had another glass of champagne, and she lit a cigarette, too, another thing he had never seen her do.

"I didn't know you smoked," he said.

"There's a lot you don't know about me."

After they'd finished the second round of drinks and were contemplating having a third, Weiss stood up from her chair, crossed her arms over chest and gave him a wink.

"Aren't you hungry?" she asked. "You look like you haven't eaten in a week. What have you got upstairs that a resourceful woman could turn into a meal?"

Weber smiled. "You don't want to cook. I'll buy you dinner."

"Come on! I want to show you that I'm not all ones and zeroes. Do you have any pasta?"

"Yes. And some pesto sauce in the freezer."

He paid the bill. She took his hand and led him out the door of the bar and down a long hall to a block of elevators.

"How did you know where I live?" asked Weber.

"Lucky guess," she answered. "Plus it's in the security profile on Marie's desk."

She took his arm, and leaned dreamily on his shoulder in the elevator. When they got to Weber's floor, she put her arm around his waist. That felt awkward, and he didn't reciprocate at first, but as she walked unsteadily toward his door, he put his arm around her shoulder to support her. At his doorway she turned her face up to him; she waited a moment for a kiss, and when it didn't come, she gently pulled his head toward her until their lips were touching.

"Welcome home," she said. "You're a hero."

He opened the door sheepishly. The apartment was tidy enough; the cleaning lady had been in with the security detail that week when he had his enforced holiday. But it was such a barren space, the kind of apartment that would be inhabited by a single man who spent all his time at work. There was the big wide-screen television, flanked by a well-used leather easy chair and footstool. The rest of the décor looked like it had been selected by an expensive designer who furnished corporate apartments for CEOs.

She took his arm. She looked confused, just for a moment.

"Would you do something if you thought you had no other choice?" she said quietly.

"Maybe. I hope I never get in that situation. Why do you ask?"

"No reason, really. Sometimes people get stuck, that's all."

Weber opened a bottle of white Burgundy in the refrigerator while she rummaged in the refrigerator for the makings of a meal. She pulled out a stale onion, some tomatoes that were inedible a month ago, and three unopened blocks of processed cheddar cheese.

"Men don't really get it about food, do they?"

"I'm sorry. I mostly eat out." He paused, embarrassed. "The truth is, you're the first woman I've had up to the apartment since I moved in. Isn't that pathetic?"

"It's touching." She brushed her finger against his face. "Where's the powder room?"

"Down the hall, first door on your left."

She walked off. There was something tentative in her manner, as if she were uncertain which hall led where.

Weber had another sip of his wine. Maybe it was the booze, or the hunger from having eaten so little the past few days, but he felt light-headed. He wasn't a man who liked losing control of himself, but in this case it seemed preordained, and he was trying to decide whether it made him comfortable or uncomfortable.

He heard a whoosh of water, and then a few moments later a closing door.

Ariel walked into the room with deliberate steps. This was a controlled, disciplined woman; a doctor of computer science. She didn't do things on a whim. She pulled herself up so that her bottom rested on the kitchen countertop. Her black sheath covered only halfway to her knees.

"Do you think I'm pretty?" she asked. She said the words haltingly, as if she had never asked the question before.

"Of course you are," said Weber, "especially tonight."

"Do you . . . ?" she began.

"Do I what?"

"Do you want to be with me?" She said it shyly, tentatively.

She took his hand and pulled him toward her. She was clutching something lacey in the other hand.

"Are you sure?" asked Weber. "There are a hundred rules against this." He looked toward her clutched fist. "What's that?" he asked.

She opened her hand and her panties fell on the countertop. She had removed them in the bathroom. Her legs parted slightly. She looked at him with desire and pulled on his arm again, but as he paused, wondering, she turned away in momentary embarrassment.

"Are you sure?" he asked again.

"Of course I am."

"But you work for me. I could get fired for this. It's wrong."

His sharp words made her blush. She closed her legs, let them dangle over the counter for a moment and then hopped down. She looked embarrassed and angry. But there was another emotion, too, of regret.

"This isn't what I wanted," she said. "I can't do this."

Weber shook his head. He felt the kind of awful that comes from encouraging someone and then pulling the plug.

"You can do anything you want, Ariel. I'm sorry I'm your boss. Try me another time."

Her eyes hardened. It might have been the look of a woman who had been aroused and then rejected. But there was something more. She was willing herself to anger.

"Try me *another* time?" She talked loud enough to be heard through the walls of the apartment building. "Is this a test run?"

"Quiet down. Everything's okay."

"You've been flirting with me for weeks. And then we get drunk, and we go up to your apartment. I take off my panties, thinking that's what you want, and then you pretend that it's all a big nothing."

"Maybe we should just forget the dinner here. Go out and have a burger somewhere."

"Fuck the dinner and fuck you, Weber."

She took the panties off the counter, turned her back on Weber and stepped into them, pulling them up and then lowering the tight dress.

"It won't work," she said quietly, walking toward the door. She looked toward the ceiling. Weber was confused.

"I'm sorry," he repeated. "What do you mean, 'it won't work'?"

But she didn't answer. She crossed the threshold into the hall, turned and walked down the hall, every step a seeming register of indignation.

40

WASHINGTON

The next morning, Graham Weber arose at his habitual hour of five a.m. He went out for a slow, groggy run along the river. He thought about Ariel Weiss and blamed himself for letting her drink too much. As he was returning to his building, he saw the familiar face of Oscar, his driver, back in his usual parking spot out front on Virginia Avenue, accompanied by the iron-necked Jack Fong, the chief of the security detail. They were sitting in a new car, a black Lincoln Navigator, the same model that the director of National Intelligence used, rather than the old Cadillac Escalade.

Weber waved to them and went upstairs to shower and shave. He had been planning to go back to Langley that morning and take up the reins, recover his sense of how to run the CIA in a government he now perceived as hostile and dangerous, perhaps give another speech in the bubble in a day or two, decide how to expose the wrong that he knew had been committed. But as he stood under the spray of the shower nozzle, an idea fell into his head that required changing his planned itinerary for that morning, and going instead to the White House.

He put on his best gray suit and an Italian silk tie from Ferragamo that he saved for special occasions.

Weber waited until seven a.m., when civilized bureaucrats were up, and then phoned the White House switchboard and asked to be connected to Timothy O'Keefe, the national security adviser. He reached O'Keefe in his car, already on his way to that grand office in the West Wing overlooking Pennsylvania Avenue. Weber asked for an appointment that morning and O'Keefe, to Weber's surprise, immediately assented. He told Weber to come to his office at nine-thirty, just after the president finished his morning intelligence briefing with Director Hoffman.

Weber spent the next two hours catching up on the newspapers he hadn't read during his involuntary sojourn in West Virginia. Reading the stories was like trying to make out an object through the refracted light of a heavy snowstorm. He could see the snowflakes, immediate and particular, and he could discern the more distant objects that were coated in white: trees, roofs, roads, buildings. But he couldn't actually see any particular object for itself, only the covered outlines.

Weber's Lincoln arrived at the West Wing just as the rotund figure of Cyril Hoffman was descending the stairs toward his car. The director of National Intelligence gave him a jaunty wave.

"So you're back, safe and sound," said Hoffman grandly, his voice conveying many emotions, but not sincerity. "What a relief."

"I'll bet it is. You must have been worried—that your guard corps would let me out."

"But you should be thanking me, Graham. We saved your life."

"Right," muttered Weber.

"And now you're a hero. Everyone says so. The president was beginning to worry that he had picked the wrong man for CIA. He was thinking of dumping you, but he's reconsidering. He told me so just now, in the Oval."

Hoffman gestured to the rear of the West Wing for emphasis. Yes, this president, this White House. He stepped up into his car, with a trademark flip of his coattails so that his jacket wouldn't get rumpled under him.

"You bastard," said Weber. "It won't work."

"Ciao," said Hoffman through the open window as the big SUV rumbled off.

Weber mounted the stairs to the West Wing lobby. O'Keefe was waiting for him in his office. The national security adviser looked as bland and impenetrable as ever, his face a milky expanse of jowl and cheek, with thin lips curving into a smile.

"Welcome back," said the national security adviser, extending his hand. Weber didn't shake it.

"You won't get away with this," said Weber. "I won't let you."

"Say what?" O'Keefe cupped his hand to his ear, as if he'd had trouble hearing, but really inviting Weber to reconsider.

"You won't get away with it," Weber repeated. "I know James Morris didn't act alone. He worked for the director of National Intelligence. Cyril Hoffman knew what Morris was doing, and Hoffman wouldn't have dared do it without a wink from you."

O'Keefe closed his eyes and smiled genially.

"Prove it!" he said. "But I can tell you now that you won't be able to. There is no evidence whatsoever that James Morris was acting with the knowledge of the United States government in his effort to sabotage the Bank for International Settlements. It's outrageous even to make such a suggestion. He was acting on his own, in secret, carrying out this monstrous hacker plot with help from Chinese recruits. And then, my god, he even tried to kill you! How could you, of all people, come to his defense?"

"There's evidence," said Weber.

"Yes, I know." O'Keefe nodded. "And you gathered it, with help from your remarkable friend Dr. Weiss: Amazing work that you did, chasing down Morris's secret activities. It has all gone to the grand jury. I wondered at your decision to put so much confidence in Morris at first; people might almost have blamed you for what happened. But you were playing a subtler hand. That's what I told the FBI last week. Graham Weber saw the light about Morris. Weber and I stand side by side. That's correct, isn't it?"

O'Keefe smiled again. He was almost serene in his repetition of this account of events. Weber looked at him for a long moment. He'd seen people like O'Keefe since he began dealing with government: They were the gamers and political fixers; they had their thumbs on the scale; they were always weighing the interest of the public against what was to them infinitely more precious, which was the political survival of themselves and their bosses. That was why he had always wanted to remain a businessman, until a few months ago.

Weber shook his head. He rapped the table in front of him for good measure.

"I won't do it," he said. "I won't play."

O'Keefe tilted his big round head.

"You know, Graham, I don't like to be challenged, especially in my own office, and especially by someone who owes his job to me. So think twice before you jump off this particular cliff."

Weber looked down at the mahogany table, and then back at O'Keefe. Yes, he was sure.

"Sorry, Tim, but I cannot back up a story that I know is false. I don't care what the so-called evidence seems to show. I won't do it. I'll go to the intelligence committees. I'll go to the Justice Department. I'll do whatever it takes to keep this big lie from succeeding."

"You're a fool," snapped O'Keefe. "And an arrogant one, which is worse: Do you think I am powerless? I have you by the balls, sir. I just haven't started squeezing."

Weber shook his head.

"Stop threatening me, Tim. I know I'm right. I'm ready for whatever bullshit campaign you're going to run against me."

"I wonder," said O'Keefe.

He stood and opened the door.

"Out, please," he said, with a dismissive motion of his hand. "Try to simmer down. And I suggest that you pay a call on Cyril Hoffman, your superior officer. I believe he would like a word."

Weber nodded. He removed from his pocket a letter he had typed out that morning on his computer, while waiting for the meeting in the White House. He handed it to O'Keefe.

"What is this?" asked the national security adviser.

"It's an invitation. I am calling a meeting of the Special Activities Review Committee. Some sensitive information has come to light the committee should know about. It's tomorrow afternoon. Don't be late. This is one meeting you won't want to miss."

Weber gave the national security adviser a little wink, and for the first time that morning he thought he saw a trace of anxiety on O'Keefe's round face.

Weber got into his car on Executive Road, the private alley between the White House and the Old Executive Office Building. Oscar asked where he wanted to go, and Weber had to think a minute. He needed to see all the cards. He dialed the private number of his boss, Hoffman, in his office off International Drive near Tysons Corner.

"Ah, Mr. Director, I thought you might be calling," said Hoffman.

"Apparently I need to come see you," said Weber. "I just left O'Keefe's office."

"Not apparently, but really. And as soon as possible, please. I just got off the phone with the national security adviser. He is not a happy man. You should take time to consider what he told you."

"I'll be at your office in thirty minutes. That's all the time I need to think."

"Drive slowly," said Hoffman. "Admire the scenery. You are not an impulsive man. You are a business executive. That is what you know. In other areas, you are accident-prone. Think about what you are doing."

Weber arrived in twenty-five minutes. The morning rush-hour traffic had already thinned on the Parkway and Route 123. He was cleared through security and pointed toward the DNI's office building, which was tucked away in a modest speck of green amid the concrete of intersecting highways. Hoffman's personal aide was downstairs to greet Weber and take him up to see the boss.

Hoffman stood with his arms open as Weber entered the office, as if he were preparing to welcome the return of a long-lost son. There was a look of merriment and also menace in his eye.

"Welcome, my boy. I hope you have been thinking hard and have recovered your wits. History is reaching out to you, Graham, and you must grab the bright ring. If you don't, well, you will miss your chance in time. It won't come back. You will fall into the abyss."

Weber stood, compact and immovable, just inside the portal of Hoffman's office.

"Why did you let Morris do it?" Weber said. "That's what I don't understand."

"Don't be an ass," said Hoffman. He walked over to Weber, put a hand on his elbow and steered him to a seat at his round conference table. Hoffman took the facing seat.

"You may decide to commit suicide, but you should at least have coffee first," Hoffman said. "Perhaps the caffeine will stimulate your thinking in a way that heretofore has not been evident."

He called for his steward, who brought in a large sterling silver tray, emblazoned with the seal of an Asian intelligence service that had made the gift to Hoffman as a token of eternal esteem. On the tray were two small white ceramic cups. The steward went to the shiny façade of the director's espresso machine and made two coffees, one for Hoffman and one for his guest. The steward laid down the cups and then offered a tray of what Hoffman called *viennoiseries*. When Weber refused, Hoffman smiled and took two for himself.

"You don't read history, do you?" asked Hoffman. "I mean, really read it."

"What does that have to do with anything?" answered Weber. He wanted to keep the conversation on message. "I read what I need to do my job."

"How simple and utilitarian, but inadequate," said Hoffman, "particularly when it comes to American history."

"I read the Constitution. I swore to uphold and defend it. That's enough."

"No, it isn't, actually. That's what I'm getting at. The Constitution is a document, written on paper, but its meaning was shaped by great men and their decisions. In particular, in my humble opinion, our history was shaped by the decision that our first president, George Washington, made, about what kind of a republic this would be: Would it be Alexander Hamilton's America, or Thomas Jefferson's? A republic of predictable order or unpredictable liberty? That was the first question."

"Very interesting, no doubt, but I want to talk about James Morris. I am going to tell the CIA workforce about him and his friends and enablers tomorrow in the bubble, and I will tell the grand jury the day after."

Hoffman was frowning and shaking his head.

"You are so eager to commit hari-kari. I am trying to prevent you, but it is not easy. You asked me to explain, why did I let Mr. Morris do it? I am trying to do so, if you will just *shut up* and drink your coffee and listen to what I have to say."

"All right," said Weber. "It's your nickel."

Hoffman nodded with gracious disdain.

"George Washington decided that America would be the nation envisioned by Alexander Hamilton, with a central bank, a funded debt, an orderly bureaucracy and a deep and unshakable alliance with its parent nation, its fatherland, you might say, which we know today as the United Kingdom of Great Britain and Northern Ireland. Washington could have opted for the alternative vision of a French-style democratic republic, with its burlesque of liberty, but he did not."

"Okay, got that," said Weber. "Now, can we move on?"

"No, not yet. I am now getting to the part of this story that is directly responsive to your question. I believe in loyalty to one's parents. Do you, Graham?"

"Of course. I revere my parents."

"Well now, this question of parental loyalty has presented itself in a very particular way for your employer, the Central Intelligence Agency. We were not created ex nihilo, you know. We have a parent. And the name of that parent is the British Secret Intelligence Service."

Weber laughed.

"The James Bond thing hasn't worked for me since Sean Connery. Sorry."

"That is unworthy of you, but never mind: I'm going to give you a tutorial. It will make a lot of other things clearer to you."

"Say what you like. It's not going to work. I'm going to take you and your friends down, no matter what you tell me."

"Be quiet and listen. I am going to tell you a great secret. In 1945, when the war ended, the British compiled a private history of the covert action program begun in 1940 that had led to the creation of the OSS and, by extension, the CIA."

"That's ludicrous. Why would the British run a covert action pro-gram against us? We were their closest ally."

Hoffman raised a finger, and then proceeded.

"The immediate aim of this covert action program was to draw the United States into the war to save Britain, but its larger purpose was to create a secret instrument that could protect the Hamiltonian version of America—and, in partnership with British intelligence, let us be frank, rule the postwar world."

"That's crap."

"I have a copy of the secret history in my desk. It is an account of 'British Security Co-Ordination,' or 'BSC,' which is the name the British gave to their clandestine effort to maintain American steadfastness, despite the isolationist weasels. Would you like me to read you a relevant passage?"

Hoffman put on his reading glasses and peered over the top of them in a way that made his eyebrows and forehead look like those of a large, balding owl.

"No," said Weber.

Hoffman ignored him. He leafed through the volume to page forty-six and began reading:

"This particular chapter is called 'Campaign Against Axis Propaganda in the United States.' It illustrates how well the British understood us, then and now. I quote:

> In planning its campaign, it was necessary for BSC to remember (as the Germans remembered) the simple truth that the United States, a Sovereign Entity of comparatively recent birth, is inhabited by people of many conflicting races, interests and creeds. These people, though fully conscious of their wealth and power in the aggregate, are still unsure of themselves individually, still basically on the defensive and still striving, as yet unavailingly but very defiantly, after national unity and indeed after some logical grounds for considering themselves a nation in the racial sense . . . But protest as they will, they remain essentially a concourse of immigrants and are unable, in the main, to cut the atavistic bonds which bind them to the lands of their origin.

"What nonsense," said Weber.

"I think not," said Hoffman. "I think the anonymous authors of this secret history have expressed the nub of the problem, which is that we Americans do not know who we are, and we need *help*; especially in administering the remains of the global empire that fell to us in 1945."

"You can't mean to say you take all this seriously. It's preposterous."

Hoffman removed his glasses and sat up straight in his chair.

"I do indeed, sir. I am heir to the Anglo-American promise. You are heir to it. The rest of the world simply doesn't understand. We must do what is right, whether others comprehend it or not. That is what I embraced when I joined this service. All the Hoffmans have understood it: Frank, Sam, Ed, Jack, every one of them knew when they joined the CIA that they must protect the secret power that is the only guarantee of order on this planet."

Weber shook his head.

"You're insane! If you really believe all this nonsense, why did you allow an anarchist hacker who despised Britain to attack the BIS?"

"Isn't it obvious?" said Hoffman gently.

"No. It's the opposite of obvious."

"Morris was the perfect foil. I was only too happy to allow him to destroy himself and discredit his silly movement. People can see them for what they are: wreckers and manipulators; liars of the worst sort. It will be years before we see another of these hacker princes like James Morris. And as for the special relationship he so despised, well, it's more special than ever, thanks to poor Morris and his unwitting assistance."

"You're out of control. What you have done is illegal."

Hoffman seemed not to have heard him, for he began to speak again with greater intensity.

"And there were *other* benefits, obviously, from letting Morris conduct his absurd attack. It strengthened American control over international finance. It let us rewrite the BIS charter. It reanimated our liaison with SIS. And best of all, it provided an opportunity to replace the unfortunate choice the president made for CIA director, which is you."

Weber shook his head. But there was a calm look on his face. He knew with clarity now what he was confronting.

"You're a traitor," said Weber.

"Hah! You sound like Peter Pingray, your unloved deputy. When we had to 'relocate' you for a week, for your own protection, he came to see me in great agitation. He also called me a traitor and, worse, a scoundrel. He said he had tried to warn you about me, too. Put a message in your desk drawer, sent another warning note in with some paperwork. But he said you were too thick to understand, thank goodness."

"Peter Pingray left those messages?" said Weber, with a tone of wonder, and then, to himself: "Of course he did. He had access to all the paper. He was trying to help me."

"Misguided loyalty. Pingray is gone, by the way, fired for cause, no pension and facing civil litigation unless he behaves himself."

"You are dangerous, Cyril, but it's over."

Hoffman looked weary suddenly, and unhappy.

"You make me very sorry, Graham. Truly. I hoped you would open your mind and listen—really *listen*—to what the past tells you about your duty. But you are thick! That was always the critique of you: A smart business executive, charismatic manager, wanting to help his country, but inexperienced; a man who doesn't know what he doesn't know. And now it has undone you."

"Not me. You're the one who's going down. I am calling a meeting of the Special Activities Review Committee to tell them the truth. Then I am going to Congress, to explain what you and Morris and all your crazy associates did. And then I am going to the Justice Department. I am going to explain this case for what it is: Espionage on behalf of a foreign power. Treason."

"No, you won't," said Hoffman.

"Try me."

"You won't do it because you can't. You're fired. I am removing you as CIA director, for cause, effective immediately."

"What do you mean, 'for cause'?"

Hoffman had a new look in his eye, a hard glint of cruelty combined with the light of mischief.

"I hoped that it would not come to this," Hoffman said. "But I am firing you as CIA director because of evidence that you have engaged in sexual harassment of one of your employees."

"What are you talking about?" said Weber, but in that instant he was startled by a recollection from just a dozen hours before.

"It is not pretty," said Hoffman, flicking a switch that turned on a video monitor on the wall. "Not pretty at all, what some men will do."

The video image showed Weber with his arm wrapped around a young woman in a black sheath who was walking unsteadily down the hallway. A second image showed Weber kissing the same woman at the doorway to an apartment. From the angle of the image, it must have been taken by a camera hidden high on the opposite wall. The video continued as the two of them entered Weber's apartment and closed the door.

"There's audio, too. Would you like to hear it?"

"No." Weber put his hands over his ears. Hoffman pushed a button, and the feed was audible, a woman's loud voice.

"You've been flirting with me for weeks. And then we get drunk, and we go up to your apartment. I take off my panties, thinking that's what you want, and then you pretend that it's all a big nothing."

"Maybe we should just forget the dinner here. Go out and have a burger somewhere."

"Fuck the dinner and fuck you, Weber."

"She will make a powerful witness, Dr. Weiss. You were her hero. You helped her to discover the truth about James Morris. And then you callously took advantage of her as a subordinate."

"How could she do that?" Weber muttered, more to himself than to Hoffman.

"She might well ask the same of you, sir. How could you? But here is the simple fact: I expect that Dr. Weiss will file a formal complaint of sexual harassment against you this morning, and we have corroborating video and audio evidence that supports her charge, as you can see. So as director of National Intelligence, it is my obligation to demand your resignation."

Weber was bowed. He rose from his chair and headed toward the door, stooped-shouldered, seemingly defeated. He was shaking his head, muttering to himself.

"I think the curtain is coming down, old boy," said Hoffman grimly. "If you try to attend your little Special Activities Review meeting tomorrow, you will be barred. As a former director, you don't have access. Sorry."

Weber turned on him. A spark seemed to come back into his eyes.

"You're a bad magician," said Weber.

Hoffman blinked. That was his only show of emotion, but he was stung by the comment.

"I beg your pardon."

"Remember what you told me about magic, Cyril? It was my second week on the job. You said professional magicians know that a trick always has three parts: what people see; what they remember; and what they tell others. I think maybe you have forgotten your own advice. In this case, the three don't fit."

"Bosh! You are an amateur, if I may be frank. I warned you that you had no idea what you were getting involved in here, but you persisted. You were repeatedly warned, even by Dr. Weiss. Review the record, sir. But you were blind. You are the opposite of a magician. You are a vain and arrogant man, I am sorry to say it, but there it is, the truth."

"How long was she working with you?" asked Weber.

"But Dr. Weiss was always working with me, and with her country. She is a career intelligence officer. There was never a moment in which she was not loyal to the president."

Weber studied him. "One of us misjudged her."

"*Ipse dixit.* You yourself said it. By the way, I did not tell you on my sailboat that I have any unauthorized investments with any Chinese company. And I never said that James Morris was a fall guy, or expendable, or anything of the sort. Any such claim is a lie."

"She told you that? Or did you install a microphone?"

"She is a patriot," said Hoffman. "Now get out of here. You are fired. They are already cleaning out your desk at the agency."

"Have you considered the possibility that I have one more card?" asked Weber.

"Considered, and rejected. You are busted. Good luck with your supposed 'card,' whatever that may be."

"We'll find out tomorrow."

Weber tipped his head toward Hoffman and left the office. Fong, his security chief, was waiting in the anteroom. So was Oscar, the driver. They rode to Langley in silence. When Weber got to the seventh floor, the entrance to his office was barred. Marie and Diana were in tears.

Weber embraced his two secretaries, which only made them weep more copiously. When they had calmed down, Weber had told them not to worry, that he had done nothing wrong. He asked them if he could use the conference room to make a few phone calls. He called two people. One was the deputy director of the FBI in charge of the National Security Branch. The other was Ruth Savin. He asked her to contact Ariel Weiss, urgently.

Weber waited for the public announcement that he had been fired, and the gruesome television footage that would accompany it. But through that night and into the next morning, the lid stayed on, and Weber suspected he knew why.

41

WASHINGTON

The meeting of the Special Activities Review Committee the next day was delayed for some minutes by procedural issues. Ruth Savin and Earl Beasley were sitting in their seats, but Cyril Hoffman argued via his video link from Liberty Crossing that the committee couldn't hold a session because the required quorum wasn't present. The chairman, Timothy O'Keefe, wasn't returning phone calls. Savin excused herself to consult some records in the general counsel's office.

When Savin returned, she said that the meeting could indeed take place. The administrative rules required that a majority of the five members be present. The tinny sound of Hoffman's voice came through on the speaker of the video monitor.

"But there are only two of you! How can you have a meeting?"

"Three," said Savin. "O'Keefe is on his way from the White House."

"No, he's not," said Hoffman.

"I just talked with him," said the general counsel. "He'll be here in ten minutes."

Hoffman's screen went dark.

Timothy O'Keefe arrived looking more than usually flustered. He greeted Savin and Beasley and took his seat at the head of the table and asked where Hoffman was. When informed that Hoffman was boycotting the meeting, O'Keefe got on the phone and ordered him to plug in, by the secure VTC line. In another minute, Hoffman's face was visible once again on the screen. His demeanor, usually so calm, was marred by a slight tic at the corner of his mouth.

O'Keefe rattled a coffee cup with his spoon to call for order and begin the meeting.

"The president has asked me to thank the members for attending. We have one piece of business only today. The general counsel will make her report."

O'Keefe nodded to Ruth Savin.

"I wish to report that at the written request of former director Graham Weber, the committee conducted a review of certain unauthorized actions by the director of National Intelligence in contacting a senior intelligence officer of the Russian federation named M. V. Serdukov. In the course of that investigation, the committee obtained a written statement from the FBI's National Security Branch describing the DNI's unauthorized activity in flying to France. We have been informed by French civil-aviation authorities that the tail number of his plane was N85VM."

On the monitor, Hoffman's face was growing more agitated. He coughed, stood up, walked away from the camera and then returned with a tissue, which he used to wipe his brow.

"That trip to France was approved by the White House," interjected Hoffman on the video monitor.

"No, it wasn't," said O'Keefe.

Savin looked to O'Keefe, who nodded. She continued.

"The committee received corroborating testimony this morning from a witness who said she spoke personally with DNI Hoffman about his planned trip to meet with the Russian official concerning James Morris. This witness met with me this morning for an hour and reviewed details of the DNI's activities, including classified documents that she gave him for delivery to the Russian official, at DNI Hoffman's insistence."

"Impossible," said Hoffman on the monitor. "Ariel Weiss would never do that. She intends to submit evidence charging Graham Weber, not me."

"I think you are mistaken," said Savin. "Dr. Weiss is down the hall, meeting with my lawyers. I can send you a copy of her affidavit as soon as it's finished."

"Perfidious," said Hoffman quietly.

"We have confirmed that the documents Dr. Weiss prepared were marked for transmittal to you. Office of Security personnel at the Information Operations Center have reviewed the paperwork that Dr. Weiss provided them before your unauthorized trip to France."

"Weiss is a liar. She's in love with Weber. He tried to seduce her."

"That's out of line, Director Hoffman."

"Shut up, Ruth," said Hoffman. He moved to turn off the camera. O'Keefe's firm voice intervened.

"Sit down, Cyril. The FBI is outside your office now. Be quiet and listen."

O'Keefe turned to Savin. She continued once more.

"I should caution you, Director Hoffman, that Dr. Weiss has told us the audio and video surveillance material was created under duress. She says you were monitoring her visit to Mr. Weber's apartment, and that you threatened to fire her if she didn't perform the actions recorded on tape. That incident is part of the criminal investigation that my attorneys have begun."

"Are you all mad?" said Hoffman. "I have files that implicate every one of you."

Savin looked at O'Keefe, who nodded once again for her to speak.

"I warn you, Director Hoffman, that such threats will only raise further questions about your misuse of office. I should also remind you that these VTC exchanges are being recorded."

Hoffman looked at them all, dumbfounded.

"They've won," he said.

"Who has?" asked O'Keefe.

"The 'enemy,' for lack of a more precise term. The people who want to give away the nation's secrets and bring down the house. The naïve innocents. Morris, Weber, all of you."

"We're not enemies of the United States, Cyril. You are mistaken."

"I am serving my country. Politicians are transitory but the nation's interests are permanent. We cannot escape the responsibility of leadership, dear friends. If you think that's possible, then you are the mistaken ones, grievously so. You are summer soldiers."

"Cyril, I would suggest that you retain a lawyer," said O'Keefe.

Hoffman rose once again. The monitor showed his large form moving toward the camera.

"Don't turn off the camera," said O'Keefe. "That's an order."

"I don't care," said Hoffman.

The monitor crinkled with static and then went dark. But the audio microphone was still working and the speakers carried a voice that spoke, oddly, with a combination of menace and good cheer.

"I'll be back," said Hoffman. "Of that you can be assured."

O'Keefe looked at the two others at the table and nodded, really in deference, to another person, unseen.

"Can we please conclude this meeting, so we can all get back to real work?" said O'Keefe.

"Don't bet against the billionaire. Didn't I say that?" said Beasley, with a croupier's smile.

"At the request of the president," O'Keefe continued, "I am seeking a motion to dissolve this committee, effective immediately. Its mandate for deception and special activities will be reviewed by the National Security Council, but its authority is suspended pending completion of that review. Do I hear a motion?"

Savin responded.

"I move that we dissolve the Special Activities Review Committee, and transfer to other, existing committees, such legitimate business as the committee may have."

"Do I hear a second?" asked O'Keefe.

"Second," said Beasley.

"All in favor?" asked O'Keefe.

"Aye," said Beasley, Savin and O'Keefe together.

"The motion is adopted, and the committee is hereby dissolved."

"Now, where is Mr. Weber?" asked O'Keefe.

"Outside," said Savin. "He's waiting in the deputy director's office."

"Bring him in," said the national security adviser.

Weber walked into the room, looking as if he hadn't slept in a week. "You need a vacation, brother," said Beasley.

"Sit down," said O'Keefe.

Weber took the empty chair next to the national security adviser.

"The president has asked me to tell you that he has chosen to ignore DNI Hoffman's order that you be fired. The White House received a letter this morning from Dr. Ariel Weiss, saying that the evidence against you presented by the director of National Intelligence was fabricated."

Weber closed his eyes, just for a moment, and then opened them again. "What does that mean?" he asked.

"It means that you are CIA director." O'Keefe extended his hand. "You remain the proprietor of the ghost hotel."

Graham Weber didn't want to be in the office the rest of that day. He didn't want to be anywhere, really. He thought of calling Ariel Weiss at the general counsel's office, where she was still closeted with the lawyers, to ask her why she had done it, or to apologize, or to thank her. He wasn't sure which, and he doubted she would answer, at least not until some time had passed. As he thought back over the events at his apartment that night, he realized she had assured him in her oblique way that Hoffman's extortion gambit would fail because she would disavow it. "It won't work," she had said. She might have been living a triple life, but she had a single and admirable purpose.

James Morris broadcast a video message from Caracas. He was accompanied by Ramona Kyle, the founder of Too Many Secrets, the civil liberties group that had renamed itself "Open World." Off camera were members of an international emergency assistance team that had been formed to help defend Morris and argue his case in the media. In that group, unseen by the reporters, was a handsome man with a slight East European accent who called himself Roger, and a starchy Yankee liberal, dressed in an old gray flannel suit and a striped rep tie, named Arthur Peabody. Peabody later gave interviews to selected reporters, on deep background, in which he disclosed that he was a former CIA officer and revealed new details about the conspiratorial activities of the agency to maintain what he called "the post-imperial order of 1945."

Morris spoke passionately. He was doing the work he had dreamed of, and he was a charismatic spokesman, if not an entirely convincing one. He admitted he was responsible for the attack on the Bank for International Settlements, just as the newspaper stories said. Indeed, he fairly boasted about what he had done, explaining that under cover of the cyber-attack he had transferred money from the accounts of wealthy nations to those of needy ones.

"I do not apologize for my actions. I didn't kill anyone. I didn't torture anyone. I didn't listen to people's telephone calls or steal their secrets. They claim that I broke the laws of the United States but I didn't break any of the laws of humanity. I left the criminal Central Intelligence Agency as an act of conscience. I revealed its secrets to give liberty to others. I took from the rich and gave to the poor. I'm proud of what I did."

Many newspaper stories, including those in the United States, described James Morris in the lead paragraphs as a "Cyber Robin Hood." A German website briefly posted an item after the press conference alleging that a Swiss hacker named Rudolf Biel had been killed by the Russian intelligence service in Hamburg to protect the secret of Morris's identity, but this informtion quickly disappeared and was nowhere else mentioned.

A month after he was reinstated as CIA director, Graham Weber went to the White House to see the president. He told the chief executive that, after thinking about it carefully, he wanted to submit his resignation. The CIA had been given a new start, he said, just as the president had wanted when he appointed Weber. But now it needed a professional.

Weber said that he wanted to suggest a candidate as his successor. He had run the name by Timothy O'Keefe, the national security adviser, who agreed that it was a good idea. He urged the president to nominate Dr. Ariel Weiss, who would be the first woman ever to be director of the Central Intelligence Agency. It would be a signal, said

Weber, that the agency had really broken the bonds of the past and was moving into the future.

The president didn't say yes on the spot, but O'Keefe had already told Weber that he liked the idea. It would be politically popular, and it had the additional benefit of being the right thing to do.

What was left for Graham Weber was empty space, to be filled, and the satisfaction that he had helped set free the haunted, necessary institution of the Central Intelligence Agency, so that it might become part of the American fabric, rather than a threadbare relic that had been crafted on the loom of another nation.

Perhaps the country would grow to love, or at least respect, an intelligence service that was its own creation rather than someone else's. Weber wanted to think about the best way he could help make that happen as a private citizen. But that could wait. Right now he wanted to take a walk along the river and watch the water cascade along the muddy banks, and let his mind go gray and quiet as the winter sky.

ACKNOWLEDGMENTS

This book began with the author's suspicion that in our digital world, the traditional themes of the spy novel—deception, penetration, surveillance—are increasingly about the manipulation of computer code through computer hacking and cyberwar. The author's problem was that he was a nontechnician. So began a long apprenticeship with people who were willing to share information and ideas.

First and foremost, I thank Matthew Devost, president and CEO of the consulting firm FusionX. I was introduced to Matt by Henry Crumpton, a celebrated former CIA officer whose consulting firm, the Crumpton Group, works closely with Matt's company. Matt was my guide and dinner companion at DEF CON XX in Las Vegas in July 2012. He continued to talk with me through the writing of this novel and was kind enough to read and comment on a draft of the book. I am immensely grateful to him. Will Hurd, CIA veteran and now business colleague of Crumpton, was also very helpful.

Other cyber experts were generous in sharing insights, starting with Sherri Davidoff, the founder of LMG Security, who spoke with me at DEF CON about her MIT adventures and whose book *Network Forensics*, coauthored with Jonathan Ham, is a must for people who want to understand this subject. I am also grateful to Jason Healey of the Atlantic Council; Christopher Kirchhoff at the Pentagon; Brian Krebs, a former *Washington Post* colleague and author of the popular blog *Krebs on Security*; Ed Skoudis, the founder of Counter Hack; Jon

Iadonisi, founder of the White Canvas Group; Richard Bejtlich, chief security officer of Mandiant; and Alan Paller of the SANS Institute. Journalistic colleagues were also helpful, especially Robert O'Harrow, author of the *Post* series "Zero Day: The Threat in Cyberspace," and Ellen Nakashima. Authors always say in thanking technical advisers that these experts are in no way responsible for errors, omissions or other lapses. That's especially true in this case. My tutors will only wish I had been a more sophisticated pupil.

I had generous help in Germany, a center for hacking and the idea of Internet freedom. The Atlantik-Brücke and its director, Eveline Metzen, brought me as a fellow to Hamburg, where I shared an unforgettable dinner with Max Warburg at his home on the banks of the Elbe. Later, as a visiting Allianz fellow at the American Academy in Berlin, I gave its director Gary Smith the task of finding me young Germans who knew about hacking. He introduced me to Karsten Nohl and Linus Neumann of the Security Research Labs in Berlin, and a roster of other German hackers and cyber-experts who will probably be happier if they go unnamed.

My fascination with the origins of the CIA and its relationship with British intelligence dates back to 1987, when I published a long article in the *Washington Post* about Britain's covert action inside America before and during World War II. That was when I first encountered Thomas Troy, a former CIA historian and the authoritative writer on this subject. I hope he won't mind that my characters quote directly from several of his books. I quote from my own copy of the secret history of British Security Coordination, which I obtained during my reporting in 1987. For texture on the Bank for International Settlements, I turned to several books, especially Liaquat Ahamed's extraordinary *Lords of Finance*, Benn Steil's *The Battle of Bretton Woods* and Eleanor Lansing Dulles's 1932 volume, cited in the novel, upon which I stumbled.

Four more tips of the hat: Cyril Hoffman's tale of the fictional French agent "Juliette" and her house in Saint-Brieuc evokes the true tale of the incomparable French spy Jeannie de Clarens, whose story I narrated in the *Washington Post* in December 1998. My references to magic were conjured with help from John McLaughlin, former acting director of the CIA, amateur magician and a wise and generous man. I owe special thanks to John Maguire, a former CIA officer who balances deep affection for the agency with bracing criticism. And what modern author could navigate the world today without the electronic tools Wikipedia and Google Earth, which were constant desktop companions and sources of information?

Though this book draws upon research, I should stress that it is entirely a work of fiction. The people, companies, institutions and events are imaginary. Where a real organization like the Bank for International Settlements or a real person is cited, it is in a fictional context only. Those who know the real background of this subject will appreciate how truly this is a work of fiction, not fact.

Three readers saved me along the way from pursing mistaken paths: My friend Lincoln Caplan, whose writings on the law have graced *The New Yorker*, the *New York Times* and many other publications, gave a careful, bracing read of an intermediate draft. I have dedicated this book to Linc and to Jamie Gorelick, former deputy attorney general and Washington lawyer extraordinaire, who have been among my closest friends for more than forty years. My wife, Eve, blessed with a doctorate in computer science and a career as a defense engineer, superbly critiqued later drafts. And finally and especially, I thank my friend Garrett Epps, a professor of constitutional law at the University of Baltimore, blogger, poet, novelist and literary critic. I have turned to Garrett for help in structuring each of my previous novels and he served in that role again, in a way that helped me see a path for my characters.

Finally, I thank Starling Lawrence, the best word editor in the business. He read each draft and offered honest, penetrating and often devastatingly funny comments in the margins. My colleagues at Norton have always been helpful, especially Bill Rusin, Jeannie Luciano, Rachel Salzman, Ryan Harrington, and my deft copy editor, Dave Cole. This is the ninth book in which I have thanked my peerless literary agent, Raphael Sagalyn. I am also grateful to supporters in Hollywood, including my longtime friend Bob Bookman and my gifted agents at Creative Artists, Bruce Vinokour and Matthew Snyder.

This book is ultimately about American intelligence in the age of WikiLeaks, and whether it can adapt to a more open digital world and still do the hard work of espionage. We'll all be living with that question for years to come. However this future evolves, the country will need a strong and freethinking press, and so, finally, I thank my friend Don Graham for being a surpassingly great owner of the *Washington Post*, and Jeff Bezos for taking the torch from Don and keeping it bright.